THE GRAVEYARD QUEEN ~~SER~~
by Amanda Stevens

"The beginning of Stevens's GRAVEYARD QUEEN SERIES left
this reviewer breathless. The author smoothly establishes
characters and forms the foundation of future storylines with
an edgy and beautiful writing style. Her story is full of twists
and turns, with delicious and surprising conclusions. Readers
will want to force themselves to slow down and enjoy the book
instead of speeding through to the end, and they'll anxiously
await the next installment of this deceptively gritty series."
—*RT Book Reviews*, 4½ stars

"*The Restorer* is by turns creepy and disturbing, mixed with
mystery and a bit of romance. Amelia is a strong character who
has led a hard and—of necessity—secret life. She is not close
to many people, and her feelings for Devlin disturb her greatly.
Although at times unnerving, *The Restorer* is well written and
intriguing, and an excellent beginning to a new series."
—Misti Pyles, *Fort Worth Examiner*

"I could rhapsodize for hours about how much I enjoyed
The Restorer. Amanda Stevens has woven a web of intricate
plot lines that elicit many emotions from her readers. This is a
scary, provocative, chilling and totally mesmerizing book. I never
wanted it to end and I'm going to be on pins and needles until the
next book in THE GRAVEYARD QUEEN SERIES comes out."
—*Fresh Fiction*

Also by Amanda Stevens

THE DOLLMAKER
THE DEVIL'S FOOTPRINTS
THE WHISPERING ROOM

The Graveyard Queen

THE RESTORER
THE KINGDOM
THE PROPHET
THE VISITOR

Look for Amanda Stevens's next novel
in The Graveyard Queen series

THE SINNER

available soon from MIRA Books

AMANDA STEVENS

THE VISITOR

MIRA

If you purchased this book without a cover you should be aware that this book is stolen property. It was reported as "unsold and destroyed" to the publisher, and neither the author nor the publisher has received any payment for this "stripped book."

Recycling programs for this product may not exist in your area.

ISBN-13: 978-0-7783-1517-9

The Visitor

Copyright © 2016 by Marilyn Medlock Amann

All rights reserved. Except for use in any review, the reproduction or utilization of this work in whole or in part in any form by any electronic, mechanical or other means, now known or hereinafter invented, including xerography, photocopying and recording, or in any information storage or retrieval system, is forbidden without the written permission of the publisher, MIRA Books, 225 Duncan Mill Road, Don Mills, Ontario M3B 3K9, Canada.

This is a work of fiction. Names, characters, places and incidents are either the product of the author's imagination or are used fictitiously, and any resemblance to actual persons, living or dead, business establishments, events or locales is entirely coincidental.

® and TM are trademarks of Harlequin Enterprises Limited or its corporate affiliates. Trademarks indicated with ® are registered in the United States Patent and Trademark Office, the Canadian Intellectual Property Office and in other countries.

For questions and comments about the quality of this book, please contact us at CustomerService@Harlequin.com.

www.MIRABooks.com

Printed in U.S.A.

THE
VISITOR

One

The blind ghost returned in the spring, and with her more nightmares. The days warmed, the magnolias opened and foreboding settled in like an unwelcome caller.

Night after night I lay in a dreamlike state, worn out from the physical labor of my cemetery restorations, but too frightened to succumb to a deeper sleep because *she* would appear to me then. The look-alike specter that had followed me back from the other side. I wanted to believe she was merely my namesake, the ghost of some long-dead ancestor, but I very much feared she was a vision of my future self. A manifestation of the tortured woman I would one day become.

Discomforted by my thoughts, I glanced over at John Devlin, the Charleston police detective who lay sleeping beside me. His ghosts were gone now. His daughter's spirit had finally been able to move on, thus breaking the tie that had kept her mother—Devlin's dead wife—bound to him. In the ensuing months since Mariama's departure, I'd allowed myself a glimmer of hope that Devlin and I might finally be together. We'd forged a strong bond since that fateful day. An unbreakable connection that neither ghost nor human could sever. Or so I wanted to believe.

But as the temperature climbed and the days lengthened, my blood only ran colder. A shift in the wind brought a whiff of something unnatural. Distorted shadows crept across my bedroom ceiling. As the pull from the other side grew stronger, I couldn't help but obsess over my visitor's ominous prophecy. *What you are, I once was. What I am, you will someday become.*

She'd only ever come to me in my dreams, but I was awake now and I could feel her presence stronger than ever. Careful not to rouse Devlin, I rose and tiptoed from the room, slipping down the hallway, through the kitchen and out to my office, which was located at the very back of the house. The long windows afforded a view of the garden where moonlight dappled the freesia. I stood there probing the shadows, the flutter of every leaf, the quiver of every limb spiking my pulse.

A draft seeped in through the windows, bringing the smell of dust and dried lavender. Hair on end, I peered through the layers of moonlight and darkness until I found her. I didn't outwardly react to her diaphanous form, but everything inside me stilled as a terrible acceptance stole over me. She *was* here. Not just in my imagination, not just in my dreams, but *here*. And now I could no longer deny that I was being haunted.

She was dressed in a white lace frock suitable for a wedding or burial. Moonlight shone upon and through her so that I had no trouble distinguishing her all-too-familiar features—the straight nose, the high cheekbones and the slightly parted lips. The same understated features that stared back at me from the mirror except for one notable exception. Her eyes were missing.

Levitating outside my window, she pressed a hand against the glass and a wintry chill shot through me, a bone cold that came only from the other side. The windows rimed, a film of ice forming in the corners of the panes. Minuscule fissions fanned out from her splayed fingers as the glass crackled beneath the pressure of her brittle cold.

Why are you here? I wanted to cry out. *What do you want from me?*

But I already knew the answer. She wanted my essence, my life force, my humanness. She wanted what every ghost craved—to be alive. That was what made them so dangerous. That was what made them so voracious.

No sound came from her moving lips, but I could hear her message clearly in my head: *The key. It's your only salvation. Find it!*

Then she dissolved into the shadows as the frost on the windows vanished.

"Amelia?"

I might have jumped at the sound of my name, but after years of living with ghosts, I'd learned to quell my reflexes. Devlin moved up behind me. The power of his presence never failed to thrill me, but I could take no pleasure in his nearness at that moment.

"What are you doing?" he asked.

"I couldn't sleep."

"What's wrong?"

"Nothing," I lied.

He placed his hands on my shoulders. "My God, your skin is like ice."

"It's cool in here."

"Come back to bed." His fingers trailed down my arm. "I'll keep you warm, Amelia."

The way he drawled my name, even more than the lingering chill, drew a shiver. "In a minute."

He rested his chin on my head with a sigh. "Something's bothering you. What is it? Another nightmare?"

I hesitated, my gaze scanning the darkness. I wanted so much to confide in Devlin, lay all my cards on the table, but that would mean telling him about the ghosts. If he remembered anything of his near-death experience, perhaps he would have been more receptive to my gift. But he'd awakened from his coma without any memory of those moments before and after the shooting. As his wounds healed, his disdain for the supernatural returned stronger than ever, leaving me to brood about how he would react to such a confession.

After everything he'd been through with the malicious and now dead Mariama, an attachment to an unstable woman was the last thing he'd want. So I'd taken the cowardly way out and said nothing.

For most of my life, I'd been sequestered behind cemetery walls, protected from ghosts but isolated from human companionship by Papa's rules. The loneliness of my adolescence and young adulthood justified my silence now. Or so I told myself. I had a right to happiness, no matter how fleeting, and so I clung to my secrets as tenaciously as the ivy roots that I tugged from my forgotten graveyards.

"Tell me," Devlin insisted.

"I thought I saw something in the garden."

He was instantly alert. "Just now?"

"A few minutes ago."

He turned me to face him. "Why didn't you wake me?"

"Because it was probably nothing more than a shadow." Why had I even mentioned it? Was I testing him? Prodding him to admit that he, too, could sense an otherworldly presence?

"I'll take a look around," he said.

"You're wasting your time. You won't find anything."

His expression remained stoic, but I felt the same mixture of exhilaration and trepidation that I'd experienced upon our first meeting. I wondered if I would always be a little unsettled in his company. His charisma could be overwhelming at times, and yet his manner remained formal and reserved. He was a beguiling puzzle, John Devlin. An enigma to his very core.

"It's not a waste if it puts your mind at ease," he said, pressing his lips to my forehead. He disappeared into the kitchen and I heard the back door close behind him. A moment later, he was in the garden, the beam of his flashlight outing tree trunks and exposing dark corners.

Moonlight glinted in the new silver at his temples, a souvenir from his journey to the other side. My breath quickened as I watched him. Without ghosts feeding on his energy, he'd lost that gaunt, desolate look. His eyes were no longer sunken, his cheeks no longer hollow, but regardless of his physical well-being, he would always be tormented by memories. There would always be an empty space inside his heart that I could never fill.

He stood in my white garden, shoulders rigid as he lifted his face to the moon before turning—with a shudder, I could have sworn—back to the house.

"All clear," he said as he came into my office. "Nothing to worry about."

He moved back to the windows and we stood gazing out into the moonlit garden, where the early yarrow gleamed like silver. Garlands of wild roses cascaded down from the tree branches, adding a touch of romance to the night as nothing else ever could.

Devlin wrapped his arms around my waist, pulling me against him once more. Safe within the sanctuary of his embrace, I tried not to think about the past or the future. The only certainty we could ever have was in the moment. I'd learned that lesson the hard way.

But even when he kissed me, I couldn't shake the feeling of doom that had been building for weeks. Something was coming. The blind ghost's visit was just the beginning.

Two

I was up and dressed the next morning and on my first cup of tea when the sun crept over the horizon. Leaning a shoulder against the bedroom door, I sipped the tea in the hazy air and watched Devlin button his shirt.

He didn't always stay over. His job made him restless and he would often get up in the middle of the night to go over the files of a troubling case. Work occupied much of my time, too. I'd been freer over the cold winter months and Devlin and I had grown close during his recuperation. But lately I'd sensed a distance.

It was easy to blame the return of the ghosts and the secrets that I kept from him, but Devlin had become increasingly pensive and withdrawn in his own right. Sometimes when he had no idea I was around, he'd stare out the window with the strangest look on his face or glance over his shoulder as if he could sense a presence that even I couldn't see. After the trauma of the shooting, his behavior wasn't unusual, I told myself. But I couldn't help worrying that something else bothered him. Something he didn't want me to know about.

I caught his gaze in the mirror and smiled. "Tea?"

"No, thanks. I barely have enough time to stop by the house and change before the first briefing. After that, I'll be off-line for the rest of the day. I'm not sure when I'll be back."

I nodded. "I understand. I have a full day myself."

"New restoration?"

"If I win the bid."

"Good luck." He draped his jacket and tie over his arm as he strode across the room to the doorway. The sun peeking through the lace curtains gave him an otherworldly glow, and for a moment, I was reminded of the shimmer of a manifestation. But John Devlin was no ghost. He was warm, human and very much alive.

Pausing at the door, he slipped his free hand through my hair, tilting my face as he leaned down to brush his lips against mine. My heart instantly quickened. It was all I could do to keep the cup and saucer balanced as I responded with a parting of my lips, a quick dart of my tongue.

He drew back, eyes gleaming. Then he threw his jacket and tie on the bed, removed the china from my fingers and, threading both hands through my hair, kissed me again. The pressure of his mouth and the heat of his body reminded me all too vividly of what had transpired between us an hour ago. The intimate whispers, the soft moans, his hand sweeping slowly up my thigh.

That was all it took. One kiss, a memory and I was lost to him all over again. In all my twenty-eight years, I'd never known anyone like Devlin. He was everything I'd ever dreamed of in a man and not at all what I could have imagined.

"I really do have to go," he said.

"I know." Rising on tiptoes, I kissed him again, lightly now, because it was time for both of us to start our day. "Will I see you later?"

A slight hesitation, so infinitesimal as to be my imagination. "I'll have to let you know. I'm not sure when I'll be back."

"You're going out of town?"

A longer hesitation and a shadowy flicker in those dark, dark eyes. "I'm having dinner with my grandfather at his house in Myrtle Beach."

I lifted a brow but said nothing because I was completely taken aback by the revelation. Devlin and his grandfather had been estranged for years, ever since Devlin had decided to become a police officer rather than joining the family law firm. I suspected the hostility between the two stubborn men ran a lot deeper than Devlin's career choice, but he had never really opened up to me about his family.

Turning away, he picked up his coat and tie. "His assistant seemed to think it a matter of some urgency, so I don't know how long I'll be there. If dinner runs late I may stay over and drive back in the morning."

"I understand. I hope he's not… I hope everything is okay."

"I'm sure he's fine," Devlin said, but the shadows in his eyes belied his casual assurance.

I made no further inquiries even though I'd always been curious about Jonathan Devlin, an illustrious attorney and philanthropist who could trace his roots all the way back to the founding of Charleston. I'd walked past his mansion south of Broad Street any number of times, but I'd never met Devlin's only living relative. I didn't like to press him about his people because my own family had more than their fair share of secrets.

Determined to put those lingering doubts behind me, I set out on my morning walk as soon as Devlin drove away. I always enjoyed a brisk stroll through downtown where the magnolias were already in bloom and the city's past lurked on every cobbled street corner. On those days when I arrived before dawn, I loved to pause on the Battery to watch the sun come up over the harbor. In that quiet time as the ghosts floated back through the veil and the tourists slept soundly in their beds, I had the city to myself. No secrets to worry about, no prickles at my nape to warn me of an uncanny presence. Just the dance of sunlight on water and the silhouette of Fort Sumter shimmering on the horizon. Right before the dew burned off, the trees would sparkle with diamonds, a fairyland of prisms so bright and beautiful I could scarcely catch my breath at the wonder of this city.

I was a relative newcomer to Charleston, having been born and raised in the small town of Trinity, but my mother was a native Charlestonian. She and my aunt had grown up in a small house deep in the historic district, in the shadow of all the grand mansions. Theirs had been a childhood steeped in genteel tradition and seasoned by middle-class reality.

As a child, I'd been captivated by the grace of their bearing and the charm of their Lowcountry accents. They were exotic creatures that bathed in rose water and dressed in crisp cotton. It was only when I grew older that I came to realize the effort that went into such elegant presentations. Like so many Southern women of a certain age, my mother and aunt's upbringing had become their vocation.

I was not my mother's daughter by nature or nurture. On most days, I dressed in jeans and sneakers and rarely bothered with makeup. My face was tanned and freckled from working in the sun, my palms callused from the hard labor of a cemetery restorer. I possessed none of my mother's or aunt's polish, and sometimes when I looked at myself in the mirror, I wondered how someone like me had caught the eye of a man like Devlin.

This was not a question born of self-deprecation or false modesty. I could acknowledge my attributes. I was well educated, well traveled and my profession kept me physically fit. I liked to think that my eyes were a standout, changing from blue to gray and sometimes green depending on my attire and surroundings. At the bottom of my irises were tiny elongated motes. When I was little, I'd discovered that if I squinted just so and used a bit of imagination as I peered into the mirror, those odd colorations gave my pupils the look of keyholes.

But no matter the color of my eyes, no matter my education, profession or intellect, I would never be one of those golden women who glided so effortlessly through life. For me there would never be yacht club luncheons or white-gloved garden parties or harmless flirtations over frosty mint juleps. That was Devlin's old world, and because of who I was and where

I came from, I would never be welcome there. For all its charm and allure, Charleston remained an insular place, one of bloodlines and traditions, a city perpetually turned inward by its rivers and harbor. I was an Asher by birth, a legacy imbued with great wealth and corruption, but I was also a Gray. My papa's people were simple mountainfolk, and it was from that branch of the family that I had inherited my dark gift. Caulbearers, we were sometimes called. Those of us born with a veil. It happened every generation or so.

But as more of Papa's secrets came to light, I was starting to suspect that my legacy ran far deeper than the ability to see spirits. I had been born dead to a dead mother. My grandmother Tilly had pulled me back from the other side by cutting away the veil of membrane covering my face and forcing air into my premature lungs, and now I sometimes felt that I belonged to neither world. I was a living ghost, a wanderer who had not yet found my purpose or place. But every new discovery, every broken rule brought me closer to my calling.

If only I could peer through the keyholes of my eyes and know the future, perhaps I could somehow change my destiny. But how did one fight preordination? How did one combat fate?

It was a question I pondered often in the dead of night as ghosts drifted past my window.

Back home and freshly showered, I carried my second cup of tea out to the garden, where I could watch the butterflies flit among the sweetspire. Somewhere down the street, a horn blared and I could hear the muffled roar of traffic on Rutledge as commuters headed to and from the Crosstown. But all was calm and quiet here in my little oasis. Or so I thought.

I must have still been on edge from that ghostly visitation because the moment I spotted the open cellar door, my heart gave a painful jerk.

Tamping down a premature panic, I crossed the yard to the steps, but before I could call down, an odor wafted up to me—the smell of musk, earth and more faintly, decay. Not the stench of active rot, but the fusty perfume of old death.

Phantom fragrances were often attached to ghosts. Devlin's dead daughter had smelled of jasmine, and the sightless apparition of dust and dried lavender.

But this was not the scent of a ghost.

A cloud passed over the sun and I shivered. When the sun came back out, a shadowy face stared up at me from the gloom of the cellar.

Three

"Amelia?"

My heart stuttered for a fraction of a second as I tried to catch my breath. The shock of hearing my name on some odious creature's lips stunned me. Then reason intervened and I realized the voice was a familiar one. A safe one.

"Hey, I didn't scare you, did I?" Macon Dawes called up.

I could just make out his features in the dusky light. Tousled hair, tired eyes, slightly pointed chin. Not a demon, not some loathsome half being from an in-between world, but the pleasantly human visage of my upstairs neighbor.

But that smell…

I clutched the stair rail as I struggled to quiet my pounding heart. "I was a bit startled. I wasn't expecting to find anyone in the cellar at this hour."

"Did the hammering wake you up?" He placed a foot on the bottom step as he continued to stare up at me. He wore black Chucks nearly identical to the ones I had on, torn jeans and an old plaid shirt thrown over a threadbare T-shirt. The ordinariness of his rumpled appearance comforted me. "Sorry about that. I should have realized all that banging would go straight up the walls to your place."

"I didn't hear a thing," I assured him. "I was just having some tea in the garden when I noticed the open door."

"Still, it wouldn't kill me to mind my manners. I'm so used to my crazy schedule at the hospital I forget there are folks like you keeping normal hours out there in the real world."

"No harm done." I went down a step or two. Now that my pulse had settled, I was genuinely curious. Macon was a student at the nearby Medical University of South Carolina, so I'd grown used to his coming and going at all hours. But so much early-morning activity was unusual even for him. "What are you building down there?"

"Building? Nothing. Just reinforcing some of the shelving so we can have a little more storage space." He motioned toward the depths of the cellar. "Have you been down here lately? This place is a firetrap. You wouldn't believe all the useless crap I've come across. Cartons of old textbooks and magazines, trunks of moth-eaten clothing and something that looks suspiciously like a mummified bat."

I descended another step. "What's that smell?"

He wrinkled his nose. "You should have gotten a whiff earlier before I aired out the place. I think something's nesting down here."

"Nesting?" I asked in alarm. "Like what?"

"Rats, maybe. Or possums. And did I mention the

spiders?" He ran fingers through his hair with an exaggerated shudder.

"Do you need a hand?" I asked with little enthusiasm because the mention of spiders gave me pause. I'd had a mild case of arachnophobia since childhood and despite my years of prowling through web-shrouded tombs and infested mausoleums, I'd never quite managed to conquer my aversion.

"Thanks, but if you'll make sure all your belongings are marked, I'll take care of the rest."

"I don't have much. Just a few boxes that were left behind when I moved in. I'll come down and take a look, though."

I started down the steps, reluctant to leave the sunlight in the garden for the dimness of the basement. The house had been built on the site of the chapel of an orphanage that had burned to the ground at the turn of the last century. The cellar was the only thing that remained of the original structure, and sometimes when I went down there, I had an uncomfortable feeling that something lay hidden and waiting behind those brick walls. Something other than spiders and rodents.

The house had always provided a shield from the ghosts—a safe haven—but sometimes I wondered if the cellar might be a back door through the protective firewall of hallowed ground. The only spirit to ever breach my inner sanctum had been the ghost of Devlin's daughter. Somehow she'd found a way inside my house, and if she could do it, how long before I experienced another intrusion?

I continued downward, my footsteps echoing eerily in the dank stillness. A second stairway at the back of the cellar led to the kitchen, but the door had been boarded up during one of the renovations. Once upon a time, that fortified passage had made me feel safer inside the house, but now I wondered if my peace of mind had ever been anything more than an illusion.

Funny how the same sealed door could make one feel secure on one side and trapped on the other. As I reached the bottom of the steps, I became overly aware of that single exit. Claustrophobia pressed in on me. For an archaeologist turned cemetery restorer, I tended to have a lot of inconvenient hang-ups.

"What's that noise?" I cocked my head with a frown.

Macon paused. "I don't hear anything."

"Listen. It's an odd drone. Sort of like an electrical hum."

He lifted his gaze to the bare lightbulb. "Faulty wiring would be my guess. I doubt this place has had a proper inspection in years. Like I said, a regular firetrap."

Rubbing my arms, I glanced around warily. Macon was right. Something had been crawling around the cellar, shredding old books and forgotten clothing while leaving behind the faint but animalistic odor of musk and decay. "I've never liked coming down here," I said. "This place gives me the creeps."

"Says the woman who restores old graveyards for a living." Macon blew dust from a box, then lifted the lid to peer inside. "Junk, junk and more junk." As he swung the carton off the shelf, something dislodged and tumbled to the floor—a card with two nearly identical photographs mounted side by side.

As I bent to pick up the curiosity, I felt a tug of recognition even though I'd never seen the man that gazed up at me from the dual images, let alone the two diminutive girls that stood in front of him. They were older than their size would suggest, in their mid-teens perhaps.

Judging by the odd attire, the photos had been taken long before I was born. The man was shirtless beneath old-fashioned bib overalls while the girls were draped in dark cloaks that covered their frail bodies from neck to ankle.

Something about the incongruity of those heavy cloaks, about the way they stood back-to-back with their faces turned toward the camera gave me an inexplicable chill.

I handed the card to Macon. "Look at this."

He moved over to the natural light in the doorway for a closer examination. "It's a stereogram," he said after a moment. "If you look at it through a viewer, the photographs merge into one 3-D image."

"I've played around with photography. Double exposure and things like that, but I don't know much about stereoscopy. The card seems quite old."

"I'm sure it is. These things were popular as far back as the nineteenth century. I had an uncle who collected them. I wonder if there's a stereoscope around here somewhere. Where did you find it?"

"On the floor. I think it must have been wedged between the shelves. You probably nudged it loose when you moved the box."

I waited patiently while he rummaged through the dusty items, a man on a mission. A few minutes later, he gave a triumphant "aha" and held up an interesting-looking apparatus mounted on a wooden handle. Taking the device back over to the stairs, he placed the card in the holder and raised the viewer to the light. "Wow, this is cool. The image is so clear it's as if they're standing right here in front of me."

He handed me the stereoscope and I lifted it to the light. My eyes took a moment to adjust and then the subjects leaped out at me, so much so that I was startled by the perception. As Macon said, they could have been standing directly in front of us, so sharp and uncanny the image. My gaze was magnetically drawn to each of those solemn faces dominated by dark, piercing eyes.

Then I began to notice other oddities. A small wagon-like contraption in the background. A fenced enclosure beneath the front porch where a dog might have been penned. I could even see a grainy face in an upstairs window staring down at the trio.

A familiar face.

The image blurred as my fingers tightened around the polished handle. I couldn't believe my own eyes. It must only be my imagination, some weird optical illusion because there was no reasonable explanation for what I saw. But I was a woman who lived among ghosts. My world didn't operate on reason and logic.

Taking a moment to steady myself, I brought the image back into focus. The girls disappeared and the man faded away until I saw only that face peering down from the upstairs window.

The eyes, the nose, the mouth—the same understated features that stared back at me from the mirror.

Four

After sipping a cup of chamomile, my nerves began to settle, but I was by no means calm. I tried to convince myself I was overreacting, but what were the chances of that stereogram turning up in the cellar at the same time I was being visited by the sightless apparition?

Macon hadn't seemed to notice anything unusual in the image or my demeanor. A phone call had pulled him away before he could study the card further, and by the time he returned, he was anxious to get on with his work. I'd escaped upstairs with the viewer and stereogram and had taken both straight to my office, where they now sat on my desk until I could decide what to do with them.

I wasn't particularly worried about having either in my house. I'd never believed that possessions or even places could be haunted. People were haunted. However, ghosts could sometimes use objects to communicate, and I had to wonder if the stereogram was yet another message from the blind ghost.

It was a big leap, and as I went about my business for the rest of the day, I reminded myself that now was not the time to let my imagination run wild. I had a bid to work up for Seven Gates Cemetery, my blog to update and a speech to write for the Oak Grove dedication ceremony. Until I had time to investigate, I would do well to put that card out of my mind.

But no matter how hard I tried to concentrate, my attention kept straying. The stereogram kept calling. Whether it was a facet of my personality or the nature of my business, I couldn't rest when a mystery needed solving.

Succumbing to temptation, I inserted the card in the holder and brought it to my eyes, turning my chair to the natural light so that I could scrutinize the three-dimensional image for messages and clues. But the only thing that meant anything to me was the face in the upstairs window.

At least now I could assume that my look-alike had once actually existed. She wasn't a vision of my future self, but a ghost from the past. That revelation should have eased my mind, but the fact remained, she'd followed me through the veil for a reason. She'd warned me to find a key, but where was I to even look?

Shivering, I set the stereo card aside and examined the viewer, noticing for the first time a small silver plate fastened to the underside. The inscription was so tiny I could just make it out: "To Mott, From Neddy. Together Forever."

In even smaller print at the very bottom of the metal tag was the name of a shop: Dowling Curiosities, Charleston.

Given the age of the stereoscope and how long it had likely been stored in the basement, I hadn't much hope that the shop would still be in business. To my surprise, however, a Google search yielded a King Street address. I'd undoubtedly passed it any number of times while strolling through the historic district. I diligently noted the information in my phone so that I could look for the place on my next walk.

For the rest of the afternoon, I remained at my desk, alternately working on bids and studying the stereogram until hunger pains disrupted my concentration. Since Devlin would be spending the evening with his grandfather, I decided to walk down the street to a little place on Rutledge for an early dinner. To my surprise, however, he was sitting on the front porch waiting for me when I arrived home a little while later. As I approached the steps, a light breeze trailed a trace of his cologne, a dark, spicy scent with hints of warm vanilla and a dangerous note of absinthe. Sultry, seductive and a bit decadent for the daylight hours, but that was Devlin.

The late-afternoon sunlight filtering down through the trees blinded me for a moment so that he became nothing more than a dark form imprinted upon my retinas. It almost seemed as if another shape hovered over him, but then I blinked and, like the mysterious stereogram, the two images merged into one.

"I thought you were having dinner with your grandfather tonight," I said in surprise.

"I am. But I happened to be passing by your house and I had the urge to see you before I head out." He paused to stare down at me for the longest moment. "Are you all right? You were scowling just now as you came through the garden."

"Was I? The sun was in my eyes." I sidestepped out of the glare and as my vision adjusted, I was struck yet again by his devastating good looks. Despite the heat, he appeared as fresh as the proverbial daisy, his cotton shirt crisp, the line of his tailored pants still neatly creased. As I climbed the stairs, it occurred to me that I'd never sufficiently appreciated a well-fitting trouser until I met Devlin.

When I got to the top step, he bent to kiss me. Normally, I would have gone willingly into his arms, drawn by that delectable scent and his innate allure, but I found myself strangely reticent, holding back my desire as I tried to resurrect defenses that had tumbled upon our first meeting.

More and more I was coming to understand Papa's withdrawal. Retreating behind the wall of his own troubled thoughts had been the only way he knew to protect himself and those around him from the ghosts.

Devlin searched my face. "I don't think it was the sun. Something's wrong. I can see it in your eyes."

"I'm just tired."

"Because you're not sleeping." He trailed his knuckles along my jawline. "I wish Rupert Shaw had never talked you into going back to Oak Grove. You've been having nightmares ever since you agreed to finish the restoration."

"It's a very dark cemetery," I said. "A troubled place even before the murders."

His gaze deepened. "But it is just a place. What happened there was human evil, not supernatural. You do know that, right?"

He wasn't entirely correct, but I could hardly argue

the point. "Not all my feelings about Oak Grove are negative. We met because of that cemetery. I certainly don't regret that. Although I'd like to think that our paths would have crossed regardless."

His eyes softened and some of the strain between us melted. "Such a romantic notion from someone usually so serious."

"The two aren't mutually exclusive, you know."

"In you, they're not. I've never known anyone so full of contradictions. You're a very complicated woman, which is only one of the many reasons I find you so fascinating."

"You find me fascinating?" I asked without guile.

"Have I not made that clear?" He cupped the back of my neck as he gazed into my eyes. "*Endlessly* fascinating."

I felt my knees go weak at the dark glint in his eyes, at the provocative edge in his drawl. Then foolishly I wondered if he'd once thought the same of Mariama, and I glanced away.

He took my chin and brought my face back to his. "Hey. What's that look?"

"Sometimes I'm still surprised by us," I admitted. "You and me. That we're together."

"Why?"

"We're so different. We come from different places."

"Maybe that's why we work. Our differences keep things interesting," he said lightly, but his expression sobered. He tucked back a strand of hair that had escaped from my ponytail. "I hate seeing you like this. So exhausted and distracted. Nothing's going to happen if you fall asleep, you know. I'll do everything in my power to keep you safe."

"I know that. Just as I'll do everything in my power to keep you safe. But some things are beyond our control. Even you have no sway over my nightmares."

"Maybe you sell me short," he said and tugged me to him.

This time I didn't pull away, proving, I supposed, that when it came to Devlin, I didn't have the courage of my convictions. If the blind ghost lurked in the shadows, I was oblivious to her presence, attuned to nothing more than my own pounding pulse and those seductive eyes peering down at me.

Devlin murmured something to me that later I would never be able to recall except for the silken drawl of my name. His kiss, when it came, was very slow, very deliberate and devastatingly effective. But his hands... Those strong, graceful hands were greedy and grasping... touching here, skimming there...making me tremble with need as I clutched at his shirt.

Somehow I found myself backed up against the porch wall, protected from the street by his body. He lifted my top, pressing his hands to my breasts and deepening the kiss with his tongue. I locked my hands around his neck and threw my head back with abandon as his mouth moved to my throat, then to my ear, then back to my lips. The traffic noises faded and the floorboards evaporated beneath my feet. Only the sound of his voice brought me back to earth.

"Sorry. I got carried away." He moved back to adjust my shirt. "I know you're not one for public spectacles."

"You didn't hear me complain, did you?" I asked breathlessly. "I wanted you to do that. All of it. When you touch me like that…"

"Like this?" he murmured, his hands sliding back inside my shirt.

Electricity sizzled along my spine. "Yes, exactly like that."

With the tip of my finger, I traced the outline of the silver medallion he wore tucked in his shirt. I fancied I could feel the coolness of the medal beneath the fabric and the quiver of power and history contained inside that ominous emblem.

"You always know how to get to me, don't you?" I said. "You know just where to touch me, how to look at me so that I can't help losing control. Sometimes I wonder how you do it."

"How I do what?"

"That," I said with a shudder as he pulled me closer. "Everything you do makes me want you even more. I've never felt this way before. That sounds like a very bad cliché, I know, but it's true. All you have to do is say my name and I melt. It's as if you've cast a spell over me."

I expected him to kiss me again after that candid and perhaps ill-advised confession and then sweep me inside to the bedroom to prove just how vulnerable to his touch I truly was. Instead, his mood seemed to shift as a disquieting shadow flashed in his eyes, and for some inexplicable reason, I thought again of Mariama, a sultry, hedonistic woman versed in the ways of dark magic. She was gone now, her ties to Devlin thankfully severed, but I wasn't foolish enough to discount the influence she'd once had over him or the things she had undoubtedly taught him.

Was that why he still wore the medallion? As protection against her treacherous grip?

He claimed he didn't believe in the power of talismans, and yet I'd never seen him without the silver emblem around his neck, the entwined snake and claw chillingly symbolic of the entanglements and dangerous alliances that came from being a member of the Order. And from being Mariama Goodwine's husband.

The mood tainted by thoughts of his dead wife, I extricated myself from his embrace. "You've a long drive ahead of you and I don't want to make you late."

"Yes, it wouldn't do to keep the old man waiting." He seemed to immediately regret his harshness. "Sorry. I don't mean to be short with you. As you may have guessed, I'm not looking forward to the evening."

I put a hand on his sleeve. "Are you sure there's nothing else bothering you? Seems to me I'm not the only one who's been distracted lately."

Now it was Devlin who detached himself from my touch, gently brushing aside my hand as he moved out of the shade into a patch of waning sunlight. "I'm fine."

He hovered at the top of the steps gazing out over the garden before he turned to glance back at me. The look on his face made me tremble even though I was hard pressed to put a name to the indefinable darkness I glimpsed in his eyes. Wariness? Resolve?

No, I thought with a jolt. What I saw in Devlin's eyes was dread.

Five

❦

That night, I turned in early with a new novel, but exhaustion claimed me before I made it through the first chapter. Saving my place with a crystal bookmark my aunt had given to me years ago, I turned off the light and snuggled down in the covers as I tried to clear my mind of secrets, stereograms and the smell of old decay in the cellar.

I must have been dreaming about that smell because the phantom scent roused me from the first deep sleep I'd had in nights. I lay very still with eyes wide-open, trying to orient myself in the darkness. The odor was so fleeting and indistinct it might well have been a remnant of my dream. I wasn't frightened. Not then. Not until I heard breathing.

The rhythmic sawing was low and croaky. Human but not human.

A thrill of alarm chased across my scalp even as I tried to rationalize the sound. It was just an old-house noise like all the other creaks and groans I heard from time to time. The doors and windows were locked tight. A human intruder couldn't get in without making sufficient racket to wake me and it was a rare occurrence for a ghost to penetrate hallowed ground. I was safe here in my sanctuary. I desperately needed to believe that.

But as I lay there drenched in moonlight and dread, the sound came again, raspy and furtive. And close. Very close. Right behind the headboard, I was certain.

My own breath quickened as I slowly turned.

Nothing was there. Nothing that I could see. *Because the sound came from inside the wall.*

I wanted more than anything to leap from bed, put distance between myself and those terrifying rasps, but instead I lay there listening to the darkness as my mind raced back to the conversation with Macon. He'd said earlier that something was nesting in the cellar. An opossum or a rat, perhaps?

An animal would certainly explain the musky smell, but what of the breathing? The ragged exhalation suggested something larger than a rodent, a sentient prowler that could invade hallowed ground and maneuver its way into my sanctuary.

Slipping a hand from beneath the covers, I reached for the lamp switch. Light flooded the room, chasing shadows from corners and momentarily staunching my terror. Nothing stirred. I saw no evidence of a visitor, animal or otherwise. The rasping had stopped, but I still had a sense that something hunkered inside the wall. I could feel an avid presence behind the plaster.

Climbing out of bed, I plucked one of my slippers from the floor and then, taking a position at the end of the bed, I flung the shoe against the wall above the headboard. I heard a muffled squeal, followed by furious scratching that now came from the hallway.

Gooseflesh popped at the back of my neck. I had no idea what I was dealing with. Human, animal… something from another realm? I couldn't imagine the space between the walls accommodating anything larger than a raccoon, but if the sound really had come from the hallway outside my bedroom… If something had found a way in through the basement…

Images spiraled through my head as I stood there trembling. The last thing I wanted to do was leave my bedroom to investigate, but what choice did I have? I needed to make sure nothing was loose in my house.

Oh, how I wished for Angus's company at that moment. Ever since the battered mutt had adopted me during a restoration in the Blue Ridge Mountains, he'd been my constant companion, a guardian against intruders from this world and the next. But he was in the country with my parents because I'd thought, foolishly perhaps, that they needed his protection more than I did.

Grabbing a flashlight from my bedside drawer, I eased through the door and inched my way down the corridor, pausing now and then to track a new sound. Was that the scratch of a claw, the faint click of a door?

By the time I reached the kitchen, I'd almost managed to convince myself that nothing was amiss. I was just about to step into my office when a soft thud brought me around with a jerk.

My gaze went straight to the cellar door and I paused there with hammering heart. Then I tiptoed across the room, and I pressed my ear to the thick wood. All was silent in the cellar, but I could feel cold air seeping through the keyhole. Not for anything would I put my eye to the aperture, but I had to wonder if something was on the other side peering in at me.

I knelt and shone the flashlight beam through the opening. A high-pitched squeal—or was it a whistle?—had me scrambling back to the middle of the kitchen floor. Drawing my knees close to my chest, I sat there quaking, my gaze glued to that keyhole.

I still didn't see how a flesh-and-bone intruder could have invaded my sanctuary. The only way in from the cellar was through that locked door…unless…

Could there be a hidden crawl space somewhere?

My gaze darted about the kitchen. The notion of a secret passageway was deeply disturbing, but I wasn't about to go exploring for the entrance. For now, all I could do was seal the keyhole with a piece of duct tape and shove a table up against the door—futile precautions that did little to calm my nerves.

Leaving lights on all over the house, I went back to the bedroom and crawled under the covers, bracing myself for another long, sleepless night. Turning to the nightstand to retrieve my novel, I froze with a gasp.

The translucent husk of a cicada, perfectly preserved and still attached to a twig, lay on top of the book. The silver bookmark with the dangling crystals was gone.

Six

I was very tired the next morning, having dozed only fitfully after I'd gone back to bed. The insect shell left on the nightstand troubled me greatly because it was concrete proof that *something* had been in my house, even in my bedroom. In hindsight, the actions of my strange visitor seemed almost childlike—pilfering my sparkly bookmark after a macabre game of hide-and-seek. But this revelation made the intrusion no less alarming. Quite the opposite, in fact.

Despite my exhaustion, I managed to rise at a decent hour and was out the door well before nine. I'd scheduled a meeting with a local historical society for late morning, but I still had plenty of time to investigate Dowling Curiosities.

I found a place to park, and as I walked along the shady streets, the sights, sounds and tantalizing smells of a Charleston morning helped soothe my ragged nerves. The tourists were already up and about, although most of the upscale shops along King Street's antiques district were not yet open.

Passing the address of the shop, I backtracked but saw no sign or shingle. I thought I'd entered the wrong address in my phone until I realized the shop was located at the back of a building. Access was through a wrought iron gate and down a cobblestone alley lined with potted gardenias.

A sign in the window informed me that the shop would open at ten so I headed over to the harbor for a walk along the water. By the time I returned, it was a few minutes after ten and I could see some activity in the shop. A woman was just leaving and we nodded to one another in passing. Bells announced my arrival and her departure as the door swished closed and I stood for a moment gazing around.

Dowling Curiosities was small, cramped and smelled of camphor. The restricted space might ordinarily have repelled me, but the light shining in through the windows was pleasant and the crowded displays had been styled by a clever hand: antique dolls dressed in mourning clothes, carnival sideshow posters in gilded frames, glass cabinets showcasing all manner of curios from ivory-handled dueling pistols to bizarre mechanical toys. And on long shelves above the display cases, dozens of antique cameras and stereoscopes.

As I approached the back counter, a man came through the curtains and stopped dead when he saw me, his hand flying to his heart.

"Oh, my," he said on a sharp breath. "You gave me a fright. I didn't know anyone was about. I heard the bells but assumed that was Mrs. Hofstadter leaving."

"We passed each other in the doorway."

"Ah, that explains it."

I looked around doubtfully. "You are open for business, aren't you?"

"Yes, of course." He stepped up to the counter with a welcoming smile and I found myself charmed by his whimsical fashion statement—plaid pants and a sweater vest over a lavender shirt with a popped collar. He looked to be in his mid- to late thirties, but the silky sweep of dark blond hair across his brow gave him a boyish look that belied the tiny crinkles around his gray eyes. "How may I help you?"

"I'm hoping to find some information about an antique stereoscope."

"Well, you've certainly come to the right place. Stereoscopy happens to be a passion," he said. "What kind of stereoscope are you interested in?"

"I'm not here to buy. I found an old viewer in my basement and I'm hoping you can tell me something about it."

As we spoke, I removed the stereoscope from my bag and placed it on the counter. He picked up the device and lifted it briefly to his eyes even though the cardholder was empty.

"This is a handsome piece. Manufactured by the Keystone View Company here in the States. You can still see their stag elk trademark on the side. See?" He pointed out the emblem. "The unit appears extremely well preserved for having been stored in a damp basement." He gave me a reproachful glance.

"I had no idea it was even there," I said defensively.

"What a wonderful find, then. I'd put the age somewhere around 1890 to 1900."

"That old?"

"Yes, indeed," he said as he carefully returned the viewer to the counter. When he glanced up, there was a shrewd gleam in his eyes. "If you're looking to sell, I should warn you that the Monarch—which you have here—was the most common viewer on the market back in those days. Handheld units were mass-produced and relatively inexpensive even in the late nineteenth century. They're collectible, of course, but not as highly prized as the larger stereoscopes."

"It's not mine to sell. As I said, I came across it in my basement and I'm trying to determine the original owner."

"That'll be next to impossible, I'm afraid." He leaned an arm against the counter and I got a whiff of orange blossoms with a dark base note of hawthorn. "A viewer this old has undoubtedly changed hands any number of times. Unless you know how it came to be in your cellar, I don't know how you'd be able to trace the provenance."

"That's why I came here, Mr. Dowling—"

"Owen, please." He flashed a beguiling grin.

"I think you may be in a unique position to help me…Owen. There's a small silver tag on the bottom with the name of this shop and an inscription."

He lifted a curious brow as he turned the viewer over. "So there is. 'To Mott, From Neddy. Together Forever,'" he read, a frown fleeting across his features as he studied the plate.

"Do you recognize those names?" I asked anxiously.

"What? No," he said with a distracted air. "I was just trying to remember when we switched from silver plating to brass tags for inscriptions." He paused, considering. "I don't recall ever seeing one like this, so I think we can safely assume the viewer was bought and sold before my time."

"I know it's a long shot," I said on a hopeful note. "But I thought you might have a sales receipt or even a record of the engraving."

"The computerized files won't go back that far, and even if they did, it would be impossible to locate a receipt without a last name. But if I may make a suggestion?"

"Please.

"If you'd like to leave the viewer, I'll be only too happy to show it to my great-aunt. She's owned the shop for nearly forty years and I believe she used to do all the engraving herself. The names in the inscription are rather unusual, so there's a chance she might remember them."

"Would it be possible for me to come back later when she's in?"

Owen Dowling shook his head regretfully. "Her visits are few and far between, I'm afraid. She rarely even comes to Charleston these days."

"I see." I pulled a business card from my bag and placed it on the counter between us. "If you or your aunt should think of anything, would you please give me a call?"

He glanced down at the card and another scowl skidded across his forehead, but when he looked up, his expression showed nothing but a mild curiosity. "You're a cemetery restorer."

"I am."

"I don't think I've ever met one before. Sounds like a fascinating profession."

"It can be. Anyway, thank you for your time."

"It was my pleasure. I only wish I could have been of more assistance."

I shrugged in resignation and thanked him again as I returned the stereoscope to my bag.

A phone rang in the back and he pocketed my card with an apologetic smile as he glanced over his shoulder. "Sorry. I'm the only one here so I have to get that. But please…" He waved a hand to encompass the showroom. "Stay and have a look around. Take your time and enjoy our curiosities."

"I have an appointment, but some other time perhaps." My voice trailed away as he disappeared through the curtain and I could hear the rumble of his voice as he answered the phone. I would have liked nothing more than to spend the rest of the morning browsing through all the oddities and treasures, but I had to get to my meeting with the Greater Charleston Historical Society.

The pleasing tinkle of the bells followed me out into the sunshine. As I started down the cobblestone alley toward the street, something compelled me to glance over my shoulder.

Owen Dowling stood just beyond the doorway peering after me. He had a phone to his ear, and as our gazes connected, he stepped back into the shadows as if he didn't wish to be seen.

I experienced the oddest sensation in that moment. Part premonition, part déjà vu. I'd never met the man before, had never been to that shop. Yet I couldn't shake the notion that I had been guided to Dowling Curiosities for a reason, and that my visit with Owen Dowling had somehow set something dark and dangerous in motion.

Seven

Later that afternoon, I headed out again, this time to see Dr. Rupert Shaw at the Charleston Institute for Parapsychology Studies. As I came around the side of the Institute after parking, I shot a glance across the street at Madam Know-It-All's, the palmist I'd become acquainted with last fall. I didn't linger to try to catch a glimpse of her. I was in too much of a hurry to speak with Dr. Shaw.

"He's expecting you," the new assistant said with a smile after I introduced myself. "I'll take you back."

She escorted me down the hallway and motioned me through a set of thick pocket doors. "Go on in. If either of you need anything, I'll be at my desk."

"Thank you."

As her heels clattered down the hallway, I stepped across the threshold and glanced around the room, relieved to see the same cozy muddle that I remembered so fondly. If anything, the stacks of books on the wooden floor had grown to a new, precarious level and an assortment of files and magazines threatened to swallow Dr. Shaw's massive desk.

The French doors stood open to the garden and I

spotted his lanky silhouette at the edge of the terrace. He stood with one hand propped against a column, his head turned slightly away from me, but I could still see his careworn profile. His profound sadness caught me off guard, and I paused before knocking or calling out his name. A second later, he stepped in from the garden, his eyes lighting when he saw me.

"There you are. Right on time as always. I was just outside getting a little fresh air." The melancholy I'd glimpsed a moment earlier was now carefully masked, but there was no disguising the ravages of grief. The past few months had not been kind to Dr. Shaw. The sorrow of losing his only son had etched deep furrows in his brow, and his eyes held the shadows of a man haunted by memories and regret—a look I'd seen often in Devlin's eyes.

Not wishing to be caught staring, I bent to remove the antique stereoscope from my bag and placed it on his desk.

He picked up the device and turned it in his hand. "What an interesting piece."

"I thought you might find it so. And this is the stereogram."

He took his time scrutinizing the images before slipping the card in the holder as he swung his chair around to capture the light. "The faces are startlingly clear, aren't they? Almost as if they could speak to us." His voice held a note of wonder. "Are there others?"

"Other stereograms, you mean? It's possible. The basement is crammed full of old boxes."

"Worth a look, I should think." He lowered the viewer and swiveled back to his desk. "The resemblance is uncanny. I'm referring to the woman in the window, of course. Is she an ancestor?"

"I have no idea." I released a breath that I hadn't realized I'd been holding. The fact that he could see her was confirmation that she'd been alive at the time the photograph was taken.

"Surely someone must have mentioned how much you favor a grandmother or great-aunt or distant cousin," he suggested.

"No, never. Until last fall, I'd been told I was adopted."

"But you're not?"

"The circumstances of my birth are unusual, to say the least."

"I see." He removed a magnifying glass from his desk and studied the images for another long moment. "Intriguing the way the camera caught her in that window. Almost as if she were a guardian watching over them," he mused.

"I hadn't thought of her that way," I said. "I wish I knew who they all were."

"You don't recognize the man?"

I glanced up at the note of excitement in his tone. "No. Should I?"

"You're much too young, I expect. Ezra Kroll's legacy is all but forgotten these days, but there was a time when the very whisper of his name could send a chill down one's spine."

"Ezra Kroll?" My pulse quickened, though I was certain I'd never heard of the man before. "Who was he?"

"The founder of a rather mysterious commune back

in the fifties. He and his followers lived in a self-sustained colony a few miles south of Isola in Aiken County. Some of his relatives still reside in that town."

Something niggled. Not a memory but a bristling awareness that this tidbit was important. A clue, perhaps?

"What about the children?" I asked. "His daughters, I presume?"

"Kroll had no offspring. But I seem to recall reading something about twin sisters. Conjoined twins," he added.

"What age were they when they were separated?"

"They were never separated."

"Never?" All of a sudden, the inscription from the stereogram flashed through my brain: *To Mott, From Neddy. Together Forever.* "What happened to them?" I asked with a shiver.

"It was very tragic if the stories are to be believed. One of the twins died. The other was so distraught that she tried to hide her sister's passing by using cloves to cover the smell. It was days before anyone caught on."

I stared at him in horror. "Is that true?"

"Cloves were used in the Middle Ages to disguise the stench and flavor of rotting meat."

"No, I mean…is it true that they were still joined even after the sister passed?"

"Who's to say? Stories become embellished over time." He dropped his gaze to the stereogram, scrutinizing it for another long moment. "Notice the way they're standing back-to-back, heads turned to the camera, expressions identical. If I didn't know better, I'd think it was an optical illusion."

I put a hand to my nape, where the flesh still tingled. "What else can you tell me about Kroll?"

"He was a distinguished scholar and scientist who seemed to have a brilliant future ahead of him, but he came back from the war a changed man. He gave up his family, career, money—everything—to pursue his vision of utopia. He gathered like-minded people around him, many of them former soldiers desperate for a quiet life. And for a time, Kroll Colony flourished. But every paradise has its serpent. No one knew anything was wrong until the smell drifted into town."

My fingers tightened around the chair arms. "What happened?"

"Mass suicide. Men, women, children…all gone. Kroll's body was found sometime later in the woods with a gunshot wound to the head."

"Self-inflicted?"

"More than likely, although there have been contradicting theories down through the years. The bodies from the Colony were buried far away from the public cemetery and sealed off by a stone fence. The place is isolated and nearly hidden by an overgrown maze that can be quite daunting to navigate, especially when the light starts to fade."

"I take it you've been there."

"Yes. A few years ago I was contacted by one of his sisters, a woman named Louvenia Durant. She owns a Thoroughbred farm in Aiken County. The cemetery is located on the property she inherited from Kroll's estate. Over the years, there have been reports of strange lights. She requested that the Institute send someone down to do some readings."

"What did you find?"

"A few pings on the EMF meter, a bit of static on the recorder, but nothing of consequence. However, the visit was well worth our time. Kroll Cemetery is the most strangely beautiful place I've ever investigated. There are thirty-seven graves inside, all of them marked with unusual headstones and tombs."

"What's so unusual about them?" I asked.

"For one thing, the symbols are unlike anything I've ever seen. Each marker is inscribed with a seemingly random number and a key—"

"A *key*?"

He gave me a quizzical look as he nodded. "No two are alike. The effect is quite eerie."

"I can imagine," I said on a breath. "Normally a key represents knowledge or, if wielded by an angel or saint, the means to enter heaven. Crossed keys symbolize Saint Peter. But the keys you've described…" I trailed off, tamping down the advent of something fearful in my stomach. I had a bad feeling that I was being led down a dangerous path with nothing but these esoteric bread crumbs to guide me. "I don't know what to make of them."

"Some claim the cemetery is a puzzle or riddle that no one has ever been able to solve. Just think of it." Dr. Shaw leaned forward, eyes gleaming. "All those clues and symbols hidden behind high walls for decades, waiting for someone clever enough to come along and put all the pieces together. And who better to solve a graveyard mystery than you, my dear?"

Eight

The breeze that blew across the Institute's parking area was warm and fragrant, but I couldn't stop trembling as I climbed into my car and started the engine. As anxious as I was to get home to my computer, I sat for several long moments, idly watching crepe myrtle blossoms pepper the hood as I tried to dissect all that I'd learned.

A twin desperate to cling to her dead sister. A commune that had ended in tragedy. A cemetery of keys and suicides. All seemingly linked by a strange stereogram that had turned up in my cellar.

I had no idea how the pieces fit together, but by the time I nosed my car onto the street, I could feel the tightening fetters of an obsession. Who in my position could resist the puzzle of that tiny walled graveyard and the mystery of all those keys? That I might somehow be personally connected to Kroll Cemetery only added to my fixation.

As soon as I got home, I went straight to the office and opened my laptop. An anticipatory thrill quickened my heart as I typed in the name Ezra Kroll and watched the links pop up. Curling a leg underneath me, I relaxed more comfortably into my chair and soon became lost in research.

Nothing I learned about Kroll would suggest the evil charisma of a cult leader or demagogue. To the contrary, he had been a gentle, unassuming scholar who'd eschewed the violent culture that had sent him and so many other young men off to war. He'd chosen, instead, to live simply and in harmony with nature, which made the tragedy at Kroll Colony all the more unfathomable.

Hours passed as I sat spellbound. Twilight came and went. The questions raised by my visit to Dr. Shaw and now by my own research spun on and on until I finally gave up and went to bed.

I'd tossed the cicada husk in the trash that morning, but as I flipped on the light to turn down the bed, I cast a wary glance at the nightstand. Nothing was there. No insect shell or bookmark. I heard nothing in the walls, smelled nothing untoward in the air. All was calm in the house, but it was a very long time before I slept.

Sometime later I was again awakened by a noise. I lay there straining to hear scratches in the wall or raspy breathing behind my headboard, but the disturbance was different this time. Distant and less distinct. It came to me that I may not have been roused by a sound at all, but by a sixth-sense certainty that I was no longer alone.

I eased open the nightstand drawer and removed a fresh can of pepper spray, which would be of no use against ghosts, but might offer a modicum of protection against the more substantive entities I called in-betweens. If a thing could breathe and scramble through walls, it could also feel pain, I reasoned. It might even be as frightened as I was. A squirt to the eyes might be enough to startle such a creature away.

That my mind would even go to such a place revealed how far I'd come from a time when ghosts had been the only supernatural encounters in my life. Now I lived in a world populated by all manner of shadowy beings.

Clutching the canister, I padded across the room and peered through the door before merging into the thicker gloom of the hallway. As I approached the kitchen, I paused once more to listen. I started to move through the doorway only to stop dead, one foot suspended over the threshold as a breeze stirred my hair. In the same moment, I realized I could hear the faint swish of passing cars out on the street as if a door or window had been left open.

I saw something move in my office then. A flickering shadow. A flash of light. Instinctively, I melted back into the darkness in the hallway and counted to ten before chancing another glance into my office.

A figure stood behind my desk, rifling through the contents of a drawer. The form was dark but well defined against the windows. I couldn't make out any features, but I took note of what I could see—black clothing, slim build, tallish. And human.

Which would explain why I'd detected no abnormal chill in the air, no death scent in the draft that once again lifted my hair. How the intruder had managed to invade my house so stealthily, I had no idea.

My first impulse was to backtrack down the hallway and get to my phone, but I was afraid that even the slightest movement would draw his attention. I couldn't know if he was armed, but I had to assume he was dangerous, perhaps even desperate. I wanted to believe all I had to do was stay out of sight and once he discovered that I had nothing of value in my office, he'd leave.

But he didn't appear easily discouraged. He closed one drawer and opened another, strewing papers all over my desk. I had no idea what he might be after, but if he decided to search the rest of the house, I was a sitting duck. As soon as he crossed through the kitchen into the hallway, he'd spot me cowering in the shadows. I couldn't remain hidden forever. I had to get to the front door or to my bedroom, where I could lock myself in and call the police.

I moved slightly, testing the floorboards. The creak beneath my feet sounded as loud as a gunshot. Before I had time to blink or even draw a breath, the intruder leaped over the desk—in a single bound I would later swear—and lunged toward me.

Stunned by his agility, I was slow to react. By the time I whirled and dashed down the corridor, he was almost upon me. His footsteps, silent earlier, pounded on the old wooden floorboards, the creaks and moans sending a sharp, cold panic up my spine.

I'd walked that hallway hundreds of times. I knew every nook and cranny by heart and as I raced toward the foyer, I searched my memory for a weapon or the nearest escape route.

He was right behind me, gaining on me with every step. I hit the wall, barely evading his grasping fingers, and sent a small table crashing to the floor. We both tripped and in those precious moments it took to right my balance, I stumbled past my bedroom door.

I'd bought myself some time, but not enough to backtrack to the phone, much less unfasten the dead bolt and chain lock on the front door. Instead, I raced through the parlor archway and flattened myself against the wall, trying to control my breathing as I scanned the room.

The windows were all closed and locked. By the time I could wrench one open, he'd be on me again. The house was a death trap. I couldn't hope to hide or evade him for long so I had to take a stand.

All this sailed through my mind as I readied my finger on the pepper spray. I knew where he was in the hall even though he was silent. He knew where I was, too. I sensed his intense concentration and the penetration of his stare through the wall.

Reflex, surprise and that puny can of pepper spray were my only defenses. All I could do was let instinct take over. The moment he appeared in the doorway, I leaped out and pointed the nozzle at his face.

The spray hit him in the eyes and he fell back into the foyer. I used that moment of shock to grab a nearby lamp and swing it at his head. The blow brought him to his knees. He collapsed between the front door and me so I sprinted into the hallway.

His hand shot out and gripped my ankle, yanking me off my feet. I hit the floor hard, air gushing from my lungs as the can skittered across the floor away from my grasp. For a moment I could do nothing but flail helplessly. Summoning my strength, I propelled myself forward on hands and knees, but the assailant grabbed me again.

I rolled onto my back and we were suddenly face-to-face. In that terrifying moment, I could have sworn I recognized the gleam of his eyes through the ski mask. Then I lashed out with my legs, pedaling them frantically until, stunned by the blows and the ferocity of my attack, he fell back into a table. In all that time, in all that commotion, he never made a sound. Not even a grunt.

Clamoring up the stairs to the door at the top, I pounded as hard as I could and called out to Macon. The door had been permanently bolted when the house had been converted into two apartments. He wouldn't be able to let me in, but if he heard my screams, he'd call the police—

Arms snared me from behind, one encircling my waist, the other clamping over my mouth.

For what seemed an eternity, we struggled at the top of the stairs until my feet flew out from under me and I tumbled backward down the stairs. The intruder fell with me and we sprawled side by side on the foyer floor. I must have blacked out for a moment because I saw faces swimming on the inside of my eyelids. Distorted visages that I didn't recognize but somehow knew. One of them said, "Where is it? *Where is it?*"

Where is what? I wanted to ask, but the question flitted away as light began to filter through the swirling darkness and my current predicament came rushing back to me.

I blinked several times, trying to clear my vision as I searched for a weapon—a lamp or vase, anything with which I could defend myself. I grabbed a leg from the splintered table as I crawled into a corner and propped myself up, preparing for another attack.

It was only then that I realized I was alone. Through a haze of panic, I heard footsteps stumbling down the long hallway toward the kitchen and Macon's voice yelling at me through the front door.

"Amelia! Are you all right? Amelia! Can you hear me? The police are on the way."

Hitching myself up against the wall, I staggered across the foyer, undid the locks and threw open the front door. The last thing I remembered was Macon's eyes going wide with shock as I pitched forward.

Nine

For most of my life, ghosts moved silently through my world, leaving nothing behind when they floated back through the veil but a lingering chill and a dread of twilight. However, once that forbidden door had been opened by my association with a haunted man, some of the spirits had started to communicate—a development that came with a terrifying suspicion that my gift was far darker, far more dangerous than Papa had ever let on.

The encounters had been mostly with entities that were somehow connected to me. I told myself those bonds were the reason certain ghosts could penetrate my defenses so easily.

But as I lay alone in a hospital emergency room cubicle, the voices inside my head were unknown to me. I had the horrifying notion that the random babble came from the morgue. Confused whispers from the newly departed mingling with the tormented moans of lost souls. The macabre cacophony rose up through the hospital floors, swelling in my brain until I pressed hands to ears to try to dull the sound.

The young resident who had examined me earlier

came through the door and flashed a sympathetic smile as he approached. "It always gets crazy during a full moon."

I stared at him in astonishment as I dropped my hands to the bed. "You hear them, too?" Then I realized he was referring to the rumble of human misery coming from the other cubicles. That was *not* the sound in my head, I was certain. "How do you stand it?"

"You get used to it." He pulled up a rolling stool and sat down at my bedside. "You look as if you could do with a little good news."

"Yes, please."

"We've got most of your test results back and everything looks normal. No broken bones or signs of internal bleeding and your vitals are all stable. For someone who took a tumble down a flight of stairs, I'd say you're a very lucky woman."

"That is good news."

"You'll be sore and bruised for a few days and you may experience headaches from that bump on your head. I don't think there's any cause for alarm, but even mild concussions are nothing to take lightly. I'd like to keep you overnight so that we can monitor your reflexes."

The last thing I wanted was a stay in the hospital, but I wasn't foolish enough to second-guess a doctor. And I wondered if a concussion might be the cause of the weird disturbance in my brain. I'd never heard anything like that noise. Not even close.

"If I do have a concussion, what can I expect in the way of symptoms?"

"Depending on the severity, amnesia, dizziness, nausea, confusion. Maybe some sensitivity to light and sound."

"Sensitivity to *sound*?"

"You seemed to be experiencing a bit of that when I came in just now." He scribbled something in my file as he talked. "That's another reason I'd like to keep you overnight. As I said, I don't anticipate any problems, but with head injuries, symptoms don't always show up right away. It's best to err on the side of caution."

"What about noises *inside* my head?"

He glanced up. "You mean like ear ringing? It's not uncommon. Are you experiencing that right now?"

"Not exactly."

"What kind of noise, then?"

I hesitated. "It's like…babbling."

"As in people talking?"

"In hushed voices. It's probably coming from the hallway," I said. "Maybe I am a little sensitive to sound right now."

He rose and rechecked my pupils with a light. "Do you have a headache?"

"A slight one."

"Blurred vision?"

"No."

He had me follow his finger with my eyes and then made another note or two in the file. "Any dizziness? Nausea?"

"Not really."

"Can you tell me what day it is?"

I complied. He asked and I answered several more questions until he seemed satisfied.

"Try to relax. Someone will be in shortly to take you upstairs. It'll be quieter up there. You should be able to rest."

Macon stopped by a few minutes later, his rumpled attire and days-old beard giving him the appearance of someone who had just wandered in off the street. But despite the late hour and circumstances, he seemed surprisingly chipper, even whistled an inane tune as he removed the chart from the door and skimmed the contents.

"What's the verdict?" I asked.

"You look like something the cat dragged in," he said as he returned the file to the holder. "But you'll live."

"That's a relief. What are you still doing here anyway? Don't you have an early shift?"

"I thought you might need a little moral support and besides, I wanted to get a look at your X-rays before I left. I don't have to tell you how lucky you are, do I?"

"That seems to be the general consensus," I said with a nod. "But I've been informed that I have to stay the night so that my reflexes can be monitored."

"Normal procedure," he assured me. Then he very casually checked the dilation of my pupils just as the doctor before him had. "Headache?"

"A mild one."

"Any other discomfort?"

"Not really. Nothing I can't handle."

"Wait until morning," he cautioned. "You'll feel as if you've been hit by a freight train."

"Thanks for the warning. And by the way, may I compliment you on your bedside manner?"

He grinned. "A piece of advice? If you're offered something for pain, take it. Don't try to tough it out."

"I'll keep that in mind." I tugged the blanket a little higher because it was chilly inside the cubicle. "Right now I'm still trying to figure out how someone broke into my house without waking me. I'm normally such a light sleeper."

"One of the cops told me that the back door was jimmied with a special tool. Whoever it was knew what he was doing. You probably wouldn't have heard him even if you'd been wide-awake in the next room."

"So he came prepared," I said with a shiver. "Doesn't exactly sound like a random break-in, does it?"

Macon shrugged. "I don't know about that. According to the cop, even petty thieves have sophisticated equipment these days. They just order whatever they need off the internet."

"What else did the officer say?" I asked anxiously.

"I only spoke with him briefly and he was pretty cagey. As far as I know, they haven't taken anyone into custody so let's hope they're still out canvassing the neighborhood. Don't worry about your place. I'll keep an eye on things until you're released."

"Thanks, Macon. For everything. I don't know what would have happened if you hadn't been home tonight."

"I'm just glad you were able to wake me. I've been told it's like raising the dead. Anyway, all I did was call 911. You're the one who fought him off."

I mustered a smile. "One rises to the occasion. You

should go home and get some sleep before your shift. I'll be fine."

"I'm headed that way now. Can I get you anything before I go?"

"No, you've done more than enough, thank you. And...Macon?"

He glanced back as he started toward the door.

"Be careful, okay? It's possible someone could still be lurking about." I was thinking about the cellar and all those dark recesses where someone—something—could hide, even from the police.

"I wouldn't worry about that. Dude's long gone by now. You just get some rest."

After Macon left, I lay alone for the longest time staring up at the ceiling tiles as all those strange sounds droned on in my head. When I was a child, I'd had a recurring dream about being lost in a tunnel. I could see a light at one end, but the other end was pitch-black. I'd start toward the flicker only to be drawn back by something unseen in the dark. The tug-of-war waged on and on while disembodied arms reached through the walls to clutch at me.

I felt that same smothering claustrophobia of my dream. I couldn't see the arms, but I had a sense that something was reaching out for me, pressing in on me. The sensation was so strong I had to sit up on the gurney to catch my breath.

A panic attack, I told myself. Surely I was allowed a lapse after everything that had happened to me. Still, I didn't like feeling out of control. I wanted to be home, safe and sound in my own little sanctuary, but even that peace of mind had been taken from me now.

My head began to pound and I felt dizzy, so I lay back down and was just drifting off when I had the eerie sensation of being watched. I opened my eyes and turned my head toward the entrance, expecting to find a nurse or an orderly who would transport me upstairs. The doorway was empty, but I was certain someone had been there a moment ago.

Swinging my legs over the side of the bed, I got up and padded across the room to glance down the hallway. I found nothing unusual in the chaos of the emergency room and was about to chalk the sensation up to paranoia when a man at the end of the corridor caught my eye. He was turning a corner so I only had a glimpse of his profile, but something about his attire and the style of his hair reminded me of Owen Dowling.

It couldn't be him. The coincidence would be too great. Unless…his presence at the hospital *wasn't* a coincidence. Maybe the stereoscope was more valuable than he'd let on.

The business card I'd left only listed my name and phone number, but finding my address wouldn't have been at all difficult. And there'd been that odd awareness as I stood outside the shop, a niggling premonition that my visit to Dowling Curiosities had triggered something dangerous.

I told myself not to jump to irrational conclusions as I returned to the bed. But I lay with my eyes wide-open until someone came in to take me upstairs. The ghost voices in my head grew even louder as I was wheeled down the hallway, but once inside the elevator, they became muffled. As the car rose to the upper floors, the sound grew dimmer until a measure of calm returned to me. By the time I was rolled into the room, the sounds had vanished altogether, leaving nothing in my head but a dull throb.

A nurse helped me settle in, and then a police detective named Prescott arrived to ask questions. I would have preferred Devlin, of course, but I hadn't been able to reach him.

This detective looked to be in his mid- to late forties with thinning hair and a condescending attitude that did nothing to put me at ease.

The first thing he did was to jot down my name, address and phone number in a small notebook he pulled from his pocket. Then he took a position at the foot of my bed, where he could peer down at me. Whether he had placed himself there deliberately to intimidate me, I couldn't say, but his impervious stare unnerved me.

"I know you already gave a statement to the responding officer, but I'm going to need you to take me through it again," he said.

"Okay." I was happy that I could think a little more clearly now that the chattering in my head had subsided. "Something roused me from sleep. I don't know what it was because I don't remember hearing anything. But I woke up with a feeling that something wasn't right in the house. So I got up to investigate."

"You didn't think about calling 911?"

"No, not then. It's an old house and there are a lot of night noises." And at that point I hadn't thought the intruder human.

The door to my room opened just then and I felt

a familiar tingle up my spine, a rush of hot blood through my veins that always signaled Devlin's arrival.

He strode in—tall, lean, purposeful—and the air seemed to crackle with electricity as he moved toward me.

Ten

Maybe it was my tattered nerves or the position from which I stared up at him, but Devlin looked larger than life and far more formidable than I would have imagined under the circumstances.

In that charged air, a shiver whispered up my backbone. Even the other detective seemed to sense the shift in energy and he scowled warily as Devlin closed the distance between the door and my bed.

He was as impeccably dressed as ever in monochromatic shades of gray and charcoal, colors that brought out the premature strands of silver at his temples. His hair was mussed, as though he'd run impatient fingers through it on the way up to my floor, and his unshaven jaw gave him a rakish air that I did not find at all unattractive.

Because of the ghosts, I learned at an early age how to calm myself in times of great stress, but Devlin's sudden appearance had a profound effect on me. A knot rose in my throat as our gazes locked, but I tried to shake off my emotional response to him. It was very important that he not think of me as weak or vulnerable, that he never need worry about my mental state as he undoubtedly had with Mariama.

"Hello" was all I said.

"Hello to you, too. Are you okay?"

"Yes, it's nothing serious. A few bumps and bruises." I nodded to the man at the end of the bed. "I assume you know Detective Prescott?"

Devlin's gaze flicked over me and darkened before he turned to Prescott. "A word, Detective?"

The older cop gave him an irritated scowl. "I'm in the middle of an interview."

"I'll be brief."

Prescott nodded curtly and walked to the door. From past observations, I knew that Devlin commanded the respect of his peers, but the privileges and connections that came with his background also bred a certain amount of resentment.

The two men conversed in the hallway for a few moments and then Prescott returned to the foot of my bed while Devlin took up a position at the window.

"Did the suspect speak to you?" Prescott asked. "Did he grunt or groan during the struggle? Did you hear anything that would identify him as male?"

I hesitated. "I don't think so."

"You don't think so?"

"I blacked out for a moment. I thought I heard a voice, but it seemed dreamlike. I'm not even sure it was real."

"What did this voice say to you?"

I strained to recall. "I don't remember."

"Nothing at all?" he pressed.

I shook my head.

Prescott exchanged a look with Devlin. "You described the assailant as being a little under six feet and thin. He wore a mask over his head."

"Yes, like a ski mask." I gestured vaguely toward my face. "I couldn't see anything but his eyes."

"So you never got a look at him. Under the circumstances, you can't be one hundred percent certain the suspect was male, can you?"

"No, I suppose not. I just assumed…the way he attacked me—"

"What about smells?" Prescott interjected. "Cologne? Perfume?"

"I didn't notice any." Which was odd given my recent sensitivity to scents.

"Rings, watches?"

I shook my head.

"Scars, tattoos?"

"It all happened so fast and it was dark inside the house…" My gaze strayed back to Devlin. He stood with his back to the window, arms folded, head slightly bowed. I felt a quiver go through me at his unwavering concentration. Would I ever get used to the fierceness of that stare?

Prescott said something to me then and I had to wrench my gaze from Devlin's. "I'm sorry. Could you repeat the question?"

"Have you seen any suspicious cars in the neighborhood? Any strangers lurking about?"

"No, but I live on a busy street. I might not notice anyone new."

"Do you have any idea what the suspect was after?"

"I don't keep cash in the house, and the only items

of any real value are my laptop and cameras, some equipment I use for work, a pearl necklace. Nothing that could be sold for very much money."

Prescott shrugged. "He may not have needed a lot. A hundred bucks can keep a meth head buzzed for a couple of days."

"What makes you think he was looking for drug money?" I asked.

"The way he went after you," Devlin answered, drawing another frown from Prescott. "It's not unusual for a meth addict to display extreme aggression, especially if he feels cornered or threatened."

"Yes, I've read that," I said. "So you think the break-in was random?"

"I didn't say that." Devlin's eyes were so fathomless I hadn't a clue what he was thinking. "What I am saying is that the suspect's behavior wasn't rational. You said he leaped over the desk to get at you and he kept coming even when you fought back. He could have escaped through the same door he entered when he saw you, but instead he pursued you despite the ski mask he wore to hide his features."

My mind spun back to the attack. The assailant had been relentless, but his behavior hadn't struck me as frenetic. To the contrary, he'd seemed in control and coldly determined.

I said none of this aloud, however, because I was anxious for Prescott to leave so that I could have a private conversation with Devlin.

To my relief, the detective closed his notebook and returned the pen to his pocket. "You'll need to come in and sign your statement once you're released from

the hospital. In the meantime, if you remember anything else, give me a call."

Devlin followed him out of the room and a moment
later, I again heard their voices in the hallway.

I was tempted to climb out of bed and eavesdrop at
the door, but the effort seemed beyond my strength.
Every bone in my body had started to ache. I didn't
dare glance in a mirror. I'd never been a vain person,
but I could only imagine what I must look like.

When Devlin returned, I was in the process of pour-
ing myself a cup of water from the insulated pitcher on
the nightstand. He came over and finished the task for
me, which was probably a good thing since my hands
weren't as steady as they might have been.

He stood staring down at me until I had the strongest urge to reach up and run my fingers through
the tousled strands of his hair, to brush my knuckles
against the unaccustomed scruff on his lower face.
But more than anything, I wanted to pull him to me
for a long, comforting kiss.

I did none of those things because in that fragile
moment, I was more aware than ever of the distance
that had been growing between us.

The silence seemed to stretch forever, but only a few
seconds passed as he waited for me to finish the water.
Then he took the cup and returned it to the stand.

"How are you feeling?" His scent enveloped me as
he perched on the edge of my bed.

I shrugged. "I'm okay. No broken bones or internal injuries. Just some bruising and possibly a mild
concussion. I was admitted to the hospital to be on
the safe side."

Devlin leaned in but he made no move to touch me. He didn't have to. His presence consumed me, in part because of my shattered poise, but mostly because he was Devlin.

His gaze lingered on the tender side of my face. "Is that where he hit you?" His expression never changed, but there was something behind his eyes, a hint of violence that made my heart jolt.

I lifted a hand to my cheek. "It's from the fall. I don't think any blows were exchanged except for when I struck him with a lamp."

"I was told you put up a fight." A stranger might have mistaken his monotone for indifference, but I recognized the flatness of his delivery for what it was—supreme control.

"I'm strong for my size. I think that took him by surprise."

"You are strong," he agreed. "And brave. Frighteningly so, I sometimes think."

"Brave? Hardly." I held out my hands so that he could see how badly they still shook.

"Being brave and being fearless are two different things." He reached over and adjusted the covers around me. The gentleness of the gesture belied the darkness still simmering at the back of his eyes. "Some of the bravest people I've met were also smart enough to know when to be afraid."

"Does that include you?" I asked, our gazes locking.

"I hope so."

"Somehow I can't imagine it…you afraid."

"Why not? I'm human."

"What frightens you?" I asked.

He didn't answer, but I saw something flash in his eyes before he turned away.

As I studied his profile, the oddest vision formed in my head. Devlin was still seated on the edge of my bed, but it was as if I could see right through him into the farthest corner of the room—or into his mind—where a tall figure with a bowed head loomed in the shadows.

For a moment, I thought someone must have entered the room without my notice, but then I blinked and the illusion vanished.

"What is it?" Devlin asked, turning back to me. "You look as if you've seen a ghost."

"I'm sorry. My attention drifted for a moment. I think shock may be setting in."

The intensity of his focus stirred me in a way that only Devlin could. "Would you like for me to leave so that you can rest?"

The sensible thing would be to let him go. I was hardly fit company and I needed time to get my emotions under control. But given the vision, the headache and the voices inside my head, I didn't think it a good idea to be alone.

"I don't want you to go." I reached for his hand and when his fingers curled around mine, the unexpected bite of frost startled me. Devlin was always so warm, so steady—so human. A counterpoint to the ghosts. The coldness of his skin filled me with an unreasonable fear and my first reaction was to release him. Instead, I clung to his hand. "Stay. I need to talk to you about something."

"What is it?"

I tugged at the covers, still shaken by the chill of his touch. "I know you and Detective Prescott think the intruder was looking for money or something to hock, but I'm not so sure."

"You think he was searching for something specific?"

"I don't know. Possibly."

Devlin frowned. "Tell me."

"Macon and I found an old stereoscope in the cellar. Do you know what that is?"

"A 3-D viewer."

"There's a little metal tag on the bottom engraved with the name of a local shop. I took it in and was told that viewers from that era are collectible but not particularly valuable. If true, I don't suppose it could be the reason for the break-in."

Devlin lifted a brow. "If true? Do you have reason to doubt the validity of the assessment?"

"No, not really. But I wasn't completely honest with Detective Prescott. I do remember what the voice said to me while I was blacked out. He said, 'Where is it? *Where is it?*'"

"Why didn't you say so earlier?"

"Because it didn't seem real. I honestly believed it was just my imagination. But then earlier before I was brought upstairs, I thought I saw the shopkeeper in the ER. I only caught a glimpse so that may have been my imagination, as well. But it freaked me out a little."

"What's the name of the shop?"

"Dowling Curiosities on King Street. The man I spoke with is Owen Dowling."

Devlin gave a brief nod. "I'll check him out."

"We also found a stereogram—the card that fits into the stereoscope. The image was of a man and two girls standing in front of a white two-story house. I took the card and the stereoscope to the Institute so that Dr. Shaw could have a look at them. He identified the man as Ezra Kroll."

"As in Kroll Colony?"

"You know about that place?" I asked in astonishment. "Why have I never heard of it?

"It's like your abandoned graveyards," Devlin said. "Years pass, people forget. And it's so far off the beaten track the only way to get there is by foot or horseback."

"Then, how do you know about it?"

"When I was a kid, my grandfather owned a Thoroughbred farm not far from Isola. Some of the old-timers that worked for him would occasionally mention Kroll Colony. They were still superstitious about that place."

"Have you ever been there?"

"A few times. It was mandatory that I spend a couple of weeks every summer on the farm to build character," he said with a humorless smile. "The housekeeper had a boy about my age. Nathan Fortner. His grandfather had once been a cop, but after his retirement, he took a job in the stables. He used to tell grisly stories about the Colony, so naturally Nathan and I would ride over to the ruins anytime we could sneak away. We'd sometimes spend the whole afternoon poking through the buildings. Some of the roofs had caved in so the place was dangerous. I'm sure that was a big part of the attraction."

"Go on." I leaned forward, captivated by this glimpse into Devlin's early years. He rarely volunteered information about his childhood.

"All I remember is an old commissary, a couple of dormitories for the single colonists and a few smaller buildings for the families. Some of the houses still had scraps of old clothing and toys strewn about and the commissary even had dishes on the table from the colonists' last meal."

"I'm surprised that stuff wasn't carted off a long time ago as souvenirs. People can be ghoulish about that sort of thing."

"I'm sure some of it was, but the locals mostly kept their distance. Like I said, it was a spooky place, difficult to get to and not much to see once you got there."

"Is it still standing?"

"All the buildings burned to the ground a long time ago. There's nothing left now but the cemetery."

"Do you know how the colonists died?"

"Cyanide most likely. Back then, you could find it in local feed stores." A grim note crept into Devlin's voice. "Death would have been quick but not quick enough."

I glanced toward the window, trying to distract myself from the gruesome imagery. "Dr. Shaw said Ezra Kroll was shot to death in the woods. Apparently, there's always been a question of whether or not it was suicide."

"Nathan's grandfather was still a cop when it happened. He had a theory that none of the deaths was suicide. He believed it was mass murder perpetrated to cover up a single homicide."

I stared at Devlin in horror. "What could motivate a person to do such a thing?"

"Same motives I see every day. Jealousy, passion, greed." Devlin's expression hardened and I wondered if he was thinking about another crime of passion and greed, one that hit a little too close to home. "Ezra Kroll came back from the war a damaged man. He'd inherited the family fortune, but had no use for earthly possessions beyond what he needed to survive. He started giving all the money away to the needy while his relatives had to stand by helplessly and watch the coffers dwindle."

"So one of them took matters into their own hands?" I could hardly imagine such a thing. Three dozen innocent people, including children, had lived in Kroll Colony.

"The colonists ate every meal together," Devlin said. "It was a ritual. But on that day, Kroll missed the communal lunch. The police believed he left to meet someone who lived nearby. A woman."

My thoughts raced suddenly. If the woman in the stereogram—my look-alike—had been involved with Ezra Kroll, maybe that explained why she'd followed me back from the other side. She couldn't rest until justice was done. Like Robert Fremont, another ghost from my past, she needed a conduit to tie up her earthly loose ends.

A nurse came in just then to monitor my vitals. She shooed Devlin into the hallway, giving me a minute to reflect upon everything he'd told me as she pumped the blood-pressure cuff.

"Your heart rate is still a little elevated," she said. "Try to relax. Best thing you can do right now is rest."

"I'll try."

"Are you in pain? I can get you something to take the edge off if you need it."

"No, I'm fine."

"Press the call button if you need me," she said. "I'll send your friend back in, but remember what I said. Rest."

"I will. Thanks."

She exited silently on rubber-soled shoes and Devlin returned a moment later. "I've been given my orders," he said.

"Not to leave, I hope."

He came back over to the bed. "No, but I think we should table our discussion about Kroll Colony. It's a gruesome story and you don't need more nightmares. When you're released in the morning, you can show me everything you found in the cellar."

"About that stereogram—"

"In the morning," he insisted.

"You're right. It's better if you see it for yourself." I took his hand to pull him down beside me on the bed. "But just one last thing. When you go see Owen Dowling, be discreet, okay? He's probably done nothing wrong and I don't want to worry or embarrass him because my imagination ran away with me in the emergency room."

"Aren't I always discreet?"

An innocent question, but the subtle shift in Devlin's drawl made my blood surge. "Yes…I suppose you are…"

He leaned in, eyes as dark and sultry as a Charleston midnight. "What if I were to discreetly kiss you right now?"

"If I didn't know better, I'd think you're trying to distract me."

"Is it working?"

I sighed. "You know that it is."

"Good." He leaned in, feathering his lips over mine in a fleeting caress that made me tingle. I tunneled my fingers through his thick hair, but when I would have pulled him to me for a deeper kiss, he held back, making me want him even more as he moved his mouth lightly against mine.

Trailing kisses across my cheek, he said in my ear, "When I find the man responsible for that bruise on your face, I'll make him very, very sorry."

I drew back in shock. "Don't say that. I would hate to think of you doing anything rash or foolish on my account."

"I'll be neither rash nor foolish," he promised. "But I will be thorough."

All I could do was stare up at him. "Sometimes you frighten me."

"Why?" His hand rested on my leg, and I wondered if he was even aware of what his touch did to me.

"I look into your eyes and I still see a stranger."

This drew a scowl. "That's ridiculous. You know me better than anyone ever has."

"Do I?" Somehow I thought that honor still belonged to his dead wife.

"Yes," he insisted. "And anyway, we've done too

much talking for one night. You should try to sleep now."

I sank back against the pillows and stared up at the ceiling, still troubled by his threat. "It's too cold in here to sleep."

He stretched out beside me on the narrow bed, tucking the covers around me as he pulled me against him. "Better?"

"Much." I cushioned my head on his shoulder as we fell silent. Through the layers of his clothing I could feel the vibration of his heartbeat, strong and steady. His skin was warm now and I pressed closer, basking in the heat from his body.

"The last time we were in this hospital, our roles were reversed," I said.

"I remember." He tightened his arms around me. "I was told that you barely left my side the whole time I was unconscious."

"I was afraid if I let go of your hand, you'd slip away from me. I wouldn't be able to bring you back even with—" I broke off in midsentence as I realized what I'd been about to say. *Even with Darius Goodwine's magic.*

After the shooting, Devlin had shown no sign of awakening from his coma so in desperation I'd reached out to his old nemesis. The powerful *tagati* had brought Devlin back to me, but not without a price, I feared.

"What were you about to say?" Devlin asked.

"Nothing."

"You're trembling," he said. "Should I get you another blanket?"

"Just hold me tighter."

He complied, drawing me into his warmth. "Try to put it all out of your mind for now. You're safe here with me. I won't let anything happen to you. Close your eyes and go to sleep."

His voice was so calming, his arms strong and reassuring. I nestled down in the covers and let the rhythm of his heartbeat lull me to sleep.

When I woke up, he was gone.

Eleven

The room was dark, but I could see a silhouette looming in front of the window. I caught my breath before I realized it was Devlin.

He stood very still, his face tilted skyward, moonlight bathing his features. The hush of the hospital heightened my senses. I could hear the murmur of voices in the hallway, even the distant ping of an elevator, but my attention remained riveted on Devlin. His presence filled the room, and I drew a long breath, drinking in that indefinable essence that belonged solely to him.

As I lay there studying his profile, a large form swooped down from the sky, casting a shadow across his face and into my room before vanishing into the night. I might have thought the fleeting image had been caused by the bump on my head except for the way Devlin took a half step back from the window.

"What was that?" I gasped.

He whirled in surprise, those gleaming eyes pinning me in the moonlight. "How long have you been awake?" He sounded taken aback, though whether from my alertness or that plunging shadow, I had no idea.

Ignoring his question, I pushed myself up on my elbows to scan the window behind him. "You must have seen it, too. It was huge."

"Yes, I saw it," he said with a shrug, but there was an unexpected roughness in his tone that his aristocratic drawl couldn't disguise. "I only caught a glimpse out of the corner of my eye, but I'm sure it was an owl. Their wingspan is impressive, especially when you aren't expecting to see one."

"An owl? In the middle of the city?"

"It's not unheard of," he said. "Barn owls are fairly urbanized. They like to nest in church steeples. And we have plenty of those in Charleston."

His tone had lightened, but neither his words nor his demeanor soothed me. I found something ominous about the way he'd been staring out into the darkness so intently. "Whatever it was flew right past the window. Close enough to cast a shadow over your face and into the room."

Devlin said nothing, but instead moved toward the bed with his customary grace, his features an inscrutable mask. He looked perfectly poised, calm and unbent, but the rigid set of his shoulders betrayed a tightly coiled tension. Where moonlight slanted across his face, I could see a hint of trouble brewing in the furrows of his brow. I noticed the phone in his hand then. I hadn't heard a ring or a vibration, much less a conversation, but something had obviously transpired to disturb him.

My gaze darted to the window, then back to Devlin. "Is everything okay?"

Normally, he was as adept as I at concealing his emotions, but I was picking up a weird vibe from him tonight.

"What is it?" I urged.

Another pause. "I have to go out for a while."

"Is it a case?"

He hesitated for so long that I thought he didn't want to answer, but then he said with a hint of dread, "It's not a case. I'm told my grandfather has taken ill."

I glanced at him in alarm. "I'm sorry. I hope it's not serious."

"He was in perfect health when we had dinner so I'm convinced he's up to something. I just haven't yet figured out his angle."

"Are you so sure he has an angle? What if he really is sick?"

"That slim possibility is the only thing tearing me from this room tonight," Devlin said. "I'll be back as soon as I can, but in the meantime I'll see to it that security keeps a sharp eye out for anything or anyone suspicious."

"Don't worry about me. Whoever broke into my house is likely long gone. I'll be fine."

"Amelia…"

I waited expectantly. He wanted to tell me something. I could see it in the flare of his eyes.

I put an encouraging hand on his arm. "What is it?"

He leaned over and grazed his lips across my forehead. "I wouldn't leave you if I wasn't certain you'd be safe here."

"I know that."

"Get some rest. I'll be back before you know it."

A moment later, he was gone.

I wanted to call out to him, to tell him to be careful out there in the dark where dangers from this world and the next lay in wait.

Instead, I got up and padded over to the window to search the night sky. I still wasn't convinced I'd seen an owl earlier. For most people a nocturnal bird would have been a perfectly acceptable explanation for that diving shadow, but I wasn't most people. I knew things. Saw things. Heard things.

The past twenty-four hours had been full of strange happenings. I felt very off center. It was as if banging my head on the stairs had awakened something inside me, making me more attuned than ever to the unnatural world around me. And yet I suffered no other repercussions from the blow. I didn't feel dizzy or disoriented. I hadn't experienced any blurred vision or memory loss and even my headache had faded. I wanted to believe the visions and voices would disappear, too, once I left the hospital.

What was it the resident had told me earlier? *It always gets crazy during a full moon.* No kidding.

The moon wasn't just full but ringed. When I was a little girl, before I knew about the ghosts, Papa would tell me stories about swamp witches and boo hags that traveled through the Carolina marshes by moonlight. I later wondered if those eerie tales had been his way of preparing me for what was to come. He used to say that a lunar halo signified a time when spirits were especially restless. A dangerous time when mirrors should be covered and babies hidden so as not to be replaced by changelings.

Maybe there had been something to that warning. If the phases of the moon could affect ocean tides and human behavior, what might they stir in creatures from the other side?

Wresting my gaze from that silvery sphere, I started to turn back to my bed when I happened to glance down at the street. It was misting and the pavement shimmered with an oily patina beneath the streetlamps. My room looked out on a busy thoroughfare, but there was very little traffic at this hour. Which might explain why my attention was drawn to a lone pedestrian across the street.

The person was small, but I didn't get the sense that I was looking down at a child. Something dark and flowing was draped over the shoulders, making it nearly impossible to distinguish the silhouette among the other shadows. Indeed, for a moment I thought I might have attached human shape to a bush or tree trunk.

I told myself there was nothing at all sinister about someone being out and about at this hour. Perhaps the person was waiting for a bus. But I couldn't dismiss the feeling that a gaze had been cast upon my room. Upon *me*.

The sensation was so intense that I took a step back; my heart beat a rapid tattoo. When I dared to glance out again, the figure had disappeared, leaving me to wonder if the shadow had been nothing more than my imagination.

I went back to bed and pulled the covers up to my

chin. Sleep came with disturbing visions. I had no idea how long I'd been dreaming when my eyes popped open, senses fully alert. It would be dawn soon, a time I always anticipated, but I could still feel the pull of the dead world.

I saw the ghost then, hovering deep in the shadows. As if sensing my awareness, she drifted out of the gloom with outstretched arms and paused at the end of my bed to turn those dark-stained sockets upon me. It was the eeriest sensation, the way she stared down at me. Could she see me or did she merely sense me? Could she feel my warmth? Had she been drawn there by my energy?

She made no move toward me, to latch on to me, but instead levitated at the end of my bed for the longest moment as if making certain that I was awake. She had manifested in the same white lace dress from her previous visit, but now I saw that she clutched a key in one hand.

Before I had time to process this turn of events, she drifted through the closed door. Her message couldn't have been plainer. She wanted me to follow.

There had been a time when trailing an entity would have been unthinkable, but the days of ignoring the other world were long behind me. The ghost knew that I could see her. She was already haunting me. Perhaps if I did as she wished, she would go away and leave me alone. Not likely, but it was the only thing I had at the moment to cling to.

Climbing out of bed, I crossed to the door and glanced into the corridor. The overhead lights sputtered from an electrical surge caused—I was certain—

by the ghost's energy. There was an elevator by the nurse's station and another at the opposite end of the hallway large enough to transport gurneys from floor to floor. That elevator went all the way down to the basement level. I wasn't sure how I knew this unless I'd subconsciously taken note of the buttons when I'd been brought up to my room.

The tiles were cold beneath my bare feet as I slipped down the hallway in the wake of the ghost. The moment I rounded a corner, out of sight of those behind me, the electrical fluctuations subsided. I entered the elevator, the doors closed and, as the car descended, the hushed voices from the morgue crept back into my head.

When the elevator stopped, I stepped out into a wide hallway with branching corridors on either side. In front of me was a set of double doors with narrow glass panels through which I could see into the receiving area of the morgue. A red sign marked the outside bay where bodies were delivered and picked up, and beyond a long counter were several closed doors, which I assumed were the autopsy rooms and coolers.

The ghost voices faded as an unnatural hush fell over the hallway. Time seemed to stop as I hovered between the dead world and the living world. The floating sensation was not at all unpleasant, but it lasted for only a heartbeat before the babbling in my head started up again, rising to a sharp, painful crescendo. The walls started to spin and I slid down the cool cinderblocks, curling myself in a ball as I clutched my ears.

Even in the grip of that debilitating vertigo, I could feel invisible hands reaching through the walls for me, diaphanous bodies squeezing in on me as I huddled on the floor breathless and trembling.

For a moment, I let myself entertain the possibility that all of this was nothing more than a terrible hallucination. A nightmare from which I would soon awaken.

But I knew better. It was real. It was happening. And in a moment of enlightenment, I realized why the blind entity had led me down to the basement. The voices were stronger in the morgue because the newly departed had somehow opened a door, allowing those trapped souls to reach out to me. Individual spirit communication was one thing, but this mass beseeching was a new development. Another terrifying facet to my dark gift.

Twelve

I staggered to the elevator and somehow managed to make it back to my room without detection. I felt very alone and frightened. Something was happening to me. Something that I'd never experienced before. The ghost voices in my head were silent now, but the echo of that cacophony lingered.

Since the age of nine, I'd avoided contact with ghosts. Papa had warned me early on that their parasitic nature made them especially dangerous to people like us because what they craved above all else was to be human again. To acknowledge their presence only deepened that craving and caused them to cling even harder to those they haunted. How was I supposed to follow all these strange clues without making myself vulnerable to them? Without compromising both my physical and mental well-being?

I couldn't. I *wouldn't*.

And yet even as I resolved to protect myself, I was irresistibly drawn to them. The blind ghost wouldn't go away until I solved her puzzle. The voices in my head wouldn't let me rest until I found out what they wanted.

Climbing into bed, I cowered under the covers until the sun came up, refusing to succumb to exhaustion until the ghosts had once again drifted back through the veil. Then I dozed on and off until the cheerful clatter of the breakfast trays awakened me, and I tried to put everything else out of my mind. I didn't want to think about that predawn trip to the morgue or to dwell on the dark direction my gift had taken me. With sunlight streaming in through the window, it all seemed like a very bad dream to me now.

And that was how I wanted to think of it. An episode brought on by the trauma of my attack and the strangeness of my surroundings. I told myself that as soon as I left the hospital and returned to my normal routine, everything would be fine.

But my life had never been normal or fine. A bump on the head hadn't brought the sightless ghost into my life or the scratching into my walls. Something was definitely going on, but I shoved every bad thought to the furthest corner of my mind as I nibbled on a piece of toast and sipped weak tea.

Devlin had stopped by earlier while I slept. He'd left a small bag of toiletries and a fresh change of clothing, which was a very good thing since I had nothing to wear home but the pajamas I'd had on when I was admitted. I was touched by his thoughtfulness and grateful for his foresight. While I waited for the doctor to make his rounds, I showered, dressed and then perched on the side of the bed, picking at my broken nails.

By the time all the release papers had been signed and my personal belongings returned to me, I barely had enough time to call a cab and get to the Oak Grove Cemetery for the dedication service. Under the circumstances, I could have skipped the ceremony and no one would have held it against me, but Dr. Shaw had asked me to say a few words and I didn't want to let him down.

And, as eager as I was to leave the hospital, I wasn't so keen on returning home alone to face the scene of the crime. Focusing on work had always been my salvation and this morning, even Oak Grove provided a welcome distraction.

But I had gone no distance at all down the cemetery pathway when I froze in trepidation. The day was sunny, not a cloud in the sky, and already a small crowd had assembled. I could hear laughter and the lighthearted chatter of a friendly gathering that would undoubtedly lavish praise upon my work.

So why the foreboding? Why the thorny dread that had manifested at the base of my neck and now scratched its way down my spine?

I'd detected a death smell, I realized. A trace of decay so faint I could almost believe my imagination had manufactured the scent. I scanned the perimeter of the cemetery as I sniffed the air, but the odor had already vanished.

Temple Lee, the state archaeologist and the closest thing I had to a best friend, sauntered over. "Admiring your own work, I see."

I tore my gaze from the wall to glance at her. "What?"

"You were obviously captivated by something and I don't see anyone in this geriatric crowd that would elicit that level of enthrallment." She caught my arm and turned me toward the light, her expression instantly sobering. "Is that a bruise on your face? What on earth happened?"

"I took a tumble, but I'm fine now. It looks a lot worse than it feels." I didn't want to begin the event with a lengthy explanation about the break-in or my attack, especially with someone as sharp and inquisitive as Temple. So I shook off the incident with a quick smile and change of subject. "This is a nice surprise. I didn't expect you to drive all the way in from Columbia for the ceremony. How did you even know about it?"

"I received an invitation a few weeks ago. I happened to be in town so I thought I'd drop by and see what you've done with the place."

"And?"

"Impressive, but you already know that."

"The restoration was a lot of hard work," I said. "And I don't mind admitting that I'm glad it's finally over."

"I don't blame you, considering all that went down here." Temple glanced out over the headstones. "Hard to believe all of that happened only last year. Seems a lifetime ago."

"I know."

Her gaze drifted to the gathering. "I don't see Devlin among the illustrious. Surely he means to show up for the big unveiling."

"I don't know if he's coming. He has a lot on his plate these days."

Temple turned to scrutinize my expression. "Do I detect trouble in paradise?"

"Not at all."

"You're still together, then?"

"Of course," I said a little too defensively. "Why wouldn't we be?"

She shrugged. "No reason except that I've always found the two of you an unlikely pairing."

"You've never made any bones about that."

"Don't be offended. I've heard you say the same thing yourself." She gave me a sidelong glance. "He's fully recovered from the shooting, I trust."

"He's back on the job if that's what you mean."

"That's not at all what I mean and you know it."

As much as I enjoyed Temple's company, I remained a private person and felt no compulsion to share with her the more intimate details of my life. "Oh, look," I said. "There's Dr. Shaw. And I believe he's headed our way."

She gave me a knowing glance. "You're very good at changing the subject, but I'll let it slide because I'm in no mood for Rupert. I'll just make myself scarce and let the two of you have a nice chat."

"I'll tell him you said hello."

"Yes, do that," she said over her shoulder as she sauntered away.

I watched her disappear down a pathway before I turned to greet Dr. Shaw. He was in the company of two women who looked to be about his age or perhaps even a few years older. One was tall and slim and appeared athletic for her age, the other tiny, stooped and walked with a cane. The latter wore a dark print dress with a smock-like jacket that covered her shrunken torso while the taller woman was attired in jeans, boots and a lightweight blazer. I wondered if they were members of the committee, the group of distinguished, often eccentric and always private Emerson University alumni that had hired me to restore Oak Grove Cemetery once it had become a candidate for the National Register.

As Dr. Shaw and his companions approached, his gaze went immediately to the bruise on my face. "My dear, what happened? Are you all right?"

"Yes, I'm fine, thank you. I had a fall, but nothing serious."

"I'm glad to hear it," he said, giving me a worried look. "I've brought along two guests who are eager to meet you. This is Mrs. Louvenia Durant and her sister, Miss Nelda Toombs. Ladies, this is Miss Amelia Gray, the cemetery restorer I told you about earlier."

My gaze flashed to Dr. Shaw but he gave an imperceptible shake of his head as if to warn me to say nothing of our previous conversation. "How do you do?" I murmured.

The tiny woman transferred the cane to her left hand and offered me her right. Her grip was surprisingly strong, although her skin felt as dry and fragile as tissue paper. "Louvenia and I are very happy to make your acquaintance, Miss Gray. Dr. Shaw has been quite effusive with his praise of your work, and I must say, he did not overstate your accomplishments. It's a beautiful restoration, isn't it, sister?"

"It's impressive, yes," Louvenia agreed. She, too, extended her hand and while we conducted the initial pleasantries, I surreptitiously studied their faces for any resemblance to Ezra Kroll.

Louvenia's eyes were the color of moonstones, soft and dreamy, but Nelda's were dark like her brother's and I imagined they could be just as piercing.

"Mrs. Durant has a cemetery located on her property that she may be interested in restoring," Dr. Shaw explained, and I marveled at his smooth delivery. His tone conveyed not the slightest hint that we had spoken recently and at length about Kroll Cemetery. "Naturally, I told them about you and invited them to meet me here today so they could see a sample of your work."

"Thank you," I said, trying to emulate his coolness. I shifted my gaze to his companions. "If there is anything in particular you'd like to see or if you have any questions, please don't hesitate to ask."

"I'm sure we'll have a great many questions once we get closer to the process," Louvenia said. "But for now, it would be helpful to know how long a restoration normally takes."

"It depends on the size and condition of the cemetery and the scope of the restoration. I'm afraid I can't even give you a rough estimate until I see the cemetery for myself."

"That makes sense," Nelda said with a nod. "However, before we take up any more of your time, perhaps we should inform you that the cemetery is said to be haunted."

Louvenia scowled down at her sister. "You know I dislike it when you speak so glibly about such matters."

"I didn't mean to be glib," Nelda said, but I thought I detected a faint twitch at the corner of her mouth. "I merely thought Miss Gray should be aware of the rumors before she commits to a restoration."

"What are the rumors?" I asked.

A shadow flickered in Louvenia's gray eyes. "Most recently, two of the workers I hired to clean up around the cemetery claimed they heard strange voices coming from behind the walls and some of their tools have gone inexplicably missing. Regardless of my sister's intent, she was right to warn you. The dead don't rest easy in Kroll Cemetery."

"Perhaps the restoration will calm them," Nelda said. "At any rate, Miss Gray doesn't strike me as the type to be overly bothered by ghosts."

"She's never been to Kroll Cemetery," Louvenia muttered.

I suppressed a shiver as Dr. Shaw and I exchanged glances.

Outwardly, Louvenia Durant appeared cool and composed, but there was something going on in the depths of her eyes. A feverish glint that echoed the nervous flutter of her hands before she clasped them behind her back.

"Tell me a little more about the cemetery," I said. "Is it a family burial site?" I knew from Dr. Shaw that most of the interred were from Kroll Colony, but I was curious to hear her response.

"Our only brother is laid to rest there," she said. "We have no other relatives in the cemetery, but since it's located on my property, I feel a responsibility to care for all the graves."

"I understand."

"You may have heard of our brother," Nelda put in. "He was once quite notorious. His name was Ezra Kroll."

I tried to sound only mildly curious. "Why was he notorious?"

She glanced at her sister and something passed between them that deepened Louvenia's scowl. "I don't see any need to go into that right now. It has nothing to do with why we're here."

"Sister is right," Nelda said. "Ezra's story can wait for another day. We've already taken up too much of your time and we've someone waiting for us."

"Dr. Shaw, could I have a quick word before we leave?" Louvenia asked anxiously.

"Of course," he replied with his usual courteous aplomb. He turned to Nelda and me. "Will you excuse us?"

"Take your time," Nelda said before I could speak. "It'll give me a chance to get better acquainted with Miss Gray. That is, if she has no objection."

"None at all."

Nelda stared after her sister. "Poor Louvenia. She would never admit it, but she's hoping Dr. Shaw can help exorcise her ghosts."

"Oh?"

"My sister has always been given to flights of fancy, particularly when it comes to that old cemetery. A guilty conscience is a powerful conjurer, Miss Gray."

I didn't know how to respond to her comment, so I held my silence and waited.

"You see, she and our brother had a terrible falling-out before he died. She's never gotten over it."

"That would be a hard thing to get over," I said.

"I only tell you this because if you decide to accept the restoration, you'll be working closely with Louvenia, and I think it only right that you know what to expect."

"I appreciate that."

"Physically, she's as strong as a horse," Nelda went on. "I've always been in awe of her stamina. Even now she works twice as long and hard as most of the hired hands that are half her age. But emotionally she's a lot more fragile than one might imagine. Truth be told, I'm a little worried about how the restoration will affect her. Dealing with that cemetery is bound to stir up painful memories. But she's right. Those graves have been neglected for far too long. The dead deserve better. Especially our dear Rose."

"Rose?"

"She was the last person laid to rest in Kroll Cemetery. Perhaps you could give her grave a little extra care if you accept the commission. She was someone very special to us." Nelda leaned heavily on her cane, her dark gaze rapt as she studied my features.

"Of course," I said, disconcerted by the intense inspection.

"Forgive me for staring…the resemblance is just so startling."

My attention sharpened. "Resemblance?"

"Did you not notice how Louvenia and I were both gawking at you earlier? I could hardly believe my eyes when Dr. Shaw pointed you out to us."

"I don't understand. I look like someone you know…or knew?"

"You are the spitting image of Rose, Miss Gray. If I didn't know better, I'd think she had somehow managed to return from the grave. I expect that's why I find it so easy to talk to you. It's like having her back after all these years."

"How…interesting." It was difficult to keep my voice even when my pulse had jumped so erratically at her revelation.

"I was quite overcome when I first saw you," Nelda said. "But now that I've had time to ponder the situation, I think you must somehow be related to her. You even share the same last name."

"She was a Gray?"

"By marriage, I think. Do you have people in the Isola area?"

"Not that I'm aware of, but I know very little about my family. I suppose it could be just one of those odd coincidences. Gray is a common last name."

"No, I don't think so," Nelda mused. "Things happen for a reason, I always say. Dr. Shaw bringing us out here to meet you… Rose moving to Isola just when Mott and I needed her the most…"

Mott.

At the mention of that strange name, it was as if a dark cloud had moved over the sun. A shadow fell across the landscape and I heard the eerie rattle of a cicada somewhere nearby.

Rustling leaves drew my attention to one of the live oaks that had been planted around the edge of the cemetery. The drooping limbs provided easy access over the wall, and for a moment, I thought someone might be up there hidden by the foliage.

A flock of blackbirds took flight, and I lifted my gaze to the cloudless sky, concentrating so intently on those flapping wings that I almost missed the stealthy shadow near the wall. A distorted form that faded so well into the gloom I wondered if my dazzled vision had played a trick on me.

But no. Something was definitely there.

The form was humanlike, female and tiny—little more than four feet tall I would guess—with a pronounced hump on her back. Not a ghost, not a shadow being, she was unlike anything I'd ever seen before.

My nerve endings bristled a warning. Here was yet another danger, another fear. The veil had parted, allowing something else to slip through.

The rules kept you safe, Papa had once told me. *But you broke them and now that the door has been opened, you're vulnerable.*

To all manner of entities, it seemed.

The silhouette moved slowly, using the shadows so effectively I had trouble tracking her. She was childlike in stature, but her features were wizened and not quite of this world. As I peered through the deep shade, she turned and looked directly at me as if to acknowledge my notice. The sensation was so creepy and invasive I took a step back, my heart flailing.

As I stood there enthralled, she threw back her head and opened her mouth wide as if to call to someone— or to something—unseen. But the sound that sprang from her throat was more insect than human. Like the rattle of a cicada, plaintive and chilling.

Thirteen

Several moments passed and still I couldn't tear my attention from the wall, even though the silhouette had disappeared into the deeper shadows.

Nelda Toombs was still chatting away beside me, oblivious to anything amiss. But suddenly it came to me that the smock-like jacket she wore over her dress not only covered her shriveled body, but also disguised what most would assume was a dowager's hump on her back.

One of the twins died. The other was so distraught that she tried to hide her sister's passing by using cloves to cover up the smell.

Even as Dr. Shaw's words came back to me, even as I turned to once again search the shadows, I reminded myself that sometimes the things I saw and heard and smelled really were products of my imagination. The sun had clouded my eyes and the shadowy form had been fleeting. Woods surrounded the cemetery. Wasn't it possible that I'd heard an actual cicada?

But what of that insect husk on my nightstand? What of that face in the stereogram, the voices in my head?

Logic wasn't going to work. I knew what I knew.

"Are you all right?" Nelda asked in concern. "You look quite pale all of a sudden."

"I'm…still shaky from the fall, I guess. It was a little more serious than I let on to Dr. Shaw. In fact, I was just released from the hospital this morning."

"Bless your heart. I don't wonder you're shaky. Perhaps you should be home resting."

I managed a faint smile. "I'll be fine. I'm enjoying our conversation. And I must say, I'm very curious about the woman you say I look so much like."

Nelda's expression turned wistful. "Rose was everything to us. Our protector and champion and the closest thing to a mother that Mott and I ever knew."

"Mott was your sister?"

"She was so much more than that, Miss Gray. We were born conjoined, you see. She was a part of me. Closer even than a mirror twin."

I swallowed past the foreboding that bloomed in my throat. "Mott is such an unusual name. I don't believe I've ever heard it before."

"When we were little, I couldn't pronounce Maudette so she became Mott and I was Neddy. We lost her many years ago."

"I'm sorry."

"Thank you, but in some ways it was a blessing. We had a difficult childhood, you see. Shunned and bullied because we were different. But…" An apologetic smile flashed. "That was a long time ago and, as Louvenia said, it has no bearing on why we've come to see you today. Besides, I've rambled on long enough and I think she's ready to leave."

I glanced down the path to where Dr. Shaw and

Louvenia still lingered. She scowled in our direction as though worried about what her sister might tell me.

Nelda leaned in suddenly and put her hand on my arm. For a breathless moment, the scent of cloves overwhelmed me. "Come see me when you get to Isola. There are things about that cemetery you should know before you agree to the restoration."

"What things?"

"Not here. Not with *him* watching."

I thought at first she meant Dr. Shaw, but then I noticed a young man just inside the gates. He stood with arms folded, back resting against the wall as he stared down the path to where we stood talking. I felt a chill go through me as our gazes connected, and I could have sworn I saw him smirk.

He looked to be just shy of six feet and so slender he might have seemed delicate except for the undercurrent of violence that belied his angelic visage. His hair was a strange silvery gold and his eyes were so light they appeared transparent from a distance. His unusual features were at once arresting and unsettling, and I couldn't seem to tear my gaze away.

"My great-nephew, Micah," Nelda said softly. "You're not the first to fall under his spell. He has a way about him, does he not?"

"He's very striking," I murmured.

"He was born with the face of an angel, but looks can be deceiving." She was still holding my arm and I felt her grip tighten. "You should know that Micah is not at all in favor of a restoration."

"Why not?"

"Not here," she said again. "Just promise you'll come see me in Isola."

I nodded, sliding my arm away as the hair on the back of my neck lifted. So many images swirled in my head as I watched her shuffle away.

The stereogram of those strange girls...

The arresting young man at the cemetery entrance...

The hunchback entity I'd seen in the shadows... The noises in my wall... The nesting in my cellar...

I had no idea how these events were connected, but like Nelda Toombs, I didn't think any of them a coincidence.

Fourteen

"That was certainly an odd visit," I said a few minutes later when Dr. Shaw had rejoined me. I moved off the trail into the shade.

"Wasn't it, though?" He chuckled as he followed me underneath the tree. "They are quite the eccentric pair," he said, without a trace of irony. "It's been a few years since my dealings with Mrs. Durant, so I was quite surprised when they turned up at the Institute this morning without an appointment. I hope you don't mind that I invited them here to meet you."

I swatted a mosquito on the back of my arm. "I don't mind. But are you telling me they just showed up out of the blue? Right after we had that long conversation about Kroll Cemetery?"

"The timing is curious," he agreed. "But I don't see how it can be anything other than happenstance. I never mentioned that conversation to anyone. Did you?"

"I told Devlin. I had to. My house was broken into last night and I thought it might be related to the viewer."

"Related how?"

"Before I came to the Institute yesterday, I took the stereoscope to a place on King Street called Dowling Curiosities. I was hoping they could be of some help in tracking down the owner since the piece came from that shop. The man I spoke to was named Owen Dowling. Probably my imagination, but I thought I saw him again later at the hospital."

"Hospital?"

"There was a bit of a scuffle during the break-in, but I'm fine."

"Was the suspect apprehended?"

"Unfortunately, no."

"Owen Dowling," Dr. Shaw said thoughtfully. "What did he look like?"

"Tallish and slender. Dark blond hair. Midthirties. Why?"

"A young man accompanied Mrs. Durant and Miss Toombs to the Institute this morning. He didn't come in, but I saw him pacing in the parking area when I walked them out to their car. He was younger than the man you described. Early twenties, I would guess, and his hair was very pale."

"I know who you mean. He was here just a few minutes ago. You didn't see him at the entrance? Nelda called him Micah. He's her great-nephew, which would make him Louvenia's grandson, I suppose."

"Ah. Then that makes sense. Mrs. Durant mentioned earlier that her grandson had been away for a number of years but had recently returned to live with her on the farm. I gather he thinks a restoration would be a waste of her money."

"Yes, Nelda said he was against it."

Dr. Shaw's expression turned anxious. "That young man… His presence was extremely unnerving. It's hard to explain, but I actually experienced a chill down my spine when he turned his eyes upon me."

"I felt it, too, but he's not the only one who unnerved me today. Do you remember what you told me about Ezra Kroll's twin sisters? When one of them died, the other tried to cover her passing by using cloves to disguise the smell. I'm certain Nelda Toombs was that girl. The living twin."

"I've had the same thought," Dr. Shaw said with a nod.

"She called her sister Mott, which is the name in the stereoscope's inscription. She also said I look very much like someone named Rose, the last person buried in Kroll Cemetery. But it's not just that I look like her. Her last name was Gray and my middle name is Rose."

His snowy brows lifted. "That would be an extraordinary coincidence, wouldn't it? Have you spoken to anyone in your family about the resemblance?"

"No. My father would be the one to know if there's a connection, but I've been reluctant to bring him into this because he's not always the easiest person to talk to." Papa's withdrawal was only a small part of my reluctance. I was afraid to uncover any more of his secrets because they had a way of changing my life.

"Dr. Shaw…" I paused, glancing up into the trees as a breeze rustled the leaves. "Something very strange is going on with these women." I didn't just mean Louvenia Durant and Nelda Toombs, but also the blind ghost and the hunchback in-between. All of them were linked. By blood, by friendship, perhaps even by death. But how were they connected to me?

"Something strange indeed," Dr. Shaw said. "However, I'm afraid further speculation will have to wait until later. The ceremony is about to start and afterward I'll be tied up with committee business for the rest of the day. Could you come by the Institute tomorrow? Say around two?"

"I'll be there."

He offered his arm. "Shall we join the others?"

"Yes, by all means," I said wearily. "Let's get this over with."

Dr. Shaw spoke first on behalf of the committee and afterward I was called upon to say a few words about my work. I made no mention of the violent history that lay beneath the cemetery but instead touched upon the methods and techniques I'd employed and how, even though cemetery restoration was my business, I always encouraged cemetery *preservation*. Too much damage to stone, layout and symbolic foliage could be wrought by the hands of the well-meaning but untrained restorer. Then I ended my remarks as I always did with what Papa called the cardinal rule of cemetery visitation: take nothing, leave nothing behind.

A smattering of polite applause and murmurs of appreciation, a few questions and it was all over. I returned the gate key to Dr. Shaw and breathed a sigh of relief at the closing of a very dark and disturbing chapter in my life.

Temple came up beside me. "You've become an

engaging speaker. You had that group in the palm of your hand."

"Thanks. I learned from the best," I said, referring to my time with her in the state archaeologist's office.

She was silent for a moment. "What I said earlier about your relationship with Devlin. That you're an unlikely pairing. I didn't mean to hurt your feelings."

"You didn't. As you said, I've thought the same thing myself on occasion."

Her expression sobered. "Can I be frank? I worry about you sometimes."

I looked at her in surprise. "Why?"

"A person doesn't go through what John Devlin did and come out unscathed. That man has darkness in him."

"We all have darkness," I said.

"Not like him. Surely it hasn't escaped your notice that bad things happen to the people around him."

My hackles rose in defense. "You can't blame him for that."

"Maybe not, but—"

She broke off, her gaze going past me to the entrance. I thought by her startled expression that she'd spotted the mysterious Micah Durant or perhaps even the hunchback silhouette. But then I felt a familiar tingle along my spine and I turned.

Devlin strode along the path toward us. Maybe it was Temple's warning or all the strange events occurring around me, but I couldn't help shivering as our gazes locked.

He was dressed in black, the European cut of his trousers and jacket giving a stylish edge to his otherwise somber attire. He was clean shaven, his hair neatly combed, and when he turned his head, the silver at his temple caught the sunlight.

And I caught my breath.

Fifteen

❦❦❦

A little while later, Devlin and I walked back to his car together.

After our initial greeting, we hadn't said much until we were through the gates and well away from Temple and the others. I could tell something was on his mind, but he didn't seem inclined to enlighten me.

I gave him a sidelong glance, studying his profile for a long moment before I broached the tricky topic. "How is your grandfather?"

"He's in the hospital having some tests run."

"So he is sick, then."

Devlin hesitated. "He's not himself."

I wasn't sure how to interpret his response, but I also knew better than to press. If and when he wanted to tell me about his grandfather, he would do so. Just like I would confess all my secrets to him when I felt the time was right. Given all that I still kept from him, I could hardly expect candor in return. Still, I missed the closeness we'd shared during his recovery. The distance between us now made me worry about the strength of our bond. Made me ponder the sustainability of a relationship between two people as insular as Devlin and I were.

"I'll keep him in my thoughts," I said, and he gave a brief nod.

"How are you feeling?" he asked.

"Other than a little soreness, as good as new. Thank you for bringing my clothes by this morning."

"No problem. You were sleeping so I didn't want to wake you."

Now it was I who nodded and we walked on in silence until I stumbled over a tree root that snaked across the path.

"Are you sure you're all right?" Devlin asked as he took my elbow. "No lingering headaches or fuzzy vision?"

"Just clumsy," I said with a smile. "It might help to watch where I'm going."

"That's generally a good rule to follow," he teased, but his eyes were dark and attentive. "I hate what happened to you."

"It's over now and it could have been so much worse."

"And preventable if I'd been with you last night."

"No one could have foreseen the break-in. You were exactly where you needed to be last night."

"This situation with my grandfather…" He trailed off with a frown. "I don't know that I'm ready to talk about it yet."

"I understand."

"He's been so deceptive in the past. It's hard to tell how much of what he's going through is manipulation and how much is delusion."

"Delusion?"

Devlin glanced at me. "It's possible he could be seriously ill."

"Then, you should go and be with him for these tests. You don't need to worry about me. As you can see, I'm perfectly fine."

"And I intend to do everything in my power to make sure you stay that way. I've requested extra patrols on your street and I had all your locks changed. That's why I was late to the ceremony." He fished a set of keys from his pocket and placed them in my palm. "As for the shopkeeper, Owen Dowling, I've run a background check. He doesn't have a criminal record and the shop is legitimate. It's been at that same location for decades and has an impeccable reputation among local collectors."

"So that's that, then. It's a dead end."

"It would appear so."

"Well, I do have a bit of news," I said. "Dr. Shaw brought Ezra Kroll's sisters to the cemetery to meet me earlier."

"How did that come about?"

"Dr. Shaw and Louvenia Durant became acquainted a few years ago when she contacted him about disturbances on her property. I gather that's one of the reasons she came to see him this morning. They've had some recent sightings."

Devlin's silence spoke volumes as he turned back to the path. His disdain for the unknown was our biggest bone of contention. How could I explain my gift to someone who clung to his disbelief as though it were a lifeline?

"Anyway, Dr. Shaw brought them to Oak Grove to meet me because they're interested in having Kroll Cemetery restored. You mentioned that you used to explore the old commune when you were a boy, but you didn't say much about the graveyard. Do you remember anything about it?"

"A little. As I recall, the entrance was hidden by a maze," he said. "As a kid, I found that pretty fascinating."

"Fascinating but not unusual. Mazes were often planted at graveyard entrances for the same purpose you'll occasionally see high thresholds in Japanese cemeteries. To discourage ghostly wanderings."

He gave me a look. "How does that work?"

"Spirits can't step over or navigate crooked pathways. A superstitious community would have been especially cautious with suicides. The ghosts of those who take their own lives are considered notorious wanderers. That probably explains the high walls that surround the cemetery. In the old days, they would have buried the bodies facedown to disorient them."

"The things you know."

I merely smiled as we continued down the path. When we reached the car, he turned to me again.

"I need to ask you something."

I tensed, because it had been my experience that conversations beginning in such a manner rarely ended well. "Go on."

"These nightmares you're having. Do they have anything to do with what happened last fall?"

A lot of things had happened last fall. I'd been targeted by an evil presence in the little town where I'd been born, and upon my return to Charleston, a powerful witch doctor had stalked me through my dreams. But neither of those predators was responsible for my current distress.

"Why do you ask?"

"Because I know something's bothering you. Even before the break-in, you were having trouble sleeping. I thought it was because of this cemetery, because of what happened here, but now I'm not so sure. Amelia…" He paused. "If you felt threatened in any way, you'd come to me, wouldn't you?"

And tell you what? That a sightless ghost followed me back from the other side and now something is nesting in my cellar, crawling through my walls, leaving insect husks on my nightstand?

"Sometimes there's no rhyme or reason to dreams and nightmares," I evaded. "You really don't need to worry about me."

"I wish that were true." He lifted a hand to my bruised cheek, emotions warring on his face, feelings that made me too breathless to contemplate. After all this time, I still wasn't used to the electric hum that raced through my veins at his slightest touch, the quiver in my stomach when he said my name. I'd never in my life experienced anyone like Devlin. I was certain that I never would again.

"It's not just the nightmares," he said. "It's a look in your eyes. The way you stare out the window. It's as if you're waiting for something. Watching for someone. And yet you won't talk to me."

His hand slipped to the back of my neck, pulling me closer. I went without protest because the intensity of his dark gaze enthralled me. I couldn't have drawn away at that moment if I'd wanted to, which, of course, I did not. I stood there frozen, mesmerized by the tiny flames dancing in his midnight eyes.

"Why is it that even with you in my arms, I can feel you slipping away from me?" he murmured.

"I sometimes feel the same about you. You're here but you're not here. There's a distance. A part of you that won't let me in."

"I *am* here," he insisted, his gaze so intense I had to look away. "When I'm with you, there's nothing and no one else."

"Sometimes I wonder."

He took my chin and made me look up at him. "There are many things to wonder about in this world, but that's not one of them."

Dipping his head, he brushed his lips against mine, and I melted into him, letting his energy wrap me in a safe cocoon. He was warm, solid, human.

But even as I settled more deeply into his embrace, I had the strongest urge to glance over my shoulder. Something was out there even now. I could feel an unnatural presence lurking at the edge of the woods, slinking through the gloom where all the dark things thrived.

Sixteen

After leaving the cemetery, we dropped by police headquarters so that I could sign my statement, and then Devlin drove me home. After a quick search of the house to make sure everything was in order, he headed out, but whether to spend time with his grandfather or on some other errand, I had no idea.

Alone, I took another slow walk through all the rooms. Devlin had had someone in to clean up the broken glass and furniture, a service he trusted, but I remained uneasy. The echo of my footsteps seemed to punctuate the utter quiet of my sanctuary as I made my way down the hallway.

I tried to distract myself by puttering around in the kitchen, but the homey sounds of clinking glass and clattering pottery reminded me of all the times I'd watched my mother move gracefully about her kitchen. The memory didn't soothe me. Our evening meals had often passed in uneasy silence. When the sun went down and the breeze picked up, the scent of roses from the cemetery would drift in through the open windows, a lush harbinger of the coming nightfall. My eyes would sometimes catch Papa's and for an instant, there would be a spark, a fleeting acknowledgment of our mutual fear before he once again retreated into his dark place.

I'd often pondered the dynamics of our family. Despite Papa's withdrawal, our "sight" had irrevocably bonded us while my mother had kept me at arm's length even when she embraced me. It wasn't until a trip to my birthplace that I understood why. Because of how I'd come into this world, she was afraid that I would be taken from her. And maybe a part of her was a little afraid of me, too.

One by one, the pieces of my life had fallen into place with that journey to Asher Falls. But there were still blank spaces, still too many secrets that had yet to be revealed. How it would all come together and where it would end remained a terrifying mystery.

And speaking of mysteries…

The stereogram once again beckoned. Succumbing to the lure, I put the card in the holder and rotated my chair toward the light, but this time, I concentrated my attention on the girls rather than the face in the window. As I studied their images, I detected a faint outline beneath the cloaks where their bodies were joined by the humps on their backs. *Together forever.*

My mind flashed back to the form I'd spotted in Oak Grove Cemetery and the smell of cloves when Nelda had leaned in. Given what Dr. Shaw had told me about the use of the spice by the living twin to cover the stench of her sister's death, I wondered if the scent had been an attempt at contact by the dead twin.

Whatever that tiny creature was, she wasn't a ghost. She had more substance, more lingering humanity

than most of the apparitions I encountered, leaving me
to wonder if the physical, spiritual and telepathic bond
with her sister had somehow changed her death course.
Perhaps she hadn't made the full journey through the
veil, but instead resided in an in-between space that
allowed her passage into this world, into my cellar,
even into my walls.

I returned the stereoscope to the desk, my thoughts
racing. Something very strange was happening to and
around me. I recognized a supernatural manipulation
as surely as I could sense the icy chill of a ghostly
presence. I was being guided—herded—to Kroll Cemetery, but to what end? The intrusion from beyond
both angered and frightened me, but I couldn't deny
a certain fascination.

Dr. Shaw had suggested that I search the cellar for
additional stereograms and I thought it was a good
idea. If there were other cards to be found, maybe the
images could provide more clues.

I wasn't anxious to explore that murky cellar alone,
but far better to go down there now with the sun still
burning brightly in my garden. I would make quick
work of the search. In and out. A matter of minutes.

It sounded so simple.

Changing into my work cargoes, I loaded my pockets with a flashlight, pepper spray and my cell phone.
Then I went out into the yard and lingered among the
flowers as I tried to bolster my courage.

Idling plucking a pink rose from a nearby bush, I
twirled the stem between my fingers as I walked over
to the cellar steps to stare down at the door while I
sniffed the air for a musty odor. I smelled nothing but

the sweet scent of the rose. Dropping the blossom on the top step, I slowly descended.

I unlocked the door and thrust my hand inside to grope for the light switch. The weak illumination cast by the bare bulb was hardly inviting so I hovered in the doorway, piercing the dreary corners with the flashlight beam. I saw nothing and smelled only the faintest trace of decay.

Propping open the door with a brick, I stepped inside. Macon had accomplished a lot after I'd fled. The shelves at the front of the cellar were all reinforced and neatly arranged, the discarded boxes and broken bric-a-brac piled to one side for easy transfer to the curb on trash day. I walked slowly through the gloom as I flicked the light over the crumbling brick walls, assuring myself that I was alone.

The old staircase was to the left and toward the back of the cellar in an area as yet untouched by Macon. The shelving that had been built over the boarded-up kitchen door was piled high with boxes and debris. I began to shuffle everything around, temporarily abandoning my stereogram search for a darker quest. How had something gained entrance to that stairwell from the cellar? Could there be a hidden passageway into the walls of my home?

Nothing seemed amiss at first, but then as I stood back and fanned the beam over the wall behind the now-empty shelves, I saw a crack near the floor. Dropping to my knees, I crawled under the lower shelf to get a better look, and then pried back one of the boards so that I could shine the flashlight up the rickety staircase.

Playing the beam over the kitchen door, I spot-lighted the keyhole as I imagined a tiny humpback being peering in at me, somehow shriveling into something minuscule enough to scurry through my walls.

As I brought the light slowly down the stairs, a flash of fire caught my eye. The crystal bookmark—I was sure of it. Proof that something had indeed been in my bedroom and had somehow exited the house via the stairwell and cellar.

But why take the bookmark? Why leave the insect husk in its place? Was there a message in the exchange that I hadn't yet deciphered?

At the bottom of the steps, I could see bits of cloth and shredded paper as if something had tried to make a nest there. Quelling my desire to flee the cellar, I went in search of Macon's tools and supplies, and then, easing back under the shelf, I set to work with grim determination. Dust rained down upon me as I pounded away, but I didn't stop until I'd thoroughly secured the stairwell.

Brushing grime and cobwebs from my hair and clothing, I returned to the front of the basement to resume my search for the cards. Even as alarm bells sounded inside me, I took my time, moving boxes around and shining my flashlight into all the dark recesses.

But the longer I remained below ground, the greater my unease. As I turned to toe a plastic carton out of my path, the light dimmed. I thought at first the over-head bulb had gone out, but then I realized that something had blocked the natural light streaming down the steps into the open doorway. I wanted to believe a cloud had passed over the sun, but I could still see ribbons of illumination trimming the edges of the door frame. Someone—or something—stood at the top of the stairs.

Slowly, I lifted my gaze to the opening, sniffing the air for a death scent. Nothing came to me and I thought—hoped—it might be Macon. I told myself to call out. What harm could it do? I wasn't exactly hidden nor could I slip away unnoticed. I was trapped. I knew it; whoever was at the top of the steps knew it. But neither of us made a move and the only sound I heard was the drumming of my own heartbeat.

As I stood there immobile, my tongue suddenly tingled with the warm taste of cloves. I saw a flash in the doorway, an arc of reflected light, and then came a metallic ping as something hit the brick floor and bounced toward me. I glanced down warily, an icy breath whispering down my collar.

Seventeen

~~~⤜◦◦◦⤛~~~

A brass key lay at my feet, the kind that would fit an ordinary door lock. Surely this couldn't be the key the blind ghost had demanded I find. How could something so nondescript be my salvation?

I supposed it was human nature that I should reach for it even as Papa's warning sounded in my head: *Leave it be, child. Remember the rules. Never acknowledge the dead. Never stray far from hallowed ground. Never associate with the haunted. And never, ever tempt fate.*

Too late. My fingers had already closed around the metal.

As I straightened, a shaft of sunlight from the doorway caught the brass. For a moment, the thing seemed to dance in my hand. The radiance mesmerized and I stood transfixed, helpless to combat whatever dark force had entered my life.

Put it back, Amelia. The door that can be unlocked by that key could very well lead to your destruction. Return it and leave the cellar without looking back.

The spell broken by Papa's imagined warning, I uncurled my fingers, but the tingle in my mouth grew stronger, as if my every distressed thought had been read and another calming message sent. A presence was trying to communicate with me, but I had no idea if the entity was ghost, human or in-between. I was too afraid at that moment to allow it into my head.

Papa's phantom caution flitted away as my fist closed once more around the key. I somehow knew it was important, another clue. What did it matter if I took it? The rules had long since been broken. A door to the dead world had already been opened.

Call it instinct, call it desperation or even defiance, but I knew I couldn't fight destiny with only half-truths. I felt strongly that my greatest weapon still lay hidden in the secrets that had been kept from me since the terrifying night of my birth.

There was only one person who could help me uncover the past. Despite my fears and reservations, I had to go see Papa, and soon.

And with that resolve, the taste in my mouth faded. Sunlight once again spangled down through the open doorway. Everything returned to normal, and if I hadn't seen what I'd seen in my life, if I didn't know what I knew, I might have convinced myself the past few moments had been nothing more than a hallucination or a waking dream.

But I *did* know.

Eighteen

I put the key and the stereoscope in a desk drawer and for the rest of the afternoon tried very hard to concentrate on work. Twilight slid in on a mild breeze, but as darkness descended, the wind picked up and the chime outside my office played an unnerving serenade. I sat with my back to the windows and didn't turn even when a tree limb scratched against the glass. I didn't want to know what waited in the deep shadows of my garden.

Around nine, I took a couple of pills for my headache and stretched out on the chaise, not yet ready for bed. I still had hopes that Devlin would call and kept the phone handy just in case.

I only meant to doze for a few minutes, but when I roused sometime later, the garden breeze had died away to an unnatural stillness. I tried to concentrate on the hum of the ceiling fan in my office and the pop of settling floorboards overhead as Macon moved about his apartment. The normal household sounds were reassuring and made me feel less alone. Pulling a soft throw over my legs, I closed my eyes and sank more deeply into slumber.

When the dreams came, they transported me back to a time in my childhood when I had not yet been aware of the ghosts. I was in Rosehill Cemetery with Papa. It was just getting on dusk and moths flitted through the air like dark-winged fairies. I sat in the grass and watched Mama's yellow tabby pounce once, twice and then disappear into the shelter of a rose thicket with something dangling from his sharp teeth.

The approach of twilight had always spooked me. Even with Papa nearby I felt the stir of an unknown fear. The day had been clear and warm, but now a chilly breeze swept through my hair, lifting the blond strands as though invisible hands were at play there. Papa didn't seem to notice the sudden nip. His head was bowed to his work and he didn't glance up even when the leaves overhead began to whisper.

Trying to ignore the tingles across my scalp, I removed a ribbon from around my neck so that I could admire the old key I'd found earlier on a headstone in the deepest recesses of Rosehill Cemetery. Shrouded in ivy and Spanish moss, that forgotten corner had become my hideaway. No visitors ever came along that way and even Papa rarely went back there. But I'd spent many an hour in the company of the forsaken, reading aloud from my Gothic romances and weaving daisy chains to adorn the crumbling headstones.

I was never to take anything from the graves. Papa had instilled that rule in me long ago, but I felt certain that key had been placed on the headstone for me to find. My aunt Lynrose was visiting from Charleston and she always brought little gifts—a book, a charm, a shiny silver dollar—which she slipped beneath my pillow or hid away in my favorite climbing tree.

Suspended from a pink satin ribbon, the key was ornate and beautiful, the kind that might open an ancient treasure box stuffed with toys and trinkets and deep, dark secrets. Draping a clover necklace over the headstone, I slipped the ribbon around my neck as a frisson of excitement coursed through me.

The key felt heavy and warm to the touch. Tucking it inside my sweater, I skipped off to find Papa.

Now as I waited for him to finish his work, I grew more and more fascinated as I spun the ribbon around one finger, watching the brass catch the fading light. Faster and faster I twirled the ribbon until the knot worked loose and the key went flying.

"Oh!" I fell to my knees to search through the thick grass.

"What's wrong?" Papa called out to me.

"I lost my necklace. The one Aunt Lynrose left for me. I've looked and looked, but I can't find it anywhere."

Papa abandoned his work and came over to kneel beside me on the ground. "Whereabouts did you drop it?"

I showed him the spot and he began to methodically comb through the grass with his gnarled fingers. We kept at it for a long time until I finally grew weary of the search.

"I'm tired, Papa. Can we come back tomorrow and look for it?"

"*No!*"

His sharp tone startled me. I glanced up at him in confusion. "Why not?"

His tired gaze met mine in the falling twilight. "You mustn't leave here until you find what you lost."

"But why, Papa?"

"Remember what I told you, child. Take nothing, leave nothing behind."

"I know, but—"

"Keep looking, Amelia. *Hurry.* We're losing the light."

There was something strange in his voice and demeanor. Something almost frenzied about the way he applied himself to the search. In that moment, he didn't seem at all like my papa but a driven, secretive stranger.

Finally, he straightened and held out his hand so that I could see the key in his palm. "Is this yours?"

"Yes! Oh, thank you, Papa!"

"It looks very old, child. Are you sure your aunt gave this to you?"

As he studied my face, a guilty conscience niggled. I'd been certain earlier that Aunt Lynrose had left the key on the headstone, but Papa's strange behavior filled me with doubt. What if I'd taken something that didn't belong to me, something sacred from a grave? Papa would be very unhappy with me and I couldn't abide his disapproval. He and Mama meant everything to me. What if they decided to send me away? Ever since I'd learned of my adoption, I'd nursed a secret worry that I might someday be returned to the family that didn't want me. What if that someday was now?

All of this flashed through my mind in the blink of an eye as I answered Papa with a vague nod.

He took my arm and drew me to my feet. "Listen to me, Amelia. Whatever you bring into a cemetery, you must never, ever leave behind. Do you understand?" His grasp tightened. "I don't mean to frighten you, but this is important. That key has special meaning to you, does it not? It was given to you as a gift. Leaving it behind might be misconstrued as an offering or barter. Or worse, an invitation."

"An invitation to what, Papa?"

His face grew even more somber. "It doesn't bear thinking about, child."

An image of the clover chain I'd left on the headstone in exchange for the key necklace flashed through my head. I wanted desperately to tell Papa what I'd done, have him reassure me that all was well, but I was too afraid. Not of him. Never of him. But of something I didn't yet understand.

He looked beyond me to the cemetery entrance. His gaze lingered for only a split second before he lifted his face to the sky. As he watched the bats swoop overhead, he said softly, "Look over toward the gate, Amelia, and tell me what you see."

His request puzzled me, but I did as he asked. "I don't see anything, Papa. Why? What's wrong?"

"Nothing, child. I thought for a moment we had a visitor, but it's just these old eyes playing tricks, I reckon. Now put that trinket safely in your pocket and let's go home. Your mother worries if we're not back by dark."

As he gathered up his tools, I couldn't resist glancing over my shoulder. For a moment, I thought…

No. It was just a shadow. Nothing was there.

There's no such thing as ghosts.

But as Papa and I set off for home, that brass key was an unwelcome weight in my pocket.

I awakened with an unsettling certainty that the dream had not been a dream at all but a memory nudged loose by the incident in the cellar. I hadn't thought about that key necklace in years. Like so many things in my life that had once seemed important, the memory faded when the ghosts came.

Now I recalled how agitated I'd been after Papa's warning. I'd spent an uneasy night with the key underneath my pillow and the next morning I'd risen early to return that found treasure to the headstone. I'd gone back a few times to see if the key was still there, and it always was, waiting for me to slip the pink ribbon around my neck.

I never asked Aunt Lynrose if she was the one who had left it because I didn't want to know. After a while, I started avoiding that hidden corner of the graveyard. I found a new hideaway in the hallowed section of Rosehill Cemetery where I could read my books and play among the statuary. And other than a few pilfered stones, I had taken Papa's cardinal rule to heart: *Take nothing, leave nothing behind.*

As I thought back to his strange behavior that day, I became certain that he'd seen a ghost at the gate. Maybe I had, too. The shadow I'd glimpsed may well have been my first sighting.

I'd always wondered why the ghosts had come into my life. For the first nine years of my existence, I'd remained oblivious to their presence. I'd been born with the gift but blinded to the dead until a veil had been lifted from my eyes, allowing me to see that which had been unseen.

Had the key been the catalyst?

And if taking that key from the headstone had somehow opened a door allowing the ghosts into my world, what might I have unleashed by removing the key from the cellar?

Get rid of it, child. Return it to where you found it!

Panic chased up my spine at Papa's imagined warning. Grabbing the key from my desk, I went out into the garden, where the air smelled of dead leaves and spent roses. Moon bursts of datura hung heavy with dew and from shadowy beds, white agapanthus rose on spindly stems. The night was very still, so eerily static I could hear the pounding of blood through my veins.

I didn't need a flashlight. Clouds of artemisia floated on either side of the walkway, guiding me unerringly to the cellar stairs where I knelt. The rose that I'd dropped there earlier was gone.

For a moment, I tried to convince myself that Macon had removed it or the wind had blown it away, but deep down I knew better. Someone—something had taken the flower and tossed the key in the cellar in exchange.

"It wasn't a trade," I whispered into the night, but I had no idea to what or to whom I spoke. "It wasn't an offering or an invitation or anything else. See? I'm returning the key." As I placed it on the top step, the brass gleamed obscenely in the moribund moonlight.

From deep within the garden came a long, strident rattle followed by several short bursts. A warning? A rebuke?

Anger fought its way up through the fear. I felt like a mouse caught in a trap, once more a helpless pawn in some dark, mystical game. I picked up the key and curled my fingers tightly around the brass as I stood. For a moment, there was no sound at all beyond the soft swish of my breath. Then an ear-piercing whistle jolted the silence and I whirled toward the garden.

Before I had time to think, I flung the key into the night.

Cold and quaking, I waited for another whistle or an insect-like rattle, but the sound I heard was eerily metallic, like the squeak of a phantom wagon wheel.

For some reason, I flashed to the stereogram, to the strange, cart-like apparatus I'd noticed in the background. Maybe it was my imagination fired by the realness of that 3-D image, but I could have sworn I glimpsed a tiny humpback creature gliding backward through the shadows of my garden.

Nineteen

"Perhaps we're reading too much into the timing," Dr. Shaw said the next day when I met him at the Institute. "Louvenia Durant knew of my work with the committee. It's not so unusual that she would ask me to recommend a restorer."

"Yes, I suppose that's true. Assuming she really is interested in my professional services."

"I believe she's sincere about the restoration," Dr. Shaw said as he sat back in his chair. "But for the sake of argument, let's assume our qualms are warranted and there really is something fishy about her and her sister's visit. What that something might be, I've no idea, but would it make a trip to Kroll Cemetery any less appealing? The other day you seemed quite intrigued by the notion of all those engraved keys."

"I still am." More so now than ever considering the events that had transpired in my cellar and garden. Intrigued…and increasingly frightened at the prospect of following all the ethereal clues being strewn before me. But follow them I must because I was being led to that cemetery for a reason. Ignoring the signs wasn't an option.

Dr. Shaw got up and began to rummage through a file drawer. "I'm certain I have some photos of Kroll Cemetery around here somewhere. Mrs. Durant had strict rules about filming and photographing the graves, but she allowed us to snap a few shots so long as we agreed that nothing would be published."

"I'd love to see them."

After a few minutes of searching, he gave up with a sigh. "The file must have been moved to storage. We've switched to digital photography almost exclusively in our fieldwork, but I distinctly remember taking those shots with my old camera. I'll ask Vivienne to have a look later for either the prints or the scans. When we find them, I'll have her drop them by your house." He closed the file drawer and returned to his desk.

"Dr. Shaw, you said the other day that some people think the cemetery is a giant puzzle that has never been solved, but it seems to me that a far bigger mystery is how that stereogram ended up in my basement. Do you believe some things are preordained?"

"I don't believe the universe is random," he said obliquely.

"Neither do I. There are no true coincidences. Everything happens for a reason. My finding that stereogram. Louvenia Durant and Nelda Toombs coming to see you."

"Your resemblance to the mysterious Rose," he added with a gentle smile.

"Exactly. That may be the greatest puzzle of all."

"And you're certain no one in your family has ever mentioned the likeness?"

"No, never. But I'm driving up to Trinity tomorrow and I'm hoping my father will have some answers for me."

Dr. Shaw rubbed a finger across his chin in deep thought. "You said the other day that the circumstances regarding your adoption were unusual. What did you mean by that? If you don't mind talking about it, that is."

"I don't mind, but it's a long story." I glanced out the French doors. The scent of roses wafting in from the garden brought a pang of nostalgia. The heady fragrance always took me back to those lonely summer evenings in Trinity. "I found out last fall that the man I'd always thought of as my adoptive father is in actuality my biological grandfather. He had an affair with a midwife named Tilly Pattershaw, my maternal grandmother. They had a daughter named Freya, but Tilly never told Papa about Freya until years later when I came along."

"Freya is your birth mother?"

"Was. Someone murdered her on the night I was born."

"My dear, how tragic," he said in a hushed voice.

I was a little uncomfortable accepting condolences for the loss of someone I'd never even known. The woman who raised me—Etta Gray—was my mother. Freya Pattershaw was just a name and a face in a photograph. And yet as I conjured her image, I felt the sting of tears behind my lids. "Actually, she died before I was born."

"*Before* you were born?"

"As I said, it's a very long and unusual story."

"Please go on."

"Tilly found Freya just moments after she'd been murdered. The body was still warm, Tilly said. So she cut me from Freya's womb and resuscitated me."

Dr. Shaw looked truly flabbergasted, which said a lot considering the tales he must have heard during his years at the Institute. "I don't know what to say, Amelia. What an extraordinary story."

"Oh, there's more. I've barely scratched the surface." Which was true, but I didn't know how to proceed. I'd sought Dr. Shaw's advice often in the past about various abnormal matters, but I'd never told him outright about the ghosts. Discretion had been ingrained in me for far too many years and walking on eggshells had become a habit.

But now I once again experienced that inexplicable urgency to lay bare my secrets. I had so many doubts and worries about my future, so many dark thoughts tumbling around in my head and no one to help me make sense of them. If I could unburden myself to anyone in the world without fear of ridicule, it would be Dr. Shaw, a man who had devoted his life to the study of strange goings-on.

Still, I hesitated. "I'm not sure what any of this has to do with the stereogram, let alone Louvenia Durant and Nelda Toombs."

"Perhaps nothing," he said. "But your resemblance to the woman in the window is remarkable, and as you said, there are no true coincidences. There must be a connection. We have to keep searching until we find one."

I glanced at him doubtfully. "The thought of that frightens me."

"Why?"

"Unless you know my whole life's history, you probably wouldn't understand."

"You can tell me as much or as little as you like," he said. "But I've always thought it far better to embrace the unknown than to fear it."

Spoken like a man who'd never had a netherworld creature nesting in his cellar.

"Maybe you're right." My voice dropped to a near whisper as my gaze flitted once more to the open door where a small shadow crept across the patio. I felt the tingle of cloves on my tongue, so weak and ephemeral I couldn't be certain the sensation was even real.

Dr. Shaw followed my gaze. "What's wrong?"

"Nothing. For a moment, I thought… Nothing. It was just a shadow," I said with a shrug. Or a materialization of my fear. Maybe Dr. Shaw was right. Embracing the unknown could take away some of its power.

"You look as though you could use a little fortification," he said. "Shall I ask Vivienne to bring us some tea? Or something a little stronger perhaps?"

"No, thank you." Although a cup of chamomile would not have been unwelcome at that moment. "If I seem a little flustered, it's because I've never told this story to anyone. Some of it will sound far-fetched, but I hope you'll keep an open mind."

"My dear, do you forget to whom you are speaking? My whole life's work is based upon the fantastic. Please continue. You have me enraptured already."

"I hope you still feel that way when I'm finished."

"So you were cut from Freya's womb," he prompted.

I nodded, taking a moment to sort through my thoughts. "When Tilly resuscitated me—pulled me back from the other side, so to speak—she felt a presence…a force. She said it was as if something evil had hold of me on the other side and didn't want to let go. When she finally brought me back, she felt this terrible *rage*."

A snowy brow peaked, but he said nothing.

"Tilly was so terrified she got in touch with Papa, a man she hadn't spoken to since he'd gone back to his other life seventeen years earlier. He drove up to Asher Falls, buried poor Freya's body and then he took me away from that place because he and Tilly were worried for my safety."

"He believed her about this presence?"

"Oh, yes."

Dr. Shaw leaned back in his chair, observing me intently. "Was Freya's killer ever caught?"

"Eventually." I couldn't help but wonder what my life might have been like if my birth mother hadn't been murdered. Would I have grown up in the woods with Tilly and Freya, or would my birth father's family and their terrible legacy have claimed me at an early age? I hated to think of the person I might have become without Mama and Papa's gentle guidance.

Dr. Shaw still watched me thoughtfully.

"Do you know what a caul birth is?" I asked him.

"Yes, of course. A baby born *en caul* has the amniotic sac still wholly or partially intact. It's not very common, but an infant born *with* a caul is even more rare. In those instances, a thin membrane actually loops around the ears and attaches to the face. But—" he paused "—something tells me you already know the distinction."

I nodded. "Caul births run in my family."

Curiosity flickered in his blue eyes. I could almost see the questions churning inside his head. "Do you know if the membrane was preserved?"

I hadn't expected *that* question. "I have no idea." Such a thought had never occurred to me and, truthfully, I was a little repulsed by the notion.

Dr. Shaw chuckled. "I can appreciate your distaste, but it was once customary to save them as protection against witches and demons. Cauls were also highly valued by seamen because they were thought to prevent drowning." He glanced at one of the bookshelves behind me. "I'm sure I have a copy of *David Copperfield* around here somewhere. You may remember that passage about his caul being advertised in the newspaper for the low price of fifteen guineas. He was offended that the only taker was an attorney rather than a sailor." His eyes danced with merriment.

I wasn't quite as amused at the prospect of selling skin casings as he apparently was. "How does one go about preserving a caul anyway?"

"In the old days, the midwife rubbed a sheet of paper across the baby's head and face, pressing the membrane onto the parchment. Of course, given what you've told me of your birth, I doubt your grandmother had sufficient time even if she'd been so inclined. The veil would have been removed quickly in order to start resuscitation. I'm surprised you don't have scars from the attachment points."

I touched a finger to my hairline. "Maybe they're just hidden." Like so many things in my life.

"That's certainly possible. However, you've always been a keen observer so I can't imagine they would have escaped your notice. Nor do I think I'm telling you anything you don't already know."

"Actually, I don't know that much about cauls. I only found out last fall about my birth and I've been busy with Oak Grove ever since."

"I see. Well, apart from the membrane itself having magical properties, caulbearers are believed by some to be spiritual guides and healers, as well as seers." His gaze on me deepened. "Are any of these attributes at all familiar to you?"

"Are you asking if I have ESP or the ability to heal? No. But ever since I found out about my birth I've had this odd sense of…" Again my gaze strayed to the garden doorway. I saw nothing this time but the brilliant flicker of sunlight through the live oaks.

"Go on."

"Destiny," I finished reluctantly. "As if my course has already been charted."

"What do you think your destiny is?"

"I don't know." I thought of all those ghost voices in my head at the hospital, all those grasping hands in my dreams. "I'm afraid to know. It's as if I've been waiting for something my whole life. Or something has been waiting for me. But I never realized it until now. Maybe because I was so sheltered and protected. Looking back, I'm convinced that every decision, every milestone, even my every thought and dream has led me down a predetermined pathway." I paused, grappling with a concept I didn't fully understand. "It started with my birth, I think. I was brought back from the other side for a reason. I believe I was *chosen*."

The word hung in the air, suspended on a stray gust that blew into the office, ruffling the papers on Dr. Shaw's desk.

"A loaded word," he said softly. "Chosen for what?"

"I've no idea." I rubbed my arms, trying to restore circulation to the frigid veins. "I was born dead to a dead mother. That has to mean something. I've been told I have power because I was born on the other side of the veil."

"What kind of power?"

"I don't know."

He looked at me in such a way that I felt almost breathless with anticipation. Or was it dread?

"What is it, Dr. Shaw?"

He hesitated, his thumb tapping an idle rhythm against the surface of his desk. "Tell me, Amelia, did you have imaginary playmates when you were a child? Did you see things others couldn't? Visions… apparitions…"

"You mean ghosts?" I asked.

"Yes, ghosts. As I said earlier, you can tell me as much or as little as you want, but I've always known there was something special about you. You have the inner radiance of someone attuned to the invisible world around us, and you seem to attract more than your share of unusual phenomena."

"Which you've always been able to explain away,"

I reminded him. "You're the one person who can help make sense of everything that's happened to me."

"And there may well be an explanation for what you're experiencing now. I don't discount any possibility. You said you feel as if you've been waiting for something all your life. That you've been chosen."

I drew a breath and nodded.

"In some cultures, people believe children who see visions and apparitions grow up to become death walkers."

"But I never said—" I stopped short as another chill shot through me. "*Death* walkers?"

"You're not familiar with the term? It isn't as dire as it sounds, although I suppose it depends on one's perspective. Death walkers are those rare individuals who have the ability to help souls pass from this world to the next. They serve a unique and powerful purpose in the circle of life. Perhaps your unusual birth has bestowed upon you this gift."

I remained silent, my stomach in knots as I resisted the inclination to press my hands to my ears, once more blocking out what I didn't want to hear. What I couldn't bear to comprehend.

"Think of it as a vocation similar to your grandmother Tilly's," he said. "She was a midwife, yes? Only you aren't meant to help souls enter this world. Your job is to help them leave."

"That's a very frightening prospect," I said on a ragged whisper.

"To the contrary," he said kindly. "Some would consider it a high and noble calling. It's what the shamans refer to as a midwife to the dead."

Twenty

After I left the Institute, I parked downtown and walked over to the Unitarian Churchyard, one of my favorite cemeteries in Charleston. A glimpse through the rear gate might lead a first-time caller to conclude the graveyard was abandoned or badly neglected, but the paths were meticulously kept, allowing visitors to wander at will through the deliberately overgrown shrubbery and wildflowers.

The heavy oaks provided a welcome respite from the heat of the street and I took my time reacquainting myself with the centuries-old headstones and ironwork. Some of the secluded corners reminded me of Rosehill Cemetery, especially this time of day with the heady scent of flowers hanging on humid air. Now and then I could hear a strand of organ music from inside the church, normally a perfect accompaniment to meditation and reflection, but my mind was much too chaotic to settle. Today, nirvana was not to be found among the primroses.

As I strolled along the shady trails, I couldn't stop thinking about Dr. Shaw's speculation regarding my birth and my destiny. Death walker. Midwife to the dead. No matter the term, I didn't want to consider the possibility that I might have such a calling. What a nightmarish thing to even contemplate.

And yet had I not tried to find some rhyme or reason for the ghosts in my life? Some higher purpose for this terrible gift that could justify the loneliness and isolation of my existence?

"Set aside the grimness of the terminology and imagery and allow yourself to explore the possibilities," Dr. Shaw had advised. "Remember what I said about your grandmother's calling. This is not so different."

But it was different, and all I could picture was a dark-shrouded skeleton ferrying the dead across the River Styx.

"A death walker might best be described as a conductor of souls. A shepherd of the dead, if you will. According to shamanism, someone born with this gift has an inner light that guides the lost to them. A spiritual magnet that attracts the lingering life force released into the universe when someone passes. Perhaps that's why you've always felt so at home in cemeteries and why you've chosen to spend so much of your life in and around them. Graveyards aren't just repositories of decaying flesh and bone, but of the unbound energy of death. All you need do is open yourself up to this force."

"But what if I don't want anything to do with that kind of power?" I'd asked. "What if all I want is to be left alone to lead a normal life?"

"A true calling should never be ignored, my dear. It invites disruption and makes for an unsettled life."

Easy to say if one hadn't an inkling of the parasitic

nature of ghosts or the evil that lay in wait on the other side. Guiding the dead through the veil might well be a noble endeavor, but it would require someone with far greater courage than I.

A couple of tourists had stopped on the path and they spoke in hushed, excited tones as they pointed to a grave. I thought at first they might have spotted a small animal scurrying through the underbrush, but then I detected a low drone that grew louder as I approached. When I passed them on the path, I heard one say to the other, "Have you ever seen anything like it?"

I glanced in the direction where their gazes were pinned. A swarm of honeybees had gathered on one of the headstones, covering the surface so thoroughly that on first glance the monument appeared to be moving. It was a very disconcerting illusion, and I stood there awestruck until I realized the incessant buzzing reminded me a little too much of the drone of ghost voices in my head. I nodded to the pair and hurried away.

I walked on, deeper and deeper into the green coolness of the cemetery. Where one path crossed another, I saw a shadow on the pavers as someone came up behind me. Ever cautious, I glanced over my shoulder.

A young man had stopped a few feet away to gaze down at a headstone. He stood in deep shade and I could see only his profile, but I recognized his slight form and the silvery-gold curls falling down over his forehead.

My first instinct was to confront Micah Durant and demand to know why he had followed me to the cemetery, but suddenly I was seized by the strangest sensation. It was as if I had the power to peer past his angelic facade all the way down into his soul, and the blackness of his essence shocked me.

He turned then, a half smile playing at the corners of his mouth as he started toward me. Neither of us spoke even when he drew even with me on the path. I opened my mouth, to say what I wasn't quite certain, but he put a finger to his lips to silence me as his other hand moved to the side of my neck.

A scream rose to my throat. I thought surely he meant to assault me, but when he drew his hand away, I saw that a honeybee clung to one of his knuckles. Bringing the insect to eye level, he examined it closely as he rotated his hand. Incredibly, the bee shifted so that man and insect remained face-to-face. They stayed that way for the longest time before the honeybee finally flew away.

And then Micah Durant turned without having uttered a word and strode down the walkway toward the King Street gate.

Twenty-One

~~~~~~~

"They say everyone has a double," Devlin said a little while later as he peered through the viewer.

I'd arrived home to find him once again waiting on my front steps. He was a welcome sight after that odd encounter at the churchyard. And as always, he smelled divine. I resisted the urge to press my nose to his neck while he studied the stereogram.

After a few moments of scrutiny, he glanced up. "Is she a relative?"

"I don't know. She's almost certainly the woman named Rose that Nelda Toombs mentioned yesterday at Oak Grove. Nelda said we bore an uncanny resemblance and she seemed convinced that Rose and I were somehow connected. But what I'd really like to know is how that card ended up in my cellar."

From past experiences, I knew that searching for a practical answer in my impractical world was often a futile endeavor. Better just to accept that some things could never be explained. But that didn't stop me from longing for a rational explanation of recent events. If anyone could uncover the logic in any situation it was Devlin. His disdain for the supernatural wouldn't allow him to consider the alternative. So I let him unwittingly play the role of devil's advocate, hoping that he could open my mind to other less disturbing possibilities.

"Are you certain it couldn't have fallen out of a box of your belongings?" he asked. "Maybe the card got mixed in with some of your things when you moved out of your parents' house."

"That was years ago and I've moved around quite a bit since then. I think I would have found the card before now. Besides, I don't ever recall seeing any stereograms or viewers in the house, let alone any images of a look-alike. When I was little I used to spend hours and hours poring through family photograph albums. If I'd seen that picture or that woman, I'm certain I would have remembered."

"Not necessarily. The resemblance wouldn't have been so noticeable when you were a child."

I let myself cling to his reasoning for a moment. "I guess that's possible. Anything's possible." As I knew only too well.

"Have you shown the card to anyone in your family?"

"Not yet, but I'm driving over to Trinity to talk to Papa tomorrow. If I'm related to this woman—Rose— he'd be the one to know."

"That sounds like a reasonable plan," Devlin said. "Are you still worried that the stereoscope is somehow connected to the break-in?"

"I can't imagine why Owen Dowling or anyone else would go to so much trouble for an old viewer. But I also don't see how the timing can be coincidental. My house was broken into only a matter of hours after I took the stereoscope into his shop. And then the very next day, Louvenia Durant and her sister showed up at Oak Grove Cemetery. The whole situation is extremely unnerving, especially seeing my face in an image that must have been taken decades before I was born." Almost as unsettling as seeing my face on a ghost.

Devlin considered the card for a moment longer before turning his attention back to me. "The resemblance really is uncanny. I can understand why you'd find it spooky. Do you know what happened to her?"

"To Rose? Only that she was the last person to be buried in Kroll Cemetery and her grave is isolated from the others."

"She didn't die with the colonists?"

"I don't think so. Nelda never mentioned how she passed. If Papa can't tell me what I need to know, I'll start digging through the county records."

"You're really getting caught up in all this, aren't you?"

"Yes, I suppose I am." I shrugged and tried to play down my growing obsession. "There's nothing like a good mystery to get the blood flowing. Searching through archives is one of the most gratifying aspects of my job. Tracking down that one piece of the puzzle that makes everything fall into place."

"The thrill of the hunt," he murmured as he moved over in front of me. Eyes glinting, he ran a knuckle down the fading mark on my cheek, and I couldn't help shivering as I remembered his troubling promise. *When I find the man responsible for that bruise on your face, I'll make him very, very sorry.*

In that instant with his magnetic gaze upon me, I sensed something dark inside Devlin. A discordant energy that I didn't yet understand. I put my hand to his chest, outlining the silver medallion through his shirt. Something very strange happened then. My mind emptied and images came flooding in.

The sensation wasn't a premonition or a hallucination or even my imagination. It was a memory, I realized. *Devlin's* memory. Without even meaning to, I'd somehow slipped into his past.

Twenty-Two

He was no longer looking down at me, but at his companion, Mariama. Behind him a dozen or more silhouettes circled a fire, their voices and laughter rising over the music that played in the background. I recognized the song. It was one that had been popular at least fifteen years ago.

Devlin himself looked younger. There were no worry lines around his mouth and eyes. No silver in his hair from his trip to the other side. No dark circles, hollow cheeks or lingering emaciation from being haunted. Instead, he looked predatory and possessive, every bit the young, privileged male.

He moved toward Mariama, eyes hooded from intoxication and gleaming with lust. It occurred to me then that I wasn't viewing the scene from Devlin's perspective or even from Mariama's. I was an onlooker inside his memory, an observer to an event that had happened a long time ago.

"You really get off on this stuff, don't you?" he teased.

Mariama flung her arms wide as she threw back her head in exhilaration. "You have no idea! It's the most intoxicating sensation in the world! When the power is fully unleashed, it feels like lava flowing through my veins, lightning in my fingertips." She drew a long, rapturous breath. "But it's not just inside me, it's everywhere. In the trees, the sky, the ground. Even the air. Can't you smell it?"

Devlin lifted his face. "That's ozone. A storm's coming."

She gave a throaty laugh and passed him a bottle. "That's *magic*."

"If you say so." He lifted the whiskey and drank deeply.

"I know you feel it, too," she said. "I can see the throb of your pulse. Your heart is racing."

"That's not magic. That's you."

She slid her hand up to the medallion around his neck, entwining the silver chain around her fingers. "So much power in this totem. So much history in this emblem. You've no idea."

"Trust me, I know the history of the Order of the Coffin and the Claw," he said with an acerbic edge. "My grandfather made certain of it."

"He hasn't told you everything. He can't. Not yet."

"What are you talking about?"

"Like the Devlins and the Goodwines, the roots of the Order go all the way back to the beginning of Charleston. My ancestors came over on slave ships. One of them was a powerful *tagati*, a witch doctor who bartered his magic to the most prominent men in the city, men like *your* ancestors, in exchange for his freedom."

"Are you saying my family was in league with yours?"

"Until the Devlin conscience got the better of them, and then they and the *tagati* became mortal enemies. Some would say the Order was born from their blood feud."

"Fascinating." Devlin was back to being amused. "Does that make us mortal enemies, then?"

Mariama was silent for a moment. "You take these things far too lightly. What we are about to do is serious. Irrevocable. Are you sure you want to go through with it?"

"Sure. Why not?" he said with an easy grin.

"Very well. Clear your mind so that our thoughts become one. A single consciousness." As Mariama spoke, she withdrew a small dagger from her pocket and, taking Devlin's hand in hers, carved a crescent in his palm.

He swore.

"The cut has to be deep to bind us." She sliced her own palm without a flinch. "Now we join hands." She laced her fingers through his. "We become one mind, one body, one soul. I'm in your blood now, a part of you. Nothing can ever tear us apart. Not time, not history, not even death. From this day forward, I will be with you always. No matter what happens, I will never leave you."

"Never is a long time," he said.

"For us it's but the blink of an eye."

She smiled over her shoulder then, peering through the shadows until her gaze lit upon me.

That wasn't possible, of course. If this were really

Devlin's memory, she couldn't know I was there. I told myself it had to be a daydream or my own fanciful projection. But I could smell the ozone of her magic. I could feel the presence of something dark and powerful behind me.

Slowly I turned to search the woods.

A tall figure stood in the shadows watching me. My heart started to race as Darius Goodwine moved into the light to confront me.

I hadn't seen him since the night we'd struck a bargain for Devlin's life. How was it we were facing off now in Devlin's memory when I hadn't known either of them in the distant past?

"Why are you here?" I asked.

A cryptic smile flashed. "The better question is, why are *you* here?"

"I don't know. I don't even know how I got here."

"Of course you do. You have a powerful gift, one that is constantly changing and evolving as your connection to the dead world grows stronger. You're not the same person as when we first met, nor will you be the same when our paths cross again. But one thing hasn't changed. You continue to align yourself with the one man who could be your undoing."

I frowned. "Devlin would never hurt me."

"Not now, perhaps. But who knows what the futures holds?" Darius cocked his head, studying me. "Do you think you're the only one wrestling with a legacy? Do you think you're the only one being guided by destiny?"

"What do you mean?"

"Once John Devlin's grandfather is gone, there will

be demands put upon him. Expectations that even you can't imagine."

"Tell me."

"Not yet. Not until you're ready. But watch your back, Graveyard Queen. You have no idea who John Devlin really is."

"Wait!" I cried as he began to fade back into the shadows. But he was already gone and when I turned, Devlin and Mariama had also vanished, leaving me to my own memories and a troubling premonition that my future with Devlin had been doomed from the moment we met.

I shook myself out of the memory, the daydream… whatever it had been. The eerie sensation had lasted only a split second, but during that moment, I'd unconsciously taken Devlin's hand. Now I turned his palm up, searching, finding and then tracing the tiny moon-shaped scar with my thumb.

He recoiled in shock, backing away from me as he stared at his palm in revulsion. Then, shoving both hands into his pockets, he paced to the windows and stood staring out into the garden.

Neither of us said anything for the longest time. It was strange how close we'd been one moment and now it seemed that miles and centuries of history separated us. I studied his rigid form, badly shaken by what I'd seen. By what I'd heard.

"John…" I said on a breath.

He turned with shuttered eyes.

I had no idea what I'd been about to say to him. Maybe I meant to ask him about his family's history and the expectations that came with his legacy as a Devlin. Maybe I wanted him to reassure me that nothing from his past or mine could tear us apart. Instead, I shifted my focus to the tiny indentation just beneath his bottom lip. I'd wondered about that scar for so long. Maybe if I emptied my mind…

No, I told myself firmly. No more playing around with a power I didn't yet understand.

"You're looking at me very strangely." His voice sounded strained, foreign. Did he have an inkling of what had just transpired? I didn't understand it myself and I still wasn't entirely convinced I hadn't imagined the whole thing. "What is it?" he asked.

"I have some photographs I want to show you."

"Of what?"

"Kroll Cemetery." I turned to the desk so that he couldn't see my trembling fingers as I tore open the package that Dr. Shaw's assistant had left on the porch. The packet had been waiting for me when I got home from the churchyard, but I'd delayed my examination of the images until I'd shown Devlin the stereogram.

Now I eagerly glommed on to the distraction because I didn't want to think about Mariama's assertion that she would never leave Devlin or Darius's warning that Devlin could be my undoing. I didn't want to dwell on my evolving gift or the history of the Order of the Coffin and the Claw or the possibility that Devlin and I might never find our happy ending.

"Where did you get them?" he asked as he moved up beside me.

"Dr. Shaw had them sent over. He told me that Kroll Cemetery is thought to be a puzzle because of all the keys and seemingly random numbers engraved on the headstones. Now I can see why." I sifted through a few of the pictures. "The symbols are unlike anything I've ever seen."

Devlin picked up one of the photographs, turning it toward the windows for a closer scrutiny. While he studied the image, I studied his profile as something distressing occurred to me. Had he been thinking about Mariama earlier when we'd been so close, or had I entered a memory that was deeply buried in his subconscious?

If his dead wife had been on his mind, why? *Why now?*

"I'm not sure there's anything mysterious about the numbers," he said.

"What?"

"The numbers on the headstones. Most of the bodies were decomposed beyond recognition. The remains were probably numbered in the order in which they were found."

With an effort, I tore my focus from the past and tried to concentrate on the here and now. On the mystery of Kroll Cemetery. "That makes sense, I guess, but I can't help thinking those numbers are a code or a message. They have significance. They're another piece of the puzzle."

"If it's a code, someone would surely have figured it out by now," Devlin said.

"Not necessarily. The cemetery is located on private property. How many people have even been allowed inside those walls?" Spreading the remainder of the photographs across the desk, I stared down at the final image, the headstone of the last person to be buried in Kroll Cemetery. *Amelia Rose Gray.*

Seeing her full name—my full name—on the headstone rattled me.

Devlin put a hand on my arm. "Are you okay?"

It was all I could do not to move away from him. Maybe it was just nerves, but I felt an unpleasant sensation where the scar in his palm touched my bare skin. I looked up, probing his face, scrutinizing those tiny new worry lines around his mouth and eyes, but his expression revealed nothing more than concern for me.

"I'm fine," I said.

He tilted his dark head, observing me carefully. "I don't think you're fine. You look upset."

"Maybe a little. First I find a photograph of a woman who looks enough like me to be my twin and now a headstone with nothing but my name on it. No date of birth or death. Nothing. It's almost as if that grave has been there waiting for me all these years."

"That's nonsense," Devlin said with a scowl. "The headstone doesn't have anything to do with you. The woman buried in that grave has been dead for decades."

"Laid to rest in a cemetery of suicides."

Was the cause of Rose's death the reason she couldn't move on? Did her cryptic message have something to do with the tragedy at Kroll Colony? After all these years, had she found a way to reveal the truth through me?

So many questions…

"Maybe she just wanted to be near Ezra Kroll,"

Devlin said. "Did you notice that her headstone is different from the others? No number or key symbol."

"You can just make out something at the top of the marker," I said. "See? Right there." I pointed to some faint etchings in a shaded area of the stone.

"Doesn't look like much to me," Devlin said.

I gathered up the photographs and placed them in a neat stack on my desk. "These images only tell part of the story. I'm more convinced than ever that I need to see that graveyard in person."

Devlin looked worried. "I'm not sure that's a good idea. The cemetery is remote. No houses or roads for miles."

"All I know is that I'm drawn to it," I said. "There's so much about my background I still don't understand. So much of my family's history that remains unknown to me. I'm not like you. You can trace your roots back centuries. You know exactly where you came from and who your people are."

"That's not always a good thing," he said obliquely.

"Still, can you blame me for being curious?"

"No, but try to keep some perspective. Just because you never knew about Rose doesn't mean there's some great mystery behind her death."

"I really hope that's true." But the signs and visitations told me otherwise. I could no more ignore Rose's clues than I could stem the tide of ghosts that came through the veil at twilight.

She had sought me out for a reason. Not to latch on to my warmth and energy or because she wanted to be human again. She needed me to find a key. Unless and until I could give her what she wanted, she wouldn't go quietly back into the afterlife.

And the logical place to start my search was in Kroll Cemetery.

Twenty-Three

Devlin and I had an early dinner together downtown and then a brief stroll along the Battery to watch the sunset. As we walked along the waterfront, I slipped my arm through his and, for a short time, pretended that neither of us had anything more pressing on our minds than watching the sailboats glide into the harbor.

The shimmering water reflected an exotic palette of ruby and cerulean, and I could smell gardenias in the warm breeze that ruffled Devlin's hair. I closed my eyes, drawing a deep breath as I rested my head against his shoulder. It was one of those moments that seemed already imprinted upon my memory, tugging loose a dreamy nostalgia that I knew from experience could too easily turn into loneliness.

Devlin had fallen prey to his own thoughts. His eyes were distant and brooding as he looked out over the sea, and I knew that he'd gone to a bad place—here or in the past—where I had no business prying. But he wasn't entirely oblivious to our surroundings. I felt him tense at the sound of a child's laughter drifting out from White Point Garden. The echo of joyous in-nocence would always be bittersweet to him.

I looked up and saw a shadow steal across his features a split second before he turned away. There was something disturbing in his eyes, a fleeting darkness that reminded me of legacies and expectations. Despite my unease, I didn't pull away a few seconds later when he bent to kiss me, even though we were far from alone on the walkway. I sensed he needed the contact. Whatever his turmoil, I was his touchstone.

He didn't kiss me, though. Instead, his head came up abruptly, his gaze going past me to scan the milling tourists on the walkway. Reluctantly, I glanced over my shoulder, but I saw nothing out of the ordinary in the crowd.

The air shifted as the sun hovered over the cityscape of steeples. The waning light brought a prickle to my scalp and I lifted my face to the wind as I detected a faint trace of ozone even though there wasn't a cloud in the sky.

I turned back to Devlin, my breath catching at the look on his face. I could sense the bristle of his every instinct. Wariness hardened his eyes and in the deeper depths, I saw a glimmer of dread.

When I would have tightened my hold on his arm, he moved away. The rejection seemed unconscious, but in that instant it hit me anew just how fragile our relationship had become. Despite everything we'd been through, despite moments of harmony and deep passion, Devlin and I were still breakable.

Long after he'd left my house to return to his grandfather in the hospital, I sat out on the porch, still warm from a shower and the afterglow of our lovemaking, and pondered the situation. Devlin was no longer haunted by ghosts, but something bedeviled him just the same. He'd been aware of something on the Battery. A scent? An aberrant presence? He would never admit it, of course, but I had often wondered if his refusal to acknowledge the supernatural was his way of keeping the demons at bay.

An image of Mariama sprang to mind and I shivered. For all I knew, she could still be lurking somewhere in the gray waiting for a chance to slip back through the veil. In which case, I should take care not to topple Devlin's defenses.

Besides, I had my own otherworldly stalkers to worry about. Until I could decipher all the clues, neither would leave me alone. I wanted to believe their banishment was a simple matter of solving an old mystery—finishing earthly business—but deep down, I knew it wouldn't be that simple. Dealing with ghosts and in-betweens was never a straightforward proposition.

As twilight slanted down through the trees and the air filled with the dreamy scent of Confederate jasmine, I got up and went inside, turning on a lamp in the foyer to guide me through the house. The rooms hadn't seemed so empty earlier, the hush quite so menacing in Devlin's company. But now with the rosy flush of sunset melting into the violet horizon, I felt the weight of an all-too-familiar presentiment descend upon my shoulders.

Trying to ignore the unease, I made a cup of tea and carried it to my office where I stood for a moment, gazing out at the gathering darkness. Then, deliberately turning my back on the shadows, I sat down at my desk for an evening of research and speculation.

My thoughts once again turned to Rose. Given her appearance in the stereogram and the location of her burial, I had little doubt that she'd somehow been involved with Ezra Kroll. Had a romantic relationship been the catalyst for all those deaths?

Passion and jealousy were powerful motivations. As old as time itself. If Rose had been in love with Kroll and his life had been cut short because of their liaison, I could well understand why her ghost would need closure if not vengeance. I tried to put myself in her place. What would I do if Devlin were taken from me? How would I ever make peace with such a loss?

It was not a question I wanted to examine at length. But no matter how hard I tried to squelch my earlier anxiety, I couldn't forget the ominous emotions I'd picked up from him as he'd scanned the crowd on the Battery. Or the way he'd snatched his hand away when I'd tried to trace that moon-shaped scar in his palm.

Hardening my resolve, I once again shoved aside those niggling doubts and buckled down to my work. I'd just found a new mention of Ezra Kroll in an obscure article about communes when a sound in the quiet house brought my head up with a jerk.

I sat very still, listening to the silence. When nothing came to me, I turned in my chair to scour the garden. Night had fallen in earnest while I worked. Stars twinkled through the treetops and I could see the faint shimmer of what might have been a ghostly face in the deepest corner of the garden. I watched for only a moment before averting my gaze.

Rotating back to the desk, I returned my attention to the laptop. But in the instant before my eyes dropped to the screen, I detected a flickering shadow just beyond the kitchen in the murky niche where the foyer light didn't quite reach. I watched and waited, my stomach knotted in apprehension. *Something was inside my house.*

My first instinct was to reach for the phone. I would call Devlin and have him rush back from the hospital. Then my hand fell away. This was no flesh-and-blood prowler. Already I'd caught a whiff of decay.

I could see nothing of substance in the dark, but I knew she was there just the same. She had come up from the basement and traveled through the walls to get to my hallway. The same intruder that, for whatever reason, had left a cicada husk on my nightstand in exchange for the bookmark. The same interloper that had tossed a key down into the cellar and made herself a nest in the stairwell. A squatter that was human but not human.

The flickering shadow vanished and the house once again fell into an intensified stillness. I sat transfixed, my breath coming quick and shallow as I waited.

Into that loaded silence I heard a flurry of scratching and scrabbling, as if something was clawing its way through the walls.

Slowly, I pushed back my chair and got up from the desk, mentally preparing myself for what I might find as I followed the sound through the kitchen, down the hallway and into my bedroom. As I stepped over the threshold and reached for the light, the noise in the walls stopped. In the half beat before I flipped the switch, I could have sworn I heard a hitched breath.

I stepped into the room and glanced around. *I know you're here.*

My gaze raked the walls, searching every corner and crevice and taking inventory of the knickknacks on my bureau—silver hairbrush and mirror, a picture frame, my mother's pearl necklace. And the basket of polished pebbles from Rosehill Cemetery that I had once been foolish enough to think would offer some protection against the dangers of the unknown.

My things were just as I'd left them and nothing else seemed out of place. If any of my belongings had been taken, I didn't miss them.

I heard nothing, saw nothing, but I knew my visitor was there, just behind the plaster. Somehow she had found a way through the boarded-up stairwell and once again crawled into my walls. I could feel her presence in the shiver down my backbone.

I slipped across the room to the wastebasket where I'd tossed the cicada husk and bent to retrieve it. As I straightened with the twig between my fingers, lamplight poured through the transparent shell, turning the insect's remains to amber. It was really quite lovely. As eye-catching in its own way as the bookmark.

Carefully, I placed the twig on top of the book jacket where I had found it and lifted my gaze to the wall behind my bed. "No more offerings," I said firmly. "No more trading. Leave my things alone and get out of my house."

Then slowly I walked to the door, turned off the light and went back to the office where I dropped, with a pounding heart, onto my chair and waited.

Twenty-Four

I wasn't sure what I expected to happen. Certainly not the intense quiet that followed. For the longest time, I heard nothing more than the hum of the refrigerator, the swish of the ceiling fan. No scrabbling in the walls. No thud on the basement stairs or ping of a dropped key.

My ears were so acutely attuned to the loaded silence that the chime of my phone had the effect of a gunshot. It was all I could do not to jump.

I checked the display but didn't recognize the number. Lifting the phone to my ear, I braced myself to hear a cicada rattle or that piercing whistle on the other end. Such an expectation undoubtedly spoke as much to the acceptance of my alternate reality as to my fear. Anything seemed possible in my world, even a phone call from beyond.

"Hello? Hello? Are you there?" inquired a concerned voice on the other end. "Amelia?"

"Dr. Shaw?" *Thank God.* I'd never been so happy to hear his voice. My grip relaxed on the phone as I let out a relieved breath. "Yes, I'm here. Sorry. I didn't recognize the number."

"I'm calling from my cell phone. Are you all right, my dear? You don't sound yourself."

"I'm fine, thank you. Just a little frayed around the edges. Too many things on my mind these days."

"I hope our earlier conversation isn't one of them. You looked distressed when you left the Institute this afternoon so I wanted to make sure you were okay. And I also want to apologize. All of that business about a calling was nothing more than speculation on my part. A bit of whimsical conjecture based upon what I know of your history. In hindsight, I feel I should have been more circumspect. Given all you've been through, I can see why you'd find even the suggestion of such a mission distressing, if not downright harrowing."

"I admit, death walker is hardly the job I would aspire to," I tried to say lightly. "But I'm not upset by the suggestion. I came to you for advice. You're the only one I can talk to about these things and I value your counsel. So, please, no apology necessary. And anyway, our visit is the least of my concerns at the moment."

"What's the matter? And what can I do to help?"

My gaze flicked warily back to the hallway. "It seems something has invaded my walls and cellar, even the barricaded stairwell that runs up to the kitchen."

"*Invaded?* I take it you don't mean the usual suspects of mold or rodents," he said carefully.

I should be so lucky. "I don't know what it is. My upstairs neighbor thinks we have something nesting in the cellar. Rats, as you said, or maybe opossums. Normally, I'd be inclined to agree as I can hear scratching behind the plaster from time to time. But there have been other incidents that I can't so easily explain away. Things I didn't mention when I came to see you earlier."

"Such as?"

"An insect husk was left on my nightstand in place of a missing bookmark. And I saw someone… something…with a hump on her back creeping through the shadows at Oak Grove Cemetery. She was very small. Shriveled, I would say, and dressed all in black. When she turned to look at me, she made this strange rattling sound in her throat. Almost like a cicada. Then last night, I spotted the same apparition—or one like her—in my garden. I can't help wondering if this… being is Mott Toombs. She's trying to make contact for some reason."

"An interesting theory," Dr. Shaw said thoughtfully. "But there may be another, less alarming explanation."

"I'm all ears."

"Would it reassure you to know that such a sighting as the one you just described isn't all that uncommon?"

"You must be joking."

"No, no, I'm dead serious, my dear. Have you never heard of the Old Hag Syndrome?"

"Papa used to tell me stories about boo hags," I said. "Is that the same thing?"

"Tales of boo hags are particular to our part of the country, but people all over the world have experienced the night-hag phenomenon."

"Which is…?"

"A feeling of being watched, of something lurking

about or standing over you. Even if nothing is actually seen, there's a common perception that the watcher is a dark, female figure, usually old and wizened. Even more common are reports of audio hallucinations—scratching, scraping, buzzing, static. The medical explanation is sleep paralysis, or more specifically, hypnagogic or hypnopompic hallucinations. A state that usually occurs right before you fall asleep or are just waking up. In other words, a visual and audio representation of a dream while you're partially awake."

"A lucid dream, you mean. I don't think that would explain what I saw at the cemetery," I said. "I assure you, I was fully awake. Nor do I think it would explain the cicada husk and the missing bookmark, let alone the key that was tossed down into the cellar."

Dr. Shaw fell silent for a moment, but I could sense his keen interest. "You didn't mention a key before."

"It happened yesterday when I went down to the cellar to look for other stereograms. I didn't see anyone at the top of steps, but the key landed right at my feet. I couldn't have missed it."

Another pause. "And you're worried that the instigator of all these incidents may be Mott Toombs?"

"Yes, that is precisely my worry." I clutched the phone. "Dr. Shaw, I believe all of these events are somehow connected to that stereogram that I brought to your office. In fact, I'm certain of it. Someone or something is leaving clues for me to follow, only I don't know how to interpret them."

"I would agree there appears to be a connection." His voice now held a note of concern.

"I feel as if I'm being manipulated. *Herded* is the

term that comes to mind. As frightened as I am by the clues, I'm even more afraid of what might happen if I don't follow them."

He must have heard the panic that had crept into my voice because he said in a soothing tone, "I'm here to help you, Amelia. We'll figure this out together. The most important thing to remember when confronting the unknown is to remain calm. Negative energy attracts even more unrest. As you know, my dear, I've conducted dozens of investigations into the supernatural over the years, and more often than not, a logical answer can be ascertained if one cares to dig deeply enough. Even in your case, I should think."

"Nothing would make me happier."

"Noises in walls, for example, are almost always caused by animals. The aforementioned rats and mice, the occasional opossum or squirrel. We've also run across our share of raccoons. Crafty little beggars with nasty dispositions and the very devil on wiring. If something is nesting in your cellar and walls, I would suggest we first eliminate the normal before we tackle the abnormal. Nine times out of ten, a vermin infestation is the source of the problem."

"And the one time out of ten?"

"Inconclusive," he said after a nerve-racking pause.

"Somehow those statistics don't reassure me."

"Better to know what we're dealing with, is it not?" he asked gently. "Then we can decide how best to proceed."

"Yes, I suppose." His logic made me feel a little better. "So what do we do first?"

"As it happens, I know of a very reliable exterminator. He's humane, discreet and very good at what he does."

"And if he doesn't find any animalistic evidence?"

"Then I can send over a team to do some readings. Or I'll come myself if you prefer. But one step at a time."

The reasonable way he laid it all out could almost make me believe that rats and mice had indeed taken up residence in my walls and that the figure I'd seen at Oak Grove and in my garden was nothing more than a visual interpretation of a dream. Hallucinations and vermin infestations had never sounded so appealing.

But something inside me balked at having my sanctuary further violated. A persistent voice warned that outsiders, even someone as open-minded as Dr. Shaw, might somehow exacerbate the problem. Might somehow stir the unrest.

"Amelia? Are you still there?"

"Yes. I was just mulling over your suggestion. I don't know that I'm comfortable having an exterminator come in without my landlady's permission."

"As I said, he's very discreet. And if you're at all concerned about having a stranger in your home, let me put your mind at ease. I've known him since he was a child. In fact, I first met him and his grandmother when my team was called in to examine a problem similar to yours."

"What do you mean 'similar to mine'?"

"He was convinced that something lived in the walls of his bedroom. His grandmother decided the best way to disabuse him of such a notion was to have the Institute launch an investigation."

"Did you find an animal?"

"Not so much as a dropping. And the absence of physical proof only strengthened the boy's conviction that a *duende* resided in his walls. I've sometimes wondered if his profession is a direct result of that childhood obsession."

"What is a *duende*?"

"I suppose you could say it's a variation of the Old Hag Syndrome. The legend differs from culture to culture, but the grandmother described a small, humanoid creature that sometimes crawls out of bedroom walls or other close places to barter with children."

A cold fist of fear closed over my heart. "What do they barter?"

"Coins, trinkets, toys…anything that would catch a young eye in exchange for the child's soul."

My mind went instantly to the key necklace I'd found on the headstone and to Papa's ominous warning in the deepening twilight of Rosehill Cemetery: *Take nothing, leaving nothing behind.*

Had I inadvertently bartered away my soul when I took the key from the grave, leaving the clover chain in its place?

I didn't really believe that, of course. As fantastical as my reality now was, I still had limits of acceptance and belief. And yet it hadn't been long after I'd found the key that the ghosts had entered my world.

"You don't really believe such creatures exist, do you?" I asked fearfully.

"I always try to keep an open mind to any possibility," Dr. Shaw said. "And despite all the logical answers that we've found over the years, there are many things in this world that will never be explained. The *duende* could have been nothing more than a hallucination or the product of a lonely little boy's imagination. Or the child might well have been the target of a poltergeist or some other form of restless spirit that was attracted to his warmth and energy. The earthbound entity either became trapped in the wall or wanted to remain there to be close to the boy."

"You said you found no evidence," I said.

"No physical evidence of an animal infestation."

"What did you do?"

"We treated the *duende* as we would any other unwelcome presence. We smudged the house to cleanse the negative energy, and we commanded the spirit to leave the boy alone."

"Did that work?"

"Only temporarily. In any case, I don't know that I would recommend such a direct approach in your situation. As you said, all of these events seem to be connected to the stereogram you found in the cellar. If you're being harassed by a spirit that's somehow bound to Kroll Colony, a confrontation could have serious repercussions."

"What kind of repercussions?"

"Think about what happened to those colonists and to Ezra Kroll himself. You may be dealing with some very powerful emotions."

I couldn't help but shudder. "I showed the stereogram to John. He once knew someone from Isola who believed the deaths weren't suicides at all but mass murder perpetrated to cover up a single homicide."

"Yes, I've heard that theory, as well. Amelia…"

Dr. Shaw trailed off as if reluctant to voice his next thought. For the first time during our conversation, I heard doubt in his voice. Maybe even a hint of fear.

"What is it?"

"You may need to prepare yourself for the possibility that the spirit you've encountered isn't just leaving clues. And the endgame may not be justice or even revenge. Indeed, you may not be dealing with a single entity at all, but a manifestation of mass rage. A pent-up fury that needs a conduit. In other words, it needs you, my dear."

Twenty-Five

$\sim\!\!\!\!\!\!\!\bigcirc\!\!\bigcirc\!\!\bigcirc\!\!\sim$

My heart thudded painfully as I picked up the congealing tea to calm myself, only to set the cup back down with a clatter. I wouldn't have thought it possible to be more unsettled than I had been earlier when I'd trespassed into Devlin's memory, or even later on the Battery with the smell of ozone in the air and dread in his eyes. But the notion of mass murder, mass rage, mass *possession* went far beyond doubt and disquiet.

I wanted nothing more than to pull Papa's rules over my head and bury myself in the twin defenses of denial and pretense. But it was too late for that. The ghost and the in-between knew that I could see them. No amount of make-believe would send either away. I hadn't yet suffered any physical ramifications of a haunting, but it was only a matter of time before the drain on my life force weakened me.

"My dear, are you all right?"

"I don't know."

"It seems I've upset you once again, and I'm sorry for that, but I felt I had to warn you. If you're to visit that cemetery, you must be forearmed. Perhaps under the circumstances, it would be better to postpone your trip."

"No, I can't do that. I *have* to go. The sooner, the better. I have to find out what they want. I can't hide or run away from this, Dr. Shaw. That would only make things worse. Following the clues may be the only protection I have left. For whatever reason, I'm being summoned to that cemetery. I think there's a message to be found on those headstones. Maybe you were right the other day when you asked who better than I to solve the riddle. I'd like to think that nothing more will be required of me than my professional expertise."

"I hope so, too," he said, the foreboding in his voice an echo of my own trepidation. "But promise me you'll take care when you get to that cemetery. I've no special intuition or extrasensory perception, but I do have a hunch that you're approaching a crossroads. A physical and spiritual turning point in your life. I would once again advise that you proceed with the utmost caution."

We talked for a moment or two longer before hanging up, and then I returned to my research. I heard nothing else in the walls and maybe it was my imagination, but the quality of the silence had shifted. Despite Dr. Shaw's warning, I no longer felt frightened or threatened. It was as if my decision to visit Kroll Cemetery had temporarily placated the interloper.

Even when I rose a little while later to get ready for bed, I didn't feel the need to glance over my shoulder as I walked down the hallway. I wouldn't say that I felt as safe and secure as I once had in my sanctuary, but my mood had certainly lifted. I showered, dried my hair and then crawled into bed, rolling to my back so that I could watch the changing patterns of moonlight on the ceiling until I grew drowsy.

Sliding down between the crisp sheets, I cocooned myself in the covers as the ceiling fan stirred the night air. I was just drifting off when I heard a tap at the window.

My eyes flew open as I lay there, listening to the darkness. The sound came again. *Tap, tap, tap.* Trying to relax my muscles so that I could move more fluidly, I shifted my position until I had a view of the window.

Something dark covered the glass. I thought at first the curtains were drawn, but I didn't remember closing them before I turned in. And once my eyes adjusted to the gloom, I could see the glisten of moonlight in the upper pane. As I focused on that pale stream, I saw an insect fly to the window and cling to the screen. Then another came and still another until I realized the darkness covering the lower panel was neither curtain nor shade, but a cloud of black moths.

Maybe I wasn't fully awake or maybe I'd become inured to the unusual, but in that first instant of awareness, I was more curious than frightened. I even entertained the notion that the beacon inside me—the unnatural light that attracted the ghosts—might also have summoned the moths.

The quiver of their iridescent wings was hypnotic and my focus became almost trancelike until a dank cold penetrated my fixation. A draft so icy I could see the frost of my breath in the remaining moonlight.

And with the plunging temperature came a scent that reminded me of damp earth and old death.

Tap, tap, tap.

My attention darted back to the window. The moths kept coming, kept clinging until all but a sliver of moonlight was extinguished. Now I could make out little more than the vague shape of furniture, but instinct told me not to reach for the lamp. It was best not to see what had entered my room.

Clutching the covers to my chin, I lay motionless as I peered through the frigid darkness. I saw no humpback silhouettes or sightless apparitions, but I knew something was there just the same. I wasn't dreaming or hallucinating. I hadn't conjured the moths or the cold. Or that smell. Whatever had invaded my bedroom was real. Not human, not any longer, but there was no denying a presence.

Mott?

I almost whispered the name into the darkened room but I held my silence as I cowered under the covers.

The chill deepened and the smell intensified as the tiny interloper moved about the space. I sensed her standing over me and I wanted nothing so much as to leap from bed and run screaming into the night. But I clung to my courage as tightly as I clutched the blanket, and I remembered Dr. Shaw's warning that negative energy stirred unrest. I took a breath, trying to calm my racing heart.

Just when I thought I had my fear under control, I felt the frosted caress of dead fingers against my cheek, the brush of frigid lips in my hair. Cloves tingled on my tongue, but I took no solace in the spice. I had come to loathe the taste.

Squeezing my eyes closed, I willed away the trespasser. *Please go. Leave me alone. Leave me in peace.*

I heard the low rasp of a breath, a guttural mutter that sounded like *"Mine,"* and then the click of long fingernails against the top of the nightstand as she rummaged through my things. A drawer opened, then another and another.

What are you looking for? What do you want from me?

After a moment, the shuffling stopped, the cold faded and I knew that I was once again alone in my bedroom. I huddled under the quilt as I listened for signs of a retreat. I heard only silence. No scratching in the walls or footsteps out in the hallway. But I knew Mott was gone and with her the moths.

Moonlight flooded the room, but still I reached for the lamp. Blinking in the sudden brilliance, I glanced around, my gaze coming to rest on the nightstand.

The cicada husk had vanished and in its place were three gleaming keys.

Twenty-Six

I swung my legs over the side of the bed and sat there staring at the keys, all lined up in a row, but teeth turned away from me, as if all I had to do was pick one up and insert it into a lock.

Which one, though? And was I really being given a choice or did each have a special purpose?

A chill lingered in the room, not from the intruder, but from my own fear. I dragged the covers over my shoulders as I scooted closer to the nightstand, wanting a better look, but not daring to touch. Not yet. I remembered the reaction I'd had when the first key had been tossed in the cellar. I'd gotten rid of it in the garden, but now here it was back on my nightstand along with two others.

I wouldn't remove any of them until I had a chance to consider the consequences. I didn't want my actions to be misconstrued as acceptance of this offering. Even worse, a trade or invitation.

I studied each key for a very long time, taking note of the shank, head and bittings as I looked for inscriptions or numbers, anything that would give me a hint of what they might unlock. One was a skeleton key with a long shank and ornate head. The fanciful scrollwork reminded me of the key I'd found in Rosehill Cemetery, right down to the tattered pink ribbon still threaded through the filigree bow. As a child, I'd imagined the treasure chest that key might open, but now I worried about the horrors that could be unlocked if I chose the wrong door.

Then I had another thought. Was the skeleton key somehow connected to Rose? Could this key be my salvation?

What if Rose had left it on that headstone all those years ago as a talisman against the ghosts? Rather than summoning the apparitions into my world, maybe it would have kept them locked out.

The head of the third key had been carved to resemble an eye. Four teeth pointed straight down from the shank like the prongs of a pitchfork. There was something distinctly menacing about that strange key. I found myself both repelled by and drawn to it.

"What am I supposed to do with them?" I whispered into the silent room. "What is it you want from me?"

As I gazed around my familiar surroundings, searching for answers to the unknowable, I caught a glimpse of my reflection in the dresser mirror. The sight stopped me cold, the resemblance to Rose filling me with a terrible dread. Our destinies were inexorably linked. What I was now she had once been. What she was I would someday become.

Rising, I walked over to the mirror and leaned in to scrutinize my features—*her* features—focusing on those tiny motes at the bottom of my irises. Had

Rose's eyes possessed those same strange markings? As a child, had she ever fancied they were keyholes?

I glanced at the odd-shaped key lying on my nightstand and then back at my reflection. Suddenly, I had the disturbing notion that those pointed teeth matched exactly the dark lines beneath my pupils.

Twenty-Seven

I was just heading out of the house the next morning when Owen Dowling called. Still on edge from the night's events, I answered cautiously when I saw the store name on the display.

"I hope I'm not catching you at a bad time," he said. "You asked that I call you the next time my great-aunt came to the shop. She's here now, as it happens. I told her about the stereoscope you found and she's very eager to speak with you about it."

"Did she recognize the names in the inscription?" I asked anxiously.

"I'll let the two of you talk about that. Would it be possible for you to drop by the shop this morning?"

"What time?"

"The sooner the better as I don't know how long she plans to be here."

"I'll come right now, then."

"Wonderful! I'll tell her to expect you. And, Miss Gray? Don't forget to bring the stereoscope."

Twenty minutes later, I found myself striding down King Street with my backpack thrown over one shoulder. It was not yet ten so most of the shops were still closed, but downtown already bustled with tourists. There were so many people out and about and the sun shone so brightly from a cloudless sky that I felt only mild trepidation as I turned down the alley toward Dowling Curiosities. Devlin's investigation had unearthed nothing suspicious on either the shop or Owen, but even if he had discovered something untoward, I doubt I would have been thwarted. After what happened last evening, a human threat would almost be welcome.

The shop was locked so I tapped on the glass until Owen Dowling appeared at the window. Drawing open the door, he flashed a charming smile as he gave a slight bow. A courtly and old-fashioned greeting even by Devlin's standards.

"Miss Gray! Thank you for coming on such short notice." He moved back from the door and motioned for me to enter.

Stepping across the threshold, I was once again assailed by the medicinal aroma of camphor. The overhead lights had not yet been turned on and I could see dust motes dancing in the beams of sunlight streaming in through the windows. The effect was unexpectedly cheery given my mood and the bizarre nature of some of the collectibles.

"Thank you for calling me. I'm so happy your great-aunt agreed to meet with me. She's still here, I hope." I couldn't see anyone else in the shop, but decided his aunt must be in the back.

"She is." Owen nodded toward my backpack. "You brought the stereoscope?"

"Of course."

"See, Auntie? I told you she wouldn't forget."

My gaze darted around the shop, but I still didn't notice anyone until the woman came out from behind one of the display cases. Her dark attire and diminutive stature had rendered her almost invisible in the shadows.

I was so taken aback by her sudden appearance that it took me a moment to recognize her. Then I exclaimed, "Miss Toombs!"

"Lovely to see you again, Miss Gray...Amelia."

I turned to Owen accusingly. "So you did recognize the inscription when I was in here before. Why didn't you say so?"

He put up a hand in protest. "I swear to you, I wasn't familiar with those names. I've never heard my aunt called by anything other than her given name. I had no idea she was the Neddy in the inscription."

"He's right," Nelda said. "Neither of those nicknames has been used in decades. No one in Owen's generation would have recognized them. Still," she turned to give him a gentle rebuke. "You might have told her who she was coming to see when you phoned her. I'm afraid I gave our visitor a shock."

"How was I to know that the two of you had already met? It seems I'm the one in the dark here." He removed a feather duster from a nearby hook and swept it along a row of antique dolls. The slight rustle of their taffeta skirts sounded like rain. "Go ahead and have your talk," he said peevishly. "I'll just be over here dusting."

Nelda's dark eyes glittered mischievously as she slipped her fingers through his suspenders and gave them a playful snap. "Don't scowl so, nephew. It'll give you wrinkles."

"Heaven forbid," he said in mock horror as he side-stepped away from her.

She turned to me with an encouraging smile. "Let's go back to the office, shall we? We'll be more comfortable there, and I've made tea."

I followed her through the curtains into a large storage room of neatly arranged boxes and crates. The office was tucked away in a corner at the back of the building. An antique writing desk faced the door, but Nelda led me past the workspace to a small sitting area furnished with a striped settee and two Queen Anne chairs. The upholstery and rugs were in soothing shades of blue and green—sea colors—that complemented the lush courtyard I could glimpse through French doors. It was all very vintage and feminine. Very old Charleston.

"What a charming office," I said.

"It was similarly furnished when I inherited the shop from a distant relative. I always liked the quaintness, but I expect Owen will redo everything once he takes over. That'll be hard for me. I'm old and I don't like change, but it's only fitting the shop be returned to the Dowling side of the family. Owen isn't really my nephew, you see, more like a cousin several times removed. But he's always thought of me as his great-aunt and I've never been one to stand on ceremony."

"I understand Dowling Curiosities has been at this location for a very long time," I said.

"Well over fifty years. I was surprised to find myself in my cousin's will, but our family is nothing if not eccentric and more than a little complex. You've no doubt noticed that I have a different last name than Ezra's." She motioned to one of the chairs and she took the settee, propping her walking cane nearby and smoothing wrinkles from the smock she wore over her dress. "William Kroll was Louvenia and Ezra's father. After he died, my mother married Harold Toombs, a weak opportunist who left her shortly after Mott and I were born. It was a difficult delivery and our poor mother had many months of recovery. Harold couldn't or wouldn't accept the responsibility for our care so he packed his bags and took off."

"That must have been hard on everyone."

"Mother never got over his abandonment. When she died a few years later, Louvenia swore it was from nursing a broken heart for so long. In truth, she succumbed to pneumonia. Tea?"

"Yes, thank you."

While Nelda busied herself with the teapot and cups, I removed the stereoscope from my bag and placed it on the coffee table.

She paused, eyes filling with emotion before she reached for it. "May I?"

"Of course."

She turned the stereoscope over, searching for the inscription. "Ah, there it is." She ran a finger over the tiny metal plate. "I gave this viewer to Mott on our thirteenth birthday. My cousin found it on one of her excursions and engraved it in this very shop. And now here it is back, after having been lost for so many years."

"I'm happy to return it to its rightful place," I said.

"That's very generous of you. The shop will reimburse you for your troubles, of course."

"No need. The viewer belongs here with you. But I do wonder how it came to be in the cellar of a house on Rutledge Avenue."

A frown flitted across Nelda's wizened brow. "I've no idea. It just disappeared one day. I never knew what happened to it."

"And this, as well?" I laid the stereogram on the table facing her.

She picked up the card and studied the dual photographs for the longest time before pressing the images to her heart. "I remember the day these were taken. Ezra had just come from the Colony where he'd been working in one of the gardens and Mott and I begged him to have his picture made with us. We adored him so. But he was always camera shy, especially after he returned from the war."

"Who took the photographs?"

"Louvenia. Mott showed her how to position the frames at slightly different angles to create a 3-D image just the way Rose had taught her. Mott was always a quick study. She became as obsessed with photography as Rose. Both were in love with stereoscopy. They claimed you could see things in the three-dimensional imagery that couldn't be glimpsed with the naked eye."

"That's Rose in the upstairs window, isn't it?"

Nelda slipped the card in the holder and lifted the stereoscope to the light. "Why, yes it is. Watching over us as always. Funny, I never noticed her there before." She returned the viewer to the table and handed me a cup of tea. "You can see why I was so startled by the resemblance."

"Yes, it's uncanny, as you said. How did you come to know Rose? If you don't mind my asking."

"I don't mind. I like talking about her. She just turned up in town one day. It seemed peculiar at the time. She had no friends or family in Isola, not even a job at first. Later, I came to suspect that she and Ezra had crossed paths in the past. She moved into a cottage he owned not far from the Colony."

"Why didn't she live in the Colony?"

"It takes a very special mind-set to adapt to communal living. Rose was much too private. Instead of paying rent, she made arrangements to tutor Mott and me. We had to miss a lot of school because of our health, you see. And there were other reasons…emotional reasons why we lagged behind. But Rose was a wonderful teacher. In no time at all, she had us doing work that was well above our grade level. Ezra was very proud of us all, especially Mott. The two of them were always so close. Sugar?" She offered the small bowl of glistening cubes, but I declined.

"I'm fine, thank you. The tea is wonderful just as it is."

She smiled, pleased by the compliment. "The secret is just a hint of cloves."

I quickly swallowed. "Oh?"

"It's a tricky spice. Overpowering if one isn't careful with the blend. I suppose I'll need to pass down the recipe to Owen along with the shop." She took a sip, savoring the taste with closed eyes before setting aside her cup. "Where were we?"

"You said Rose used to tutor you and your sister."

"I don't think she ever even saw anyone else, except on those rare occasions when she went into town for supplies. She certainly didn't socialize. I know she must have been lonely, the cottage being so isolated. There wasn't a road and barely a footpath. The terrain was difficult for Mott and me so Rose came to us most of the time. But every now and then, we'd venture to her place. She always made such a fuss when we visited. Treated us like little princesses. After everything we'd endured, Rose's affection and unconditional acceptance meant the world to us."

"She was a special person, sounds like."

"Beautiful inside and out," Nelda said, still with that misty smile. "And, as I mentioned, an avid photographer. For a time, she even had a darkroom in her house. Mott and I spent many a happy hour in that tiny space watching her work. She used to say that looking through the lens of a camera was like peering through a keyhole. All it took was an open mind to see many strange and fantastical things."

I glanced at the stereogram, wondering if there were things in the images that I had yet to notice. Fantastical things. Ghostly things. "That's a very intriguing observation," I said.

"Oh, Rose had a lot of such notions even before she became so ill."

"What was wrong with her?"

Nelda's dreaminess turned to melancholy. "What happened at Kroll Colony hit her very hard. And then only a short time later, we lost dear Mott. So many tragedies that year. It was all too much for her, I think.

That and the loneliness. Something inside her snapped and she began to lose touch with reality."

"She stayed on in Isola after your brother died?"

"Yes, in that same little house. Sister and I always assumed that Ezra had made provisions for her before he passed since she had no visible means of support. He was a generous soul, and like the rest of us, he had a soft spot for Rose. I'm sure she could have lived quite comfortably in town or anywhere she wanted, but she seemed to prefer the solitude. And, of course, she had her work at Kroll Cemetery."

I leaned in. "What kind of work?"

"The locals were very vocal about not wanting to taint the public burial ground with all those suicides. Some believed it to be a mortal sin, you see. Rose made arrangements for the bodies, even the former soldiers, to be buried near her home so that she could mind the graves herself. She even went so far as to have walls erected around the cemetery and a maze planted at the entrance to keep out the gawkers and mischief makers."

Or to keep something else in, I thought with a shiver. "Your family didn't mind about the cemetery? It was built on Kroll land, I assume."

"No one objected. It seemed the right thing to do and I think Louvenia was glad to have someone else take care of all the details."

"Was Rose also responsible for the headstones?"

"Yes. She had each carved and engraved to her precise specifications."

"I've seen photographs of the cemetery," I said. "All those numbers and keys etched into the headstones—

I've never come across anything like them. Do you know what they mean?"

"Rose had a fascination, a fixation, if you will, with keys. She must have collected dozens, if not hundreds, of lost keys over the years."

"Did she ever explain her fascination?"

Nelda shrugged. "I don't recall that we ever asked her."

I stared down into the teacup for a moment. "Dr. Shaw said there are those who believe the cemetery is a puzzle or riddle that no one has ever been able to solve."

Nelda smiled. "Perhaps because it's unsolvable. You have to take into account Rose's mental state when she designed Kroll Cemetery. What made sense to her would undoubtedly seem nonsensical to the rest of us. By the time the cemetery was finished, she was already living in her own world. Withdrawn and paranoid even with me. At some point, she suffered a complete breakdown. That's the only way to explain why she did what she did."

"Build the cemetery, you mean?"

"No, dear. Rose killed herself."

My hand jerked slightly, clattering the porcelain cup against the saucer. "How tragic, especially after all those other suicides."

"You've no idea. I was the one who found her hanging in the tiny dark room, a key still clutched in her lifeless fingers. I'll never forget the way the blood dripped down her face like crimson teardrops."

"There was blood?"

Nelda lifted her gaze to mine. "You see, before Rose died, she used that key to put out her eyes."

Twenty-Eight

I left the shop with more questions swirling in my head than when I had arrived. Nelda was so preoccupied with the viewer that she barely noticed my exit. I'd meant to ask about her insistence that I come see her before I agreed to the restoration, but after her grisly revelation about Rose, I hadn't felt like lingering.

My look-alike and namesake had lost touch with reality, put out her own eyes with a key and then hanged herself. Of course, Nelda had been little more than a child at the time and she may not have known all the facts. If someone had murdered Ezra Kroll and the colonists in cold blood, who was to say Rose hadn't met the same end?

But what if the ghosts *had* driven her insane? What if she'd killed herself to escape them?

What if the same fate awaited me someday?

I always assumed my destiny was a dark one. I had only to look at Papa. He'd withdrawn inside himself to escape from the ghosts, and he kept things from me about my past and my gift because he wanted to shelter me. His motives were selfless, but his secrets made me vulnerable. I could see that now. The rules had hobbled me as much as they had protected me. Instead of growing stronger and learning how to fight for my future, I'd spent most of my life sequestered behind cemetery walls, hiding and pretending.

That time was long gone. My eyes were open now and I could no longer deny the changes that were happening inside me any more than I could hide from the ghosts.

But I was tired of dwelling on the direness of it all. It was a beautiful May morning, cloudless and breezy. I didn't want to think about my gift or Rose's prophecy or the unbound power left behind by the dead. I wanted to shove every bad thought to the furthest corner of my mind and retreat into my work as I always had.

There would be time enough later to reflect on Rose Gray and Ezra Kroll and the cemetery she had built for him. Time enough to obsess over those keys on my nightstand and the motes in my eyes and the gruesome way in which Rose had met her end. But for now, for a little while longer, I would lose myself in the withering beauty of one of my forgotten graveyards.

And for most of the day, I was able to do exactly that in a little cemetery just outside Charleston. But on my journey to Trinity late that afternoon, the forbidden images crept back in. The possibility that a key I'd found on a headstone in Rosehill Cemetery nearly twenty years ago had turned up on my nightstand made me contemplate again the notion of predestination and how all the strange occurrences in my life were somehow connected.

The sun still hovered over the treetops when I pulled into the empty driveway. I knew from an earlier phone call that my mother was away for the day with my aunt. I'd started to go straight to the cemetery to look for Papa, but I'd wanted to spend a few minutes with Angus. He bounded across the yard to greet me as I climbed out of the car, but the moment I held out my hand to him, he stopped short, his lips curling back in a low growl.

His threatening behavior stunned me. He wouldn't have forgotten me in so short a time. I could only surmise that he had intuited the supernatural turmoil around me. Maybe he'd even sensed the unbound energy of death that I had unwittingly attracted.

Still in shock, I knelt and spoke to him in my softest voice. "It's me, Amelia. Don't you recognize me? You know I won't hurt you."

His head came up and he stared at me for the longest time with those dark, soulful eyes. Then he took a cautious step closer as if he wanted to believe I was still the old Amelia. Almost immediately he halted with a snarl, his tail dropping and his hackles rising.

He looked to be on the verge of more serious aggression so I stood slowly and began to ease back to my car. "It's okay, Angus. It's okay, boy," I soothed over and over.

He was getting ready to lunge. I could tell by his stance. If I made one wrong move, I had no doubt he'd be on me.

As I felt for the door handle, he rushed forward and then retreated, repeating the action until I was back inside my vehicle. Then he began to pace, teeth bared, body hunched low as I started the engine and drove away.

His rejection devastated me. Of all the beings that had come and gone in my life, Angus was my constant, my touchstone, as close to a soul mate as I would likely ever know. We understood each other because we both had the sight.

He had turned on me once before, but only because he'd been afflicted by the evil that resided in the woods and hollows around Asher Falls. Even then, he'd somehow managed to banish the influence and come to my rescue.

Now it was something inside me that threatened him. That repelled him.

Even after I'd glimpsed the darkness inside Micah Durant, even after I'd slipped into Devlin's memory, I hadn't wanted to accept the evolution of my gift, but it was hard to discount Angus's response to me. Suddenly, Darius Goodwine's words came back to haunt me.

You're not the same person as when we first met, nor will you be the same when our paths cross again.

Still shaken, I parked on the shoulder of the road and took a shortcut through the woods, emerging only a short distance from the entrance to the old section of Rosehill. The gate was unlocked, but I didn't go inside. Instead, I turned to stare down into that secluded glen where I'd found the skeleton key necklace all those years ago.

I'd once asked Papa why the people buried there hadn't been laid to rest on the other side of the wall, in consecrated ground. He had explained to me that in the old days, it had been customary to keep the bodies of criminals, suicides and other undesirables separated from the traditional burials. Not only were the remains exiled from hallowed ground, but they were also relegated to the northernmost part of the cemetery, where it was cold, dark and damp.

My gaze followed the dipping path into the copse. When I was a child, I hadn't minded the gloominess of that corner. I'd felt very sorry for the outcasts who were buried there and had taken it upon myself to visit each grave so that the dead would know that I'd been there. But Papa refused to linger. He'd always made quick work of his duties, seemingly anxious to be back out in the sunlight. He'd never forbidden me to play there, but I wondered if he'd known just how much time I'd spent inside that shadowy enclave, reading aloud to the dead and weaving daisy chains to adorn their headstones.

I could feel a tug toward that murky place now, but I told myself the attraction was nothing more than my own curiosity. I really wanted to believe that. As I hovered there clutching the straps of my backpack, it came to me that I was standing on the exact spot where the two pathways diverged. A crossroads. Straight ahead lay the safety of hallowed ground. To the left, a slanting stone trail into perpetual twilight. I had a choice of destinations. I wanted to believe that, too. But even as the notion of free will flitted through my head, I was already picking my way along the broken flagstones, guided by the melancholy fragrances of damp earth and dead leaves.

A breeze drifted through the crowding oaks, rippling the leaves and stirring long curtains of Spanish moss. Despite Papa's care, the years hadn't been kind to this part of the cemetery. I could see a handful of fallen stones while others had succumbed to the tenacious clutches of ivy roots and vandals. The crumbling markers were mostly rough fieldstones and simple slate tablets. No angels resided here. No saints marked my progress along the winding pathway.

Deeper and deeper I traveled, my footsteps silenced by moss. I hadn't been back that way in years and wondered if I would even recognize the headstone on which I'd found the key. But presently my gaze came to rest on a crumbling marker, and the flesh at my nape started to crawl. Time, weather and perhaps even a bolt of lightning had blackened the face of the stone so that the name was completely obscured. I had no idea who was buried in the sunken grave nor did it seem to matter.

I paused on the trail, gathering my courage before making my way through the dead leaves and underbrush to the back of the marker so as not to tread upon the grave. Pushing aside tendrils of ivy and brambles, I scratched away some of the lichen and then ran my hand lightly across the rough surface. I could feel a slight indentation in the stone and leaned down for a closer inspection. Perhaps it was the hazy light or the power of suggestion, but I fancied I could trace the outline of a shank, teeth and bow.

I removed the skeleton key from my backpack and placed it in the hollow. It was a perfect fit.

How many years had that key remained on the

headstone, waiting for me to return? Why had it come back to me now? And how could it possibly be my salvation?

The wind picked up and the leaves started to quiver as the light faded. In the outside world, dusk hadn't yet fallen, but here in this forsaken corner, the veil had already thinned and the ghosts were getting restless.

My gaze was still riveted on the headstone. As the chill of a manifestation settled over me, the key started to glow.

Twenty-Nine

"Amelia? What are you doing, child?"

At the sound of Papa's voice, I snatched the key from the headstone and stuffed it in my pocket, guilt niggling as I turned to face him. I'd brought the key into the cemetery, so I wasn't breaking any rules by taking it with me, but I had a bad feeling that Papa might consider my rationalization a matter of semantics.

"I was looking for you," I told him. "I thought I heard you back here."

"Come along. It's getting on dark and your mother will be back soon."

He took my hand as we walked back toward the gate. I could feel the unwelcome weight of the key in my pocket and I felt the same fear and confusion I'd experienced on that long-ago twilight because I somehow knew my life was about to take another terrifying turn.

Papa must have sensed my distress. He clung to my hand until we got to the end of the path, and then he opened the gate and we both stepped through onto hallowed ground. We walked in silence through the monuments and markers until we reached the stone angels. I dropped to the ground and Papa lowered himself more tentatively. Drawing my knees to my chest, I watched the statues come alive in the fiery glow of a Carolina sunset.

When the dance was over and the sun had dipped beneath the horizon, Papa finally turned to me, his grizzled features taut with worry. "What's wrong? Why are you here?"

"Something's happened," I said.

"What is it, Amelia?"

I hugged my legs tightly, assembling my thoughts as the sky deepened and the bats came out.

"Tell me, child," Papa urged gently. He looked old and tired, the stoop of his shoulders even more pronounced than when I'd last seen him. In that moment I realized how fragile he and Mama both were these days. Time was slipping away and I couldn't bear to think of a future when they would no longer be with me in the living world.

I hadn't allowed myself to imagine that time too often, but every once in a while, a thought crept in. Would they be able to move on or would they linger, drawn by the warmth and energy that had been lost to them in death?

I banished the unwelcome image with a shudder as I turned to Papa. "I'm being visited by the ghost of a woman named Rose Gray. She's been coming to me in my dreams for months, but now she's manifested." I paused, wondering how best to proceed. I was desperate for answers, but I also knew that pressing Papa too hard might send him back into the dark sanctuary of his own thoughts. I had to tread carefully. "I've seen a photograph of her. She looked very much like me. She even had my name. It can't be a coincidence. Who was she, Papa?"

"She was my mother."

I drew a harsh breath, though not from shock. Rose and I shared the same name, the same face. It wasn't a leap to assume we shared the same bloodline. But to have it confirmed was more emotional than I would have expected. "I asked you so many times about my family. Why did you never tell me about her? You must have noticed how much I looked like her. You even gave me her name."

"Some things are best left in the past," he said.

"That's not true!" I said angrily, and then immediately regretted my outburst because he was my papa after all. "You've always remained silent to protect me. I know that. But you can't keep secrets from me any longer. It's too dangerous." I ran my hand aimlessly over the ground between us, idly plucking at the blades of grass where we had once searched for the key necklace. "Something is happening to me, Papa. I don't just see the dead anymore. I sense things. Thoughts and emotions of the living. Sometimes I can even glimpse memories. What I'm becoming…" I trailed off, hardly daring to voice what had been preying on me for a very long time. "I think whatever is happening to me was set in motion at my birth. Grandmother Tilly was able to save me for a reason."

Papa stared straight ahead into the deepening twilight, refusing to look at me. Refusing to acknowledge my fear. But I wouldn't be dissuaded so easily.

"I believe I have a purpose. A calling. And it has something to do with Rose. Somehow our destinies our intertwined. That's why I'm here. I have to know about her. I have to find out what happened to her so that I can protect myself."

He remained silent for the longest time, so motionless I was afraid he'd drifted off into his faraway place. But then he said wearily, "Much of her life remains a mystery to me. She left when I was just a boy."

"Why?"

"To protect me from the ghosts."

My pulse quickened. "She was like us? A caulbearer?"

"The Grays are caulbearers, but my mother was a Wysong and she had a special gift. A curse, some would call it. Like you, she had a light inside her that drew them."

I put a hand over my heart as if I could somehow quell the beacon inside my own chest. "What was she?" I asked in a near whisper. "What am I?"

"I don't know, child."

But I knew. I was a perfect storm. A Gray and a Wysong on Papa's side. An Asher and a Pattershaw from my birth parents. I was the culmination of all their dark gifts and, on top of it all, I'd been born dead to a dead mother, giving me an even stronger connection to the other side. No wonder Papa didn't know what to call me.

A breeze blew through the trees, carrying the summer perfume of honeysuckle and rain. There was moisture in the air and the faintest crackle of electricity that foreshadowed a midnight storm. It was an odd, loaded moment. Dark and portentous. Where Papa had looked old and fragile before, now he seemed ageless as nightfall drew down upon us.

"Do you know what happened to Rose?" I asked him.

"She died. But she had been away for a long time by then."

"How old were you when she left?"

"Nine or ten. I don't rightly recall anymore."

"Did you already know about the ghosts?"

"Yes. My first sighting was the ghost of a boy named Jimmy Tubbs. He'd been killed in a logging accident a week before I spotted him at the end of our lane."

"What did you do?" I asked, remembering my first sighting and how Papa had sat me down in this very cemetery and told me what I had to do to remain safe.

"I ran across the yard to the porch where my mother sat peeling peaches. I told her I'd seen Jimmy standing at the end of our road staring up at our house as if he was contemplating paying us a visit. A part of me wanted her to scold me for making up stories, but instead she made me promise to never tell anyone about Jimmy, especially my father. If I saw the ghost again, I was not to look at him or speak to him. I was not to acknowledge him in any way."

"She gave you the rules," I said.

"After that, I saw other ghosts, mostly in the woods behind our house. My mother said they came because of her. It was dangerous for me to be around her now that I had come into the sight."

I tightened my arms around my legs, trying to ward off the growing chill of his words. "Go on," I urged.

"One day my father came home and found a note from her. She wrote that she was tired of living in the mountains and wanted to go back to her own people. He was livid at her betrayal, but I knew the truth. She left to protect me."

"Did you ever see her again?"

"Only once, the summer I turned twelve. I'd just come in from doing the evening chores when I overheard Pa and his new wife talking about her. I thought it peculiar because we never spoke of my mother. They forbade it. I was never allowed to even mention her name. But I heard them say that someone had seen her down here in South Carolina. They said she'd taken up with some man that she'd known before she married my father."

Ezra Kroll, I thought. "What did you do?"

"The next morning, I packed a change of clothing and what little money I'd saved up and hitchhiked down the mountain. It was just getting on dusk when I finally came upon her house."

He paused for a breath, and in the ensuing hush, I could hear the cicadas. Their abrasive serenade filled me with dread. Overhead, night birds circled and swooped and outside the safety net of hallowed ground, the veil to the dead world thinned.

"What happened then, Papa?"

"The ghosts came. Dozens of them swarming her house like a horde of locusts. I never saw anything like it."

Resting my chin on my knees, I thought of those

ghost voices I'd heard in the hospital morgue. The invisible bodies pressing in on me through the walls. After all these years, I only now had an inkling of my destiny. A nebulous understanding of just what my gift entailed and what I might have to do to protect the people I loved.

"Did you see your mother?" I asked Papa.

"Not until daybreak. When the sun came up and the ghosts disappeared, I left the woods and went up to knock on her door. I barely recognized the woman who answered. She'd aged far beyond her years. Her hair had gone gray and she was frail. So slight a puff of wind could have blown her away."

"Was she alone?"

"Yes. I'd heard in town there'd been some tragedy. A lot of people had died, and I thought maybe that explained the ghosts."

I shivered thinking of all those entities seeking my great-grandmother's help, needing retribution before they could finally move on. And I wondered again why I was being summoned to Kroll Cemetery. "Did she recognize you?"

"She seemed leery of me at first, but then she brought me inside, fixed me some breakfast and sat with me while I ate. After that we took a walk in the woods."

"How long did you stay with her?"

"Just for the day. When the sun went down, she sent me away and made me promise not to come back. I was never to return even after she was gone."

"After she was gone? Why?"

"She wouldn't say. But I had the sense she was afraid of something."

Afraid of something or someone? I wondered. By that time, Rose must have had her suspicions about what had happened at Kroll Colony.

"Sometime later, I received a package from a girl who had known her," Papa said. "My mother had taken ill and died. The girl's family had seen to the burial. She'd put together some remembrances—photographs, trinkets and such that she thought I might like to have. She even included a picture of my mother's grave."

"Who was this girl?"

"She never gave me her name."

I wondered if it was Nelda Toombs. She and Rose had been so close it seemed only natural that she would have reached out to Rose's son. "You never went back to visit her grave?"

"I made her a promise that day. Keeping my word was the last thing I could do for her."

"You…never saw her after that?"

"Her ghost, you mean? She never came to me. She must have been waiting for you."

"But why?"

"You're like her. You share her gift." He turned to me in the deepening twilight. "But a ghost is a ghost, child. Even my mother's ghost."

"I know, Papa."

I understood only too well his trepidation because helping Rose's ghost meant facing both known and unknown dangers. In order to solve the mystery of Kroll Cemetery, I would have to use facets of my gift that I was only now discovering. Tapping into the unbound power of death would set me on a course from which I feared there would be no return.

But did I really have a choice? What did I have to look forward to if I didn't help her? Swarms of ghosts? Insanity?

"Was there a key in the package the girl sent to you?" I asked Papa.

"A key? No, why?"

"Did Rose ever tell you about a key? It would have been special to her, I think."

Papa looked at me strangely. "Where did you get this notion?"

"From Rose's ghost. She told me to find a key. It's my only salvation, she said."

"She *told* you?"

"Not in words, not aloud, but I could hear her in my mind."

Papa suddenly seemed overcome with emotion. He wiped a hand across his eyes as he stared out over the angels.

I laid a gentle hand on his arm. "Papa, Rose had all the headstones in the cemetery where she was buried engraved with key symbols. All except for her own. You don't have any idea what those keys meant to her?"

"A key represents knowledge," he said vaguely.

"Yes, but I think there's more to it than that. I think she used those keys to leave a message or a riddle. It makes me wonder if…" I could still feel the weight of the skeleton key in my pocket. "When I was little, be-fore the ghosts came, I found a key here in this cem-etery. I told you that my aunt had given it to me, but I really found it on a headstone. I returned it the next day and tried to forget about it, but now I can't help wondering if Rose left that key for me to find."

Papa said softly, "She'd been dead a long time by then. Decades."

"We both know she could have still found a way."

His eyes closed briefly. "Why did you lie to me about that key?"

"I was afraid I'd done something very wrong. You said that I must never take or leave anything behind that could be misconstrued as an offering or invitation. But people leave flowers and mementos behind all the time in graveyards. That rule only applies to us, doesn't it? To *me*." I clutched his arm. "Why, Papa?"

His voice lowered to a ragged whisper. "It invites them in."

"Into the living world?"

"Into *you*."

I drew a sharp breath. "You mean possession?"

I could see the rising moon in his eyes and it made me shiver. "Before my mother left, she taught me how to protect myself from the ghosts. Just as I taught you. She told me about the ravenous spirits that feed on human warmth and energy, about the restless ghosts that can't move on because of unfinished business. The day I went to see her, she told me about a different kind of entity, one that lingers in the living world for the sole purpose of creating chaos. Malcontents, she called them. Wraiths that prey on the weak and the innocent. They cajole and seduce and barter in order to find a conduit for their evil. Once they crawl inside you, child, the only way to rid yourself of them is death."

Thirty

I sat in the grass, watching the bats as Papa gathered up his tools. It was pointless to try to continue our conversation because he'd already shut down, disappeared into that black space where no one could reach him.

I didn't mind so much at the moment because I needed time to process all that he'd told me. Not only about Rose, but about those entities that preyed upon the innocent. I couldn't stop thinking about the key I'd taken from the headstone and how, after all these years, it had turned up again on my nightstand. Had I been preyed upon by one of those ghosts? Had I unwittingly been selected to be the conduit of a malcontent's evil?

Far better to believe that Rose had left that key for me to find, but as Papa had warned, aligning myself with my dead great-grandmother didn't come without a price.

I was so lost in thought that the tingle down my spine was the first warning I had that we were no longer alone. I glanced up to see Devlin walking toward us on the path. As I watched him approach, a barn owl swooped down over the graves and flew across the flagstones in front of him. He stopped short, but instead of following the winged predator with his gaze, he glanced over his shoulder. When he turned back around, I could see his face in the moonlight and the intensity of his expression startled me.

As Devlin entered our realm of stone angels, Papa nodded a greeting before excusing himself and setting off toward the gate. I waited until he was out of sight before rising. I thought it odd that Devlin made no move to close the space between us. Perhaps not so odd, considering my conversation with Papa, that I keep my distance from him.

"What are you doing here?" I asked, in a voice I hardly recognized as my own.

"You said you were coming to see your father today. I took a chance you'd still be here."

"Why? What's wrong?" I asked anxiously.

"Nothing's wrong. I was on my way back from Columbia and had the urge to see you."

"Why were you in Columbia?"

"I had business to attend to." He slanted his head, studying me. "Are you okay?"

"I'm fine. I'm just surprised to see you."

"Are you sure that's all it is?"

"Yes. Why wouldn't it be?"

"I don't know. All these questions are starting to feel a little like an interrogation."

"I'm sorry."

"And I can't help wondering why you're still standing all the way over there."

"I could wonder the same about you."

He closed the distance between us. "Better?"

"Yes," I said on a breath.

Weaving his fingers through my hair, he tilted my face, teasing open my lips with his. My mind still churned with everything Papa had told me, making me slow to respond.

Sensing my reluctance, Devlin pulled back, his fingers still threaded in my hair as he searched my face. "It's obvious I've come at a bad time. Maybe I should have called first."

"No." My hand flitted to his chest. "It's not you. I'm glad you're here. You've no idea."

"But something is wrong," he said. "I take it you spoke to your father about Rose."

I sighed. "I don't want to talk about any of that right now."

"That bad?"

"It's complicated and unsettling and I'm all talked out. Right now I just want you to kiss me again."

He pulled me to him. "Not a problem."

"I want you to…" My eyes closed briefly. "Make me feel normal."

"Is normal how you usually feel when I kiss you?" he teased. "We'll have to work on that."

He wrapped his arms around me then, lifting me so that I hovered over him. I stared down into his eyes for the longest time and then, cupping his face in my hands, *I* kissed *him*, with a hunger that startled us both. I could feel the heat of his skin through his clothing and where his hands clutched me to him, my own flesh burned. I wanted him, right then, right there. Nothing else mattered. Not Papa. Not Rose. Certainly not any of the Krolls. The night belonged to us now.

Slowly, he slid me down his body until my feet touched earth once more. "Nothing normal about that kiss," he murmured.

"Come with me." I took his hand and pulled him beyond the angels into the deeper shadows of the cemetery where we wouldn't be disturbed by ghosts or humans. The statues and vines concealed us from prying eyes and hallowed ground would keep the door to the dead world firmly closed.

"I wasn't expecting this," he said in that old-world drawl after I'd kissed him again with the same aggression.

"Nor was I," I said on a shiver. "But it's that kind of night."

A bemused smile tugged at the corners of his mouth. "There's something different about you." He picked a leaf from my hair and let it drift to the grass. "Your smile, your eyes. The way you kissed me just now. You seem…"

"Not normal?"

"Normal is highly overrated. You seem *more* somehow."

I knew what he meant. I was more. I had a new sensitivity to everything around me, including him. My nerve endings quivered with an awareness I'd never experienced before. My senses were unnaturally heightened. I was focused on Devlin, but also hyperaware of our surroundings. The whispering leaves, the scratch of tiny claws in the underbrush. I could still smell honeysuckle and roses, but the air was now punctuated with the decadent scent of Devlin's cologne. I drew in the fragrance like an addict.

I turned in his arms, pressing back into him as I lifted my lips to his neck. He held me tightly, one arm over my breasts, the other hand sliding down my abdomen, into my jeans, tempting me in ways that had nothing to do with the evolution of my gift.

He nuzzled my ear and whispered my name, using that irresistible drawl to melt me. His fingers moved softly against me and yet I had never felt such a delicious tension. My head fell back against his shoulder as I stared up into the treetops through half-closed eyes.

Something was up there staring down at me. Gleaming eyes in a snowy face. A barn owl, probably the same one that had winged across the path in front of Devlin.

I told myself this was nothing out of the ordinary. I'd seen owls in the cemetery before. But this one… The way he perched there, so still and knowing…

It's not an omen. It's not a harbinger of dark things to come. Don't look at it.

But I couldn't tear my gaze away. "Something's up there," I said.

Devlin lifted his head. "What?"

"The owl that flew across the path in front of you. It's watching us."

He was silent for a moment as he searched the branches. "So it is." I felt his lips in my hair. "Ignore it."

Slipping free of his hold, I turned to face him, lifting both hands to undo the buttons of his shirt until the silver medallion lay gleaming against his chest. The moment I touched the cold metal, I felt a jolt. *Like lava flowing through my veins, lightning in my fingertips.*

It would have been so easy—too easy—to close my eyes and let Devlin's thoughts and emotions pour into me. To crawl inside his head and search through his memories until I discovered what made him tick. I'd always held a fascination for his time at the Institute and a perverse curiosity about his relationship with Mariama. Even dead, she loomed larger than life.

But I wouldn't invade his privacy. I wouldn't use that facet of my gift with Devlin because I still wanted to believe that we could someday have a normal life together.

"What's wrong?" he asked as I drew away from him.

"Papa could come back at any moment."

"He's gone up to the house."

"He could return, though."

Devlin sighed and brushed a strand of hair from my face. "You're killing me here. You know that, don't you?"

"I'm sorry."

"No, you're right. He could come back." He glanced over his shoulder at the trail. I could sense a sudden wariness in him, but I didn't think he was worried about Papa.

"What is it?"

He searched the path for another long moment before turning back to me. "Nothing. Just making sure we're alone."

"We are. Except for the owls and the bats." We

stood very close, but I sensed a subtle distance between us now.

"Are you ready to tell me what happened tonight?" he asked.

"With Papa, you mean?"

"What did he tell you about Rose?"

"She was Papa's mother. My great-grandmother."

"That's not a surprise," Devlin said. I saw his gaze dart back to the path. "Even apart from your shared name, the resemblance is too uncanny to be a coincidence. Did he say why he'd never mentioned her?"

"Papa doesn't like to talk about his past," I answered truthfully if not altogether candidly. "He keeps a lot of things hidden."

That simple observation seemed to give Devlin pause. His gaze brushed me for a split second before he glanced back up at the owl. "He isn't alone in that regard. I sometimes think we Southerners have a predilection for secrets."

"Yes. I sometimes think the same," I said as I watched him closely.

It was a strange moment. A subtle acknowledgment of the barrier that would always be between us. I fretted endlessly about all the things that I kept from Devlin, but he was just as secretive. There were parts of his past I would never be privy to, like his time at the Institute and his membership in the Order of the Coffin and the Claw. The medallion he wore around his neck had been the emblem of secrets and dark deeds since the founding of Charleston.

"Why did you go to Columbia?" I asked. "Were you working a case?"

"No. The trip was personal."

"Is your grandfather okay?"

"The trip wasn't about him, either. And yes, he's okay. There's been no physical change. I'm meeting with his doctors tomorrow for a psych evaluation."

"I know the two of you aren't close, but this must still be so difficult for you."

Devlin shrugged. "Dealing with my grandfather has never been easy. Old age hasn't tempered his disposition or his demands."

"Or his expectations, I imagine."

He shrugged again. "I'm not here to talk about my grandfather. If you want to know the truth, I stopped by here to make sure you hadn't taken off for Kroll Cemetery without telling me."

"Why didn't you just call me?"

"I can be more persuasive in person."

I could certainly attest to that. "If you mean to try to talk me out of going, you're a little late. I've already made arrangements to meet with Louvenia Durant tomorrow to go over the details of the restoration."

"Then, I'd better tell you what I found out today," he said grimly. "I drove to Columbia to meet with Nathan Fortner."

"Nathan Fortner." I searched my memory until the name finally clicked. "He's the friend you mentioned before. The boy you used to explore the ruins with."

"He's an attorney in Columbia these days, but he also maintains a small office in Isola. The last time we spoke he mentioned that his firm had done some work for the Kroll family."

"What kind of work?"

"Something to do with the estate. Evidently, there's been contention among the various branches of the family for decades. After Ezra's death, a will was never found, so the money was eventually divided among the surviving relatives. Somehow the eldest sister ended up with all the land, which was a sizable fortune even apart from her portion of the cash and investments. According to Nathan, a rumor later surfaced that the sister had destroyed Ezra's will because she'd been disinherited. That sister was Louvenia Durant."

"They did have a falling-out," I said. "Nelda Toombs told me that Louvenia had never gotten over the estrangement. That's why she's so emotional about the restoration. And speaking of Nelda, I found out today that she's the owner of Dowling Curiosities. Owen Dowling is her great-nephew."

"How did you find that out?"

"Owen called and asked if I would come by the shop so that his aunt could see the stereoscope. Nelda was there when I arrived."

Devlin scowled. "How did he explain withholding the information from you?"

"He claims he didn't recognize the inscription because the nicknames haven't been used in years."

"Do you believe him?"

"I'm not sure. He's hard to read. But Nelda did back him up."

Devlin rubbed the back of his neck as if the fatigue of a long day was finally setting in. "Do you know anything about Louvenia Durant's grandson?"

"I've seen him around. His name is Micah Durant

and apparently he isn't very happy about the restoration. He thinks his grandmother is squandering her money."

"Maybe there's another reason for his disapproval," Devlin said. "It's something Nathan hinted at. He could only speak hypothetically, of course, but it got me to thinking. If Louvenia or any of the Kroll relatives wanted to put that land on the market, the expense of moving the cemetery could diminish the value. It would be easier just to get rid of the headstones and pretend the cemetery never existed."

"I don't think Louvenia would stand for that."

"Maybe not while she's alive," Devlin said.

I stared at him for a moment. "You don't think her own grandson would try to harm her, do you?" But even as I played devil's advocate, I couldn't help remembering the visceral reaction I'd had to Micah Durant.

"All I know is that I don't trust these people," Devlin said. "There are too many coincidences and deceptions in the way they've made contact with you." He rested his hands on my shoulders. "I wish you would wait until I'm free to go with you, but at least promise me you'll keep your eyes and ears open. If there's even a hint of danger, you call me."

"I will." I wanted to reassure him that I would be fine on my own and that he needed to stay focused on his grandfather's health.

But truthfully, I also had a bad feeling about the Kroll family. Something dark had happened within their ranks. Something that had kept the ghosts of Kroll Colony restless for decades.

This was no simple visitation or restoration. I was being pulled to that walled graveyard by both the living and the dead, and whatever the outcome, I wouldn't leave Kroll Cemetery unscathed.

Thirty-One

The next day, I left for Kroll Cemetery. I set out with my tools, camera equipment and a change of clothes because tramping through cemeteries could be a hot and dirty business during the spring and summer months. Dr. Shaw and his associate were already in place and I kept the map he'd drawn for me nearby in case the navigation system couldn't deal with the country roads. The three keys were safely stored in a zippered compartment of my backpack. I wished that I still had the stereoscope and card because I felt certain they were important clues, but I'd left both with Nelda Toombs.

Surprisingly, my mood was lighter than it had been in days. For one thing, I felt relieved to finally be taking action, and for another, I'd had no visitations since my talk with Papa. I hadn't heard scratching in the walls or witnessed any manifestations, which I hoped meant that I was on the right track. So long as I did as the entities wished, they would leave me alone.

With so many things swirling around in my head, the miles sped by. Soon enough, I left the coastal area behind and entered a dark green landscape of hunting forests and timberland. Aiken County was known as Thoroughbred country, and the horse farms I passed along the way ranged from modest clapboard houses and outbuildings to stately plantation homes and elaborate stables reminiscent of the estates where the Vanderbilts, Astors and Hitchcocks had once summered.

The sunshine streaming in through the windshield lulled me, allowing the lush landscape to captivate my imagination. Before long I started to relax and enjoy the journey. I often traveled to the far corners of the state and beyond for work, and I'd come to appreciate the solitude of those long drives.

Just outside Isola, I put in a call to Dr. Shaw to let him know when he could expect me.

"I've been hoping to hear from you," he said with cautious excitement. "Where are you?"

"I'm still a few miles outside town. Why? Is anything wrong?"

"No, quite the opposite, in fact. I've made a rather extraordinary discovery on Rose's headstone."

My own excitement surged. "What is it?"

"I think it would be better if you see for yourself."

My fingers tightened around the steering wheel and I found myself leaning forward as if I could somehow will away the remaining miles. "You can't just leave me hanging! At least give me a hint."

He paused. "Very well. The last time we spoke you mentioned some markings that you'd noticed at the top of Rose's headstone. You thought they might be imperfections in the stone or a photographic artifact. But your first instinct about them was right."

"Meaning?" I asked on a breath.

"The markings are an inscription, possibly even a message written in braille."

"In *braille*?"

"I don't know how I missed it when I toured the cemetery the first time. But the placement is discreet. Easy to assume they're blemishes or anomalies in the stone if one doesn't take a close enough look."

The discovery was indeed fascinating, but also disturbing given what Nelda had told me about Rose's passing. She'd blinded herself right before she took her own life. The bloody key had still been clutched in her hand. Why a braille inscription if she had only lost her sight a few moments before her death?

Somehow it had been easier to believe that my great-grandmother—my look-alike and namesake— had succumbed to a temporary madness that had driven her to commit such a horrifying act. But a braille inscription on her headstone, one that she had undoubtedly arranged for herself, suggested that she had been planning the grisly mutilation for quite some time. But *why*?

"Do you know what it says?" I asked.

"Not yet. I've photographed the inscription from various angles and emailed the images to my assistant to look up the translation for me. I also sent a scan of a rubbing I made of the stone. I should hear back by the end of the day."

"It's a very interesting find, Dr. Shaw."

"Yes, I think so, too. I would imagine a headstone inscription in braille is rather rare."

"I've seen only one, in Nunhead Cemetery in London." I'd gone the year after my aunt had treated me to a visit to Père Lachaise in Paris. Nunhead was a much darker place, more Gothic and lush. I could still remember the scent of the lime trees as I'd wandered along the overgrown walkways, ignoring the ghosts.

"There are so many things I want to show you in Kroll Cemetery," Dr. Shaw said in a strangely subdued voice. "It's such a beautiful place, but rather forlorn, I'm afraid. I find myself lingering over each of the headstones, trying to imagine those last moments in Kroll Colony. Wondering if the colonists knew when they awakened in the morning that it would be their last day on earth. Or were they betrayed? Blindsided by someone they trusted? Left to die horrifically, their legacy tarnished for all eternity."

"It's a mystery that desperately needs a resolution," I said.

"Indeed it does," he agreed. "And I'm more certain than ever that you're the one who can finally unravel this graveyard's secrets."

A half hour later, I left the town of Isola behind as I headed out to Louvenia Durant's horse farm. With Dr. Shaw's map still resting on the seat beside me, I felt confident I could find her place without too much trouble. As I crossed over the city limits, traffic thinned and the four-lane thoroughfare gave way to a narrow country blacktop lined with pine trees. Other than an occasional farm vehicle, I had the road to myself.

Five miles out of town, I slowed to look for the turn, afraid that I might miss it because of the thick woods. I needn't have worried. The entrance to the Durant property was prominently marked with an impressive archway and two metal horses mounted on brick columns built on either side of the paved lane.

As I drove through, I cast a wary glance around me. Suddenly, I felt a very long way from civilization. A world away from my beloved Charleston. I was on my way to meet Louvenia Durant, a woman I barely knew, in the middle of nowhere. Perhaps not the smartest thing I'd ever done, but despite my distrust of the Krolls, I couldn't imagine that anyone in the family meant me harm. Too many people knew of my whereabouts. A mishap on their turf would be hard to explain. At least that was how I reasoned away my unease.

The narrow road wound through mile after mile of solid evergreens. With my window down, I could smell pine and cedar mingling with the darker scent of the hawthorn. I had the sense that I was traveling through the black forest of a childhood fairy tale and was glad when the trees cleared and I could see patches of sunlight ahead.

As I topped a ridge, the woods gave way to rolling pastures dotted with wildflowers. Behind well-tended fences, magnificent horses grazed peacefully in the afternoon heat, the only interruption to their rural paradise the distant crack of a rifle.

Rounding a curve, I finally caught sight of the house, a sprawling three-story plantation home with a small army of chimneys rising from the rooftop. The spread was beautiful in the somnolent light. Even the outbuildings and stables had the well-cared-for look of a place where money had never been a concern.

A uniformed maid answered the door, her dark eyes at once appraising and dismissive. "Whatever you're peddling, we already got a dozen more'n we need."

Her bluntness took me aback. "I'm not selling anything. I have an appointment with Mrs. Durant. My name is Amelia Gray."

The shrewd gaze narrowed as she rested a hand on her scrawny hip. "That cemetery gal from Charleston she told me about? Didn't nobody call you this morning?"

"No, I haven't heard from anyone all day."

"Well, don't that beat all." She threw up her hands in frustration. "I swan, I don't know why Miss Vinnie keep that gal on, not worth a plug nickel, you ask me, never do a thing a body tell her to do." The woman heaved a weary sigh as she gave me another doubtful scrutiny. "I reckon you better come inside, but mind them feet. Don't go tracking dirt in here on my rugs."

"It seems I've come at a bad time," I murmured. "Maybe I should just wait outside."

"Come in," she barked. "Before you let the flies in."

"Yes, ma'am." Quickly, I wiped my shoes on the mat before stepping into a large foyer with aged pine flooring and thick plaster walls. A ceiling fan stirred currents of chilled air and I had to suppress a shiver.

"Wait right here while I go fetch Miss Vinnie." I had a feeling the woman wanted to caution me not to touch anything but managed to curtail the impulse by tightly pursing her lips before she turned and disappeared down a long, spacious hallway.

Left alone, I gazed around curiously, craning my neck to see into the well-appointed parlor on one

side of the stairs and the dining room on the other. I
would have expected to find family portraits lining
the magnificent walls, but the artwork was mostly
equine in nature. Through a row of French doors, I
spied a peacock strutting across the lawn, and beyond
the garden, a horse and rider jumped hedges at the
edge of a pasture.

I watched for a moment, mesmerized even from
this distance by the grace and symmetry of both animal and human before turning back to my immediate surroundings. I couldn't help wondering if Ezra
Kroll had once lived in this house and if he had ever
regretted leaving behind such a comfortable life for
the meager existence of the commune.

"Miss Gray?"

I whirled at the sound of my name.

Louvenia Durant had come through the dining
room while my attention had been diverted and now
she stood in the large doorway observing me. As our
eyes met, I had the unsettling notion that she knew
exactly what I had been thinking.

"Your trip over was pleasant, I trust." Her gaze was
very direct and vaguely anxious.

"Yes, it was a nice drive, thank you."

"I'm sorry my assistant wasn't able to reach you
before you left Charleston." Her face darkened as her
gaze went to the window that looked out on the front
grounds. The rider I'd glimpsed earlier had left the
pasture and now walked the magnificent chestnut
sedately up the long drive. For a moment, Louvenia
seemed struck by the sight and then she collected herself. "I'm afraid there's been a change of plans."

"Oh?"

"Something unexpected has come up. A family matter that can't wait. Our meeting will have to be postponed. I'm terribly sorry. I can't apologize enough for the inconvenience."

"No worries. I hope it's nothing serious."

"That remains to be seen," she murmured, her gaze darting back to the window.

The rider was still some distance away, but when he removed his helmet, I saw the spill of silvery-gold curls across his forehead. I sensed a mounting tension in Louvenia as Micah Durant drew closer.

"My grandson," she finally said. "He's only been back a short time and already he has the household in an uproar. Not to mention that poor horse in a lather." Her lips thinned in disapproval as he steered the chestnut off the road, taking a shortcut across the lawn to the stables. She tore her gaze away and offered a strained smile. "I'll be tied up with family business for the rest of the afternoon, but I'd like to reschedule our meeting as soon as possible. That is, if you're still agreeable."

"Of course," I said, trying to curtail my disappointment. Or was it relief? "Shall I call you in a day or two to set something up?"

"I don't want to wait that long. I feel that time is of the essence and we should get started on the restoration as soon as possible." She brushed her hands down the tail of her shirt, a nervous tic that made me wonder what was going on inside her head. "I know this is terribly presumptuous of me, but I wonder if you'd be willing to come back in the morning. Say around eight?" Before I could answer, she quickly added, "I don't expect you to drive in from Charleston at that hour, but maybe you'd be willing to stay over. I've taken the liberty of arranging accommodations for you in town at my sister's bed-and-breakfast. Dr. Shaw and his associate are occupying the upstairs guest rooms, but there's a small cottage in the garden that I think you'll find cozy. And of course, I'll be more than happy to reimburse you for your time."

"That's very generous of you, Mrs. Durant."

"I'm a businesswoman, Miss Gray. If I were in your shoes, I would expect no less. Please do consider the offer. As I said, I'm anxious to get started on the restoration. I've put it off for far too long, but now that I've made up my mind, I find myself impatient to have it done with."

"I'll make a call and see about rearranging my schedule," I said, mentally going over my commitments for the rest of the week. "Will it be all right if I let you know later this afternoon?"

"Yes, of course. Just leave a message with Grace Anne. She'll make sure I get it."

I nodded my agreement. "I won't keep you, but may I ask a favor before I go?"

She lifted a curious brow.

"I understand Dr. Shaw has already begun his investigation at the cemetery. I'd like to drop by there to see him this afternoon if you've no objection."

"I've no particular objection, but the cemetery is difficult to get to. Are you sure you can find it on your own?"

"Dr. Shaw gave me a map and I can always call him if I get lost."

She gave a brief nod. "You're anxious to see Rose's grave, I expect."

"I'm interested in the whole cemetery, but I can't deny a fascination for a grave with my name on it."

"You do look so much like her," Louvenia mused. "At least, the way she looked when she first came here."

"Miss Toombs said she and her twin were very devoted to Rose."

"They adored her. She was always so gentle with them and so very protective. I'm thankful they had her in their lives, even if for only a short while. God knows they had little enough joy. People can be so unspeakably cruel."

"Yes, unfortunately that's true."

She glanced at me with a frown. "You must know about my sisters. It seems you've spoken with Nelda at length."

"She mentioned they had a difficult childhood," I said carefully.

"To put it mildly. In this day and age, my sisters would be favorable candidates for separation since they shared no vital organs, but back then surgery on conjoined twins was tricky. We were told the lengthy operation might result in one of their deaths. How do you choose?"

It was a rhetorical question so I said nothing.

"Mother wouldn't accept the risk," Louvenia went on. "Had she lived, things would have been easier— on all of us—but after she passed, the care of the twins fell to Ezra and me. When he came back from the war, he could barely look after himself. I'll be the first to admit that I should have been a better guardian." Her fingers tangled in the tail of her shirt as if she were trying to wipe away something unpleasant from her hands.

"I'm sure you did the best you could," I murmured.

Her smile was wan. "You're very kind to think so. My only excuse is that I wasn't much more than a girl myself and wrapped up in my own affairs. Rose offered the twins sanctuary. A safe haven where they didn't have to worry about being bullied by the other children."

"Your sister said Rose was their tutor."

"She was so much more than that. I believe they came to think of her as a surrogate mother. I'm certain they would have gone to live with her if given the opportunity. As it was, they spent every waking moment thinking about her, talking about her, making little gifts for her. It was a harmless obsession. Nelda was always the stronger of the two. The dominant twin, I suppose. Someone at the Colony built a little device, a sort of cart with a special harness so that she could pull Mott along behind her. Off they'd go. Sometimes at night, I can still hear the squeak of those wheels." She paused and I could have sworn I saw a shudder go through her. I, too, suppressed a shiver as I remembered the metallic sound from my garden.

"They must have had a very strong bond with Rose," I said.

"A bond," Louvenia mused. "Yes, that's an apt way of putting it. I think in some ways, Rose clung to them just as tightly. I often wondered if she'd lost a child of her own before she came here. There was such a sadness about her."

"Your sister mentioned that Rose became ill."

Louvenia nodded. "When she got really bad, she'd wander the countryside at all hours, mumbling to herself, pointing to things that no one else could see. It was really quite eerie. And the way she would look at you. As if she could see all the way down into your soul." Louvenia closed her eyes. "The memory of it still brings a chill."

"Who took care of her during her illness?"

"Nelda did what she could, but she was still so young, only fourteen or so, and the surgery after Mott passed left her weak. A local doctor looked in on Rose from time to time, as did I, but there was no one else. Most of the townsfolk were afraid of Rose. And of Nelda, too, I think."

I was hesitant to pursue the conversation. How much did I really want to know about Rose's descent into madness? But I couldn't leave it alone. I couldn't ignore the squeamish details when there might be a chance I could learn something that would keep me from the same fate. "Did Nelda arrange for Rose's burial in Kroll Cemetery?"

"There really was no other place for her," Louvenia said.

"Because of the suicide?"

Another hesitation. "Yes, of course. The suicide."

Before I could say anything else, the front door opened and a man breezed in with a leather overnighter strapped over one shoulder. His slacks and shirt were neatly pressed, his loafers polished to a high gleam. He turned his back to me as he closed the door, but I knew who he was at once.

"Sorry I'm late," Owen Dowling called over his shoulder as he hung the bag on a hook near the door. "I had to take care of a few things before I left Charleston. I'm afraid Micah may not be our only problem—"

He turned toward the foyer and froze when he caught sight of me.

His sudden appearance seemed to have rendered Louvenia speechless. The fingers of one hand tangled in her shirt while the other hand crept to her throat.

Thirty-Two

"O wen," she finally managed. "I— You surprised me."

"Really? Aunt Nelda told you I was coming, didn't she?"

"Yes, of course. I guess I lost track of the time. Anyway, I'd like you to meet Amelia Gray. She's the cemetery restorer Nelda and I met with the other day in Charleston."

"I've already had the pleasure," he said with a flash of his usual charm. "I'd like to thank you again for returning the stereoscope to my great-aunt. She was quite overcome with emotion after you left the shop."

"I'm happy it's back with its rightful owner," I said.

"What's this about a stereoscope?" Louvenia asked.

"I'll explain later," Owen said. "No need to bore Miss Gray with a story she already knows."

"No, of course not," Louvenia murmured. She seemed subdued, perhaps even a little cowed by Owen, but I found that hard to imagine from a woman who had managed a sizable estate and run a successful horse farm for most of her adult life.

"So you're here about Kroll Cemetery," Owen said.

"It really is nice of you to come all this way. My aunt tells me that we've another visitor from Charleston. A ghost hunter and his assistant have taken rooms in her B and B."

That seemed to rouse Louvenia from her daze. I saw a flare of the same impatience she'd shown Nelda that day at Oak Grove. "Dr. Rupert Shaw is not a ghost hunter. The work he does at the Charleston Institute for Parapsychology Studies is highly regarded all over the state."

"I meant no disrespect," Owen said gently.

Louvenia was not appeased. She lifted her chin. "You've been listening to Nelda, haven't you?"

"She's expressed some concern," Owen admitted.

"I'm sure she has. She thinks I'm a fool or even worse, demented. But I'm telling you something is out there." Louvenia seemed to be addressing Owen, but her gaze was on me. "How do you explain the fact that no horse or dog will go near that place? Or birds. You won't find so much as a wren's nest in the trees growing around the wall."

"Now, Louvenia," Owen soothed. "I wouldn't go getting all worked up about it. Especially when we've other things to worry about at the moment." He gave her a meaningful glance.

"I warned you. I warned you all," she said with mounting agitation. "You shouldn't mock things you know nothing about. I don't like it and neither do they."

Owen shot me a look. "Of course you're right, but perhaps this is a subject best discussed later. After all, you wouldn't want to frighten Miss Gray away, would you?"

"I was just leaving," I rushed to say.

Louvenia seemed to have forgotten my presence. She stared at me blankly for a moment before the fog lifted. "If you still plan to go out to the cemetery this afternoon, please take care," she said, slipping back into her cordial if somewhat reserved demeanor. "It's a very disorienting place and the woods that surround it are dense. You might find yourself lost even with a map."

"I'll be careful," I promised.

"Are you headed out there now?" Owen asked. "Why don't I walk you to your car and at least point you in the right direction?"

"I won't put you to the trouble," I said. "I'm certain I can find the way."

"It's no trouble. I need to fetch something from the car anyway." He turned to Louvenia. "I've brought you a gift. Just a little something from the shop I think you'll enjoy."

She nodded absently. "Make sure you tell her about the maze. And the latch on the gate. There's a trick to both of them. And please let me know if you decide to stay over, Miss Gray. I'll make sure my sister takes good care of you."

"I will. And thank you for the chat," I said.

"Oh, it was my pleasure. I hope to speak with you again very soon."

With that, I followed Owen Dowling out the front door and across the wide veranda. We were both silent until we reached the steps and then he stopped and turned to me with an apologetic smile. "Louvenia tends to have some strange notions. I hope she didn't scare you away with all that talk about something being 'out there.'"

"No, of course not."

"I didn't think so, but some people are easily spooked. I guess when you work alone in abandoned cemeteries you can't afford to let your imagination get the better of you."

"I take it you don't think there's any basis for her concern."

"Why, Miss Gray," he said in a teasing voice. "Don't tell me you believe in ghosts."

"I try to keep an open mind."

"Please don't tell Louvenia. She doesn't need the encouragement." He glanced worriedly over his shoulder. "Normally, she's the most down-to-earth, business-minded person I know, with the possible exception of Aunt Nelda. Both of them are extraordinary entrepreneurs, Louvenia with the farm and Aunt Nelda with all her little businesses. But ever since I can remember, Louvenia has had an almost pathological superstition about that old cemetery."

"Is that why her grandson is against the restoration?"

"You've met Micah?" Owen asked in surprise.

"Not formally, but I've seen him around."

He lifted a brow. "May I ask where?"

"He was at the cemetery in Charleston the day I first met with your aunts."

"Ah. Well, to answer your question, I doubt his motives are at all altruistic. I'm quite certain he has his own agenda. Which is another reason Aunt Nelda and I are so worried about Louvenia. If she gets too caught up in that old cemetery again, she's apt to overlook the real threat that's living right here under her nose."

"You think her own grandson would try to harm her?"

Owen paused. "The problem is none of us really know Micah anymore or what he's been up to. Even before he left, he was a troubled young man. In and out of institutions since boyhood."

"I see." I put a hand to the back of my neck as my skin started to prickle.

"Is something wrong?" Owen asked.

"I didn't notice all those bees at the end of the veranda earlier. But their drone now is really distracting."

He listened for a moment before turning back to me. "Louvenia keeps a number of colonies around the farm. The family has a long history of beekeeping."

I took a few steps into the yard, distancing myself from the incessant buzzing.

"There's no need to worry," Owen said. "Bees aren't aggressive when they're swarming. Unless they feel threatened, of course. I suppose that's one of the good things about Micah's return. Possibly the only good thing. He's taken over the beekeeping duties. It's very hard work and Aunt Louvenia has never been one for delegation. But Micah has always had a way with the bees. A rapport. The most successful beekeepers do, you know." Owen's gaze shifted away from me and he frowned. "Speak of the devil," he muttered.

I turned to find Micah Durant staring across the lawn at us. He'd removed his shirt and I could see the outline of his ribs along his emaciated torso. The back of my neck still tingled as if a bee had crawled inside my collar. I resisted the urge to put up a hand because I somehow knew that was what Micah wanted.

I must have made some involuntary sound or movement because Owen said, "Yes, he's always had that effect on people. It's really quite disconcerting the way he stares you down like that."

I wanted to turn away, break eye contact with Micah Durant, but I couldn't tear my gaze away. Lifting his face to the sky, he slowly unfurled his arms and froze in that rapturous pose while Owen and I stood enthralled.

All of a sudden, the droning in the flower beds became so loud that my first instinct was to run for cover. I started to flee to my vehicle but halted when a cloud of honeybees rose from the blossoms and flew across the yard toward Micah. Within a matter of seconds, every inch of his scrawny body was covered in thousands of droning, crawling honeybees until he no longer resembled anything human.

"My God," I breathed.

"No worries," Owen said. "They won't hurt him. They know he means them no harm."

"How do they know that?"

"Because he told them."

I thought of the way Micah had lifted the honeybee from my neck, rotating his hand so that man and insect remained face-to-face.

Owen smiled. "You look skeptical, but honeybees are very communicative. Back in the old days, they were highly revered by the community. If the keeper died, someone from the family was dispatched to the hive to inform the bees of the news so they wouldn't die or fly away."

"That's fascinating."

"When Micah first left home, Louvenia actually lost some of her hives. But they seem to be thriving now." His gaze was still on Micah. "You're familiar with the term 'bee bearding'?" He put a hand to his chin. "There's a trick involving a caged queen that most keepers use to attract the workers. Micah doesn't do that. He's a natural lure."

My attention was still riveted on the swarming bees. How did they not smother him? I wondered. His face was entirely covered. I started to ask Owen that very question, but just then Micah jumped up and down, gently dislodging the workers. After a moment, they scattered into the trees.

"Show's over," Owen said.

I had no doubt the spectacle had been for my benefit. Perhaps it was even meant as a subtle threat.

I'd seen and heard enough for one day. "I won't keep you. I'm sure you and Louvenia have a lot to talk about."

Owen was still scowling at Micah. "Don't you have anything better to do?" he yelled.

Micah didn't respond. He merely stood there smiling at us before he, too, turned and disappeared into the trees.

"Don't mind him," Owen said. "He likes to show off and you're a fresh audience."

"It is quite an impressive trick," I said, edging toward my vehicle.

"We all have our talents," Owen muttered. "Anyway, about those directions…"

"I'm sure I can find the cemetery on my own."

"You may think that now, but wait until you're in the woods." He gestured toward the end of the driveway. "You'll need to go back a couple of miles the same way you came in. Once you're around the first sharp curve, start looking for an old iron marker to your left. Ironically, it looks like a cross now that the sign has rotted away, but it used to be a no-trespassing warning. The entrance is overgrown with vines and branches, so you'll be apt to miss it if you don't spot that marker. The road through the woods is passable in a vehicle like yours, but you'll have to take it slow."

I nodded. "Okay."

"Eventually, you'll come to a dead end. From there you'll have to go the rest of the way on foot. There's a path of sorts, but it'll still be a rough hike. Louvenia was right. The woods are dense and the scenery is disorienting. You can easily get lost if you don't pay attention to where you've been and where you're going."

"She also said something about a trick to the maze."

"It's simple. Bear left, always. There's a spot in the middle where your instincts will tell you to go right. You'll recognize what I mean when you get there. Ignore the impulse and keep left."

"And the gate?"

"The latching mechanism is released by pulling out a loose brick in the wall. You'll know it by the markings. Again, easy to overlook if you don't know it's there. Got all that?" he asked.

"Yes, thank you."

I climbed into my car and closed the door, but the window was open and an errant bee landed on the back of my hand. Before I could shake it off, the barbed stinger sank into my flesh. I felt the prick of a red-hot needle, followed by a slow-spreading heat. The angry bee circled for a moment and then fell to the ground outside the car window. Quickly, I flicked the stinger from my skin.

Owen moved up to the car, transfixed by the dead bee.

"I thought you said they wouldn't sting unless they felt threatened," I said.

He lifted his gaze. "They must perceive you as a threat."

"Why?"

He glanced over his shoulder toward the spot where Micah had disappeared into the trees.

I gave him a skeptical look. "You're not suggesting Micah told them I'm a threat, are you?"

Owen turned back with a shrug. "I don't exactly know how his rapport with them works. It goes beyond that of any normal beekeeper."

"What do you mean?"

"The first time he was sent away was because he let loose a colony in the school playground. They swarmed a boy that Micah didn't like. One of the other kids swore he'd heard Micah whisper the boy's name to the bees before he released them."

"Was the boy all right?"

"He lived, but it was touch and go for a while."

"And the authorities believed Micah had deliberately set the bees on him?"

"They believed he deliberately released those bees in the playground. That was enough to send him away, especially after a number of similar incidents. But enough about Micah. You should probably put something on that sting."

I glanced down at the welt on the back of my hand. "I guess it's a good thing I'm not allergic to bee venom," I tried to say calmly.

"It's not the poison from a single sting you have to worry about. It's the alarm pheromones left behind on your skin to warn the other workers of danger. If the colony decides to attack, there's not much you can do to get away. Even if you jump in water, they'll just wait you out."

"Thanks for the warning," I said. "And for the directions."

"No problem. Mind that sting," he said. "If I were you, I'd be on my way before the colony gets wind of those pheromones."

Thirty-Three

⟨⟨◦⟩⟨◦⟩⟩

I didn't let up on the gas or breathe easy until I was well away from all those bees. Once I no longer felt threatened, I started to worry about Dr. Shaw and the remoteness of Kroll Cemetery. I comforted myself with the knowledge that he wasn't alone. He had at least one investigator with him.

Even so, I felt the need to warn him of my growing unease about the Kroll family. Micah wasn't the only one who had left me unsettled. Louvenia Durant was an enigmatic woman who seemed haunted by her past. This alone was not enough to make me distrust her, but I did have to wonder about her guilty conscience and the falling-out she'd had with Ezra. If he really had cut her out of his will—a will that had never been found—then she was the one who had stood to gain the most from his death.

All of this rolled around in my head as I placed a call to Dr. Shaw. When he finally answered, I told him of my trepidation and then repeated Owen's maze in-structions to him to make certain that I hadn't been deliberately misled.

"Directions don't mean much in the maze or even

in the woods," Dr. Shaw warned me. "They're both quite disorienting. I've never experienced anything like them. I think it best that I meet you at the end of the road and walk you through."

"That's probably a good idea, but please be careful, Dr. Shaw. Maybe I'm being overly cautious or even paranoid, but despite Louvenia's invitation, I'm not sure either of us is particularly welcome here."

His voice sharpened. "Has something else happened?"

"I'll tell you all about it when I see you. For now just please keep an eye out."

"You as well, my dear. I'm heading out now, but in case you arrive first, wait for me in your car."

"I will."

We said our goodbyes and then I turned my full attention to the road. The light shining through the windshield was warm and so bright I found myself squinting even behind sunglasses. As I came around the first curve, I slowed the vehicle, my eyes on the passing hedgerows as Owen had instructed.

Even though he'd been exact in his directions, I still ended up making three passes before I finally spotted the cross. It was set back from the road and so tilted from decades of wind and rain that it was nearly invisible against a backdrop of weeds and brambles.

The road to the farm was private so I didn't have to worry about traffic. I sat with the engine idling as I searched for the entrance. From my vantage, the road looked to be nothing more than two dirt tracks disappearing into the trees. As I scanned the access, I detected the remnants of an old wrought iron archway covered almost entirely by ivy. The vines were entwined around and through the scrollwork so that the dangling curlicues provided a natural curtain over the entrance.

I made the turn cautiously, easing through the lush tendrils as my apprehension mounted. I'd been looking forward to a tour of Kroll Cemetery with Dr. Shaw, but now as I headed straight back into the forest, I couldn't forget something he had said to me the other night on the phone. He had the sense that I was approaching a crossroads in my life, a spiritual turning point from which there would be no return.

I glanced in the rearview mirror. The vines falling back over the entrance seemed symbolic—like the closing of a door.

Taking a resolved breath, I forced my attention to the overgrown trail in front of me. It was cool and dark in the woods. I rolled down my window, allowing the intoxicating scent of honeysuckle to seep in, along with the woodsy aroma of the evergreens.

But as I drove deeper into the trees, a heavy stillness settled over the trail, a claustrophobic oppression that didn't come from the heat of the afternoon or the closeness of the woods but from something unnatural. Quickly, I raised the window as if a layer of glass could protect me from those dark things that slithered through the underbrush. Things I couldn't yet see but knew were there just the same. I tried to ignore my newfound perception, but the feeling of being watched, of being *sought*, grew more and more pervasive.

A quick glance at the map assured me that I was still some distance from our rendezvous point, and yet I could sense Kroll Cemetery as though it were a living, breathing entity. Such a notion would have seemed strange even to me a few days ago, but now I wondered if I really had crossed a threshold.

The noise in my head began as a low rumble that ebbed and flowed as the vehicle bumped along the tracks. Not the droning of Micah Durant's bees, but a humming of what I imagined to be the dark emotions of all those trapped souls. I could feel the vibration all the way through my being. My own heart started to pound in unison, as if I were becoming one with that pulsating throng.

The awareness intensified as a gust of wind blew through the trees, rippling the leaves in an isolated pattern that reminded me of a wave crashing to shore. As the undulation swept toward me, the windows fogged and the whole car began to tremble as though caught in a powerful vortex. The air grew thick and fetid and flies began to gather on my windshield.

It was hours until twilight and yet I could feel something bearing down on me from beyond. A collective presence straining against the shackles of death.

I wanted nothing so much as to lower the window and let a fresh breeze scrub away the foulness inside my car, but I didn't dare. I didn't know what was out there. I could feel the chill of the ghosts, but there was something else pushing me *away* from Kroll Cemetery. It was as if I'd been caught between two opposing forces.

I'd come to a complete stop without even realizing it, my hands still gripping the wheel. The sense of dread overpowered me as I sat there scanning the woods. Every now and then I glimpsed something white and wispy floating through the trees. If I stared long enough, I spotted diaphanous bodies crouched on low branches, pale faces with hollow eyes and gaping mouths staring down at me.

The forest was deeply haunted. A thin place. A dark place.

Find the key, I could hear Rose whisper. *Save yourself.*

Carefully, I removed the three keys from my backpack and placed them on the seat beside me—the key that had been tossed into my cellar, the key that had been left in Rosehill Cemetery and the strange key that matched the motes in my eyes. All three were different. Each served a special purpose.

I hadn't wanted to touch any of them when they'd first been left on my nightstand. I'd been too afraid my curiosity would be misconstrued as acceptance of a gift or offering. Or worse, barter for my soul.

But the keys no longer frightened me. Instead, I felt compelled to keep them close. On impulse, I slipped the pink satin ribbon over my head, allowing the skeleton key to rest against my chest. The metal instantly illuminated as it had in Rosehill Cemetery. The voices grew louder, screaming for release as the pressure in my chest tightened. I could feel a rush inside me, almost like a strong wind being sucked through an open doorway.

It was a terrifying sensation, and my first inclination was to rip the key from around my neck and fling it into the woods. The last thing I wanted was to open yet another door.

But instead of removing the key, I turned it so that the teeth pointed away from my heart. Why I did so, I couldn't say. Perhaps it was instinct or divine intervention. The guidance of an unseen hand.

Oddly and perhaps coincidentally, the noise in my head quieted and the pressure eased. The dark things in the woods grew still and watchful. The flies scattered and the odor faded as the wind died away. I didn't know why or how, but a door had been closed.

I sat for a moment, clutching the skeleton key to my breast. I knew the ghosts weren't gone for good. I could still feel the chill of their presence. Rather, the key had granted a temporary reprieve. Maybe like hallowed ground, the metal provided a layer of protection, if not salvation.

The other two keys still lay on the seat beside me. I picked up the eye key and held it in my palm. The metal didn't glow like the key around my neck, but I fancied I could feel a throb. And with the vibration came a disturbing notion as to why Rose had blinded herself. Maybe her only way out had been to *unsee* them. If the function of the skeleton key was to provide a reprieve, then the key with the pointed teeth could have offered my great-grandmother a final solution.

Thirty-Four

━━∽⟲⟳∽━━

I soldiered on toward Kroll Cemetery. Up ahead where the trees thinned, beams of sunlight spangled down through the branches and I could see a butterfly dancing among the wild columbine that grew beside the trail. The weight of the dead world had lifted from me, but I cautioned myself not to let down my guard. Not to be fooled by the reprieve or the cathedral-like tranquillity of the woods. The peace was only a stay, an illusory calm before a gathering storm.

The road ended abruptly and I came to a rocky halt. A wall of green rose before me. The fingered leaves of the oaks and sycamores tangled with the feathery bowers of the cedars to create an impenetrable canopy. Evergreen saplings sprouted so thick at the end of the trail that I could barely make out the footpath.

I had expected to find Dr. Shaw waiting for me, or at the very least, his parked vehicle, but I saw no sign of either. No footprints or tire tracks to indicate anyone had been this way in years. I knew better, of course. I'd spoken to him only a short time ago. He was undoubtedly on his way to meet me at that very minute. All I had to do was sit tight.

But as I huddled over the steering wheel, listening to the engine tick down, I began to wonder if I might have taken a wrong turn after all. He should have been here by now.

I took another quick glance at the map, satisfied that I had come to the right place. Drumming fingers on the seat, I waited another few minutes before taking out my phone to call him. But after several rings, I gave up.

His absence niggled as I sat there. If something had delayed him, he would have alerted me or at the very least kept his phone handy so that I could call him.

I got out of the car and stood in the shade as I contemplated what I should do. On the surface, the countryside was quiet and still, but if I listened intently and concentrated hard enough, the forest came alive. An owl hooted in the distance as the underbrush rustled from the scurry of tiny feet. A flock of blackbirds took flight and circled for a moment before drifting back down into the leaves. I was so spellbound, my senses so heightened, I could hear the swish of their feathers and the click of tiny claws as they resettled themselves on the branches. I found it strange that I could be so attuned to my surroundings and still feel so completely out of my element, a million miles away from the safety net of my sanctuary.

Checking my phone for a signal, I placed another call to Dr. Shaw with the same result. The phone rang and rang. I was just about to hang up when I became aware of a new sound, distant but jarring in the hush of the woods. I lowered the phone and turned my ear to the trees, closing my eyes so that I could vector in on the disturbance. From somewhere deep in the woods came the sound of a ringtone.

I ended the connection and the ringing stopped. Then I called the same number and the sound came again, even fainter than before, as if Dr. Shaw was moving away from me.

An icy panic stole up my backbone. He was getting on in years, and the previous autumn he'd survived a terrible trauma. No doubt the stress had taken a toll. I had visions of him suffering a breakdown like poor Rose and wandering around lost in the woods or lying unconscious somewhere from a fall or a heart attack. Or even worse, what if Micah Durant had taken a shortcut through the woods and intercepted him at the cemetery or in the maze? Dr. Shaw would never have seen him coming.

I tamped down my runaway imagination as I pressed the call button yet again. I told myself there might be any number of reasons why he couldn't or wouldn't answer. Maybe he wasn't getting a signal. Maybe he'd set the phone down and forgotten to bring it with him when he came to meet me.

My first instinct was to hightail it back to the main road and get someone to help me search. Despite all my ghost sightings and years of working in isolated cemeteries, I didn't want to be alone in that forest. Not after the terrifying incident on the trail. The foulness of an unknown presence and the opposing rush of wind had left me frightened, not to mention the fact that two of the keys had somehow come alive as I approached Kroll Cemetery. This did not bode well. I wanted nothing so much as to hurry off to the nearest bit of hallowed ground where I could protect myself from what was coming.

But I couldn't shake a shivery premonition that the ghosts should be the least of my worries at the moment. Time might be of the essence for Dr. Shaw. If I left the woods only to find out later that something had happened to him, I'd never forgive myself.

Taking one last survey of my surroundings, I grabbed my backpack from the car after safely stowing the two loose keys in the zippered pocket. Then I locked the door before setting out on the footpath.

The closeness of the woods soon engulfed me. I could hear water dripping somewhere nearby, but I couldn't pinpoint the source. If I stopped on the path and turned in a circle, the sound seemed to follow me. Working alone in remote locations as I had for so many years, I'd developed a good sense of direction. But Dr. Shaw was right. The lack of sunlight and the sameness of my surroundings proved disorienting.

I kept going, stopping periodically to take out my phone. No matter how many times I called or how far along the path I traveled, the ringing seemed to come from somewhere ahead of me.

But if the scenery could be disorienting, it stood to reason that sound might also be distorted. I wanted to call out to Dr. Shaw, shout his name at the top of my lungs, but my every instinct warned that it might not be wise to broadcast my whereabouts. If he was moving away from me, back toward the cemetery, then he must have a good reason.

The trees along the path grew ever denser, the hardwoods and evergreens gradually giving way to overgrown hedges of boxwood, honeysuckle and gardenia. The shrubbery formed a tunnel with narrow channels breaking off on either side. I stopped and glanced around with quickening breath. I had come to the entrance of the maze.

The opening was shrouded, but I could see where the vines and bushes had recently been chopped back to reveal bits of rusted metal beneath the greenery.

The maze was so much larger than I had expected. I could hardly imagine Rose in her state of confusion planning something so intricate. The planting alone would have taken a very long time, and I couldn't help wondering about her original intent. Had she meant to thwart trespassers or to keep the ghosts trapped inside Kroll Cemetery?

As I stepped through the entrance, the untamed shrubbery rose twenty feet or more. The tapestry of leaves and limbs was so tightly interwoven that I could see nothing of the other channels. It had been cool and dim in the woods, but the dense vegetation constricted airflow. I started to perspire and soon found myself a little short-winded as I trudged along. I remembered Owen's instructions and followed the path wherever it veered or broke left, keeping my eyes peeled for footprints in the dirt or broken twigs in the hedges that would let me know someone had passed this way before me.

Eventually, I came to a spot where the main path seemed to angle to the right, but there was no branching trail to the left. I had the strongest urge to keep going. It was almost like a magnet pulling me forward, but even as I felt that strange tug, I realized I was experiencing a very clever illusion. There was, indeed, a path to the left, another choice, but the hedge wall curved in such a way as to obscure the entrance. I would never have noticed without Owen's warning.

After making the turn, I soon arrived at the cemetery gate, a wrought iron affair so cloaked in ivy that I couldn't see through into the graveyard. The brick wall in which it had been set was at least ten feet high. I could have climbed a tree and jumped over, but not without some difficulty.

Slipping off my backpack, I searched for the loose brick that would release the catch. As I moved in closer, I noticed that the gate stood ajar and rocked slightly as if someone had passed through it just before me.

I paused, listening to the silence. There was no sound at all now, no matter how focused my attention. No scurrying feet. No rustling leaves. Just the soft rush of my own breathing. I tried to steady my nerves as I called Dr. Shaw's number yet again. The ringtone was definitely louder. Without a doubt, the phone was inside the cemetery.

As I pushed open the gate, I became aware of the weight of the skeleton key around my neck. Perhaps it was nothing more than my imagination, but I could have sworn I felt the heat of it against my skin.

As I slipped through the entrance something occurred to me. Here in Kroll Cemetery, I was the visitor. A welcome one I hoped, but who could say for certain?

Thirty-Five

❧❧❧

As a child at Papa's side, I'd learned to appreciate the grace and beauty of old graveyards. They were withering gardens, unique unto themselves and dedicated to the ancestral worship of our Southern culture.

During my time as a restorer, I'd traipsed through countless burial sites, raked endless graves, cleaned hundreds of headstones. I'd restored graveyards large and small, old and ancient, the forgotten and the revered. But nothing had prepared me for Kroll Cemetery. It was, as Dr. Shaw had promised, the most strangely beautiful place I'd ever encountered.

The graveyard was small in comparison to the maze, completely contained within the crumbling brick walls and shaded by an immense live oak. A rambling rose had snaked all the way to the top of the tree, spreading its feelers along the branches and snowing petals down upon the graves beneath. Where light shone through the leaves, the trunk and limbs took on a fragile glow from the thousands of cicada husks that clung to the bark. The effect was breathtakingly ethereal, as if the whole cemetery had been trapped in amber.

Somehow I knew the cicada shell placed on my nightstand had come from this place. I had been right to worry about the unwitting trade of my bookmark.

My fingers crept to the skeleton key around my neck—yet another accidental barter and one that I feared would have far-reaching consequences. The key had kept the ghosts at bay earlier, but not for a second did I think that I'd discovered its true purpose.

Reluctantly, I tucked the key back into my shirt as I gazed around. The lush fragrance and riotous color from the wildflowers was nothing new in my line of work. I had seen many beautiful graveyards. But Dr. Shaw's photographs hadn't done justice to this one. He'd focused on the keys and numbers etched into the headstones while ignoring the whimsical whorls, spires and arched embellishments that added a story-book charm to the cemetery.

The layout was also mazelike, with stone pathways curling around and through the graves in no discernible pattern. Against the far wall, a tabletop tomb rose on curved legs, the intricate domed top reminiscent of an old-fashioned jewelry box. One of the legs had succumbed to time, weather and the spreading roots of the ancient oak tree so that the structure rested at a precarious angle. It was the only exposed vault in the cemetery and I was curious to learn if Ezra Kroll's remains were interred there. However, my first priority was finding Dr. Shaw.

I scanned every shadowy corner of the graveyard. Either he was long gone or concealed within the scented enclave created by the climbing rosebush. Or—and this thought really frightened me—he lay prone in the tall weeds near the tomb. But where was his investigator? Surely both men couldn't have disappeared or fallen prey to an ambush.

Placing one final call, I followed the sound of the ringtone along those spiraling pathways, resisting the urge to stop and study the inscriptions, numbers and all those key engravings. Nor did I take the time to hunt for Rose's grave. As much as I wanted to see my great-grandmother's final resting place and as intrigued as I was by Dr. Shaw's braille discovery, the solving of that riddle would have to come later.

I located his phone lying in the grass near a headstone. The case felt warm, as though someone had just dropped it, but I told myself the sun or even the battery could have heated the metal.

Glancing around anxiously, I called out his name. The responding echo sent icy fingers skidding down my spine. Then I heard nothing but silence.

The utter absence of sound and movement unnerved me. Bees should have been busy in the honeysuckle, birds picking at the early blackberries. It was as if that abandoned graveyard really had been suspended in amber, frozen in time and space for all eternity. I was reminded of Louvenia Durant's observation that no dog or horse would come near the place.

But there was some noise, I realized. A slight buzzing in my ears that propelled me into a slow circle as I searched in vain for a physical source. Daylight had always been my refuge, but now it seemed the entities could reach out to me even when the veil was at its thickest. If the unbound power of death had bestowed upon me uncanny perception and ghostly telepathy, it had also left me with a dangerous vulnerability.

The droning in my head grew louder and the ground tilted as a wave of dizziness rolled over me. I collapsed in a cold sweat as the cemetery walls started to spin and the voices in my head rose to a desperate crescendo. I felt enormous pressure in my chest, a kind of suction in my lungs and that same rush of wind.

Fumbling with the ribbon around my neck, I pulled the skeleton key free from my shirt and clutched it in my fist, willing whatever power it contained to help thwart those insidious voices inside my head.

Nothing happened at first and I thought the earlier incident must have truly been a fluke. But after a moment, the voices faded to a whisper. The pressure eased. Once more the key had temporarily locked the door to the dead world.

Released from the spell, I sat up and squinted into the sunlight. The entire event had lasted only a matter of moments, but I had the unsettling notion that a chunk of time had passed me by. Fear pricked at the base of my spine as I rose on rickety legs. The sky was cloudless, but the air had the same electric calm that came before a storm.

I'd dropped Dr. Shaw's phone in the grass and now I grabbed it and tucked it away in a pocket. As I turned to retrace my steps to the gate, a feeling came over me that I was no longer alone. Someone had entered the cemetery without my notice.

My gaze swept over the walls, the oak tree and finally the tabletop tomb. I saw someone lurking behind the domed lid and my breath quickened as I recognized Micah Durant's shimmering hair.

Nervously, I called out to him. "Hello?"

He didn't answer, just stood staring out at me through the gloom.

"My name is Amelia Gray," I said as I began inching toward the gate. "I saw you at the house a little while ago. Your grandmother invited me to take a look at the cemetery."

I could hear the drone of a hive somewhere in the woods behind him where earlier I'd heard no sound at all. I'd no sooner recognized the buzzing than Micah tilted his head skyward and slowly lifted his outstretched arms.

He meant to summon the bees, maybe even the workers from the same colony as the one that had stung me in Louvenia's driveway. If they zeroed in on the lingering pheromones, there would be no running away from them, no place to hide from them.

All of this passed through my mind in the space of a heartbeat. I tried to concentrate my every thought on survival as I mentally sifted through the contents of my pockets. The phone would do me no good. We were miles from anyone. The pepper spray would only help if I could spray it directly in Micah's eyes, and I had no intention of allowing him to get that close to me. If I could make it through the gate and into the maze, I might be able to elude him, but I wouldn't be able to outrun the bees. I had to find shelter and quickly.

I felt the crawl of tiny feet at the back of my neck, on my arm and in my hair. And then something very strange happened. Extraordinary even by my standards. A terrible noise arose within the walls of the cemetery as a winged horde descended from the branches of the live oak.

I thought at first Micah had summoned the bees and my arms instinctively flew up to cover my face and head. Then I realized that honeybees did not make the kind of high-pitched whine that sprang forth from the swirling brood, a sound that could only be described as a chain saw slicing through concrete.

Cicadas.

Thousands and thousands of cicadas.

The insect cloud grew so dense, I could no longer see Micah, and it came to me in a flash that this was the cover and distraction I needed.

Engulfed in that clattering cyclone, I fled from the cemetery.

Thirty-Six

The din of the cicadas followed me through the gate, but once I entered the maze, the sound died away as if the graveyard walls were somehow able to contain it. I couldn't help but think those cicadas had been summoned. I wondered if Mott had been there all along lurking in the shadows, perhaps crawling through the walls as she observed my every move. A wizened guardian whose intent I had yet to determine.

But I wouldn't contemplate her motives at the moment. I needed to keep my wits about me so that I could find my way back to the road. Before I'd gone too deeply into the maze, I paused to gather my bearings, mentally reversing Owen's instructions. I heard no sounds of pursuit, human or otherwise, and after a while, I began to wonder if Micah had only meant to frighten me away.

I still couldn't come up with a rational explanation for Dr. Shaw's absence unless he and his investigator had also been scared off. I found that prospect unlikely, but wherever they'd gone to, I needed to find them.

I'd been traveling through the maze at a good clip,

senses on alert for any threatening sound or movement when I ran into a dead end. I had been careful
with my turns, but somehow I must have missed one
in my rush to get away. I backtracked a few steps only
to realize that I was hopelessly disoriented.

Stopping to regroup, I reminded myself that I'd been
lost in a laurel bald once and had managed to find my
way out. That particular thicket had covered the whole
side of a mountain, the vegetation so dense in places
that I'd had to drop to my hands and knees and crawl
through the narrow channels with a killer on my trail.

This maze had been planted by my great-
grandmother, and though it seemed large from the
inside, I doubted it covered much more than a few
acres. Since the cemetery lay directly south of where
I'd left my car, all I had to do was use the position of
the sun and the compass app on my phone to work
my way out.

With that plan in mind, I resumed my journey, taking the time to carefully chart a new course each time
I came to a dead end, heading due north whenever possible. As I made my way through, I tried to listen for
snapping twigs or hurrying footsteps—or the drone
of bees—but all was silent inside the hedges.

The farther I traveled, the more convinced I became that I was in no real danger. Micah hadn't made
a move toward me in the cemetery nor had he threatened me that day in the Unitarian Churchyard. Maybe
I'd overreacted, giving him exactly what he wanted.

I trudged on until the shrubbery thinned and I could
see an archway just ahead. But I hadn't found my way
back to the road or my car, I soon realized. Somehow

the wrong turn had taken me to another opening in the maze.

The first thing I saw when I stepped out of the hedges was a dilapidated house. It had once been white, but most of the paint had peeled away and the rotting boards had weathered to gray. Pieces of lattice-work clung to either end of the sagging front porch and I could see the jagged teeth of broken windows both upstairs and down. Beyond the yard, the remains of an outbuilding peeked up out of the trees, and the rusty squeak of a weather vane sent a shiver down my spine.

Despite years of neglect, I recognized the house from the stereogram. Rose had once lived in those shadowy rooms, sequestered from her family and tormented by a horde of angry, restless ghosts. She may even have gouged out her eyes and hanged herself because of their relentless pursuit. If ever a place could be haunted, it would be my great-grandmother's home.

The tumbledown dwelling seemed to call out to me, but this was not the time for exploration. I needed to find my way back to the car and make sure Dr. Shaw was safe. Now that I was out of the maze, I had a better sense of direction and felt certain if I kept heading north, I would eventually come out at the road.

Checking the compass and the position of the sun, I set out once again only to freeze at a sudden noise. Somewhere in the maze, a ringtone had gone off. The sound of civilization beckoned even as I held back in alarm. As much as I wanted to believe that I was in no real danger from any of the Kroll relatives, I would be foolish to let down my guard, especially in such a remote location.

As I stood there with an ear turned toward the maze, the ringing stopped but I feared that Micah or one of the others was headed straight toward me. I could go back into the maze and try to elude him or I could hide out in the woods. But if he released the bees, my only hope was shelter.

I whirled back to the house. The stare of all those darkened windows was like a silent invitation.

Skirting the edge of the yard so as not to leave a path of flattened weeds, I made my way around to the back of the house where the woods had long since encroached.

Piles of bones from small prey littered the clearing and the putrid odor of a fresher kill drifted out from beneath the porch. As I neared the back steps, a feeling of oppression descended and the smell of rotting flesh turned my stomach. Kneeling at the bottom of the stairs, I peered up under the porch. I could just make out a small gate in the enclosure. As my gaze traveled along the fence, I suddenly had the sense that something was holed up in the shadows watching me.

I jumped to my feet and scrambled back into the yard. I would take my chances in the woods, I decided. Or I would go into the maze. I would seek shelter anywhere but inside that house. Bad things had happened there. It wasn't just the smell emanating from beneath the porch or the skeletal remains that littered the yard. I could sense the creep of something cold and dark and inhuman from behind that fence.

The urge to retreat consumed me, but even as I backed away from the porch, a little voice reminded me that I had come here to find out why Rose's ghost haunted me. To solve the mystery of her cemetery puzzle. The answer might well lie within the peeling walls of her long-abandoned home.

Not to mention that I still needed cover if Micah Durant decided to summon his bees.

Climbing the precarious steps, I carefully navigated across the sagging porch to the back door, which hung on a single rusted hinge. I slipped through and glanced around the dim interior, trying to quell the dread that something underneath the floorboards watched me through the cracks.

The house smelled dank and musty, but thankfully the death scent had faded. Mindful of cobwebs, I eased my way through the kitchen into a narrow hallway that led to the front entryway and a small parlor that looked out on the maze. Beneath the collapsing staircase was a locked door with a brass knob and back plate. I jiggled the handle a few times and then hurried into the parlor to glance out the front window.

Micah Durant had come out of the maze and stood staring up at the house. I could see the glint of sunlight in his hair, could feel the piercing stare of those pale eyes as he remained motionless at the edge of the overgrown yard.

Flattening myself against the wall, I inched back into the hallway. As I turned to cast another glance over my shoulder, my backpack caught on a nail. I heard a rip and then the ping of metal hitting the floor. I still wore the skeleton key around my neck, but the other two had fallen from the torn compartment and landed at my feet. As I scooped both up to stuff them in my pocket, my gaze lit on the plain brass door key.

Each key served a purpose, I thought. Each opened an unknown door.

Slipping across the hallway, I slid the brass teeth into the lock beneath the stairs. The key fit perfectly. The door swung open and as I slowly rose, I found myself gazing into a small, windowless room.

I hovered on the threshold, an errant breeze from the broken windows stirring my hair and what I thought at first was a wind chime. Then as my eyes became accustomed to the gloom, I realized the tinkling came from hundreds of keys hanging from the ceiling.

Thirty-Seven

I caught my breath and started to back into the hallway, but the sound of footfalls on the front porch checked me. I lingered on the threshold of that tiny room, torn between the unknown danger that lurked within and the human threat that approached from without. Then, drawing a breath, I stepped quickly inside and closed the door, groping for and engaging the lock. I could see nothing now except for a beam of light streaming in through a tiny hole in the outside wall.

The keys tinkled overhead, an eerie serenade that tore at my nerves.

Turning my back to the sound, I pressed an ear to the door, tracking the creak of floorboards as Micah crossed the porch and stepped inside the house. I could imagine him pausing to scan the corners and niches for any telltale movement, then lifting his gaze to the second floor as he assessed the possibility of my having braved the broken staircase.

The footsteps came slowly down the hallway, halting outside the stairwell door to rattle the knob once, twice, three times before continuing on into the kitchen and out the rear door.

I hoped he'd keep going, back into the maze, the woods, anywhere but here. I even let out a breath of relief when I didn't hear his returning footfalls. But I didn't open the door. Instead, I fished a flashlight from my backpack. The light refused to come on at first, but after a couple of thumps, the bulb flickered on and I played the beam over the walls.

The hanging keys were certainly an oddity, but my great-grandmother had left behind another peculiarity. Another obsession. She'd scrawled numbers all over the walls in no apparent order or pattern.

My heart thudded in excitement and trepidation as I took a tentative tour around the room. In one of the darkened corners, the numbers were so tiny that I had to kneel and lean in closely to make them out. I could imagine Rose hunkered there on the floor, frantically scribbling out a coded message that only she could decipher while the ghosts swarmed her tiny house.

In another corner, a row of candles had been aligned on the floor before a cross that had been crudely fashioned from twigs and the same cotton twine used to hang the keys. Several stereograms had been stacked in front of the cross, and as I sifted through the cards, I decided that Rose must have used the cramped space as her sanctuary. A safe haven where she could hide away during the dark hours.

I spread the cards on the floor and held the flashlight over them. The shots were of Rose's house, taken from different angles at various times of the day. I had no idea why she'd been so fascinated by the structure.

Without a viewer through which to study them, the images didn't reveal any secrets. But the photographs must have meant something to her or she wouldn't have placed them at the makeshift altar.

I was still deeply engrossed by the images when the flashlight bulb sputtered out, leaving me in near darkness except for the light streaming through the tiny hole in the wall. Maybe the placement of that minuscule opening was just happenstance, but something niggled. I had a feeling that as random as everything in this room appeared to be, there was a method to Rose's madness. Like Kroll Cemetery, the sanctuary was a carefully designed puzzle.

I tapped the flashlight back on and fanned the beam once more over the numbers. If the chaotic scribbling had order or reason, I couldn't discern it. I gathered up all the cards and carefully placed them in my backpack. Then I moved the light around the room, searching for other clues. As the shadows dissolved, I saw a deeper form in the darkest corner.

My hand jerked violently and the flashlight crashed to the floor. The beam arced over the numbers and then went completely dead. I huddled in the dark, clutching my backpack and trying to convince myself that I was alone in the room. No one living or dead had followed me inside.

Just your imagination, I tried to convince myself as I crawled on all fours across the floor, feeling for the flashlight.

The rough planks creaked beneath my weight. The keys tinkled overhead as if stirred by an unseen hand.

Don't look back.

A breeze brushed through my hair like the glacial fingers of a ghost. My jeans caught on a loose board and for a terrifying moment, I was certain something tugged at my leg. I jerked the fabric free, and then continued my search, flattening my hands over the dusty floor until I bumped up against the rubber housing. Grabbing the flashlight, I spun around while simultaneously flicking the switch.

Nothing happened.

As I frantically slapped the flashlight against my palm, the air suddenly grew cold and dank and a familiar scent drifted in. Not the dust and lavender that accompanied the blind ghost or the smell of ancient decay that heralded the withered in-between. This was an old-fashioned scent. Medicinal and not entirely unpleasant. It reminded me of the witch hazel Papa used to splash on after he shaved.

The scent grew stronger as the entity moved toward me, coming so close I could smell something fetid beneath the witch hazel. I didn't dare move or even breathe. For the longest time, I cowered motionless as the presence crouched beside me. This was not a ghost that needed my help to move on. This was something more powerful. Something with a nefarious purpose. A malcontent that had used a familiar scent to disguise its foulness.

Despite Rose's best effort, evil had found a way into her sanctuary.

Thirty-Eight

I hunkered in the dark until the scent faded and I knew without a doubt that I was alone. I had no idea where Micah had gone off to, and at the moment, I didn't really care. My primary motivation was to get out of that house.

But as terrified and rattled as I was, I somehow had the presence of mind to lock the sanctuary door before I fled. The walls of numbers and any other clues contained within that room would need to be carefully examined and photographed at a later date, but not now, not alone, not with that thing lurking in the shadows.

I turned and dashed down the hallway, heedless of the creaking floorboards and grasping cobwebs. I didn't stop to look behind me until I was at the edge of the yard and only halted then because I had to chart a course through the maze. The last thing I wanted was to stumble around aimlessly through those endless channels.

Once I got my bearings, it was easy enough to retrace my steps to the cemetery, and from there, I made my way back to the original entrance. As I emerged from the woods, I spotted Dr. Shaw pacing in front of my car. He grasped my arms as I rushed up to him, searching my harried appearance, taking in the twigs and dead leaves still clinging to my hair and clothing. "My dear, are you all right? Where on earth were you? I've been worried sick about you."

"We should get out of here," I said on a breath.

He frowned. "Why? What's happened? The way you looked just now…it was as if the devil himself were at your heels."

"I'm not so sure you're that far off the mark. That's why we need to get out of these woods and head back to town. We're not safe here."

His eyes clouded with concern. "Of course. Whatever you say. But we'll have to take your vehicle."

I glanced around anxiously. "Where's yours?"

"I sent my colleague for some equipment." He scoured my face once again. "I wish you would tell me what happened."

"I will, but let's get away from here first."

My frenzied behavior must have gotten through to him, because he nodded without another word and climbed into the SUV. I started the engine and began the delicate operation of turning the vehicle on the narrow road. I knew that Dr. Shaw was bursting with questions, but to his credit, he held his silence and allowed me to concentrate on my driving as I maneuvered along the narrow trail.

I had to fight the impulse to step on the gas. I couldn't wait to be out of those woods. The trees seemed to close in on us from both sides and the ghost voices were starting to chatter. I lifted a hand to wipe a trickle of sweat from my brow as I forced myself to take it slow and easy so that we didn't bottom out in a hole or crash into a tree. The last thing I wanted was to be stranded in that creepy place with the voices of the dead filling my head and flies gathering on my windshield.

Only when I eased onto the blacktop did I feel a weight lift from my shoulders. I glanced in the rearview mirror. There was nothing but clear road in our wake.

I could feel Dr. Shaw's gaze on me and I spared him a glance. "I noticed an abandoned gas station just outside town. We can stop there for a bit. My hands are still shaking. I need to get my nerves under control before we reach a main road."

"That's a good idea," he said, and then he turned his head back to the window to watch the passing scenery. A few minutes later, I spotted the faded sign and slowed to make the turn onto the gravel drive. By the look of the building, the business had been out of operation for decades. The twin pumps had long since disappeared and kudzu had claimed most of the roof. The derelict station was a forlorn-looking place and I didn't much like sitting with my back to it. But I thought it best to face the road so that we could spot anyone or anything trying to sneak up on us.

Dr. Shaw rummaged through his rucksack and produced a thermos. "Tea? It'll help settle your nerves."

"Yes, thank you. You're a lifesaver." I accepted his offering and wrapped my fingers around the cup so that I could absorb the warmth through my palms. Despite the outside temperature, my blood remained chilled.

"Now," Dr. Shaw said briskly, after he'd allowed me a fortifying sip. "Tell me what happened."

I watched a passing car on the highway as I gathered my thoughts. I wasn't quite ready to revisit what I'd experienced in Rose's sanctuary. The confrontation with Micah Durant in the cemetery was an easier place to start. "Do you remember the discussion we had at Oak Grove about Louvenia's grandson, Micah? About how unsettled we felt by him?"

"Yes, of course, I remember. Why?"

"I had the oddest run-in with him back at the cemetery. But even before that, I think he may have been following me." Quickly, I recounted my previous encounter with Micah at the Unitarian Churchyard. Then I described the incident with the swarming bees and Micah's later appearance in Kroll Cemetery. I even told Dr. Shaw about fleeing under the cover of a cicada cloud.

"The great Southern horde," he said in awe. "How fortuitous that their seventeen-year cycle culminated at the precise moment you needed a distraction."

I didn't think it fortuitous at all. Somehow Mott had awakened those cicadas. I hadn't seen her in the cemetery or even sensed her presence. But I suspected she'd been there all along, scrabbling through the cemetery walls or hovering in the gloom watching me.

"What do you suppose that young man is up to?" Dr. Shaw mused.

"Micah? I'm not entirely certain, but I know I don't trust him." I paused, taking another quick survey of our surroundings. "I don't think I trust any of them. They're an eccentric family, to say the least."

"Eccentricity is hardly a crime, my dear, and I must say, his behavior with the bees has me intrigued. However, I can't help wondering if there's something more you're not telling me." His gaze swept over my features. "I've never seen you like this."

I closed my eyes on a shudder. "Something else did happen, but not in the cemetery. I lost my way in the maze and stumbled upon my great-grandmother's house."

"Your great-grandmother?"

"Rose Gray. The woman in the stereogram."

"Ah. So she was related to you, then."

"She was Papa's mother. She died a long time ago by her own hand, according to Nelda and Louvenia."

"She committed suicide?" He shook his head. "What a tragic ending to her story."

"I don't think it was the end of her story at all. There's so much more I have to tell you, Dr. Shaw."

"Take your time," he said. "We're safe enough here. We can see anyone approaching for miles."

I nodded and took another sip of tea. "There's a small room underneath the stairs in her house. I believe Rose used it as her sanctuary. I found some of her stereograms on the floor and brought them with me, but I'm not sure that I should have. It seems wrong taking those cards from her house when they've been there for decades."

"You can always return them," he said reasonably. "Have you had a chance to look at them?"

"Only by flashlight and without a viewer. But that room… It's a very strange place."

"In what way?"

I clutched the cup tighter. "Hundreds of keys hang from the ceiling and the walls are covered with numbers."

"Keys and numbers," he said thoughtfully. "Like the headstone engravings."

"Exactly. They mean something. They're pieces of the larger puzzle. But that's not all I found." I turned to him, lifting a hand to the skeleton key necklace at my throat. "There was something else inside Rose's house. In that room. A presence that seemed to know me."

He looked alarmed. "What do you mean?"

"It used a scent from my past to mask its putrid odor."

"It?"

"A ghost, an entity…" I trailed off helplessly. "You were right about caulbearers. We do have a special sight. At least Papa and I do. We see ghosts. I don't talk about it because most people wouldn't believe me."

"But I'm not most people," he said gently.

"No. I should have told you a long time ago, but old habits are hard to break. I suspect you've known all along anyway."

"I've always known you were special and I can't say that I'm surprised by your revelation." I saw a gleam of excitement in his faded eyes. "Naturally, I'm curious about your experiences. Anyone in my position would be. But none of that matters at the moment. I keep going back to the look on your face when you came out of the woods. You were terrified, so I assume the presence you felt in Rose's house wasn't a ghost."

"I don't know what it was. The entity may be what

Papa calls a malcontent. A wraith that lingers to create chaos. Have you ever heard of such a thing?"

"I've never heard it called by that name. The kind of presence you're talking about is usually described as demonic."

A shiver went through me as I closed my fist around the necklace. "Earlier, on my way to the cemetery, I experienced the strangest sensation. It was as if I was caught in the middle of something. As though I was being tugged back and forth between two opposing forces. I think the ghosts of Kroll Cemetery want me here. For whatever reason, they need me to solve Rose's puzzle. But this thing, this malcontent wants to drive me away."

"That's not so hard to understand," he said. "You said its purpose for lingering in the living world is to create chaos. Perhaps it derives some, if not all, of its energy from the pent-up rage and frustration of all those trapped souls."

"I had the sense that it had been there for a long time. I think Rose somehow managed to trap it beneath her house, but it found a way into her sanctuary."

Dr. Shaw sat quietly for a very long time. "I was afraid of something like this," he finally said. "Do you remember what I told you the other night on the phone?"

"Yes. You warned me about a collective rage. About being used as a conduit. But I don't think that's why I've been brought here. I don't think the ghosts want to use me. I think they need me to find a way to free them. They can't move on until the puzzle is solved."

"Perhaps we need to take into account the human

equation, as well," he said. "I don't just mean you. It seems as if Louvenia's grandson may somehow be connected to all this."

"Maybe the entity, this malcontent, is using him. Owen Dowling told me that Micah has been troubled since childhood. He's been in and out of institutions for most of his life. It seems to me he would be easy prey. Although there could be another, less esoteric reason he'd want to thwart the restoration. Devlin said the cemetery could cause problems if the land were put on the market. It would be easier and far cheaper to make the graves go away than to try to relocate them."

"That makes sense, I suppose. Although I don't think Louvenia would agree to such a plan."

"Nor do I. But if she were to meet with an accident or be declared incompetent, it would certainly open the door for her beneficiaries."

"That's a very serious accusation, my dear."

"I know. But it would explain a lot, wouldn't it?"

I lowered my window to allow in a cool breeze. It was still early afternoon, but it seemed an eternity since I'd left the Durant farm for the cemetery. Amazing how so much could happen in such a short amount of time. Frightening how quickly one's whole world could change forever.

I turned back to Dr. Shaw. "As long as I'm coming clean, there's something else you should know. Do you remember the silhouette I told you I saw in Oak Grove the day of the dedication? I had a sense that she was connected to Nelda Toombs, that she might even be her dead twin, Mott."

"I remember," he said. "We discussed the possibility of your having experienced the Old Hag Syndrome."

"I've seen her again. And now I know she's not a vision or a hallucination or a waking dream. She's real. She exists. Not as a human, not as a ghost, but as a being that dwells in the shadowy space between the living world and the dead world."

"Half in, half out," he said.

"What do you mean?"

"It's an old saying about cats. They're half in this world, half in the next. In mythology, if someone needed to enter the underworld, they would sometimes use a cat to guide them. Maybe it's the same with Mott. She's half in, half out. Neither alive nor dead but something in between."

"It sounds crazy, doesn't it? I mean, I've seen her. I know she's real. I know she exists. But I don't understand how such a thing can be possible."

"As I've said many times, there are things in this world that will never be explained simply because we don't have the capacity to conceive of them. The scope of our reality is too narrow. Your visitor at one time was as real as you and I. Flesh-and-blood real. Perhaps when she died, something of her essence was left behind. A physical and spiritual bond to her sister so powerful that rather than moving on, she evolved into something else. Not human, not ghost, but a being that retained enough of her humanity to mimic life."

"What do you think she wants from me?" I asked.

"Undoubtedly, she's another piece of Rose's puzzle. We can only speculate as to her purpose, but if your calling is to help the dead move on, then maybe a

being that's half in and half out is the means by which
the door to the dead world can be opened. In any case
I don't think you have anything to fear from her. Think
of her as your guardian and protector. I would surmise
the gifts she's left around your house are her way of
making contact."

"As innocent as all that."

He smiled. "Sometimes the most obvious answer
is the correct one."

"I hope you're right."

"I suggest we drive back into town and regroup,"
he said. "If what you suspect about Micah Durant is
true, I should warn my colleague. I don't think it a
good idea that any of us be alone in that cemetery."

It was a sensible plan and one I agreed with whole
heartedly. But as I started the engine and eased onto
the highway, I felt an almost irresistible tug from the
direction of Kroll Cemetery.

Thirty-Nine

Once we were back in town, Dr. Shaw directed me to the bed-and-breakfast where he and his colleague had taken rooms. The house was a charming Tudor cottage located on a quiet, tree-lined street far from the hustle and bustle of the main thoroughfare.

I pulled up to the curb and parked, taking a moment to admire the colorful window boxes and beds of purple verbena that lined the flagstone walkway. Then I got out of the car and followed Dr. Shaw up the steps.

The small foyer was light and airy with a step down into a parlor furnished with a hodgepodge of antiques. Through French doors, I could see out into the garden where a woman in an old-fashioned bonnet clipped roses from well-tended bushes.

Nelda Toombs gave us a cheery wave as she placed her basket and clippers on a nearby table. She wore cotton gloves to shield her hands from the thorns and an artist's smock that not only protected her clothing, but also partially disguised the hump on her back.

"How nice to see you both!" she exclaimed as she peeled off her gloves. "Louvenia said you might stop by. The guest cottage is ready and waiting if you require it for the night. It's just across the garden." She gestured to a pitched roof rising above a large magnolia tree. "I think you'll find it cozy."

"I'm sure I will."

She cocked her head as her gaze flitted over my features. "Forgive me again for staring, but I find myself taken aback every time I'm in your presence. The resemblance to Rose is still so startling."

"It might interest you to know that since our last meeting, I've learned that Rose was my great-grandmother."

She smiled. "I'm not at all surprised. You must be Caleb's granddaughter."

"You knew Papa?"

"I knew about him, and only the little that Rose chose to share. She loved him very much, but as you can imagine, her son was a painful topic."

"I would love to hear more about her, but I don't want to be a nuisance."

"You're nothing of the kind," she said warmly. "As I told you before, I like talking about her. And speaking with you is like visiting with a dear old friend." Her eyes were still on me and I saw something flicker in the shadowy depths. Something that might have been meant just for me. "Even after all these years, I sometimes feel as though Rose and Mott are still with me."

Was she trying to tell me that she had seen them, too? Or at the very least, felt their presence?

Dr. Shaw cleared his throat. "If you ladies will excuse me, I'll leave you to your conversation. I've some phone calls to make."

As he moved away, Nelda took my arm. "Let's sit

for a spell, shall we?" She motioned to a pair of green metal chairs tucked back in the shade of the magnolia.

"This is such a beautiful garden," I said. "So lush and cool."

She glanced around with pride. "The place was a mess when I inherited it from an elderly uncle. I've put a lot of blood, sweat and tears into it over the years. Of all my business endeavors, the bed-and-breakfast holds a special place in my heart because it gave me a home and a means of providing for myself so that I didn't have to rely on Louvenia's good graces. I'm not a Kroll by birth, but I seem to have a knack for making money. Or maybe I've just been lucky."

"You've certainly done a lovely job here," I said. "But it must be difficult running Dowling Curiosities from a distance."

"Owen's been a godsend. But enough about me." She gave me an encouraging smile. "You wanted to hear about Rose."

I nodded. "You told me the other day that she had a fascination for all kinds of photography. I'm an amateur photographer myself. Do you know if any of her pictures or equipment were saved?"

"Not many, I'm afraid. After you left the shop yesterday, I went through some of my boxes of keepsakes. I did find one of her old viewers, and now that I know you're her granddaughter, I'd like for you to have it."

"That's very generous of you."

"It's the least I can do after you so kindly returned Mott's viewer to me. I'll bring it by the guest cottage later."

"Thank you so much. It would mean a lot to me to have something of hers," I said in earnest.

"Then, so you shall. It was Rose's first stereoscope, I think. She picked it up in a secondhand shop along with a box of travel cards. That was the start of her interest in stereoscopy. We used to sit out on the front porch and daydream about visiting all those exotic places. Of course, none of us would ever stray far from home, but there was no harm in pretending."

She sat back in her chair, letting her gaze drift over the garden. "Did you know that Rose also had an interest in the occult?"

I tried to keep my tone neutral. "As in séances? Tarot cards?"

"As in ghosts. Mott and I never told anyone for fear we would be forbidden to see her again. Rose believed the living world and the dead world existed side by side. Like a stereogram. She claimed there were times when the two worlds merged, making it possible for the dead to cross back over into our world. I think that's the reason she was so enthralled with stereoscopy. The concept of duality fascinated her."

"Miss Toombs—"

"Call me Neddy, won't you? No one has called me that in years. Not since Rose passed."

"Neddy…" The name felt strange on my tongue. "I visited Rose's house a little while ago. Just before I came here, in fact. The room beneath the stairs… That's where you found her, isn't it?"

Her eyes closed briefly. "Who took you there?"

"No one. I stumbled upon it by accident. Those keys

hanging from the ceiling and the numbers scribbled over the walls... Do you know what they mean?"

"I've wondered from time to time if those keys were still there," Nelda murmured. "Mott was always fascinated by them, too—she used to spend hours sorting through them. Sometimes she would pull certain keys aside and Rose would make up stories about them."

"Do you remember any of the stories?"

"That was a long time ago and so much has happened since then. Although there is one thing you might like to know." Nelda's fingers fluttered to her throat. "Rose used to wear some of the keys on a ribbon as a necklace. As I recall, there were three in particular that she seemed to favor. The one I remember best was very old and ornate. Quite beautiful as I recall."

I felt the weight of the skeleton key around my own neck and tugged the ribbon from my collar. "Like this one?"

Nelda stared at the key for a moment before slowly lifting her gaze to mine. "Where did you get that?" she asked in a strained voice. "You didn't find it in Rose's house."

"It was given to me years ago when I was a child. It only recently came back into my possession."

Nelda pressed a hand to her heart. "Forgive me if I sounded abrupt, but I was just so startled to see that key, even though I know it's not the same one. It can't be. Rose was buried with her key."

My fingers trembled as I tucked the ribbon back in my collar. "Are you sure?"

"Oh, yes. I remember seeing it around her neck at the viewing."

"Then, you're right. This key can't be the same one."

"It only *looks* like hers," Nelda insisted.

"Yes, of course." But I somehow knew that it *was* the same key. It had been transported by ghostly means from Rose's grave to my hideaway in Rosehill Cemetery and then later to my nightstand. "You said she wore three keys around her neck. Were the other two buried with her, as well?"

"No. They didn't seem to mean as much to her. One of them was to the room beneath the stairs. I don't know why she kept that room locked. Her house was so remote, and other than Mott and me, her only visitor was my brother. As for the third key..." Nelda trailed off.

"Was it the key you found clutched in her hand the day she died? Do you know what happened to it?"

"I assumed the police took it. I never asked. I made an effort to put that awful day out of my head. But when I saw you at Oak Grove Cemetery looking enough like Rose to make me wonder if she'd come back from the grave..." Nelda drew a shaky breath. "So many memories came flooding back."

"Can you tell me anything else about those keys?"

"Only that the skeleton key had been in Rose's family for generations. Supposedly there had once been a sister key, but it had been lost a long time ago."

"Do you think that could explain her obsession with collecting keys? Maybe subconsciously she was searching for the lost key."

"Given her fragile mental state, it's certainly possible," Nelda said. "Rose had a tendency to fixate. The keys, the stereograms, all those numbers. To her, everything had meaning, but I think her obsessions had more to do with her illness than anything else. She did say something about that lost key once that I've always wondered about. I suspect it was just another of her fairy tales, but I've never forgotten it."

"What did she say?"

"That her life would be very different if she still had the key."

"Different how?"

Nelda leaned in with shimmering eyes. "According to Rose, the lost key had the power to close the door to the dead world forever."

Forty

❧◉❧◉❧

I desperately wanted to believe that such a key existed. That it really could be my salvation. But Rose had lost her grip on reality before she died and I couldn't take her story seriously. I couldn't afford even a glimmer of hope that the door to the dead world could be locked forever, thereby allowing for a normal life without all the ghosts, without all the secrets. I couldn't put my faith in that missing key because the moment I started to believe in Rose's fairy tale was the moment I became as lost as she.

After I left Nelda in the garden, I hauled my spare set of clothes out of the car and settled into the guesthouse. It was a small space, but charmingly appointed with whimsical antiques. After I'd had a look around, I walked over to the town center to pick up a few items I would need for my overnight stay. When I returned, I found Rose's viewer on the nightstand. As curious as I was about the stereograms I'd taken from her sanctuary, the claw-foot tub beckoned. It had been a long and emotionally exhausting day, and I hoped a long soak would help relax me.

Releasing my ponytail, I turned on the taps and

opened the small window over the tub to allow some of the steam to escape. Then I eased down into the water, sighing as I rested my head on a folded towel. But I still couldn't let go of all that had happened. The lavender body wash conjured the memory of Rose's ghost and I found myself dwelling again on the gruesome way she'd died and the lonely way she'd lived. I lay there in the bubbles, washcloth over my face, thoughts churning with everything I'd learned about my great-grandmother. All those numbers and keys. The stereograms. So many obsessions. Rose had left behind an intricate web, one that I wasn't at all certain I was up to untangling.

I lay there trying to sort through the confusion until the water grew tepid, and then I climbed out of the tub, dripping and shivering as I reached for a towel. I must have been soaking for a very long time because outside the tiny bathroom window the garden lay in deep shadows. The sun was setting and twilight would soon fall.

The urgency that had driven me to hallowed ground since childhood propelled me into the bedroom, where I slipped the skeleton key around my neck once more. I placed the other two keys on the nightstand, lining them up just as I'd found them and wondering what remaining purposes the two might serve.

Restless and claustrophobic, I dressed and took the photographs and viewer out to the porch to study them in the remaining light. The air had cooled as the shadows grew longer, and the scent of roses wafted from the garden.

Plopping down on the top step, I placed the first

card in the viewer and lifted it to my eyes. The dual
images came together to form a three-dimensional
view of Rose's house. I could see curtains at the
windows and flowerpots on the front steps. It was a
pleasant-looking place if one didn't notice the shadows from the woods that crept across the yard. If one
didn't speculate about the fence that enclosed the space
beneath her house.

I viewed one card after another until I'd gone
through the whole stack. All of them were of Rose's
house, and as I'd observed earlier, they had been taken
from different angles at different times of the day.

What an odd collection, I thought as I went back
to the first card.

This time I studied the images more carefully, turning the viewer slightly until I caught the best light. I
tried to peer into the windows of Rose's house, into
the treetops, even underneath her front porch. The
longer I studied those photographs the more unsettled I became.

I was certain the shots weren't random. Rose had
deliberately set out to photograph her house from
every possible angle in every conceivable light. But
why?

As I scoured the images for clues, I suddenly had
the feeling of being watched. The sensation was so
strong that I lowered the viewer to scan the garden.
Then I lifted my gaze to the windows at the back of
Nelda's house. No one was around. No one watched
me. So why the crawl of flesh at the back of my neck?
Why the tingle at my spine?

I glanced over my shoulder. The door to the guest

cottage was closed. I saw no one at the windows. No one in the shadows.

I turned back to the garden, bringing the viewer to my eyes once more. I started to remove the card from the holder when my gaze lit on the enclosure beneath the front porch.

Something was there staring back at the camera lens. *At me.*

I couldn't see anything. No gleaming eyes. No flash of pale skin or hair. But something was there just the same.

I inserted another card, my gaze going straight to the enclosure. Something was still there, still watching.

I went back through the whole stack, circling Rose's house through the lens of the viewer.

And suddenly I knew the purpose of all those images. I knew what Rose had wanted to show me.

She'd been trying to capture in three dimensions what she had trapped beneath her house.

Forty-One

~~~~

Slipping the ribbon from my neck, I traced the skeleton key with my fingertip, wanting to believe that, like hallowed ground, the metal could protect me from the ghosts and the malcontent and any evil that I'd yet to encounter. It had some power, I felt certain. There must have been a reason why Rose had worn it to her grave.

A breeze swept through the garden, deepening the scent of Nelda's roses. My senses were so heightened, I could hear the flutter of moth wings in the four-o'clocks and the satin-like whisper of the moonflowers unfurling. A songbird trilled in the magnolia tree. A train whistle sounded in the distance. Loneliness settled over me as twilight crept in from the garden.

I sat alone on the steps, clutching Rose's key until the mosquitoes drove me inside. Then I locked up, slipped out of my clothes and into my new cotton nightgown before climbing between the cool sheets.

I placed the viewer on the floor and shoved it underneath the bed. I wouldn't look at those images again tonight. Whatever Rose had trapped beneath her house could wait until morning.

Maybe nothing had been there at all, I tried to convince myself. Maybe it was best not to borrow trouble.

But trouble found me just the same.

It came with a tapping on my door, a sound so tentative that I thought for a moment I might still be dreaming. Then it grew louder, more insistent, and my eyes popped open as I bolted upright in bed. Something was out there on the porch wanting in.

My instinct was to huddle under the covers, but instead I slid out of bed and padded to the door. A lace curtain hung over the glass, and I parted the panels to peer out. The moon had gone behind a cloud and the porch lay in darkness.

I had almost managed to convince myself that I'd imagined the sound when I heard it again. Not a knock or a tap as I'd first thought, but the click of a lone cicada.

I spotted her in the shadows then. The humpback inbetween. The childlike entity that was half in, half out.

Why I unlocked the door and stepped out on the porch, I couldn't say. Despite my fear, I was drawn to her.

She was dressed in a garment blackened with age, and she clutched something in one hand that I couldn't make out in the darkness. When the clouds drifted away, I could see her face in the moonlight. Her nose, her mouth, her eyes. Features that were no longer human and hadn't been for a very long time.

Her skin looked dark and leathered and yet somehow fragile, as though it might crumble to ash from the slightest touch. And I could smell her. The same odor of must and old death that I'd detected in my cellar.

We stood with gazes locked for the longest time, but when I made a slight move, she stopped me with a sound that was only a little less aggressive than the rattle. Her mouth was open and what might once have been teeth clacked together in a chilling staccato.

I heard the squeak of the same phantom wheel that had manifested in my garden. As the sound grew closer, the entity threw back her head and an ear-splitting whistle vibrated from the back of her throat. She flung out her arms in supplication a split second before she was sucked backward into the darkness.

I was so utterly flabbergasted by what had transpired that I failed to sense the newcomer. He stood at the edge of the garden gazing up at me, his expression unfathomable in the moonlight.

Forty-Two

—◦◦◯◯◯◦◦—

"Amelia?"

My heart fluttered as I watched Devlin move through the garden and mount the steps. He must have come straight from work because he still had on his usual attire of dress pants and crisp cotton shirt. He'd removed his coat and tie, and his shirt was unbuttoned at the throat so that I could see the gleam of the silver chain around his neck.

When he reached the top stair, he took my shoulders. Then his gaze scoured the porch behind me, an indefinable expression on his face as if he'd seen something he couldn't explain. A shadow? A flicker of light? If he'd caught a glimpse of Mott, he would never admit it. He would search and search until he came up with a logical explanation.

"Everything okay?" he asked, leaning in to brush my lips with his.

As distracted as I was by Mott's strange visit, my senses were still so attuned to the night that it almost seemed as if I could hear his beating heart through his clothing. The sound was deep, steady, primal. I put a hand to my chest, where my own heart still pounded.

"Everything's fine. You gave me a start, though. I had no idea you were coming."

"It was spur of the moment." He cocked his head. "Are you sure you're all right? What are you doing out here on the porch so late?"

"It's not that late, and why are you really here?"

"Dr. Shaw called. He said you had a scare today."

"He shouldn't have bothered you with that," I said in annoyance. "You have enough to worry about right now, and anyway, nothing happened that I couldn't handle."

"What did happen?" He was still holding my shoulders, still studying my face in the moonlight. "What's this about Louvenia Durant's grandson following you?"

"I've seen him around in a few unexpected places, but I don't think there's any cause for alarm."

Devlin was silent for a moment. "You're being awfully cavalier about all this."

"I don't mean to be cavalier. But nothing happened with Micah Durant." I summed up my interaction with the beekeeper in as succinct a manner as I could muster, but my brevity only deepened Devlin's concern.

"This guy sounds like trouble. Did you contact the local authorities?"

"No, because he didn't *do* anything. If he'd wanted to hurt me, he had ample opportunity when we were alone in Kroll Cemetery. But he never made a move toward me. He didn't even threaten me. I think he just means to scare me off."

Devlin's grip tightened. "And what happens when

you don't scare off? You think he'll just give up? I can tell you almost certainly that he won't."

I tried to shrug off his worry. "It may not matter anyway. I haven't agreed to the restoration. Louvenia and I haven't even discussed the details. Once she hears my price, she may decide she doesn't need my services after all."

"When are you meeting with her?" Devlin asked.

"Tomorrow morning at eight."

He nodded. "That seems a good time for a conversation with Durant. It won't hurt to let him know that you have a police detective watching your back. Maybe he'll think twice before escalating his behavior."

My hand flitted to his chest. "Are you sure you have time for all that? You don't need to get back to your grandfather?"

"He's in good hands, don't worry. Tonight, I'm exactly where I need to be." I saw the briefest of scowls before he curled an arm around my waist and drew me to him. When he bent to kiss me, I felt the cool brush of silver against my fingertips as the medallion slipped from his shirt.

So much power in this totem. So much history in this emblem.

I'd sworn not to dip back into Devlin's past, not to use my newfound abilities to intrude upon his privacy. But before I could stop the process, my mind emptied and a flood of images stormed in.

I almost expected to find myself in the same disturbing tableau as before, but instead of hovering at the edge of the woods, observing Devlin and Mariama from afar, I found myself in a strange room that smelled of leather and old books. For a moment, I thought I was in Dr. Shaw's office, that I must have slipped into a memory of Devlin's time at the Institute. But the room was more opulent and orderly and it reeked of very old money.

Devlin stood at a long window with his back to the room while an older man with gray hair sat scribbling at an ornate desk. He was tall and slender like Dr. Shaw but without the stooped shoulders. This man's posture was at once rigid and regal, and I knew he was Devlin's grandfather even though I'd never met him. I could see a resemblance in the set of his jaw and in the way he carried himself.

How I had come to be in that room was unexplainable. How I had become an invisible voyeur to events in Devlin's recent and distant past, I had no idea. All I knew was that the transformation of my gift had somehow connected us in a way that I'd never experienced until a few days ago.

Like Mariama, Jonathan Devlin seemed to sense my presence. He glanced up, peering into the space where my shadow self lurked before bowing his head once more to his work.

"Come away from the window, Jack. You don't know who could be watching."

Devlin turned with a scowl. "I'm not Jack, Grandfather. I'm John."

"I know who you are," the elderly man grumbled. "Why must you always interpret everything as a personal affront? Your father never minded the nickname. It goes back for generations in our family. But then, you've never cared much for tradition, have you?"

"Maybe I just don't like the name," Devlin said.

"Still as stubborn as the day you came to live with me, I see. And twice as infuriating." His grandfather tossed the pen aside and swiveled his chair toward the window. "Have you given any more thought to the matter we discussed a few days ago?"

"No. And if you intend to start in on me again, save your breath. Nothing you say will convince me."

"Even after what happened to the other one?"

Devlin turned, leaning a shoulder against the window frame as he folded his arms. "By accident or intent, Mariama drove off that bridge by her own hand. No one else was responsible."

"How do you know that?" his grandfather demanded.

"Because I know. End of story. Now take your medicine so we can both get some rest," Devlin said wearily.

"I won't take another pill until you hear me out. I'm eighty-five years old. I don't know how much time I have left. After I'm gone, certain obligations and expectations will fall on your shoulders."

"I'm well aware," Devlin muttered.

"There has been a Devlin serving in the ranks of that organization for over three hundred years. With your father gone, you're the next in line, and you know what that will entail. Everyone around you will be scrutinized, including that woman. She may fly under their radar now, but once the vetting process starts, they'll find out about her and it won't be pretty. She is anathema to everything they stand for."

Devlin just shook his head. "This is pure fantasy,

Grandfather. These people aren't real. You dreamed the whole thing up or maybe you read it in a book and now you're confused. Or maybe this is your way of trying to get me to do what you want. Whatever the case, let me make something perfectly clear. I'm not going to stop seeing Amelia Gray because her profession and background don't meet with your exalted standards."

His grandfather's fist came down hard on the desktop. "This isn't about standards! It isn't about her profession or her people. Don't you understand that? It's about *her*."

"Grandfather—"

"Open your eyes, Jack. Use your instincts. *You know what she is*."

What am I? I wondered as I spun up out of the memory.

I had asked Papa that very question and he'd had no answer. How was it that Jonathan Devlin, a man I'd never met, seemed to know something about me that my own grandfather couldn't explain?

This is pure fantasy, Grandfather. These people aren't real.

I was still swirling in a haze, lost in all those questions when I realized Devlin was peering down at me through narrowed eyes.

"What did you call me?" he asked in a strained voice.

I shook my head slightly trying to clear the fog. "What?"

"Just now. You called me Jack." His grip tightened.

"No one but my grandfather has ever used that name. You've talked to him, haven't you? Did he call you? Come to see you? What did he say to you?"

His sudden agitation startled me. "Nothing. That is…I haven't spoken to him. I've never even met him."

Devlin's expression hardened. "There's a reason for that. He isn't to be trusted. But if you haven't talked to him, why did you call me Jack just now?"

I shook my head helplessly. "I've no idea. I don't know anyone by that name. But your grandfather has been so much on your mind lately. Maybe it was some sort of telepathy."

Something flashed in his eyes. The memory of his grandfather's warning perhaps. *You know what she is.*

"I don't see how that could be possible," he said.

"There are a lot of things in this world that can't be explained."

"Now you sound like Rupert Shaw."

"I can think of worse things."

He ran a hand through his hair as he glanced out over the garden. "You know I don't put stock in that sort of thing. It's a dangerous road to go down."

"If there's nothing to it, why is it dangerous?" I asked in a reasonable tone.

His expression darkened. "It's been my experience that it can lead to obsession and a false sense of invincibility. And it's a good way to lose touch with reality."

He was thinking about Mariama now. I didn't like the intrusion of his dead wife so I put my hand on his arm to draw him back to me. Where our skin touched, lightning danced.

"Did you see that?" I asked in awe.

"Static electricity," he said. "There's a storm brewing."

That was certainly the logical explanation. The wind had picked up and I could hear a distant rumble that might have been thunder. But the weather didn't account for the sudden quiver of my nerve endings or the surge of heat through my veins. It didn't explain the intimate sounds that bombarded me—the rhythm of Devlin's heartbeat, the saw of his breath, the throb of his pulse. The infinitesimal clink of the medallion against the silver chain around his neck.

My senses were already heightened by the night and by the evolution of my gift, but now everything inside me came alive in a way I'd never felt before. It was as if I'd been accustomed to the world as a flat image, but now I could experience everything around me in 3-D. The perception was as daunting as it was exciting.

I stood on tiptoes and touched my lips to Devlin's. A white-hot shock bolted down my spine and tingled in my fingertips. I drew in a sharp breath and shuddered. "Did you feel that?"

"Yes, I felt it."

I started to touch him again, but he caught both my wrists in his hands and held them for the longest time before slowly pressing me back against the porch.

"Do you feel this?" he drawled, sliding his hand along my inner thigh.

My head fell back against the wall as he shoved my nightgown aside, teasing me with his fingers until my blood thrummed and my whole body felt electrified. If my senses were heightened, so was my desire. I had never wanted anyone as I wanted Devlin at that moment. Urgent and trembling, I tugged him closer as I fumbled with his belt and zipper.

And then it was my fingers that teased, my hand that encircled and stroked and drew a low groan as I brought him to the very brink. He lifted me, pushing into me, and where our bodies touched, sparks exploded. I could see tiny flickers of light out in the garden where manifestations were trying to break through, but I wouldn't let them. I was stronger than the ghosts now, stronger even than the Others. I held the unbound power of death in my fingertips. Drunk with passion and a dangerous sense of omnipotence, I yanked the nightgown over my head and tossed it toward those flickering lights.

Devlin said against my ear, "There's a light on in one of the upstairs windows. This porch may not be as private as it seems."

He backed me through the door, kissing me deeply as I helped divest him of his clothes. Then we moved as one to the bed. I lay back against the pillows and lifted my hands to the headboard, an artful surrender. Devlin stood at the foot of the bed staring down at me. Then, eyes gleaming in the moonlight, he put a knee on the bed and crawled up between my thighs, trailing the tip of his tongue over my abdomen and up to my breasts.

The medallion glistened as the chain swung with his movements. I wanted to touch it again, feel the coolness of the metal between my fingers, slide inside Devlin's mind the moment he slid into me.

Instead, I closed my eyes and lifted my hips to him. I could feel him there, pressing against me. His breath was hot against my neck and yet the hand that trailed along the inside of my arm was icy. A guttural moan sounded in my ear as a tongue darted out to lave along my jawline. My eyes flew open on a terrified gasp.

An odor came to me then, a fetid breath that was masked only slightly by the scent of witch hazel. The thing from Rose's sanctuary was there in the room with us. It had followed me through the maze and back to the guesthouse. I couldn't see it. But I could feel its presence. In bed beside me. Touching me. Taunting me. *Wanting inside me.*

My first instinct was to bolt out of the cottage and run screaming into the night, and I might have done exactly that if Devlin's expression hadn't stopped me cold. He was still kneeling over me, his gaze riveted on my hair where I could feel those frigid fingers plunging through the lose strands. There was something in Devlin's eyes beyond the glimmer of moonlight, beyond the dawning horror. For a moment, I could have sworn I saw the reflection of a shadowy form hovering at the top of the headboard before it turned to crawl up the wall.

I tried to scream, tried to reach out to Devlin, but I couldn't move and neither could he, it seemed. He remained motionless as his gaze moved slowly up the wall as if tracking the entity all the way to the ceiling.

Forty-Three

~~~

In the space of a heartbeat, it was gone.

The smell vanished, the cold faded and Devlin seemed to shake off his trance as he leaped from bed and reached for the lamp. Light flooded the room, revealing nothing amiss in that tiny space but the rumpled bedsheets and our discarded clothing.

I scrambled out of bed and into my jeans, hands trembling so badly I couldn't manage the snap. Drawing on a T-shirt, I curled up in a chair and hugged my knees to my chest as I watched Devlin move about the room, shirtless and barefoot. He'd pulled on his pants, not bothering to buckle the belt as he checked windows and doors in full police-detective mode. I heard him moving around in the bathroom and when he came back out, he even searched under the bed.

"You saw it, didn't you?" I asked on a shaky breath.

He shot me a glance that I couldn't decipher as he opened the front door and scanned the porch. "I saw something," he admitted. "Wait here while I take a look outside."

I jumped up from the chair. "Don't go out there!"

He turned with a scowl. "It's okay. I'll just be a minute. Where's your flashlight? All I have is a penlight."

I unzipped my backpack and fished out the light. "There's a loose connection. You may have to give it a thump."

He tapped it on. "Lock the door behind me."

That won't do any good! "Maybe I should wait for you on the front porch."

He looked as if he wanted to argue, but then nodded. I followed him out the door, watching from the top step as he disappeared around the corner of the cottage. My gaze lifted to the back of Nelda's house where the light in the upstairs window still shone. I wanted to take comfort in that lonely beacon, but instead I found myself wondering who was still awake at this hour and what were they up to.

Devlin came back around the cottage, playing the flashlight beam all along the edge of the porch.

"Did you find anything?" I asked anxiously.

"I saw some fresh footprints in the dirt below the bedroom window. Someone may have been looking for a way in."

"Someone or some*thing*?"

That seemed to give him pause. "Let's go back inside."

I turned with trepidation toward the doorway. I could see the bed from where I stood, and my gaze automatically scaled the wall over the headboard.

Devlin came up behind me. "Nothing's in there. It was only a shadow."

I tightened my arms around my middle. "It wasn't a shadow. I felt it on my skin. It was touching my hair."

I remembered the phantom tongue along my jaw and shuddered. "I know you saw it."

"What I saw was the breeze stirring your hair," he insisted. "The wind is up because a storm's moving in. That also explains the static electricity."

"There was no breeze inside. The doors and windows were closed."

"The window in the bathroom was open."

Had I not shut it earlier after my bath? I couldn't remember, but it hardly mattered because the entity didn't need an open window or an unlocked door. It could just have easily come up through the cracks in the floorboards.

"What about the smell?" I asked.

"The jasmine?" He flicked the beam down into the garden. "There's a trellis of it near the patio."

I gazed back at him in shock. I'd smelled Papa's witch hazel, but the entity had manifested Devlin's daughter's favorite flower to entice him. It could use any scent. Invade any space in search of a conduit through which it could work its evil.

"We both know it was there," I whispered.

Devlin took my arm. "Come back inside. I want to show you something."

Reluctantly, I let him lead me back through the door and then I watched anxiously as he moved around the bed to turn off the lamp. Darkness and claustrophobia enveloped me and I had to fight the urge to flee back outside to the porch.

"Look at the wall over the bed," Devlin instructed.

I didn't want to. I wanted to squeeze my eyes closed

so that, like my great-grandmother before me, I could unsee the unspeakable.

"Do you see it?" he asked and I shifted my focus to the space above the headboard. Something moved on the wall. My pulse jumped before I realized it was the silhouette of a tree branch thrashing in the breeze.

"That doesn't explain the look I saw on your face," I said. "You were frightened."

"I was alarmed," he said. "And with good reason. Someone stood outside that window looking in on us. Whoever it was cast a shadow on the wall, and the wind in the tree branches created an illusion of movement."

I almost wished I could buy the explanation of a Peeping Tom. The notion of Micah Durant or anyone else spying on us made me ill, but the alternative was far more distressing. "That still doesn't explain the look I saw on your face," I said stubbornly. Or the reflection I'd glimpsed in his eyes.

He turned on the light. "I admit, I let my imagination get the better of me for a moment."

"What about my imagination? Do you think we conjured the exact same thing at the exact same time? How do you explain our simultaneous reaction?" I'd been hovering just inside the door but now I took a tentative step toward him. "Besides, you're not the type to let your imagination get the better of you."

"Normally, no. But all this business with my grandfather must be taking more of a toll than I realized."

I gazed across the bed at him. "What business?" I asked carefully.

"All the fantasies he's cooked up. For a moment, I

let myself get dragged into his delusions." His voice was so calm and measured he almost had me convinced.

"You really think all you saw was a shadow?"

"I do." He walked around the bed and put his arms around me. "Whatever either of us saw or felt, it's over. Nothing else is going to happen tonight."

"I hope you're right," I said uneasily.

He brushed his fingers through my hair and I couldn't help shivering. "I'm here and I'm not going anywhere. If it'll make you feel better, we can leave the light on for the rest night." He was teasing me now, but when I pulled back to search beyond his coaxing smile, I saw a flicker of something in his eyes that I knew was dread.

Forty-Four

Devlin was already up the next morning when I roused. I hadn't closed my eyes until just before daylight and when I finally did doze off, my dreams were dark and disjointed. Like Rose's puzzle, I couldn't make sense of them, but an overwhelming feeling of loss plagued me, so much so that I awakened once with tears on my face.

Even curled in Devlin's arms, I couldn't go back to sleep. I lay fully dressed on top of the covers and listened to the distant rumble of thunder as a feeling of doom descended. It wasn't just the insidious nature of the malcontent or the persistent chatter of all those ghostly voices in my head that tormented me. Something was wrong between Devlin and me.

The growing gulf had troubled me for weeks and now the memory I'd slipped into earlier only solidified my doubts. I didn't know why or how, but I sensed our relationship had reached a turning point—perhaps the crossroads that Dr. Shaw had warned me about. I wanted to believe that eventually all would be well, but I had a bad feeling that rather than uniting us, ur shared encounter had changed things in ways I ouldn't yet understand.

A part of me wanted nothing more than to rush back o Charleston and put the incident behind me. Distance myself as quickly as I could from the manipulations f a malicious entity. But that wouldn't end the hauntngs. The ghosts would follow me wherever I went, arassing me night and day until I found a way to reease them. I was as trapped as they, and the sooner I eturned to Kroll Cemetery, the sooner I could solve Rose's puzzle and be free of them.

The urgency to act drove me out to the porch, where found Devlin staring out at the garden.

"Good morning," he said easily. "Did you finally manage to get some sleep?"

"A little." I went over to stand beside him at the ailing. "Did you?"

"Enough." He lifted his hand so that I could see the wig he held between his fingers. "I found this on the orch when I came out."

I took the stem so that I could examine the attached icada shell. I thought at first it was the same one that ad been left on my bedside table. But when I held he husk up to the light, the amber glow was muted ecause something remained inside. The casing had ailed to open all the way so that the winged nymph ad become trapped. Half in, half out.

The flesh at my nape tingled and I felt something npleasant curl in my stomach. Was this a gift? A varning? Another clue? Something about that amber rison made me inexplicably sad. I thought about Mott nd what she had become because her sister wouldn't release her from their earthly bond. Or perhaps their connection had been so strong that Mott had lingered of her own accord. Whatever the reason for her unfinished journey, I didn't want to take the chance that our motives could be misconstrued, and so I quickly returned the twig to the porch.

Devlin watched me curiously. "Don't you wonder where it came from?"

"There are cicada shells all over the place," I said. "Wait until you see the cemetery. That is, if you want to go with me this morning."

"I wouldn't miss it. And besides, I don't think it a good idea for you or Dr. Shaw to be alone out there. Not after everything I've heard about this Micah Durant."

"After what happened last night, Micah Durant is the least of my worries."

Devlin scowled. "After last night, you should be even more worried about him. I wouldn't be at all surprised to find out those are his footprints beneath the bedroom window."

"You're still convinced that what you saw on the wall was a shadow."

"And apparently, you're still equally convinced that it wasn't." He skimmed his knuckles briefly down my bruised cheek as his gaze softened. "Believe it or not, there is a reasonable explanation for all of this."

"So you keep saying."

"Years ago when I worked at the Institute, we were always sent in pairs to investigate any unusual activity. Sometimes my partner and I would see or feel or hear the same thing at the same moment only to discover later that we'd experienced a sort of shared delusion brought on by the power of suggestion. It still occasionally happens in police investigations. No matter your best efforts, your mind will go where it's predisposed to go."

"You think that's what happened to us last night? A shared delusion? Brought on by what?"

"The gruesome history of Kroll Colony. It's been on both our minds for days."

I wanted to believe it was that simple. A shared delusion conjured by our preoccupation with all those mysterious deaths, but I knew better, and deep down, Devlin did, too.

Nelda came through the garden just then and gave us a cheery wave. "Looks as if the storm blew itself out last night. The breeze was pleasant though, wasn't it? I trust you had a good sleep."

I smiled and murmured something noncommittal as her gaze slid to Devlin.

"Good morning," she said. "I don't believe I've had the pleasure."

"Miss Toombs... Neddy, I'd like you to meet John Devlin. He drove in from Charleston last night. I'm hoping to show him the cemetery this morning after my meeting with Louvenia."

If she was surprised by his presence at the cottage, she didn't show it. Instead, she seemed quite taken with Devlin as he went down the steps to greet her.

"How do you do, Miss Toombs?"

"Quite well, Mr. Devlin. Thank you." She smiled demurely as she offered her hand. "I trust you had a good sleep, as well?"

"The cottage is very comfortable," he said with a neat sidestep. "You have a lovely place here."

"I try my best." Reluctantly, she shifted her focus back to me. "About that meeting with Louvenia. I'm to tell you she's running late and will meet you later at the cemetery. She would have telephoned you directly but she didn't want to disturb you."

"Thank you."

"And there's a message from Dr. Shaw, as well. I'm afraid he's feeling under the weather and would like for you to come up to see him before you leave."

"It's nothing serious, I hope."

"Just a bug, I imagine. Anyway, I'll be serving breakfast shortly. Would you like some coffee or tea in the meantime?"

"Coffee would be great," Devlin said, and she beamed.

"Maybe tea a little later," I said. "Right now I'd like to check on Dr. Shaw."

"Do you want me to go with you?" Devlin asked when Nelda had gone back inside the house.

"No, just sit here and enjoy your coffee. I'll be back soon."

"Amelia..." He caught my arm and I turned to glance up at him.

He looked as if he wanted to tell me something, but instead he bent to kiss me. "Go see about Dr. Shaw. We'll talk when you get back."

I left him in the garden while I went up to Dr. Shaw's room. He answered the door in his robe and slippers, looking frailer than I'd seen him in months.

"Dr. Shaw, are you all right? Nelda said you're not feeling well."

"It's nothing to worry about," he said as he motioned me into a small sitting area. "I expect I've overtaxed myself. I'm used to spending all of my time in the office these days. Field investigations are a young man's work."

"Can I get you anything?" I asked in concern. "Do you need to see a doctor?"

"No, thank you, my dear. As you can see, Miss Toombs is taking very good care of me." He sat down at the table where a tea service had been placed and motioned for me to join him. "A morning's rest and I should be as good as new."

But I wasn't so certain. The pallor of his skin worried me and I couldn't help noticing how badly his hand trembled as he poured our tea.

"Where's your associate?" I asked as he handed me a cup. "He hasn't already left for the cemetery, has he?"

"He had to return to Charleston on another matter and I'm not sure when or if he'll be back. So I'm afraid neither of us will be able to accompany you this morning. However, I did hear from my friend about the braille inscription."

"Oh?" I leaned in anxiously. "What does it say?"

"It's from a seventeenth-century poem by Henry Vaughan. I'll forward you the email, but in the meantime, take a look." He opened up his tablet and handed the device across the table to me. "Vaughan was one of the metaphysical poets. Welsh, I believe."

I read aloud from the screen:

"O calm and sacred bed, where lies
In death's dark mysteries
A beauty far more bright
Than the noon's cloudless light."

"What do you think?" Dr. Shaw asked.

"'A beauty far more bright than the noon's cloudless light,'" I mused. *A beauty far more bright.* The line niggled, but I didn't know why. I glanced up. "Other than the obvious death reference, I don't have a clue. But the poem must have been important to Rose or she wouldn't have gone to the trouble of hiding it in braille. I must say, I'm thoroughly intrigued by the inscription. And even more eager to visit her grave."

Dr. Shaw took a tentative sip of his tea. "You're not going out to the cemetery alone, I hope."

"John is going with me, but you already knew he was here, didn't you? Why did you call him?"

"After our conversation yesterday, I was concerned for your safety. I can hardly be blamed for that, can I? I've grown quite fond of you, my dear. You're like a daughter to me. But if I've overstepped my bounds, I apologize."

I was very touched by his acknowledgment and said so. "And please don't apologize. I appreciate your concern. I'm glad to have John's company. Although..." I stared down into my teacup for a moment. "Something happened after he arrived last night. There was an episode."

A snowy brow lifted. "What kind of episode?"

"We both felt a presence in the cottage. And I could tell from John's face that he actually *saw* something.

He wouldn't admit it, of course. He still won't. He insists it was nothing more than a shadow."

"But you know better."

"I believe it was the entity from Rose's sanctuary. I could smell the witch hazel it used to cover its stench. But the odd thing is, John smelled jasmine. That was his daughter's favorite flower."

"How did he explain the scent?"

"The bathroom window was open and Nelda grows jasmine in her garden."

Dr. Shaw observed me through tired eyes. "That's a reasonable explanation, isn't it?"

"Not if you'd seen his face." I set the cup aside, realizing my own hands had started to tremble. "You've known him far longer than I have. Why do you think he clings so rigidly to his disbelief? Why can't he allow for even the slightest possibility that there are things in this world that can't be explained? He hasn't always been like that, surely. He would never have been involved with the Institute if he hadn't at least been curious. It's almost as if he experienced something terrifying in his past, something he may not even remember, and now he uses his denial as a means of protection."

"I can't answer those questions, Amelia. That is something for you and John to work out. But perhaps I've given you the wrong impression about his time at the Institute. Even back then he was a skeptic."

"You once told me he was one of your best investigators."

"Precisely because of his incredulity. I'm sure that trait also serves him well in his police work." Dr. Shaw grew pensive. "I will say this, though. Losing a child can change you in ways you never could have imagined. In essence, the person you were dies, too, making it easy to turn your back on whatever beliefs you once held."

I sat quietly riveted. I could never fully understand what he and Devlin had gone through, but at times their pain seemed tangible, as if I could reach out and pull the hollow ache of their loss into my own chest.

Dr. Shaw absently twisted his pinky ring, and for a moment I was mesmerized by the play of light on the emblem. It was the same symbol that Devlin wore around his neck. Dr. Shaw had never spoken of his affiliation with the mysterious Order of the Coffin and the Claw, but I had no doubt that both he and his son, Ethan, had been members.

"John was always a skeptic," Dr. Shaw continued. "But he also had the kind of sensitivity I've rarely come across in my line of exploration."

"Sensitivity to what?" I asked.

"People, places." Dr. Shaw shrugged. "Perhaps what you witnessed last night was a reawakening of sorts. An unconscious prod by an intuition he long ago buried. But I would caution you about putting too much emphasis on that one incident or pushing him beyond his comfort zone. Whatever he experienced, he obviously needs time to process it."

"Yes, I'm sure that's true. It's strange that we should be talking about his time at the Institute. He mentioned it himself this morning and that's so unlike him. He almost never talks about his past. There's still so much about his life that remains a mystery to me." I paused. "Do you know anything about his grandfather?"

"Our paths have crossed on occasion." I waited for him to elaborate, but he merely frowned.

"And?"

"From what I've observed, he's a cold and imperious man. A bit old guard for my taste."

"Do you know anything about the Devlin family history?"

"Only that they are one of the oldest and most influential families in Charleston and Jonathan Devlin would be the last to let you forget it." Dr. Shaw observed me from across the table. "Why the sudden interest in John's lineage?"

"I overheard something recently. But…it's not important. I shouldn't bother you with so many questions when you obviously need your rest." I stood. "Are you sure there's nothing I can get you before I leave?"

"I'll be fine." He started to rise to see me out, but I waved him back down. He sank heavily onto the chair as though the feeble effort had exhausted him. "Be careful at the cemetery today. My own intuition is telling me that things are apt to get darker before this is over. Even with John at your side, I can't help worrying about you."

"You just rest," I said. "John and I will take every precaution."

But my trepidation only mounted as Devlin and I neared the cemetery a little while later. I gripped the steering wheel tightly as we bumped along the trail and the woods seemed to close in on us. I didn't see or hear anything untoward, but I knew the ghosts were waiting. I knew the entity watched us from the shadows.

Devlin could feel the oppression of those woods, too. I sensed a building tension as he stared out the window. I would have liked nothing more than to slip inside his head and prowl through his past, but I'd made an important discovery during those hours when sleep had eluded me. I couldn't call upon the ability at will. I had no control over when and where it happened. On both occasions when I'd been able to penetrate his memories, I'd been touching the medallion, which led me to wonder if the power lay within the metal or emblem rather than inside me.

I shot him a glance, but his gaze remained fixed on the passing scenery. In the instant before I turned back to the road, I thought about Dr. Shaw's suggestion that Devlin might be going through a reawakening. A renewed sensitivity to people and places. Maybe that explained why he considered last night's encounter nothing more than a shared delusion. Rather than seeing or sensing the entity for himself, he'd somehow experienced it through me.

Open your eyes, Jack. Use your instincts. You know what she is.

"What did you say?"

I glanced at him, startled. "I didn't say anything."

He gave me a silent appraisal. "How much farther?"

"It's just ahead. Another ten minutes, maybe."

He scanned the road in front of us. "I'd forgotten how remote this place is. How thick the woods are. The timber alone must be worth a fortune. No wonder

Micah Durant is so protective of his grandmother's property. Makes me wonder if he already has a buyer lined up. Maybe that's why he's so keen on chasing you off."

"Or maybe he just likes causing trouble," I said.

"A malcontent," Devlin said. "I've run across a few of those in my time."

My blood went suddenly cold. "I've never heard you use that term before."

"It fits, doesn't it? Dr. Shaw told me that Durant has been in and out of trouble since boyhood."

"Yes, it fits," I said slowly as my hand lifted to Rose's key.

I thought about that shadow creeping up the wall last night and the footsteps outside the window. Maybe the malcontent hadn't followed me through the maze after all. Perhaps someone had brought it to the cottage last night and released it into the bedroom to wreak havoc.

"Now we go the rest of the way on foot," I said as we came to the end of the road. I killed the engine and we both climbed out of the vehicle.

"It's hot out here," Devlin said. "But at least there's still a breeze."

Yes, that breeze, I thought with a shudder as we sprayed ourselves with mosquito repellant. The wind seemed heavy and unnatural. The voices in my head had gone eerily silent, but the ghosts were still there. I could *feel* them. They knew I was coming and so did the entity.

"Which way?" Devlin asked.

"Follow me." I took the lead as we walked single file along the trail through the woods. Every now and then I paused to listen as tiny claws foraged in the underbrush or a flock of birds took flight. I wanted to believe the animal activity was a good sign. If something evil skulked in the forest, the living creatures would surely have fled.

But as soon as we left the trees and entered the maze, I grew nervous and claustrophobic. I didn't like the notion of being trapped inside those impenetrable hedges. We had gone no distance at all when I heard the snap of a twig somewhere behind us.

I drew up short and strained to listen. Was that the thud of stealthy footfalls behind us? The scrape of limbs, the rustle of fabric?

I thought of Micah Durant and his bees and how easy it would be for him to let loose a colony inside the maze.

"What's wrong?" Devlin asked.

"I thought I heard a twig snap."

He lifted his head, senses on full alert as he swept the narrow pathway behind us. "We should keep going. We'll have a better view of our surroundings in the cemetery. If someone comes through the gate or over the wall, we'll have ample warning."

I nodded. "Just in case we get separated in here, always bear left even when your instincts tell you to go right. You'll eventually come out at the cemetery gate."

"We won't get separated," Devlin said, but even the metallic click of his weapon as he checked the cartridge failed to reassure me.

* * *

We were both perspiring by the time we approached the vine-shrouded gate. The day seemed abnormally humid and I could feel static in the air even though there wasn't a cloud in the sky.

Devlin warily scanned our surroundings. "Place looks deserted. And just as creepy as I remembered it."

"Wait until we get inside."

We stepped through the gate and the surreal beauty of Kroll Cemetery struck me anew. As we hovered at the entrance, a hush fell over the graves and I once again had that strange sensation of floating, of time stopping. But despite the outward calm, I could feel the stir of restless energy all around us.

"I must have been here at a different time of day when I was a kid. I would have remembered the light," Devlin said. "The way it shines down through all those cicada shells is extraordinary."

"Like the whole cemetery is suspended in amber."

"Or trapped in time. It's a little unsettling," he admitted.

I watched him for a moment as I once again returned to my conversation with Dr. Shaw. Was it possible Devlin was undergoing his own transformation? Approaching his own crossroads?

I didn't want to dwell on the consequences of such a metamorphosis so I shoved the notion aside and turned down one of the pathways. "I think Rose's grave is this way."

We made our way through the headstones, pausing now and then to examine a key engraving or to read a name aloud. When we finally located Rose's grave site, I moved to the opposite side so that we both had a clear view of the inscription.

Kneeling, I ran my hand over the top of the marker. "This is the shadow we saw in Dr. Shaw's photo, remember? We wondered if it was a photographic artifact or an anomaly in the stone. But as you can see, the markings are braille."

"She was blind?" Devlin crouched across from me. "Has anyone said how she died?"

"Yes. It's a horrific story," I said, fighting back a wave of inexplicable sadness. My great-grandmother had died long before I'd been born, but I wondered now if she had always been with me, an ethereal guardian drifting in and out of my life. Waiting, sensing, perhaps leaving a key necklace on a headstone for me to find. I hadn't been able to see her, but I'd picked up on her feelings of loneliness and isolation. The terrible sense of loss that had lingered after Ezra Kroll's passing.

I tried to shake off the melancholy as I stared down at her grave. "Nelda Toombs said she found Rose hanged in her home. She was still clutching a key that she'd used to put out her eyes."

Devlin's shocked gaze met mine. "That is horrible. Suicide is one thing, but self-mutilation to that extent is rare. What could have driven her to do such a thing?"

"Apparently, she'd been ill for some time."

"Was she being treated?"

"I doubt it. At least not in any meaningful way. She probably didn't even realize anything was wrong until it was too late."

Devlin's gaze was still on me, but he was silent for

a very long time. I could only imagine what must be going through his mind. Was he recalling my strange behavior of late? Was he thinking about the incident last night and my obsession with Kroll Cemetery? Was he putting two and two together and wondering whether or not Rose's illness had been passed down to me?

"I think she blinded herself because of something she saw," I said. "Something she couldn't accept."

"Do you think she witnessed what happened at Kroll Colony?"

"Either saw or figured it out. And she left clues here in this cemetery."

"That's a lot of trouble to go to," Devlin said. "Why not tell the police?"

"Maybe she was afraid to. After Ezra Kroll died, she would have had no one to protect her. Imagine how alone and vulnerable she must have felt."

"Have you been able to translate the braille?" Devlin asked.

"Yes, it's from an old poem." I removed my phone and read from Dr. Shaw's email:

"O calm and sacred bed, where lies
In death's dark mysteries
A beauty far more bright
Than the noon's cloudless light."

"Death's dark mysteries. Noon's cloudless light." He shrugged. "Seems an obvious reference to what happened at Kroll Colony. The colonists died during the noonday meal."

"Then, why hide the lines in braille when the time of the event had already been established? If Rose blinded herself on the same day she died, she must have already made arrangements for the headstone. She would have had to plan everything months in advance."

"Or someone did."

I glanced up. "You think she was murdered? You think her killer arranged for her headstone?"

"I don't know about the headstone. But if Rose knew something about the deaths at Kroll Colony, I'd say murder is a distinct possibility. The mutilation… The blindness…" He stared down at the inscription. "Seems like a warning to me."

"A warning? Then, why kill her so quickly?"

"Not a warning to Rose, but for anyone else who might have known what she knew."

Or someone who might come along and try to solve her puzzle.

"That's a disturbing theory," I said with a shiver.

"More disturbing than blinding herself?" Devlin asked. "I'd say both scenarios are equally grim."

I glanced out over the whimsical cemetery, letting Rose slip into my head as my gaze traveled from gravestone to gravestone. I thought about all those keys and numbers she'd left behind and her fascination for photography and stereoscopy. I pictured her crouched and scribbling in her sanctuary while the keys tinkled overhead. Cowering in that tiny dark room as something prowled the shadows beneath her house.

That tiny dark room…

Darkroom. Dark...room.

Just like that, a puzzle piece clicked into place and the revelation set my heart to pounding. How had I not seen it before? The answer had been right in front of me as I'd huddled in Rose's sanctuary. *A beauty far more bright than the noon's cloudless light.*

Forty-Five

I felt an urgency to return to Rose's house at once, but if my calculations proved correct, we still had plenty of time. Rather than unveiling my revelation prematurely, I decided we should use the interval to explore Kroll Cemetery. Devlin sensed something was up. I could feel his curious gaze on me from time to time as we roamed the overgrown pathways.

As the hour approached, I took his hand and led him back into the maze. I'd always had a reliable sense of direction and I seemed to have instinctively committed the layout to memory. We followed a northerly course and after a false turn or two, eventually came to the entrance that opened into Rose's overgrown yard.

"Have you been here before?" I asked as we stood gazing up at the house.

He shook his head. "I don't think so. We explored the ruins of the Colony pretty thoroughly back then, but I don't remember stumbling across this place."

"It wasn't part of the Colony. This was Rose's house. Ezra allowed her to live here in exchange for tutoring the twins."

"I take it you've already been inside." Devlin's voice

held a note of censure as he scanned the tumbledown structure. "Looks dangerous. No wonder Dr. Shaw was so worried. The whole place could have come down on top of you."

"It's sturdier than it looks. Come on."

He followed me to the back of the house, where we paused once again so that he could reconnoiter. I could hear the eerie squeak of the weather vane on the outbuilding, and the sound raised goose bumps as my gaze dropped to the enclosure around the house. We seemed a million miles away from civilization, but I worried we weren't alone.

"Smells as though something crawled up under there and died." Devlin hunkered down to peer between the steps. "That's a strange place for a gate. It's barely accessible."

I tried to rub away the chill bumps. "It's a strange place for a fence, if you ask me."

"It wasn't uncommon to use the space beneath these old, raised houses for storage." Before I knew what he was about, he dropped to his hands and knees and crawled up under the steps.

"What are you doing?" I asked in alarm.

"Just having a look around." He withdrew the penlight from his pocket and angled the light toward the gate.

"Can you see anything?"

He voice came back muffled. "Not much. A bunch of boxes and trunks. Some kind of metal contraption." He shook the fence. "There's an old rusted lock on the gate."

"Please don't try to get inside," I said uneasily. "And

please stop rattling the fence. No point in announcing our presence." Although I had no doubt that if the malcontent lurked in the shadows beneath the porch, it was well aware of our arrival.

Devlin backed out from under the steps and dusted his hands on his pants as he stood. "Relax," he said. "There's nothing under there that can hurt us."

"I wouldn't be so sure," I muttered.

"Should I check all around the house? Would that put your mind at ease?"

"Let's just go inside. What time is it anyway?"

"Almost eleven. Still over an hour until noon if you're going by the poem."

"But we're in daylight saving time. If I remember my state history correctly, South Carolina reverted to standard time after World War II. Which means if we were back in Rose's day, the time would be nearing on noon. And as luck would have it, the sky is cloudless."

"So we are here because of the poem," he said.

"Yes, but the time doesn't have anything to do with what happened at the Colony. I believe it's a reference to what happens every day in Rose's dark room. Dark room. Two words."

This seemed to pique his interest. "Let's have a look, then."

We went up the back steps and entered the shadowy house. We moved stealthily, but every pop and creak reminded me of the lurking presence beneath the rotting floorboards. I shuddered to think what would happen if one of us fell through.

Removing the brass key from my pocket, I opened

the door beneath the stairs and then paused to listen as a draft stirred the keys inside.

Devlin came up behind me. "How is it you have a key to that lock?"

"It's a long story and we don't have much time. I'll tell you whatever you want to know later, but right now we need to get settled."

"So mysterious," Devlin murmured, but I could hear the anticipation in his voice. The discovery excited me, too, but I'd been in Rose's sanctuary before. I knew what might be waiting for us in the dark.

Devlin played the penlight over the walls as he walked around the room. I took out my larger flashlight and tapped on the bulb.

"Any idea what these numbers mean?" he asked.

"I'm pretty sure I know of one purpose. That's why we're here. But as to the larger picture, I wonder if the walls are a map of some sort."

"To what?"

"I've no idea. It's just a theory." A far-fetched one at that, but a part of me couldn't help wondering if the numbers could somehow lead me to Rose's long-lost key. As much as I tried to dissuade myself from giving credence to Nelda's story about a sister key that could lock the door to the dead world forever, the hope continued to burn that one day this might all be over.

I let my gaze travel around the space, searching the corners for lurking shadows. "To the right of where you're standing, you can see sunlight streaming in through a tiny hole in the wall. The opening is an aperture. This whole room is a camera obscura."

"Camera obscura?"

"It means dark room in Latin."

Devlin placed his hand in front of the beam, temporarily blocking the light. "It's like a pinhole camera."

"Yes, exactly. Except on a large scale. Do you have your phone handy? We need an alarm for straight-up eleven our time." Once he'd set the timer, I nodded. "As soon as I close the door, turn off your flashlight and put away your phone so the display doesn't shine into the room. We'll need enough time for our eyes to become accustomed to the dark before the alarm goes off."

I shut the door, we doused our torches and darkness descended. I felt my way across the room to Devlin.

"Steady," he said as he took my arms.

I put my hand against his chest and felt his heartbeat. It was only slightly elevated whereas my own heart thudded painfully. I didn't sense another presence in the room or beneath the floorboards, but the malcontent's absence worried me. Where was the entity and what did it have planned for us?

By the time the ringer sounded, my eyes had sufficiently adjusted to the gloom so that I saw what appeared to be the roofline of the outbuilding upside down on the wall. The weather vane mounted on the peaked roof served as a pointer. I watched in fascination as the inverted finial came to rest on the wall of numbers.

On the number seven to be precise.

Forty-Six

"How could you possibly know that would happen?" Devlin asked in awe. We were still sitting in the dark watching the pointer hover over the number seven.

"I didn't. But I knew the time in the poem meant something important."

"But the poem doesn't take into account the position of the sun at various times of the year. Tell me how you knew that would happen *today*," he insisted.

"I knew because Rose knew."

"Rose is dead. She's been dead for decades." His voice held a strained, hushed quality that made me shiver.

"There's a reason I was drawn to this place at this particular time. None of this is coincidental. Don't you see? Rose summoned me here so that I could find this."

"Amelia—"

"I know you don't believe me, but I can prove it. Let's go back to the cemetery and find the number on a headstone. If nothing's there, then maybe I'm wrong. But if we uncover another clue…"

He rose and pulled me to my feet. "Then what? Where does it end?"

"When the puzzle is solved." When the murderer was revealed and the ghosts were finally free. Only then would my great-grandmother be able to rest in peace.

A few minutes later, we were back in the cemetery and had located the corresponding headstone. Like all the other markers, the number was etched into the face, but I could detect nothing extraordinary about the grave or the monument. The name in the inscription meant nothing to me. The deceased was but one of three dozen colonists whose lives had abruptly ended on that fateful day.

I dropped to the ground beside the grave, tracing the symbols with my fingertip as I searched for the next clue. Devlin knelt on the other side and smoothed his hand over the surface of the stone.

"Do you feel anything?" I asked.

"No, do you?"

"There's something strange about the key engraving," I said. "The bow looks a bit like an eye. And see those three tiny perforations? I believe that's a keyhole."

I removed the strange eye key from my pocket and held it in my palm for a moment.

"Another long story?" Devlin's gaze was dark and inquiring.

You have no idea, I thought as I wordlessly inserted the pointed teeth into the punctures and felt something catch. The tumblers clicked and then Devlin and I watched in fascination as a compartment slid open at the base of the headstone.

"Now do you believe me?" I asked.

He glanced up. "Have you ever seen anything like this?"

"Yes, but usually in older graveyards. Hidden compartments in coffins and tombs were once very common. They were used to keep grave robbers from finding valuables buried with the deceased."

Devlin removed a small pouch from the space and handed it across the grave to me. "You should do the honors."

I didn't know what I expected to find. A part of me had been hoping that Rose had squirreled away her long-lost key inside. I tried to tamp down my disappointment as I withdrew yet another stereogram.

Devlin came around the grave to examine the card over my shoulder. "Is that who I think it is?"

"It's Nelda Toombs. The photos must have been taken not long after Mott died. Look at her awkward posture and the odd angle of her body. It's almost as if her sister were still attached to her."

"Maybe after the surgery she experienced something akin to the phantom-limb syndrome." Devlin cocked his head as he studied the dual images. "The composition seems off. Nelda is standing far to the side, but there's nothing else in the frame except the house in the background."

"That's because Nelda wasn't the focal point," I said. "At least, I don't think she was. I found a stack of similar stereograms in Rose's dark room yesterday. They were all shots of her house taken from different angles at various times of day. I know this sound strange. Unbelievable even. But I think Rose was try ing to capture a three-dimensional image of somethin; that couldn't be seen with the naked eye or even in . regular photograph. Something she'd trapped beneat! her house."

Devlin didn't say anything to that, but he must hav again wondered if I'd taken leave of my senses. I coul hardly blame him. I sounded unbalanced even to m' own ears, but for once, his incredulity didn't thwar me. I plunged on, speaking almost to myself as I trie to work it all out. "I thought she'd installed the enclo sure around the house to keep the entity inside, bu that doesn't make sense because what we encountere last night had no real form or substance. She mus have had another means of containing or controllin; it." My hand strayed to the skeleton key around m' neck. "The fence was never meant to keep the entity in, but to keep the unsuspecting out."

"The unsuspecting?" he asked in the same carefu voice I'd heard earlier on the porch.

"Rose knew the entity preyed on the weak and the innocent, and there were children living nearby ir Kroll Colony. All it would have taken was a taunt o a dare for one of them to crawl up under the house."

Devlin placed his hands on my shoulders and turnec me to face him. "That's an interesting theory, but you know it's based on nothing more than imagination anc conjecture, right?"

"Then, how do you explain the timing of my visit' How do you explain what we saw in the dark roon and what we found in the cemetery?"

"I can't. But I refuse to buy into this fantasy you've hobbled together from an inscription on an old headstone and your great-grandmother's bizarre obsessions. Not to mention the general creepiness of this place. It's not real, Amelia. None of this is real."

So many things went through my mind at that moment. I might have told him I knew he'd said something similar to his grandfather recently because I had the ability to invade his memories and eavesdrop on his past. I might have reminded him that despite his adamant refusal to believe in the unknown, he'd had an encounter with his daughter's ghost only moments before he'd been shot last fall. I might have confided in him about my gift and my legacy and a growing fear of where all of this might lead us.

I might have told him any number of things that would have irrevocably changed the course of our relationship forever. But the sound of a ringtone interrupted me. Or at the very least, delayed me.

We both glanced at our displays.

"That's you," Devlin said, and I lifted the phone to my ear.

"Amelia Gray?" a tentative voice inquired.

"Yes?"

"This is Nelda… Neddy. I got your number from Dr. Shaw. I'm sorry to be the bearer of bad news, but I thought you'd want to know that he's been rushed to the hospital. The ambulance just left a little while ago." She paused. "I don't mean to alarm you, but he was very pale and he couldn't seem to catch his breath."

"No, no, I'm glad you called me. What's the name of the hospital?"

"County General. It's on Main Street. You can't miss it."

"I'm on my way," I told her.

"What is it?" Devlin asked when I ended the call.

"Dr. Shaw's been taken to the hospital. I don't know how bad he is, but Nelda sounded worried. We have to get back to town at once."

"Of course." He nodded toward the stereogram I still clutched in my hand. "Should I put that back where we found it?"

I hesitated. "I need to study it through a viewer first."

He knelt and closed the compartment while I stored the card in my backpack. As we hurried through the cemetery gate, Papa's warning rang in my ears, and I couldn't help but wonder about the consequences of breaking yet another of his rules.

Take nothing, leave nothing behind.

All the way to the hospital, I kept picturing Dr. Shaw lying prone in a hospital bed, pale, unconscious and hooked up to all manner of wires and tubes. Instead, I found him sitting up in bed in a private room with a single IV connected to the vein in the back of his hand.

"I'm sorry to have worried you," he said. "I'm still undergoing some tests, but the main culprit seems to be dehydration."

"That's nothing to take lightly," I said. "I'm glad Nelda was there to call an ambulance."

"Yes, she was quite distressed. Please let her know that I'm fine."

"I will."

He leaned back against the pillow and closed his eyes. "Tell me about your morning at the cemetery."

"I'll tell you all about that later, but right now you need to rest."

He nodded weakly. "I am very tired."

"Then, sleep. I'll be right outside if you need me."

I found Devlin—phone to ear—pacing in the courtyard off the waiting room. He looked agitated and angry, but a mask descended as soon as he saw me. He put away the phone as I approached. "How is he?"

"The doctors are still running some tests, but they think he's suffering from dehydration, probably from all the hours in the sun over the past couple of days. He's not used to the heat. He's feeling better but still pretty weak. I'd like to stay here with him just to make sure he's okay."

Devlin nodded. "That sounds like a good idea. I wish I could stay, too, but something's come up. I have to get back to Charleston."

I noticed the worry lines across his brow then and the shadow that darkened his eyes. "Is everything okay?" I asked anxiously.

He glanced away as he seemed to gather his thoughts. "My grandfather has disappeared."

His calm manner of delivering the news was almost as disturbing as the revelation. "Disappeared? From the hospital?"

"No. He talked his doctor into releasing him yesterday afternoon, and he insisted on going back to the beach house. Apparently, when his assistant went to check on him this morning, he wasn't in his room. She and the others searched the house and grounds before calling the police."

"Why didn't they call you?"

"I doubt I'm high on his contact list."

"No one has any idea why he left? Or where he might have gone?"

"There was no sign of a struggle and no reason to suspect foul play. The best anyone can tell, he got up this morning, walked out the door without being detected and vanished."

"What about his car?"

"None of the vehicles are missing, nor was his driver notified. It's possible he called a taxi or had someone pick him up. It's also possible this could be another of his manipulations. He hasn't had much luck getting me to come around to his way of thinking, so he could be trying a different tactic."

"You don't really believe that, do you?"

"If you knew my grandfather, you wouldn't ask that question," Devlin said. "But in any case, I have to go."

"Of course. You'll let me know as soon as you hear anything?"

"Yes. And when I come back…" There was a slight hesitation before he said, "We need to talk."

My heart turned over at the look on his face. After everything he'd seen and heard since his arrival last night, I couldn't blame him for needing answers or for questioning my sanity. I wanted to assure him that all would be well, but I had my own doubts so I merely nodded.

Devlin was still staring down at me. "What you said earlier in the cemetery is eerily reminiscent of

e things my grandfather has been saying lately. Yet
e two of you have never met."

"What do you mean?"

"Ghosts. Demons." He shook his head as his gaze
:epened. "I still can't give credence to any of it, but
also can't deny that something strange is going on.
ntil I can figure out what he's up to, I need you to
omise me you'll be careful. I'll be back as soon as
:an, hopefully by nightfall. In the meantime, just sit
ght. Don't go back out to the cemetery or to Rose's
ouse alone. It's not safe."

I nodded vaguely as my mind churned with more
uestions. What had his grandfather told him about
hosts and demons? And how could any of it possibly
e connected to me?

Forty-Seven

Dr. Shaw was dozing when I came back into h
room. I slipped quietly into the chair beside his be
and opened the paperback novel I'd found in the wai
ing room. Perhaps it was the sleepless night I'd spe
or the pressure I'd been feeling for days, but I foun
myself growing drowsy as I tried to make sense of th
story. Twice I nodded off only to jerk myself awak
The second time I opened my eyes, I found Dr. Sha
watching me.

"I thought you'd gone," he said.

I set the book aside and tried to shake off the gro
giness as I got up to fuss with his covers. "I've bee
here the whole time. Can I get you anything?"

"No, I'm fine, my dear. I'm still feeling a bit dor
in. I think I may try to go back to sleep for a while.

"That's an excellent idea. I'll be right here whe
you wake up."

He reached for my hand. "There's something I mu
tell you first. Something you need to know."

"What is it?" He motioned for me to come closer.
sat down on the edge of his bed and leaned in. "Wh
is it, Dr. Shaw?"

His skin felt icy as his fingers closed around mine. wanted to pull away, but I was afraid of upsetting m. "You have to go back."

The urgency in his voice startled me. "Where? To arleston?"

"To the cemetery. You have to find a way to free em."

My breath caught at the look on his face. "The osts?"

"Think how long they've been waiting. How long e've all been waiting for you." His eyes glazed and s voice softened. The chill of death descended and I gan to tremble because I knew that I was no longer eaking to Dr. Shaw. I tried to wrench myself free, t those glacial fingers tightened around me. "You're e last of us, child."

My heart pounded so hard I actually felt faint. What do you mean? The last of who…what?"

"The Wysongs. The chosen."

Something fearful skittered down my backbone and hivered.

"You've always known you were different. You've ways felt the ghosts even when you couldn't see em. Now as you come into your own and your en- gy strengthens, more and more will come, drawn · your light and the promise of release. Others will me, too, child. The pernicious and the sly. They will so be lured by your light, but the dark ones will seek destroy the very thing that attracts them."

I thought of the entity beneath Rose's house, the el of its phantom fingers in my hair, the taunt of its ostly tongue against my face. I drew a shuddering breath. "Why are you telling me this? What is it you want me to do?"

"You must hunt them down, the dark ones. You must find a way to contain them."

"How?"

"Use the key. Study the stereogram. Let the numbers guide you."

I jumped and startled myself awake. The book slipped to the floor with a thud and I looked around in confusion.

A nurse stood at the side of the bed writing something in Dr. Shaw's chart. She smiled when she saw that I was awake. "I didn't mean to scare you," she said. "You were both sleeping so peacefully I was hoping not to disturb you."

I sat up in the chair. "What time is it?"

"A little after five. Are you all right? You seem disoriented."

"Still half-asleep, I guess."

"Why don't you take a walk and stretch your legs. We'll be bringing the dinner trays in soon. Maybe you'd like to go down to the cafeteria and grab a bite. You don't need to worry about Dr. Shaw. He's in good hands."

"Thanks." As I reached down to pick up my backpack from the floor, I thought of the stereogram that Devlin and I had found in the headstone.

Use the key. Study the stereogram. Let the numbers guide you.

My gaze shot to Dr. Shaw. Had I dreamed the conversation or had Rose somehow spoken to me through my old friend?

As I hovered at his bedside, he opened his eyes and smiled up at me.

Forty-Eight

I had every intention of following the nurse's advice and grabbing an early dinner in the cafeteria before returning to Dr. Shaw's room. Instead, I found myself driving back to the guest cottage to collect the viewer that Nelda had given to me the day before. I'd promised Devlin I wouldn't go back to the cemetery or to Rose's house alone, but I could at least study the stereogram we'd found.

I entered the main house first to give Nelda an update on Dr. Shaw's condition, but when I couldn't find her, I went out through the French doors and crossed the garden to the cottage.

Someone had been in to tidy up while we were out. The bed was made and fresh towels had been left in the bathroom. I couldn't imagine that Nelda did all the work herself, but as I moved about the tiny space I detected the faintest hint of cloves.

The cottage unsettled me so I snatched up the stereoscope and hurried back outside to sit in a patch of sunlight on the steps. I would linger only for a moment, I told myself. Just a quick look at the stereogram and then I'd drive back to the hospital.

I inserted the card in the holder and lifted the viewer to the light. As I searched the house in the background, I once again experienced the sensation of being watched. Shifting my focus to Nelda, I peered into her three-dimensional eyes and the feeling grew stronger. The intensity of her gaze startled me and my first instinct was to set the viewer aside. I wasn't certain I wanted to uncover whatever Rose had meant to reveal.

But the secret was right there in front of me. Literally staring me in the face. A mask had lifted when the shutter opened, allowing a glimpse of something feral in the curl of Nelda's lips, in the angry flare of her nostrils.

A breeze swept through the trees and as I looked up from the viewer, I saw the real, flesh-and-blood Nelda standing before me. She hovered in the shadows of her garden watching me.

"What has Rose left for you now?" she asked in a pleasant voice.

I didn't respond. I was still reeling from the weight of my discovery.

Placing one hand on top of the other, she leaned heavily on the head of her cane. A subtle change came over her features and I could see something cold and calculating in her eyes. "You don't know it," she said in a raspy voice. "The energy you call an entity. But it knows you."

Fear stole my breath as my heart began to pound. "Who are you?" I gasped, but I really didn't want to know the answer. "*What* are you?"

"Oh, I'm still Nelda. Only stronger and smarter.

A better Nelda, you might say." Her eyes cleared and her voice lightened. "My visitor is here, too. My dark caller. We've coexisted quite nicely all these years."

"How?"

"Oh, I think you already know the answer." Her lips curled again as she hobbled toward the steps, but I didn't feel threatened. Not at that moment. The entity that used Nelda Toombs as a conduit was limited by the constraints of her body. I could outrun her. I could get away whenever I wanted. Right now, I had a compulsion to hear what she—*it*—had to say.

"Rose has been waiting a long, long time for you to come into your own. We all have, I suppose. But for very different reasons."

"What do you mean?"

"The rules kept you safe even from Rose. So she waited until you were free of them and strong enough to help her. She was clever luring you here with that old stereogram. Very clever indeed."

"Did you send someone to break into my house to get it back? Why?"

"I had to find out what Rose was up to. I needed to know what she'd revealed to you in that image." Nelda cocked her head as she gazed up at me. "The resemblance still amazes me, but you're not as cunning or as clever as your great-grandmother. Truth be told, you're a bit dense about all this. But you're stronger than Rose ever was. You've got that going for you. I doubt you realize how much power you possess, let alone how to wield it. You're the only one left who can truly do us harm."

I clutched the viewer to my chest. "How can I harm

ou? By finding out the truth? Are you afraid of what
'll uncover in the cemetery? In Rose's house? Are you
vorried I'll reveal what you did to all those colonists?
'hat was you, wasn't it?"

A sly smile flashed. "That was *us*. The idea was
nine, though. It's what made me so desirable."

"Desirable?" I stared at her for the longest moment
s a revelation washed over me. "It was attracted to you
ecause of what was already inside you. Darkness…
vil…" I paused. "You let it in, didn't you? Your dark
aller. It didn't have to cajole or seduce or barter. You
vanted that thing inside you."

Impatience flared as her head came up. "Don't you
nderstand anything? It *chose* me. Not Rose, not Mott,
ot any of the others. *Me*." She put a foot on the bot-
om step and I caught a strong whiff of cloves. The
cent was overpoweringly sweet, but the spice couldn't
isguise the putrid essence of the malcontent inside
er. I rose and retreated to the porch.

She laughed. "Oh, are you afraid of me now? Imag-
ne that. Someone so young and vibrant threatened by
he likes of me."

"You enjoy that, don't you? Creating fear and chaos.
'ou thrive on negative emotions. Is that why you
vanted all those colonists dead?"

"What do you think, Amelia?"

My heart lurched at the sound of my name coming
rom her odious lips. I took another step back from
er. "I think there was another reason. You said the
lea was yours. You wanted them dead before the en-
ity possessed you. Why?"

"Why does it matter?" she returned.

"You were little more than a child at the time. What could have motivated you to do such a thing?"

"Very well, if you must know." She stirred restlessly as if bored by all my questions. Later I would realize that her apathy was only an act. My distress and curiosity must have been highly entertaining while she killed time waiting for her conspirator. "Ezra wanted to take Rose away from us. He wanted to leave the Colony and go somewhere new, make a fresh start. I couldn't allow that to happen. Rose was the only mother Mott and I knew. She was our protector. What do you think would have happened to us if she'd left? Louvenia would have undoubtedly placed us in a home or a hospital, where we would have been poked and prodded and stared at like some carnival sideshow attraction."

She climbed to the next step and paused in a beam of sunlight. I could see the entity clearly in her eyes now and in that rictus smile.

"Why kill all the colonists? Why not just Ezra?"

"Because *it* wanted me to. And because poison was so much easier for us to manage. A simple matter to take the container from the barn and sprinkle it into the food. Mott and I went to the Colony so often that no one paid us any mind that day."

"But Ezra wasn't there. He'd gone to see Rose."

"His absence made things more difficult, but not insurmountable, as you know."

"And Mott? Did she want him dead, too?"

Nelda sighed as a shadow flicked across her features. "My sweet little twin, always facing backward

Always at my mercy. Always wanting to see the best in people. She knew nothing until it was all over."

"But she must have known about Ezra. She was right *there*. Even if you managed to fool her about the poison, she would have heard the gunshot. She would have felt the recoil in her body."

Nelda nodded. "There was no help for that, I'm afraid. She was horribly upset, as you can imagine, but I convinced her to remain silent or we'd be put away. Still, it tormented her. She couldn't eat or sleep and I knew it was only a matter of time before she cracked, so she had to be gotten rid of, too."

"How?"

The eyes gleamed. "I drowned her like an unwanted puppy."

A shudder ran through me at the image. Poor Mott, trapped by the confines of her body and bound for eternity to the twin that had become a monster.

"You used cloves to cover the smell, but not from the decay of Mott's body. From the stench of the entity inside you."

"So you've finally figured it out. You've solved Rose's puzzle."

Despite her taunt, my mind was still working frantically to put it all together. To connect all the dots. "Rose knew about you, didn't she? She could see it inside you. So you blinded her. And then you killed her."

"She'd been slowly losing her sight for years. That's why she'd learned braille, in anticipation of her coming darkness. Given her gifts, perhaps she saw it as a blessing."

"Is that what you told yourself when you put ou[t] her eyes with that key?" I asked angrily.

Her eyes darkened. "You should have heeded th[e] warning. At least Louvenia was smart enough to sto[p] asking questions. But *you*. You had to keep digging You had to keep poking." She started up the steps using the cane for support. I backed away, keeping my distance, still certain that I could outrun her. Stil[l] certain I was in no immediate danger.

Suddenly, the door to the guest cottage flew ope[n] and the sound caught me by surprise. As I whirled to ward the newcomer, Nelda whipped the cane acros[s] my shins and I went down hard on the porch.

Then she struck me across the back. Still I tried t[o] rise. I even managed to get to my knees before a blow to the head flattened me.

"I'm surprised that one didn't kill her," Owe[n] Dowling said as he came to kneel beside me.

I tried to lift a hand to the explosion of pain at m[y] temple, but I couldn't muster the strength. I lay ther[e] paralyzed as the world spun around me.

"Take her phone," I heard Nelda say. "And that key around her neck…give it to me. Quick!"

The last thing I heard was Owen's chuckle. Th[e] last thing I felt was the ribbon sliding from my neck

Forty-Nine

I woke up in complete darkness with no sense of where I was. Disturbing images floated through my mind. The stereogram…the keys…all those numbers. Nelda staring up at me from the bottom of the porch. The door of the cottage flying open…a struggle…a blow to my head…an explosion of stars…

As I fought my way out of the confusion, I realized I was lying on my back in a very close space. I lifted my hands reflexively and discovered a flat surface only a few inches above me.

My first panicky thought was that I had been placed in a tomb or coffin, probably somewhere in Kroll Cemetery. A scream rose to my throat as I pressed against the lid with the heels of my hands and then pounded with my fists until my knuckles grew raw. I felt sick, disoriented and on the verge of a claustrophobic meltdown.

With an effort I forced myself to lie back and slow my breathing. *In…out. In…out. Don't think about the walls closing in on you. Don't think about the weight of a tomb pressing down on you. In…out. In…out.*

Once I felt calmer, I tried to take stock of my prison.

I wasn't in total darkness as I'd first thought. I could see the silhouette of my hand when I held it in front of me and I had a sense of space when I peered straight ahead or to the side. And I could feel a draft. Which likely meant I wasn't buried underground or enclosed in a tomb.

But that breeze carried a scent. A trace so foul that I thought at once of the odor wafting from beneath Rose's porch.

I knew where I was then. I was under Rose's house. Locked inside that strange fence where she'd once trapped the entity that now resided in Nelda Toombs's body.

Terror gripped me and I lashed out, kicking and pounding the floorboards in a blind frenzy. But the rotting planks held fast, and in a flash of reason, I realized that a dislodged support could bring the whole house down upon me.

I fell back against the ground, spent and shivering. I had to get control of my fear. Panic was the enemy. I'd been in close places before, dangerous places, and I was strong. Stronger than I even realized, Nelda had said. I could get out of here. All I had to do was remain calm. Concentrate. Make my way to the side of the house and find an opening.

Breathe. In...out. In...out.

And hurry.

I had no idea if Owen Dowling had left me there for dead or if he would return to finish me off. A vague recollection niggled. An overheard conversation so hazy I couldn't be sure it had really happened. I had been floating at the edge of consciousness. Dreaming, perhaps…

"*Is she dead?*"

"*No, there's a pulse.*"

"*You'll have to finish her off, then.*"

"*Oh, God, Auntie. I'm not cut out for this.*"

"*Do you want your money or don't you? And let me remind you, there are bigger stakes to consider. Once we take care of Louvenia, all of the Kroll holdings will someday be yours.*"

"*What about Micah? He won't just roll over and play dead, you know.*"

"*Micah will never again see the light of day once Louvenia's body is discovered. Why do you think I brought him back here? His troubled history makes him the perfect scapegoat. Now he can take the blame for Amelia's demise, as well. Everything is falling into place, nephew. You just have to do your part.*"

"*All right. Give me a minute—*"

"*Not here! That cop could come back at any minute. Take her out to Rose's house. There's a crawl space underneath. She won't be found until we've had time to set everything else in motion…*"

As the conversation faded, I came back to my original question. Had Owen left me for dead or would he return soon to finish the job? I had no weapon with which to defend myself. I'd been stripped of my phone, and the pepper spray was still in my backpack. I felt weak and disoriented. My head throbbed miserably. My whole body ached from the beating and perhaps from being dragged through the woods and the maze.

But I had to rally and get moving because my only hope was to be long gone if and when Owen returned.

Rolling to my stomach, I began easing my way over the hard ground. In such a confined space, I had no sense of direction and the discarded junk beneath the house obscured my view. All I could do was crawl toward the draft and hope that I could find the gate or another way through the barrier.

Gravel cut into my hands as I inched along. I paused to pick what I thought was a pebble from my palm, but the texture made me think of bone. I wouldn't dwell on that. Not now. I had to keep moving. I had to keep breathing. *In...out. In...out.*

An obstruction lay directly in front of me. I thought it was nothing more than a heap of old rags and I put out a tentative hand to shove them aside. Then I recoiled in horror. The barrier was a body.

My first thought was of Louvenia. Nelda and Owen had planned to do away with her and pin the blame on Micah. They must have gone through with their scheme, probably after dumping me here.

I eased back up to the body, running my hand along the motionless arm until I found her wrist. I couldn't feel a pulse, but in that moment of contact, the tingle of cloves on my tongue overwhelmed me.

I drew back in shock. The dead woman was not Louvenia after all, but Nelda. How she had ended up under the house I had no idea, but I could only surmise that Owen had betrayed her. Maybe he'd decided with both Nelda and Louvenia out of the way, the Kroll fortune would fall to him sooner.

Her skin was cooling but not cold. She couldn't have

been dead long. She may even have drawn her last breath while I lay unconscious only a few feet away.

As I lay there beside the body, a dreaded certainty washed over me. I wasn't alone. I could feel and smell a presence, though I couldn't see it. The entity was not unlike the one I'd encountered in Asher Falls. It was no longer a ghost, if it ever had been. It was colder and darker than any ghost. Negative energy that had evolved into pure evil. And it was there with me under Rose's house. At the moment of death, it had left Nelda's body and was now crouching in the gloom observing me.

The tingle of cloves faded as a hint of witch hazel wafted from the shadows. I could sense it moving closer, slithering unfettered through the piles of debris as it sniffed and circled, a netherworld predator on the hunt for a conduit. I still couldn't see it or hear it, but the underlying stench of its being overwhelmed me.

My hand flew to my chest, seeking Rose's key. It was gone, of course. Nelda had ordered Owen to take it from me. But he wouldn't have understood the significance unless she'd told him. Was it possible he'd left the key on her person? Could it still be in one of her pockets or around her neck?

Hope surged as I steeled my resolve, inching toward the body only to be propelled backward by an unnatural gust. I grabbed on to the nearest thing I could find, a wooden support beam, as that strange vortex swirled around me. Then the wind died away as suddenly as it had risen. I huddled in the dark, the air so stale and fetid I couldn't breathe without retching. The entity was right there, squatting beside me, touching my hair, running a finger down my arm as it tried to find a way inside me.

From outside the enclosure, I heard the abrasive rattle of a cicada. Almost at once, the entity retreated back into the shadows and I could sense its wariness. For whatever reason, it had a healthy respect for Mott's power.

I took advantage of the reprieve and eased back up to the body, running my hands over the stiffening torso, searching one pocket of Nelda's smock and then the other. I wanted to scream in frustration. *Where is it? Where is it?* But then as I jostled the body, I heard the faint tinkle of metal.

Mott's diversion had been momentary. Already I could feel the entity creeping back in as the smell grew stronger. It was coming for me. Getting nearer with each passing moment...

One hand pressed to my nose and mouth, I thrust the other hand back into Nelda's pocket, searching, searching until my fingers finally grasped the skeleton key.

I turned, clutching the key to my breast, but the talisman seemed to have no effect. Prowling and predatory, the malcontent kept coming. Closer and closer. Stroking its icy tentacles down my face, sliding feelers into my memories, seeking darkness or a weakness that would allow it to enter my soul.

I wanted nothing so much as to roll over and vomit up the filth of its presence, but something inside me held fast. I gathered my strength and every ounce of my courage. I would not let that thing in. I would not.

I sensed hesitation. Then frustration and rising anger.

The tentacles snaked around me, poking, prodding and then finding no way in, they withdrew. The odor faded. The entity hunkered there in the darkness, thwarted and enraged.

I kept moving. On and on until I reached the fence. Darkness had fallen outside and clouds drifted across the moon. I smelled rain in the air and I drew in a long, cleansing breath as I curled my fingers around the chain links and peered out. The maze was a dark outline against the horizon. I wanted to take comfort in the sight, but another scent drifted to me on the night air. *Smoke.*

The acrid smell was hardly discernible at first, but the scent grew stronger as the wind rose. I could see wisps drifting up into the sky, and a fresh terror seized me. I realized then why Owen hadn't bothered to finish me off. He'd intended all along to come back and burn down the house, turning the evidence of his dark deeds to ash along with Rose's numbers and keys. Along with any clues still undiscovered in her sanctuary.

I shook the fence in desperation and then lay on my back and tried to kick the supports loose. The enclosure held fast, and as smoke seeped down through the floorboards, hysteria bubbled.

Turning, I crawled along the edge of the house. The back porch lay straight ahead, but I felt certain Owen would have locked the gate. Still, I had to try.

Defeat bore down on me, and I could feel the en-

tity slithering back through the haze of smoke as i
attracted by a whiff of my vulnerability.

Think. *Think*. There had to be a way out.

The trio of keys had been left on my nightstand fo:
a reason. Each served an important purpose in solving
Rose's puzzle. The plain door key had allowed me en
trée into her sanctuary. The pointed teeth key had un
locked a secret compartment in Kroll Cemetery. The
skeleton key had the power to keep the ghosts at bay
but might it also serve a real-world purpose?

Even as all this flashed through my head, I was al
ready scrambling for the gate. With trembling fingers
I inserted the teeth into the keyhole. The rusty latch
clicked open and I crawled out of my prison as the
floorboards over my head began to pop from the heat

Fifty

I took only a moment to relock the gate and then I was up, half running, half stumbling away from the house. I could see smoke rolling from some of the broken windows. I didn't know if that was a good thing or not. If Rose's house burned to the ground, would the entity still be trapped or would it then be free to go in search of another conduit?

I still didn't understand how or why Rose had been able to confine the malcontent beneath her house. Somehow she must have used the skeleton key to contain it, but then Nelda had come along, hiding her own malicious nature beneath a vulnerable facade. She'd given the entity a way out once, but her death under the house had imprisoned it again.

I glanced over my shoulder as I ran and a dangerous thought came to me. Smoke billowed from the upstairs windows, but I couldn't yet see any flames. Rose's sanctuary might still be safe. All those numbers that she'd painstakingly scribbled on the walls…what if they really were map coordinates that could lead me to her long-lost key? To a future without ghosts and malcontents and those incessant voices in my head? How could I leave it all to burn? I needed to photograph those numbers, copy the map, do something, *anything* to preserve the clues that Rose had left for me.

Whether I would have had the nerve to enter the house, let alone Rose's sanctuary, I would never be certain. As I slowed my steps contemplating the fool-hardy move, Owen Dowling came around the corner of the house and stopped cold when he spotted me.

He had been carrying a gas can, but now he tossed it aside as he started toward me, slowly and deliberately at first and then accelerating as I backed away from him. I sensed no hesitation in him now. Gone was the reluctant man who had knelt at my side as his aunt had goaded him to violence.

Head lowered resolutely, he circled around to block me from the maze, where I might have been able to lose him. When I would have turned and darted toward the woods, he sprang forward with the same speed and agility that I'd witnessed from the intruder in my office.

I knew then that he had been the one to break into my home and attack me. Nelda had sent him to retrieve the stereoscope and card, and the adrenaline must have gotten the better of him. Or like Nelda, he knew how to hide his true nature.

I tried to dodge him, but shock and fear made me clumsy. I tripped over something in the weeds and before I could regain my balance, he lunged.

The momentum of his body knocked me to the ground and then he was on me in a flash, pinning my arms to my sides with his knees so that I could do nothing but thrash helplessly beneath him.

He was stronger that I would have guessed, or maybe my injuries had weakened me. No matter how hard I bucked and kicked, I couldn't dislodge him.

His hands closed around my throat and tightened. The pressure against my windpipe made my eyes feel as though they might pop from my head. The pain made me struggle even harder, but only for a moment. A dangerous lethargy crept over me and my muscles went limp. I was barely conscious now, but I could have sworn I heard someone call my name and then Owen's. A shot rang out and the pressure on my neck eased as Owen toppled backward.

The next thing I knew, Devlin was at my side. "Are you all right? Amelia, say something!"

I couldn't speak at first. My eyes still burned, and I put a hand to my aching throat as I gulped in air and coughed. "I'm okay," I finally croaked.

I tried to sit up, but Devlin pushed me gently back to the ground. "Take it easy. The police will be here soon and I've called for an ambulance."

I clutched his arm. "Owen—"

"He's alive, but he's not going anywhere." Devlin stroked a hand down the fading bruise on my cheek before gently tracing the fresh marks at my neck. "He won't be going anywhere for a long, long time, I promise you that."

"He was in on it with Nelda," I said. "It was her all along."

"Don't talk. We'll sort it out later. The only thing that matters right now is you."

I lay back and closed my eyes. I could feel moisture on my face and I thought at first it was tears, but then I realized it had started to rain. I rose up on my elbows to gaze at the burning house. "All those numbers and keys… I don't know yet what they mean. What if they really are clues or coordinates on a map?"

"Doesn't matter now," Devlin said. "It's too late. The place is gone."

"But—"

"Let it go, Amelia. It's over."

I might yet have struggled, but at that very moment, flames exploded through the upstairs windows and licked along the roofline. Devlin helped me to my feet and we took refuge at the edge of the maze as ash and embers swirled down upon us.

The rain was coming down harder now. It would protect the surrounding woods and the cemetery, but Devlin was right. The house was already gone.

Owen was wounded and Nelda was dead, but what about the entity? Was it trapped beneath the burning house or had it escaped? Was it out there even now, searching for another conduit?

I swept my gaze across the burning roof, over the yard and along the edge of the woods. As I peered into the trees, I realized with a start that something stared back at me.

I could just make out the hump on Mott's back as she separated from the shadows. She appeared to me as she had that day in Oak Grove Cemetery, a tiny, wizened in-between slinking through the darkness, turning to scrutinize me intently when she felt my gaze upon her. She watched me for the longest moment before throwing back her head and emitting that spine-tingling rattle.

Glancing up into the dripping trees, I wondered if she meant to summon the cicadas. Something blew toward me through the maze. An unnatural gust that whipped at my hair as I clutched Rose's key to my heart.

The voices in my head started to chatter, the sound ebbing and flowing as the wind undulated through the hedges. I could feel that strange suction, as if the ghosts of Kroll Cemetery were being inexorably pulled toward the light inside me. But I no longer felt resistance from the malcontent. Whether Nelda's dark visitor was gone for good, I had no idea. Maybe the ghosts had somehow overcome it in their frenzied quest for release.

On and on they came, the forgotten and forlorn. I could see them now, wispy and ethereal as they swept toward me. Sparks erupted over the treetops as the veil thinned and the dead world grew closer. The moment was strangely beautiful. Like nothing I had ever experienced. I was frightened and awestruck by the power of the release. And perhaps for the first time, humbled by my gift.

As the ghostly wave crashed over me, I thought for a moment I might be carried along with them to the afterlife. But the vertigo came and went quickly this time. The wind died away, the voices in my head faded and I felt a peaceful emptiness as I stood there with embers swirling overhead and raindrops clinging to my lashes.

When it was all over, when the last of them had finally crossed over, I glanced back at Mott, remembering what Dr. Shaw had suggested about her purpose. *If your calling is to help the dead move on, then maybe a being that is half in and half out is the means by which the door to the dead world can be opened.*

She turned toward the smoldering house, to the upstairs window where Rose's ghost still lingered. I could see the spirit of my great-grandmother clearly through the smoke. She was young again, her eyes restored now that Ezra and the colonists had been freed.

The wind wasn't as strong this time, nor was the suction. Their release was over in the space of a heartbeat. As Rose's form waned, Mott, too, began to wither, crumbling away to ashes that floated away on the breeze. But I somehow knew they were together. Walking hand in hand into the light.

I turned to Devlin, wondering if he had sensed any of what had just taken place, but his attention was riveted on the burning house.

I followed his gaze to the upstairs window where Rose's ghost had hovered only a moment ago. His features were frozen, utterly devoid of animation. But there was something disturbing about his stillness, something almost frightening about the look on his face. I had never seen him like that before.

"You saw her," I whispered.

He shifted his focus, staring down at me in the rain. I reached out a hand to him, but he backed away from my touch. His rejection was like an arrow through my heart.

In that moment, I knew for certain that something had changed between us. Something I still didn't understand. I felt cold all of a sudden and overwhelmed by the same feeling of loss that had plagued my dreams for weeks.

Fifty-One

The rest of the night passed in a blur. Once the local police and EMTs arrived on the scene, Devlin and I were quickly separated. I was taken first to the hospital and then later to police headquarters, where I gave a lengthy statement to one of the detectives assigned to the case.

The story sounded far-fetched even to my own ears, but surprisingly, Owen Dowling corroborated my account from his hospital bed. He admitted to his part in my assault and abduction, but he claimed that Nelda's death had been an accident. She'd lost her footing on the porch steps and the fall had broken her neck. He'd thought her dead when he'd put her underneath Rose's house—or so he claimed. Maybe he was savvy enough even after having been shot to try to avoid murder charges, but I tended to believe him. His tale of a wayward and impressionable boy being groomed from an early age to do Nelda's bidding held the ring of truth, especially given what I knew about her possession.

Louvenia Durant had also been called to the station, and I'd spoken to her briefly on my way out.

She'd been distraught by the evening's events, but not overly shocked. Her calm demeanor made me wonder if she'd suspected Nelda's role in the Kroll Colony tragedy all along. Maybe Louvenia's guilt for failing to protect her sisters had kept her silent and mentally fragile for decades.

Even so, she'd seemed as determined as ever to go through with the restoration. "It's the least I can do for those poor souls," she'd said, and I had sensed her pain so strongly that I'd offered to meet with her before I left town.

As for Micah Durant, he'd vanished before the police had had a chance to question him. Louvenia had appeared visibly relieved by her grandson's sudden departure, and given what I knew of *him*, I could hardly blame her.

After the police concluded the interviews, Devlin and I had found a nearby hotel room since the cottage was now a crime scene. Not that I would have wanted to go back there anyway. I was more than ready to put Nelda Toombs and her machinations behind me. Devlin must have felt the same way because we didn't talk much about what had transpired. We were both so mentally and physically exhausted by that time that we'd fallen asleep almost immediately. The next morning, he'd risen before me, having once again been summoned to the police station. After a cup of tea and a brief stop at the hospital to check on Dr. Shaw, who was thankfully on the mend, I'd set out for Kroll Cemetery alone.

And so here I was.

I welcomed the solitude of the cemetery. I needed

some time at Rose's graveside to try to process everything that had happened. To try to make sense of our connection. I still didn't completely understand my role in recent events. Nelda said that Rose had waited to make contact until the rules were broken, until I was strong enough to help her, but with what? Had she summoned me here to release all those lost souls? To uncover the real killer? Or had she wanted me to find and contain the entity?

Why had she left the skeleton key in Rosehill Cemetery all those years ago? Would it have protected me from the ghosts if I'd kept it or would it have opened the door to the dead world even sooner?

So many questions left unanswered.

Kneeling at her grave, I traced a finger along the braille inscription. Our journeys were still intertwined, but where did I go from here? Where did I search for clues now that her house was gone?

I felt oddly bereft by the loss. I still didn't know my purpose or place. The only thing I understood with any certainty was that my experiences in Kroll Cemetery had brought me closer to my destiny.

The back of my neck tingled and I lifted a hand to my nape. When I drew back my fingers, a honeybee clung to one of my knuckles. I gazed around warily, searching the darkest corners of the cemetery. My gaze lit on a shadow at the top of the wall, moved on and then darted back as my heart started to hammer.

Micah Durant crouched on top of the crumbling stones staring down at me through the amber glow of the cicada shells. As our gazes locked, I experienced the strangest chill at the small of my back, as though an icy fist had gripped my spine.

An errant shaft of sunlight set his silvery-gold hair ablaze and I was once again struck by his ethereal appearance. But beneath the angelic facade, I detected something feral in the curl of his lips, something dark and bestial in those colorless eyes.

I know you, I thought. *And you know me.*

His smile broadened as if he'd read my mind. He shifted on the wall, squatting in the gloom as his arms hung loosely in front of him. He made no effort to hide the entity inside him. To the contrary, the malcontent wanted me to know that it had found a willing new vessel.

I was unnerved by the encounter, but I wasn't afraid because I knew they meant me no harm. Not at that moment. Micah Durant and his dark visitor had come there to taunt me. To challenge me. *Come and find us if you dare.*

Someday, I silently promised.

"Amelia?"

I whirled at the sound of my name. I hadn't heard Devlin come through the gate and my heart thudded at the sight of him. When I turned back to the wall, Micah Durant had vanished.

"Are you all right?" Devlin asked as he approached. "What were you staring at so intently just now?"

"Micah Durant was here."

Devlin's voice sharpened as he scanned the area behind me. "Where is he?"

"He was sitting on the wall, but I think he must

have jumped down on the other side when he heard your voice."

"The police would like to have a word with him. So would I, for that matter," Devlin muttered as he started forward, but I stopped him.

"Don't bother. He knows this area too well. You won't find him unless he wants to be found."

"What did he want?" Devlin asked with a scowl.

"To let me know that he was still around."

His frown deepened. "I don't like the sound of that. He may not have been involved in Owen and Nelda's scheme, but he could still have his own reasons for wanting you out of this cemetery. I don't trust him."

"Nor do I, but he hasn't done anything illegal that we know of, so there's nothing we can do."

"There is one thing." Devlin's gaze swung back to me. I could see something dark in the depths of his eyes, a foreshadowing. "You can come back to Charleston with me this morning. Put this place behind you. You've accomplished what you set out to do."

"Have I?"

"You solved Rose's puzzle."

I drew a breath and nodded. "Part of it, yes. But there's still so much about my great-grandmother that I don't know. And anyway, I can't leave while Dr. Shaw's still in the hospital. He's much better this morning, but I still wouldn't feel right leaving him here alone. But if all goes well, we should both be back in Charleston soon, possibly as early as tonight."

"I'll be gone by then," Devlin said. "I'm only going back long enough to pack up a few things."

The look on his face sent the coldest chill cours-

ing through my veins. "Where are you going?" Then
something occurred to me. "Your grandfather… Has
something happened to him? Is he still missing?" I put
out a hand to touch his arm and I could have sworn
I felt him flinch. I lifted my gaze, studying his features for the longest moment before I let my hand drop
back to my side.

"My grandfather is back home safe and sound,"
Devlin said. "I have some things I need to take care
of, so I've asked for a leave of absence from the de-
partment."

"A leave of absence," I repeated numbly. "Just like
that?"

"It has to be this way."

"Why? What's going on? You can't just spring this
on me without an explanation." I didn't reach for him
again, but I wanted so badly for him to reach for *me*,
to draw me into his arms and tell me that my fear was
irrational. My premonition had no real basis. Everything was fine. We were fine. Instead, I found myself
withdrawing into my own lonely little world, as if I
could somehow protect myself from what was coming.

I wrapped my arms around my middle and glanced
away.

"Amelia."

The soft drawl of my name brought tears to my
eyes, but I blinked them away and sought refuge in my
anger. "How long have you known you were leaving?"

"The decision was made suddenly. I'm sorry I didn't
give you more warning. I didn't know myself until…"
He trailed off. "This is not how I wanted to tell you.
I thought we'd have more time—"

"Something's wrong. Something's happened that ou don't want me to know about. You don't make ecisions like this out of the blue. You're methodical nd stoic."

"Amelia…"

"This is about last night, isn't it? You saw Rose's host in that window. I know you did. You saw some- iing in the cottage that wasn't a shadow. Why won't ou just admit it?"

His gaze swept over the headstones before coming ack to settle on me. "I don't know what I saw. I'm not ure I can believe my own eyes anymore. All I know s that I can't be around this right now."

"Around me, you mean."

"The things I've learned about my grandfather and bout my family, about the expectations of my birth- ight. I don't know if I can accept what my grandfa- ier told me, or if I even believe him. But if a fraction f what he told me is true, I can't be with you right ow. It's too risky."

My anger instantly melted. "Risky? *Why?*"

Devlin hesitated. "There's a chance he's involved /ith some very bad people."

My heart started to pound in earnest at the look on is face. "What people?"

"The less you know, the better."

I took a step toward him, and this time he didn't iove away. He reached for me as my fingers slid up to ie hollow of his chest, tracing the medallion beneath is shirt. "I may already know more than you think."

"You don't. This goes much deeper than the Order f the Coffin and the Claw. You have no idea how dan-

gerous these people are." He took my forearms, grip
ping me so tightly for a moment that I winced. Th
pressure from his fingers eased, but the darkness i
his eyes held me enthralled.

"You're going after them," I said. "That's wh
you're taking a leave of absence. You don't want to b
encumbered by a badge for what you're about to do.

"I'm not going after them," he said in a strang
voice. "I'm going to join them."

I might have backed away from him then, but h
held me fast.

My finger was still on the medallion. I wanted t
trace the outline of the emblem until his thought
opened up to me, until I could slip into his memorie
and find out what had happened. Find out how I coul
help him. Stop him. But his mind remained closed t
me. Whether he'd done so consciously or not, he'
erected a wall to keep me out.

He drew me to him and I went easily into his arm:
"This isn't the end," I said fiercely.

"No." His gaze on me darkened. "I'm afraid it's ju
the beginning."

* * * * *

THE GRAVEYARD QUEEN *series continues*
with THE SINNER *by Amanda Stevens.*
Look for it wherever MIRA books are sold.

Discover the fifth book in *The Graveyard Queen*
series from award-winning author

AMANDA STEVENS

**Every cemetery has a story.
Every grave, its secrets.**

THE SINNER

My name is Amelia Gray—the Graveyard Queen.

I'm a cemetery restorer by trade, but my calling has evolved from
that of ghost seer to death walker to detective of lost souls. I solve the
riddles of the dead so the dead will leave me alone.

I've come to Seven Gates Cemetery nursing a broken heart, but
peace is hard to come by…for the ghosts here and for me. When the
body of a young woman is discovered in a caged grave, I know that
I've been summoned for a reason. Only I can unmask her killer. I
want to trust the detective assigned to the case, for he is a ghost seer
like me. But how can I put my faith in anyone when supernatural
forces are manipulating my every thought? When reality is
ever-changing? And when the one person I thought I could trust
above all others has turned into a diabolical stranger?

**Available September 27,
wherever books are sold!**

Be sure to connect with us at:
Harlequin.com/Newsletters
Facebook.com/HarlequinBooks
Twitter.com/HarlequinBooks

MIRA®

www.MIRABooks.com

MAS1784TALL

Discover the next spine-tingling
Krewe of Hunters tale
from *New York Times* bestselling author

HEATHER GRAHAM

Between the *evil* and the deep blue sea.

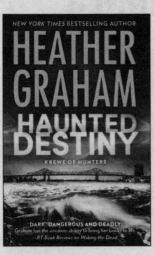

A historic cruise ship, a *haunted* ship, sets sail from the Port of New Orleans—with a killer on board. Known for displaying his victims in churches, with a different saint's medallion placed on each, he is called the Archangel Killer.

Jackson Crow—head of the FBI Krewe of Hunters, a special unit of paranormal investigators—is assigned to the case, along with local agent Jude McCoy.

Alexi Cromwell works in the ship's piano bar. She and Jude share an attraction, and not just because of their mutual talent. When a victim's ghost appears to her—and to Jude—they are forced to rely on each other to catch the killer…if they hope to save Alexi from his evil plans.

Available May 31, wherever books are sold

Be sure to connect with us at:
Harlequin.com/Newsletters
Facebook.com/HarlequinBooks
Twitter.com/HarlequinBooks

MIRA®

www.MIRABooks.co

MHG1895T

Lock the doors, draw the shades, pull up the covers and be prepared for *Thriller* to keep you up all night.

Edited by #1 *New York Times* Bestselling Author

JAMES PATTERSON

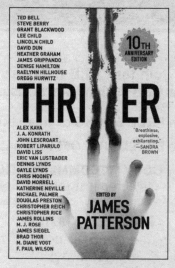

TED BELL
STEVE BERRY
GRANT BLACKWOOD
LEE CHILD
LINCOLN CHILD
DAVID DUN
HEATHER GRAHAM
JAMES GRIPPANDO
DENISE HAMILTON
RAELYNN HILLHOUSE
GREGG HURWITZ

10TH ANNIVERSARY EDITION

THRILLER

ALEX KAVA
J. A. KONRATH
JOHN LESCROART
ROBERT LIPARULO
DAVID LISS
ERIC VAN LUSTBADER
DENNIS LYNDS
GAYLE LYNDS
CHRIS MOONEY
DAVID MORRELL
KATHERINE NEVILLE
MICHAEL PALMER
DOUGLAS PRESTON
CHRISTOPHER REICH
CHRISTOPHER RICE
JAMES ROLLINS
M. J. ROSE
JAMES SIEGEL
BRAD THOR
M. DIANE VOGT
F. PAUL WILSON

"Breathless, explosive, exhilarating."
—SANDRA BROWN

EDITED BY
JAMES PATTERSON

Revisit these heart-pumping tales of suspense, including thirty-two of the most critically acclaimed and award-winning names in the business. From the signature characters that made such authors as David Morrell and John Lescroart famous to some of the hottest new voices in the genre, this blockbuster will tantalize and terrify.

Available April 26, wherever books are sold!

Be sure to connect with us at:
Harlequin.com/Newsletters
Facebook.com/HarlequinBooks
Twitter.com/HarlequinBooks

MIRA®

www.MIRABooks.com

MJP1957TALL

Turn your love of reading into
rewards you'll love with
Harlequin My Rewards

**Join for FREE today at
www.HarlequinMyRewards.com**

Earn **FREE BOOKS** of your choice.

Experience **EXCLUSIVE OFFERS** and contests.

Enjoy **BOOK RECOMMENDATIONS**
selected just for you.

PLUS! Sign up now
and get **500** points
right away!

Earn
FREE
REWARDS
Join
Today!
HarlequinMyRewards.com

MYR16RTALL

REQUEST YOUR FREE BOOKS!

2 FREE NOVELS
FROM THE SUSPENSE COLLECTION
PLUS 2 FREE GIFTS!

YES! Please send me 2 FREE novels from the Suspense Collection and my 2 FREE gifts (gifts are worth about $10). After receiving them, if I don't wish to receive any more books, I can return the shipping statement marked "cancel." If I don't cancel, I will receive 4 brand-new novels every month and be billed just $6.49 per book in the U.S. or $6.99 per book in Canada. That's a savings of at least 19% off the cover price. It's quite a bargain! Shipping and handling is just 50¢ per book in the U.S. and 75¢ per book in Canada.* I understand that accepting the 2 free books and gifts places me under no obligation to buy anything. I can always return a shipment and cancel at any time. Even if I never buy another book, the two free books and gifts are mine to keep forever.

191/391 MDN GH4Z

Name _____ (PLEASE PRINT) _____

Address _____ Apt. # _____

City _____ State/Prov. _____ Zip/Postal Code _____

Signature (if under 18, a parent or guardian must sign)

Mail to the **Reader Service:**
IN U.S.A.: P.O. Box 1867, Buffalo, NY 14240-1867
IN CANADA: P.O. Box 609, Fort Erie, Ontario L2A 5X3

Want to try two free books from another line?
Call 1-800-873-8635 or visit www.ReaderService.com.

* Terms and prices subject to change without notice. Prices do not include applicable taxes. Sales tax applicable in N.Y. Canadian residents will be charged applicable taxes. Offer not valid in Quebec. This offer is limited to one order per household. Not valid for current subscribers to the Suspense Collection or the Romance/Suspense Collection. All orders subject to credit approval. Credit or debit balances in a customer's account(s) may be offset by any other outstanding balance owed by or to the customer. Please allow 4 to 6 weeks for delivery. Offer available while quantities last.

Your Privacy—The Reader Service is committed to protecting your privacy. Our Privacy Policy is available online at www.ReaderService.com or upon request from the Reader Service.

We make a portion of our mailing list available to reputable third parties that offer products we believe may interest you. If you prefer that we not exchange your name with third parties, or if you wish to clarify or modify your communication preferences, please visit us at www.ReaderService.com/consumerschoice or write to us at Reader Service Preference Service, P.O. Box 9062, Buffalo, NY 14240-9062. Include your complete name and address.

FEB 2 7 2017

AMANDA STEVENS

31400 THE RESTORER	___$7.99 U.S.	___$9.99 CAN.
31339 THE PROPHET	___$7.99 U.S.	___$9.99 CAN.
31277 THE KINGDOM	___$7.99 U.S.	___$9.99 CAN.

(limited quantities available)

TOTAL AMOUNT	$ _____
POSTAGE & HANDLING	$ _____
($1.00 for 1 book, 50¢ for each additional)	
APPLICABLE TAXES*	$ _____
TOTAL PAYABLE	$ _____

(check or money order—please do not send cash)

To order, complete this form and send it, along with a check or money order for the total above, payable to MIRA Books, to: **In the U.S.:** 3010 Walden Avenue, P.O. Box 9077, Buffalo, NY 14269-9077; **In Canada:** P.O. Box 636, Fort Erie, Ontario, L2A 5X3.

Name: _____

Address: _____ City: _____

State/Prov.: _____ Zip/Postal Code: _____

Account Number (if applicable): _____

075 CSAS

*New York residents remit applicable sales taxes.
*Canadian residents remit applicable GST and provincial taxes.

MIRA®

www.MIRABooks.com

MAS0416BLTALL